Praise for *Your Name Here*

"*Your Name Here* is an ouroboros—and a big one at that—of a postmodern yarn that threatens to swallow itself at any moment. Rachel Zozanian is a 'notorious recluse misanthrope,' author of the decidedly centrifugal tome *Lotteryland,* which just happens to share a display table at the local chain bookstore with Helen DeWitt's *Your Name Here.* The two share more than that: There's an alter-ego dimension here as DeWitt and her co-author, Australian journalist Gridneff, play off Charlie Kaufman's *Adaptation.* As is her wont, announced in her brilliant debut novel, *The Last Samurai* (2000), DeWitt ranges across time to pepper her pages with references to the greats: Foucault, Homer, Debord, the X-Men. The dominant second language throughout is Arabic, reflecting the author's current passions—to say nothing of statistics, the classics, and 'Habermasian ideal speech situations.' If there's a plot, it hinges on efforts to shake Rachel out of her torpor, on a slowly declining film director's attempts to figure out how to film the unfilmable, and on DeWitt and Gridneff's attempts via email to wrestle down whatever the hell their collaboration is supposed to yield. To call the book experimental is to understate. At once bewildering and beguiling, and a groaning-table feast of words."

—*Kirkus Reviews*

"Peerless." —Lauren Oyler, author of *Fake Accounts*

"Helen DeWitt and Ilya Gridneff's *Your Name Here* has been the novel of the century for almost two decades, despite almost no one having read it. Now, at long last, *Your Name Here* is here. Not a rumor, not an excerpt, not a PDF: this is the real thing—a hilarious, insatiably imaginative meta-meta-meta-novel that takes every risk and plays every card and captures, maybe like no other novel, the internet's jarring dislocations and formal possibilities. Still wildly ahead of its time, *Your Name Here* contains a multitude of voices so funny, so dark, so alive to every contingency that I wish it were twice as long. What a blast!" —Mark Krotov, coeditor, *n+1*

"Although the book may appear, to begin with, to be plotless, it turns out to be tightly organized: a Godard-like enfilade of shaftings, a frontispiece-of-Leviathan-type portrait of the world as a great 'Biz' made up of millions of little bizzes . . . *Your Name Here* is a novel that doesn't really believe in novels. The writing is delightfully shameless, disheveled and dissolute; globalized and pornified and digitized somehow, bit after bit after bit."

—*The London Review of Books*

OTHER BOOKS BY HELEN DEWITT

The Last Samurai

Lightning Rods

Some Trick

The English Understand Wool

Your Name Here

Helen DeWitt

&

Ilya Gridneff

Dalkey Archive Press
Dallas, TX / Rochester, NY

Deep Vellum | Dalkey Archive Press
3000 Commerce Street
Dallas, Texas 75226

Deep Vellum is a 501c3 nonprofit literary arts organization founded in 2013 with the mission to bring the world into conversation through literature.

First edition, 2025

Support for this publication has been provided in part by grants from the Texas Commission on the Arts, the City of Dallas Office of Arts and Culture, and the Addy Foundation.

LIBRARY OF CONGRESS CATALOGING-IN-PUBLICATION DATA

Names: DeWitt, Helen, 1957- author | Gridneff, Ilya author
Title: Your name here / Helen DeWitt & Ilya Gridneff.
Description: First North American edition. | Dallas, TX : Dalkey Archive Press, 2025.
Identifiers: LCCN 2025013933 (print) | LCCN 2025013934 (ebook) | ISBN 9781628976267 paperback | ISBN 9781628976274 ebook
Subjects: LCGFT: Experimental fiction
Classification: LCC PS3554.E92945 Y68 2025 (print) | LCC PS3554.E92945 (ebook) | DDC 813/.54--dc23/eng/20250530
LC record available at https://lccn.loc.gov/2025013933
LC ebook record available at https://lccn.loc.gov/2025013934

Cover art and design by David Wojciechowski

Interior design by KGT

PRINTED IN THE UNITED STATES OF AMERICA

1
High Society

My favorite solution was to make the insta-death choice very rare (You chose door number two? You're dead!) and focus on a wide range of variables to track choices within the main story. Players don't have cut-and-dried choices that point in obvious directions, but more subtle choices that could each turn out well. Each choice has real consequences and real rewards far beyond issues of death and survival. They take the player along differing paths through the main story and result in a range of consequences and endings, depending on the preponderance of choices made throughout the game. This lets the player feel more in charge of his destiny.

Daniel Greenberg
(*Marc Saltzman,* Game Creation and Careers)

Boogie mornings

You're going to Paris. It's an eight-hour flight from New York. You want something to read on the plane. You've been meaning to read Robert Fisk's *Pity the Nation,* but you're not sure you'll be able to concentrate. The last four days have been wrecked.

The name on the ticket is Antonios Demetriakis. It matches the name on the passport. The picture in the passport doesn't match what you saw in the mirror. The feeling that aliens from Planet Zworg have performed plastic surgery while you slept is not unfamiliar.

The plan suggested by the documentation leads inexorably doomwards, to passport officials, security guards, petty teetotalitarian apparatchiks unlikely to be open to the Zworg hypothesis. Failure to follow the plan may prompt swift reprisals from Zworg. You want something to read on the plane, but this is no time for *Pity the Nation.*

The book is on a table in Barnes & Noble, part of a 3-for-2 offer. You've also been meaning to read Seymour Hersh's *Chain of Command,* and this too is in the 3-for-2 deal. They've got *Gravity's Rainbow* by the notorious recluse Thomas Pynchon. *Mao II* by DeLillo, *The Border Trilogy* by McCarthy, *The Catcher in the Rye* by Salinger, notorious recluses to a man. They've got *The Loser,* a novel about the notorious recluse Glenn Gould by the notorious misanthrope Thomas Bernhard. They've got *Lotteryland* by the notorious recluse misanthrope Zozanian. You feel surly and uncommunicative, you hate your fellow man, reclusiveness and misanthropy could be the hair of the dog. They've also got Helen DeWitt's new book, *Your Name Here.*

Your friend Mike has been telling you for years to read DeWitt's first book, *The Last Samurai* (which is not on the 3-for-2 table). He went to his friend Dan's place in Seoul in 2002; the book was lying on the bed, which took up 60 percent of the studio apartment. (Dan is now a big pop star with a bigger apartment.) Mike didn't much like the cover; he asked: "Is this a romance novel?" "It's fantastic, you should definitely read it," said Dan. The book was in surprisingly good condition. "You finished it?" "Just the first chapter. But it's good." Mike was bored, needed a book, smuggled it out in his bag, read it in two days, called Dan. "Yeah, what's up?" said Dan. "Yo, *Last Samurai* is so good. It's so fuckin' good." "Yeah, I told you it's good. Did you take my fucking book?" Mike hung up, smoked five cigarettes, went to sleep. Told all his friends, including you, to read the book. You'd heard the book was full of Greek and Japanese, a much-needed gap in your life, and Mike said, "No, no, you have to read it, it's fucking great, there *is* Greek and Japanese, but it's *motivated.*" But Mike is the first-son-of-the-first-son-of-the-first-son-of-the . . . for 11 generations going back to King Sejong, inventor of the Korean alphabet. This may be the warped perception of a descendant of Korean royalty with alphabetic obsession in the DNA. Also, Mike is not unconnected with your present hatred of the world. Not unconnected with bad, baaaaaaaad nights at Kim's Korean Karaoke. Not to be trusted.

Something's bothering you, but you can't put your finger on it.

You pick up *Your Name Here*. There's a quote on the cover.

"I give it 8½!!!!!!!!!!!!!" Janet Maslin, *New York Times.*

You open the book. Who *are* these people? What's going *on*? Where is it *going?*

THROBBING UNCIRCUMCISED MEMBER OF DR. RAOUL DUKE

I've been talking to my John Malkovich, who tells me he feels like Ingrid Bergman in *Casablanca*. What's going *on*? Where is this *going*? What do you want me to *do*? I have no idea what the character is supposed to be *doing*. People ask me what the book is about and I don't know what to tell them. Can you just explain to me what it's actually *about*?

The reason we had the meeting is that earlier in the week he had had a brilliant idea: his character could go to Cambodia and engage in sexual tourism à la Michel Houellebecq.

DeWitt: Why would you do that? If Houellebecq had your sex life he wouldn't be going to prostitutes. His access to sex has been dramatically improved by money and a Mercedes; you're a penniless paparazzo who has coke-fuelled sex romps with investment bankers.

"Malkovich": Look, Helen, I don't want to go down in history as a great fuck, I'd rather be known as a great writer. Just what is the nature of your interest in me, anyway?

What did I do to deserve this? What did I do to deserve this? And what *is* the character supposed to be doing? What is *Your Name Here* about? What's going *on*? Where is it *going*? How should *I* know, I'm just a writer with a character who tells me he is not being a prima donna. If I'd made him up I could kill him off and take the plot elsewhere. For better or worse, he actually exists. What's it all about? How did I get into this, anyway?

OK.

"John Malkovich" is Ilya Gridneff, a 26-year-old Australian journalist. I first met him in an East London pub when he was 24. I gave him my e-mail address on a receipt and went to New York to take up a fellowship at the

Cullman Center. Got an e-mail a month later, anarchic, obscene, insanely funny, Hunter S. Thompson meets the Byron of the Empty V generation.

I had problems of my own. Did not reply. Big mistake.

Ilya Gridneff was in London upstaging the BAs formerly known as Y, trading insults with Jake & Dinos & Damien & Tracey & other newly neurotic former Saatchelites. He was in Cairo chasing Angelina Jolie for the *National Enquirer.* He was in Berlin chasing Britney Spears for some other rag. He was reading Deleuze, DeLillo, Burroughs, Bukowski, Houellebecq. He used his tabloid money to go off to the Middle East, wandering around Iran in search of pharmaceuticals with a dodgy phrasebook: "Give me painkillers, the strongest you have." Lebanon, Jordan, Iraq, Turkey, Kurdistan, Iraq (not necessarily in that order), Pakistan, Kyrgyzstan, the who what where why when remains unjournalistically unclear.

I went to Berlin, sent him an e-mail after two years, got more anarchic e-mails. He turned up a month later. He talked about London, drink, drugs, everything to excess, blackouts when he can't remember what happened. "I met him at the train station. Woke up in my room next day and he wasn't there. Something didn't feel right." He says he can turn any situation to his advantage with a flick of the wrist, clickclickclick. I say: "Tell me more. Tell me more. Tell me more."

I love *The Sweet Smell of Success.* I love Malkovich in *Les Liaisons Dangereuses.* I love Kaufman's *Being John Malkovich*; I love *Adaptation.* Brilliant idea! We could write a book about this! Write a book about writing a book about this! Bad idea.

I say: Look, Ilya, everything's going to be all right. How's the Arabic coming along?

He takes out a softened, stained, much-folded piece of paper. Down the center of the page are two columns of typing

انجيلينا	Angelina
انجيلينا	Angelina
انجيلينا	Angelina
انجيلينا	Angelina
انجيلينا	Angelina
انجيلينا	Angelina
انجيلينا	Angelina
انجيلينا	Angelina

Beneath the typing, in the margins and on the back are a handwritten scrawl:

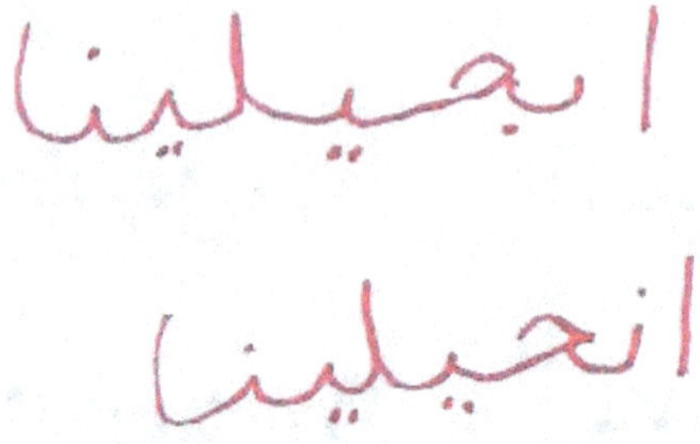

This is not the time to quibble about missing dots. I say: This is *great*! This is *great*! Look, Ilya, what this shows is that Arabic is something everyone can enjoy, it's not just for specialists, it's something that can appeal to a character they can identify with (i.e. a manipulative, calculating, promiscuous drink and drug fiend, an engaging potential serial killer). Look, Tolkien wrote *The Lord of the Rings* to provide a background for languages he invented, and by 2003 the books had sold *100 million copies*. 100 million copies, Ilya! 100 million copies! What would the world be like if someone had done that for the languages of the Middle East?

He says: Yeah. *Yeah*. So the *point* of the book is to get the *message* across, without actually coming out and *saying* in so many *words*, You stupid fucking *morons*, you're learning fucking *elf* languages!

I say: Exactly. Exactly. It's about building bridges. Look, don't worry, Ilya, everything is going to be all right. Everyone will know you're a great writer. David read the draft with your e-mails and he talked about your Joycean gift for language. The e-mails are there, everyone will say you're the best thing in the book. So look, I think this has been a productive meeting, thanks for your constructive comments. I think the plot and characters will be clear in the next draft. Everything is under control. Leave everything to me.

Later in the day I get an e-mail in which he says "about being a great fuck, no such thing as bad publicity, go ahead, send it out and let's make a million!"

I then get an e-mail from my ex-husband David, who says

> It seems to me that there are works which are more destabilising than that, and where it is often hard to see the status of the distortions and the relationship between different bits - I'm thinking of things like Bertolucci's *The Spider's Stratagem,* where it is frequently hard to see whether a particular scene is supposed to be in the present or the past. And I think works like that can be brilliant, as indeed the Bertolucci is; I suppose I felt that the occasional difficulties in *Your Name Here* were because you were aiming at something similar.

This is, on the one hand, good (comparison with brilliant Bertolucci) and, on the other hand, bad (I have just calmed my star by talk of Tolkien's 100 million copies sold). A comment which could cause untold damage if it fell in the wrong hands (those of Miss Bergman). One to be shared on a need-to-know basis (what he doesn't know can't hurt him).

The sexual-tourism-in-Cambodia idea has undermined my faith in the project, but the difference between a professional and an amateur is that a professional pushes on in the face of discouragement.

Sometimes a plot and characters sort themselves out if you think about something completely different. I go to the jazz cafe on the corner for a beer and start reading the correspondence of Hunter Thompson. I think Thompson is grossly underrated and Wolfe grossly overrated, so it's good to see Thompson calling Wolfe a worthless cocksucker for touring Europe in a white suit promoting *The Electric Kool-Aid Acid Test.* (Herr Gridneff was always on the Thompson side of the fence.) Three beers into the afternoon I find a letter to Thompson's agent, Lynn Nesbit, written while he was finishing *Fear and Loathing in Las Vegas.* Thompson did not want the book to be sucked into his existing two-book deal with his publishers; he wanted Nesbit to submit his novel, *The Rum Diary,* to satisfy the contract, or rather suggested rewriting *The Rum Diary* as the Final Pornographic Novel:

> I kicked the fucking door off its hinges. The girl backed into a corner, trying to cover herself with a curtain. I could see she was

> going to scream so I bashed her against the stove. She fell. I sat on her naked chest and pulled her front teeth with my Chinese bolt-cutting pliers. Then I grabbed her by the hair and forced my throbbing, uncircumcised member into her mouth . . . etc. etc.
>
> Yeah, one of those. I figure that kind of opening would make Ian Ballantine cry—and god only knows what it would do to his wife . . .
>
> Anyway, if faced with the specter of having to use *Vegas* as a contract breaker, I'd prefer to send in a tentative draft of *The Rum Diary*, rewritten as above. I don't think I'd have to submit more than 10 pages, to get us off the hook. You could explain that my numerous experiments with LSD have changed not only my writing style but my whole personality—and that' I'll never be the same again.

I've had to do this kind of dirty work for myself, so I warm to HT for purely personal reasons, but that's not the important thing. The important thing is that this is the character! This is the character! *This* is what we're trying to achieve! I write an e-mail to my sister about the throbbing uncircumcised member. In an earlier e-mail my sister had said

> Your use of the f-word (as we always say in elementary school!) jars me, but that's probably just because I seem to have inherited the old Vermont puritanical streak and Grandmother's Victorian sensibilities. I know most people don't respond to "colorful" language in that way.

But the throbbing uncircumcised member has her laughing out loud! My mother (who likes the f-word in the gerund) says she was rolling on the floor! David likes it! Tony Holden likes it! Tony Holden thinks we could get illustrations by Ralph Steadman! Ilyaaaaaaaaaaaaaaaaa! The throbbing uncircumcised member is our "Springtime for Hitler"! We're going to be rich!

Credit where credit's due. I thought the fucking-a-family-of-five-in-

Cambodia idea was an idea of unsurpassable stupidity. Unfunny. Why would this be in character for a journalist who has written about the white slave trade in Trabzon? Who has never paid for sex in his life? What *conceivable*—But it has led us out of the Bertoluccian labyrinth to the *Cock and Bull Story* which is the very essence of the book.

The boy's a genius. Everything is under control. Everything is going to be all right.

So yeah. You bought it. You fell for the uncircumcised throbbing member and coke-fueled sex romps. You did. They were not actually actively funny in the store, where *why don't more people shoot more people?* was the question of the hour, but you thought this was something your future, unhungover self might find good for a laugh. So, what the fuck?

You had to show up three hours before the scheduled departure of your flight. Sure enough, you're unable to concentrate. You're in seat 65B, neither window nor aisle, fish nor fowl. You open *Your Name Here,* the new novel by Helen DeWitt.

Within a page you are cursing your "friend." Now you know what was bothering you. You find yourself in some kind of pastiche of Italo Calvino's *If on a winter's night a traveler,* a book with 10 first chapters, narrated in the second person, something always goes wrong so "you" can never finish the book, you thought it was fucking brilliant when you were 19. Now you know you'll never read it again. *Invisible Cities* is the one that will last. Why didn't you buy *Invisible Cities* while you had the chance? Why don't they sell books on planes? Bastards. *Bastards.*

You turn the page.

فيلّيني Fellini

فيسكونتي Visconti

كوروساوا Kurosawa

You'd like to call your "friend" on your cellphone and point out that THIS IS NOT MOTIVATED. It is not required by the story because there IS NO STORY, it's not integral to the characters because there ARE NO CHARACTERS, and you are still trapped in a pastiche of the ultimately unsatisfactory *If on a winter's night a traveler*. You turn the page and find

كافكا

and a little voice in the head says Kafka! Kafka! Kafka! It says Kafka! Dude! Mom! Dad! I can read Arabic! Cool! Awesome! Way-hay!

This is actually not unexciting, but the voice of reason observes that this too is completely unmotivated, there's *no* story, *no* characters (except you and you never wanted to be here in the first place), THIS IS NOT LITERATURE, and you are *still* trapped in a pastiche of the ultimately unsatisfactory *If on a winter's night a traveler* . . . and you turn the page and find

تكساس

And suddenly everything falls into place! The book is some kind of Philip K. Dick alternative universe spin-off! An alternative universe where the Moors kept Granada, conquered the New World, colonized Texas!!!!!!!! But you *love* Philip K. Dick! You *love The Man in the High Castle*! You *love* the wisecracking slime molds! This is *great*! This is *great*! This is *great*! And you feel a little glow of satisfaction, because if the plane is hijacked to some remote village of feuding Sunnites and Shiites (see *Yojimbo*, which you have inflicted on a succession of reluctant girlfriends, see *A Fistful of Dollars*, ditto) *you* may be able to decipher a few signs and get back to civilization, while all the readers of *The Da Vinci Code* and *Harry Potter* are deservedly miming anguish for video ransom demands. Cool. All is forgiven, DeWitt. Strut your stuff.

The fat guy in the next seat is reading a real page-turner. *The albino drew a pistol out of his coat*, you read out of the corner of your eye, and now the fat guy has to answer the call of nature. You and the girl on the aisle get up. When you get back into your seat you see that the book on the empty seat lies open to a page on which is displayed:

بانانا   Banana

تيتيكاكا   Titicaca

In the words of the immortal Manuel,

¡¡¡¡¡¡¿¿¿¿Qué????!!!!!!!

Or as we says in America,

¡¡¡¡¡¡¿¿¿¿What the fuck????!!!!!!!

And the voice at the back of the head says: "*Huh.* Okay, *I* geddit, the straight line is a, the thing like a dotted i is *n*, the thing like a dotted i with a dot *below* is *b*, Mom, *Mom*... Titicaca, now this is seriously cool, the one like a dotted i with two dots above is t, the one with two dots below is i, ka ve have seen zis sing before.' This is an interior monologue you have been trying to silence for years, but you can live with it because you *love* Laurie Anderson's "Babydoll," in fact, wait, if they have *conscripted* you into being a character in this book does that mean you can quote the song and someone else will clear the permission? You didn't sign a contract or anything, you just found yourself here, you're not quoting any songs if they're going to make you clear permissions.

Anyway, the voice in the head says No *way* are we buying *The Da Vinci Code* for this, so you take out a pen and copy

بانانا　Banana

تيتيكاكا　Titicaca

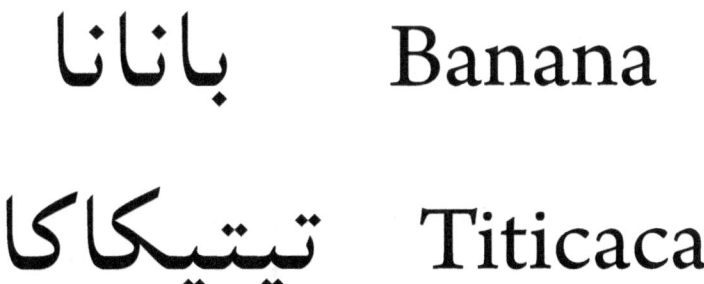

onto a napkin and put it in your laptop case for future reference. One thing, Titicaca looks so much *better* in Arabic, this is the way it would have looked for the last five centuries in fact if Boabdil had kept Granada in 1492, reversed the *reconquista* and replaced their Catholic Majesties as the conqueror of the New World. Possibly not exterminating the Aztecs in the process.

You still don't know what's going on. The fat guy is back. You and the girl get out of your seats, the guy wrestles his bulk to the window, you and the girl return to your seats. The girl is reading an adult edition of a Harry Potter, not Harry Potter plus leather fetishist lesbian triangles, just same old same old with a marginally less juvenile cover, which means this could not be the beginning of a beautiful friendship. You return to *Your Name Here,* the new novel by Helen DeWitt. To your left, the girl murmurs softly: Beckett!

You glance, startled, to your left; implausible as it may seem to argue that the unspeakable Potter "gets people reading" so that they can ultimately move on to *Murphy* and *Malone Dies*, it's surely infinitely *less* plausible to imagine a reading trajectory that starts with *Waiting for Godot* and moves on to *Harry Potter and the Philosopher's Stone* when the reader is old enough to appreciate it.

Your eye falls to the open page. You see

بيكيت　　　　Beckett

In the words of the immortal Manuel,

¡¡¡¡¡¡¡¡¡¡¡¿¿¿¿¿¿¿¿¿Qué??????????!!!!!!!!!!!

What's going *on*? Is *everyone* writing PKD spin-offs these days? Is this something everyone knows about but you, something you would have known if you had taken out a slash-and-burn trial subscription to the *New Yorker* or *Harper's* or the *New York Review of Books*? If so, you wish you'd known sooner and soberer. You like keeping up with new literary trends, but if everyone is doing it you'd rather read an example that doesn't involve revisiting Calvino's ultimately unsatisfactory *If on a winter's night a traveler.*

You decide to make a trip down the aisle before the drinks trolley is wheeled out. You apologize smilingly to the girl, head toward the back.

There's a short line. While you kick your heels, your eye is caught by a book open on the lap of the kid in seat 103C. 103C is reading Jonathan Safran Foer's new novel, *Extremely Loud & Incredibly Close*. Except that a page displays the following:

فوكو **Foucault**

قونو **Queneau**

ITWOTIM,

¡¡¡¡¡¡¡¡¡¡¡¡¡¡¡¡¿¿¿¿¿¿¿¿¿¿¿¿¿¿¿Qué?????????????!!!!!!!!!!!!!

This is a book you've *read*. From cover to cover. This was not in it. You might not remember every little twist of the plot (and *this* was a book with a *plot*, unlike *some* you could name) or every single character (and this was *definitely*, but *definitely* a book with some *characters* other than *you*), but if the Arabic for Foucault and Queneau had made an appearance you would have remembered. The Cuba Libres and caipirinhas and Tequila Sunrises have taken their toll on the little grey cells, where once you would have expatiated on [Habermas/Wittgenstein/Kripke/Kant/Braudel/Gramsci/Foucault/Adorno/Jameson/Bourdieu/the Vienna Circle/New York School/Chicago School/Frankfurt School/Paris Commune/other (delete/add as appropriate)] you find yourself adroitly shifting ground. But the Arabic for Foucault and Queneau you would have remembered. This was *not* repeat *not* in the book.

You feel disoriented, bemused. Foucault has fared less well than Kafka, arabized to a Manx cat.

Now the kid turns the page, and on the following page is a letter from the young narrator to

John Negroponte
Director of National Intelligence
Washington, DC 20511

Dear Mr Negroponte, explains Oskar, *As I am sure you know, J.R.R. Tolkien wrote* The Lord of the Rings *to provide a saga of war, loss and exile for languages he had invented. The last volume was published in 1955, a year before the Suez Crisis. By 2003 100 million copies had been sold, disseminating the languages of the elves and the dwarves in a mass market paperback. I think national intelligence would be improved if Arabic, Hebrew, Farsi, Pashtu and other so-called "exotic" languages were to be introduced to a text of comparable popularity. The Office of the Director of National Intelligence is well placed to promote this. Could I design your program?*

This was NOT in the book you read. There was a letter to Stephen Hawking, yes. There was no letter to John Negroponte. No.

So, is this, have you actually stepped *into* an alternative universe, a world where Texas is an arabophone state?

A world where plastic surgery from Zworg goes unchallenged by passport control?

Or are you in one of the more paranoiac PKDian alternative universes, nothing to do with Boabdil, just the kind of universe that looks like heavy-handed paranoiac *satire* in PKD, a universe where the Patriot Act and the Department of Homeland Security and the Director of National Intelligence reign supreme, the kind of universe that only dogfood-chomping amphetamine-munching self-pitying hallucinating PKD could dream up?

There's some kind of initiative on the part of the Department of Homeland Security, say, or the Office of the Director of National Security, some kind of gimmick to prepare people in case of a hijacking? Say you had a whole planeful of passengers who had been hijacked, and among them they could pool the ability to read the words Kurosawa, Kafka, Fellini, Visconti, Banana, Titicaca, Beckett, Foucault and Queneau, this might improve their chances of survival. Farfetched, daft, getting the pages in the books, just how much taxpayers' money was spent on this? And they're also rewriting author's books? Not just inserting a couple of Arabic words in the text, like ads in a magazine, but actually changing the text? And now PKD, or possibly J. G. Ballard, anyway an undisputed writer of cult classics has dreamed it up and either you're dreaming his dream or he's dreaming your dream—

When you were 15 you actually in your heart of hearts believed in the Thomas Covenant, the Unbeliever series.

Whatever this is, it's the actual world, some kind of Big Brotherism we know not of. Deal with it.

So is this some new encroachment on our rights that you would have known about if you'd taken out a discount subscription to the *New Yorker* or *Harper's* or the *NYRB*? Or just read Salon.com more regularly? Or is it, could it be an encroachment on our rights backed up by an encroachment forbidding mention in the press backed up by an encroachment censoring the web backed up by an encroachment censoring public mention of the fact of censorship backed up by

It's your turn for the cubicle. You spot several letters you know in the Arabic injunction against smoking! You emerge, head back down the aisle.

A woman in 103D says: Ti-ti-ca-ca. A man in 98C says: Nin-ten-do. A book at 100C is open to

before the reader turns the page, swept up, perhaps, in a book with plot and characters, a real page-turner. Ti-ti-ca-ca, Ba-na-na, Be-ckett, Fou-cault, Que-neau, the soft syllables float up, row after row.

You're back at row 65. You slip in smilingly past the girl. She's no longer reading the Harry Potter (have you misjudged her? Was it an unwanted gift? A favorite nephew's favorite book? Now that you think of it, she was only up to page 3) and is deep in *Lotteryland.*

You return to the Arabic map of Texas, hoping for PKDian plot-twisting. But wait a minute. *Wait* a minute. If the Arabic in *Your Name Here* is just an act of compliance with some edict from the Department of Homeland Security, it's not *unmotivated,* not in fictional terms, because it's just a page in a book, like an ad for Dell in *Time* or an ad for Brooks Brothers in the *New Yorker.* People don't write to John Updike saying "you lazy talentless son of a bitch, what the fuck was that quarter-column pic of a Brooks Brothers shirt doing in your story, it was completely unmotivated, it had nothing whatsoever to do with the characters, and what about the bookrest and reading lamp, John, you're over the hill. Finding your inner Breton, John? I don't think so." The Arabic, the map of Texas, were forced on DeWitt. But in *that* case, you're not reading the great Philip K. Dick alternative universe *spin-off,* whether one where the Moors kept Granada, conquered the New World and settled Texas, *or* one of creeping paranoia dashed off by a rabid writer high on Pedigree Chum.

You're back where you started, trapped in a pastiche of Italo Calvino's ultimately unsatisfactory *If on a winter's night a traveler.*

So long, and thanks for all the Quidditch

You got an aisle seat, 65C. You're sitting next to someone who looks like a *Blade Runner* android cunningly aping human scum. It's reading *Your Name Here,* the new novel by Helen DeWitt.

You're not the kind of girl who'd be in a place like this at a time like this. Not the kind of girl who'd sit next to a guy who's the kind of guy who'd be in *Bright Lights, Big City II* and be so [spaced out/coked up/polypharmaceutically prepositioned/(Add/delete as appropriate)] that he thinks he's the kind of guy who'd be in a pastiche of Calvino's *If on a winter's night a traveler.* It was pre-assigned seating.

You gave Harry Potter your best shot. Your sister gave you a copy of the adult edition (no leather fetishist lesbian triangles, just a slightly less juvenile cover and the Arabic for Beckett marooned on a page), urged you to get on-message with the only book the sprogs will read. You tried. Couldn't.

Your father went to Christ's Hospital, hated it, ran away five times. The last time he was sent to a psychiatrist who offered him lithium: This will give you Dutch courage, Vickers. Your father, very stiff upper lip, said he thought he could manage. *You will take this.* So long, and thanks for all the Quidditch.

So you went back to *Lotteryland,* by the reclusive Rachel Zozanian.

LTOTEYRALDN

1. OUT OF LUCK

1.

A crowd passed over London Bridge. No time to talk.

I said: Any spare chance. Any spare chance. Spare any chance? Spare any chance?

Thousands of legs with no luck to spare legged it by.

I thought: The odds are 50,000:1 that I am a genuine Lottery Loser with a 1 in 5,000 chance of sleeping inside in a bed 3 nights in 10. The odds are 1:100,000,000 that I am a millionaire cunningly disguised as a Lottery Loser, wrapped *in* a blanket, *in* the rain, *in* March, just to make it convincing.

If you analysed the situation purely on the odds, everyone was running a very high risk of being a shit.

Actually I just made up the odds. Well, how was I *supposed* to check them? Whatever they were, they were bad. The question was only, how bad.

It's not against Lottery regulations to lose, obviously—*somebody's* got to—but it's against the Rules to be seen to lose. It's against the Rules to be seen to win. It's not just that you break the Rules by sitting there. It's that you put everyone else in the position of ostentatious Rulebreakers, maneuvered into flashing their luck just by walking to work.

Then someone stopped, and I tried not to look up a short skirt. She was about my age, with glossy dark hair and brilliant dark eyes; she dropped five hard chances in the paper cup. She seemed to have a vague sense of the scale of the odds she was defying: the odds against stopping, against giving so much, against smiling.

She said she was sorry it wasn't more, and she was sorry I was out there, and she said she was sorry but she had to go.

2.

The next time she stopped she said her name was Gabriella, but her friends called her Gaby.

I said: That's what friends are for.

She asked about me. I thought that the odds that she had more than five minutes to spare were 578,999:12, so I explained quickly that my name was Richard, that I came from Dublin, that I had gone to Milan to train as a croupier and come to London looking for work and hadn't found it.

She said: Really? That sounds interesting.

She said: You know, I actually have a couple of contacts. I mean, maybe a publisher would be interested. I'll give them a call! You never know your luck!

3.

Unfortunately, it turned out the story was not interesting enough. It was a sad story but the mere fact of being true did not make it interesting. Lots of people lose the Lottery unfortunately and the bit about the croupier though interesting was not enough.

Gaby added avoiding my eye that they had also said she had no way of knowing if it was true.

I thought: Look, these people are not mathematically trained. In all probability. Let's be charitable here.

I said: Look, Gab, you get this kind of confusion the whole time with non-mathematicians, the best thing is to

She said: You're a mathematician? I thought you said

I said hastily: Look. We have four possibilities: Interesting truth. Uninteresting truth. Interesting non-truth. Uninteresting non-truth. What has happened is beyond our control. What's done is done. Les jeux sont faits. So we just make the non-truth more interesting.

Gaby said: You mean

I said: Leave this to me. I'll write something today and you can send it in.

I said: The thing I really miss is my lottomonitor. You don't know what it's like, not being able to run a luck check.

4.

I had been looking forward to writing *Croupier: How I Lost on the Roulette Wheel of Life*, and I was sorry Gaby's friend hadn't taken to the story. It really was someone's story, and I was glad I did not have to tell him it did not make the grade. I thought: Regrets are fruitless. Let's get on with the show.

I still came from Dublin and my name was still Richard. I had been trying to get into one of the 362 struggling Dublin boy bands, but my problem was I couldn't decide whether I wanted to be the cute one or the moody one. Because of the intense competition you had to start specialising very young; that's a big decision to make at 17. I kept putting it off and meanwhile younger guys who had got their act together were going to auditions and getting lucky.

Then I decided to go to London because I thought people would be more open to ideas. I had a couple of job offers but they weren't really what I was looking for, in retrospect I should have accepted anything but I was afraid of being locked into something, once you're perceived as one thing it can be quite hard to move over to something else. Naming no names just look at George Michael, a classic example of an artist who started out as the cute one and had an incredibly hard time being taken seriously as the dangerous one or even the moody one.

There were not so many legs now. I tried to think of what went wrong for

Richard. I thought he probably compromised, he actually took a job as the moody one that looked as though it had some room for creativity and then he got into arguments with the manager. One night the manager would take him aside and say 'Mick' and he'd say 'Richard.'

Manager: Whatever, the point being Shane is the dangerous one, you're getting very borderline in your interpretation

So he would swallow his pride and tone it down and the next night the manager would say 'Look Mike, in this business we don't have room for the egos, we're looking for people who can take a professional approach, Jason is the cute one, you know that, I know that, last night you were all over the place,' and Richard would say 'Fuck you then' and walk out. It could happen to anyone.

5.

Gaby picked it up on her way home. She sent it off to her friend and a week later she got a letter saying it was not quite what they were looking for.

I said: Did they say what in particular they didn't like?

Gaby said: Giles said he thought it sounded as though you were just making it up as you went along.

I said ruefully: Fuck. Well look, it's no reason to get discouraged, Gab. The number of things that happen not to be true is infinite; some of them have got to be plausible as well as interesting. I'll just have to keep trying.

Gaby flashed her large dark eyes to my face, then to the ground. She said awkwardly: I sort of get the impression they don't like the idea of the project, Richard.

What project? I protested. The *project* is exactly what we're trying to *decide*!

I don't know, said Gab. Something about your attitude

I said You mean they don't like *me*? But they don't know anything *about* me.

That's what they don't like, said Gab. It comes across as insincere and calculating.

I thought: Fuck.

I did not need a lottomonitor to tell me that I had been drawing PHYSICALLY REPULSIVE for the last few months. The odds against making a good impression on someone who drew FANTASTICALLY BEAUTIFUL on a daily basis were astronomical; the one chance in all the handfuls of millions had to be of drawing ENGAGING PERSONALITY which in turn probably depended on drawing APPEARANCE OF CANDOUR.

I thought: But the odds are that any Lottery Loser wants regular meals, a bath, a place to sleep; only a non-mathematician could believe in the genuine possibility of anything else.

I said, reverting to the story, that it was probably true of someone, given the cutthroat nature of the boy band industry worldwide and especially in Dublin.

I said: You know, there really aren't that many chances, the other options are liberating consumer durables or drug dealing, if they have the looks they can go the boy band route. They only have a few years before they're too old, and only three or four bands make it to the top. But it's still the best chance so they all really work at it, three or four hours a day weight training, a couple of hours working on the dancing, a couple of hours guitar work, plus the gigs. But even if they make it there are problems, people burn out really fast, and if they don't they have all this powerful material they start wanting to bring into the music when they're secure commercially and then all the 13-year-old girls defect. I saw a lot of it when I was over in Dublin.

Gaby said: I thought you were *from* Dublin.

I thought: Fuck.

6.

I thought: If I jump off the bridge this conversation will end without further contributions from me.

I stood up, letting the blanket fall to my feet, and looked down the river to Tower Bridge. The river was like a piece of chainmail, of tiny linked scales gleaming and glancing with the lure of pure liquid luck. It was as if someone had sewn together millions of Tickets and cast them down. By the bank the water was the dark dully glinting grey of a Pewter Ticket, a little further out it was the cheap bright glare of Tin, perhaps there was oil on the water because there was a smooth polished slick of Silver just beyond. Where the light flashed from building to building before striking the water it was the white of Platinum, and where the light from the west struck off the great glass panes it reached the water in floating squares of Copper and Bronze and Gold. A boat passed under the bridge, and in its wake tossed out the glittering crystals of Diamond.

I thought: It's no use. I've got to try again.

I said: I'm sorry. I know you want to minimize your chances of aiding and abetting a cunningly disguised millionaire, but it's too complicated.

She said: It's not that, it's just that

I said: There is one thing I haven't tried. I'll try it now.

She said: You mean your family?

I said gloomily: No.

I said: I'll have to go to the Lubavitch.

There was a short pause.

Gaby said: Isn't that a Jewish sect?

I said: Yes, exactly, it's a mitzvah to give to charity. The strictly Orthodox take it very seriously. In a really religious community you never see homeless people; if you really have nowhere to go you can just knock on any door and be invited in.

Gaby said: But I thought you were Catholic?

I did not think Fuck because there are limits.

I said: Look, I'd really like to explain all this if you'll give me the chance, it's just rather involved. Let me see if there's any chance I can start winning again. You don't have to tell me how to contact you, I know you don't want to trust a potential serial killer with that kind of information, but maybe you could write to me. In a month or so.

I took out a piece of paper and a pen. I said: I *think* my ether address is still in luck. If not you can write to me care of U2. I haven't been there for months but if you write to me there's a fair chance they'll forward it.

Gaby looked at the piece of paper.

She said: I thought your name was Richard.

The android in seat 65B is writing

بيكيت

on a paper napkin. You pretend not to see; you don't want to get dragged into conversation with this replicant.

You don't mind looking up from *Lotteryland* to find yourself in some kind of *Bright Lights, Big City* revival, as long as you don't have to talk to the local lowlifes. You don't mind finding yourself in an appropriation of *If on a winter's night a traveller,* but the Calvino's tour de force omits everything you know about books.

You know too much. You know that Thomas Pynchon is married to his agent, Melanie Jackson. You know that Julian Barnes is married to his agent, Pat Kavanagh. You know that Don DeLillo is married to Barbara Bennett, a banker. Or rather, Bennett was a banker for many years, and this was what took DeLillo to Greece, where he wrote *The Names,* but now you think you read she has retired.

You know too much. Your ex-stepmother was a coalminer's daughter who went to Cambridge in the early 80s. Thatcher was already cutting back on entitlements for students; they could not sign on for the dole in vacations, they could not claim housing benefit. Your ex-step's pa beat the shit out of her when she went home. She wrote for Black Lace, which was quite a feminist thing to do in the 80s; she wrote for Mills & Boon, which was not a feminist thing to do even in the trashy 80s. Martin Amis was one of her heroes, but Black Lace and Mills & Boon were the publishers who accepted unsolicited manuscripts.

You've seen the Photobooth photos of the black eye, the broken nose, the missing tooth. Her life is a trail of paperbacks, glossy black, glossy red, matte pastel, marking the fact that her father was not an agent or a banker or, for that matter, Kingsley Amis.

Calvino had his gimmick, a gimmick you loved when you read the book at 19, his imaginary reader reads a first chapter, something is wrong with the book, the first chapter is bound in the book ten times, the reader goes hunting for a physical object, a book with the missing chapters, each book that seems to promise continuation turns out to be a completely different book, the imaginary reader finds himself in pursuit of more and more and more books to complete the . . . The point is, look, let's not sneer at plots. The hunt for a physical object or objects is a perfectly good plot. What would it mean to go in search of the books displaced by the glossy paperbacks? Hunting across possible worlds for a world where Thatcher stayed home with the sprogs? Where your stepma did not get bashed to a pulp?

You're just a Bolshevik, you're a theory nerd, you're an avant-garde situationist manquée. *Your* view is that your stepma was behind the times. You read Kathy Acker, you warmed to *Blood and Guts in High School, you* think your stepma should have published a limited edition of 100, preferably in matte pastel (you *loved* the matte pastel), with her black-eyed broken-nosed glamour-puss pic on the back cover. She could have been an Emin or a Lucas, she had the chance to be *transgressive,* the chance to be transgressive while at the same time getting White Cube shows, programme notes citing Adorno, a shot at the fucking Turner Prize, and instead, look, this is someone who wrote a whole fucking doctoral dissertation in New Historicist shtick on Jacobean City *Comedy* and yet she just *accepted* the, she owns a flat in Chiswick because she scored a heroin deal which could conceivably also have been a feminist thing to do in the 80s, but there's this literary *purism*

You know you're just blaming the victim.

You're a romantic at heart.

You want writers to be rebels, revolutionaries, you want them to break the machine or be broken.

BUT MR MALKOVICH WRITES

From: Ilya Gridneff <anarchicus@hotmail.com>
To: Helen DeWitt <Helen.DeWitt@gmx.net>
Subject: 'I want to be considered great writer not fuck'
Date: 30 Aug 2006 15.05 Uhr
Frau DeWitt

yes. I gushed. But I guess my initial comment was a slight hesitation at such sexual overtones in the opening stages, linked also to all this praise for Ilya's writing. I felt like boasting or bragging and yet one shouldn't talk too much perhaps or /// . . . I like the conflict of not wanting to be considered a good fuck but a great writer but . . . perhaps this could be turned into a grander character conflict, like all these (book) industry types (penned pent up London office types or brashy Nu-yorkers looking for some 'real' dangerous action . . . all keen to meet on the rumour of sexual prowess and as he enters a more and more fantastic Byron-esq right the cute koala bad boy-boy band dilemma strengthens. Lots of 'I want my writing to be taken seriously!' 'shut up and lick, I didn't fly from London to talk shop!'

but perhaps, and perchance, the real interest or comedic affect is that he in turn becomes, or *is* prostituting himself within the very process of not wanting to prostitute himself. Like 'we' see 'him' playing the game, writing e-mails with subject headlines *'I want to be considered a great writer not fuck'*, (un)knowing the significance of such comments. It's enjoyable to be the next Henry Miller or Hunter s Thompson, like the winding of the Tristram's father's clock but it's all becoming HARD WORK. Cue rolling stones: *I can't get no . . . jouissance*!

but really, you think 'the gap' stays? A midline diastema is a blessing and a curse. I hear dentistry in Hungary is cheap. Paris would be a good backdrop, everywhere I walk the Eiffel tower will be in the picture, even when in the poor neighbourhoods.

Ilya

Subject: 'I want to be considered great writer not fuck'
From: Helen DeWitt <Helen.DeWitt@gmx.net>
To: Ilya Gridneff <anarchicus@hotmail.com>
Date: 30.08.2006 17.05 Uhr

Herr Gridneff
I think this AMAZING e-mail is exactly what the book needed. It should be finished by next week. Not to worry, everything is under control.
Helen

From: Ilya Gridneff <anarchicus@hotmail.com>
To: Helen DeWitt <Helen.DeWitt@gmx.net>
Subject: fiction fuck factory
Date: 31 Aug 2006 11.17 Uhr

Dewitt,
Yes. Tuff- tug-o-warped moniker making! What is in the na-I-me? (*Deleuze*) Perhaps, Steve Coogan as Steve Coogan/Tristram Shandy/Sir Walter Shandy rather than *Malkovich* "Being Malkovich" as my true progenitor in this fact/fiction we are unravelling. If a fictional name & false beard or Shandean wig/merkin & high-heeled shoes are required to assist the reader, perhaps, perhaps, perhaps, Misha Krapponov from Drinking Bleach, my first (great) unpublished novel, makes an early appearance?

Ilya, allegedly. Or, some random generated spam persona offering names.

P.S
Does Rachel take on a name when pulling tricks?
Ilya (for real this time)

From: "Helen DeWitt" <Helen.DeWitt@gmx.net>
To: "Ilya Gridneff" <anarchicus@hotmail.com>
Subject: Re: fiction fuck factory
Date: 31 Aug 2006 13.54 Uhr

Rachel picks a new nom de guerre each day from her many friends in Boca Raton, spam capital of the western world: Blake Alexander, Krause Kitty, Rolando Bishop, Gladys Cano, Gordon Adams, Dulce Taylor, Ross Lott, Clayton Thompson, Kim Bowen, Marlin Dejesus, Damon Cox, Gwen Yarbrough, Barbara West Sophie Crockett and others too numerous to mention. This didn't make it into the book though b/c it was getting too long (and I think you are giving away the plot).
Krapponov is not much like yr character in this book. How about Pechorin, hero of our time?
h

From: Ilya Gridneff <anarchicus@hotmail.com>
To: Helen DeWitt <Helen.DeWitt@gmx.net>
Date: 31 Aug 2006 15.02 Uhr
Subject: A zero for our Tine

Hell- en (back),
Yes! I read *Hero* a while ago and did think I was often making a fool of myself with various princesses in London or thereabouts. While my fictional doppelganger, or '*dabble-ganger*,' may represent *"our generation's vices in full bloom"* and I did see Perochin as a friend, a 'sensitive rascal' somewhat but I

think maybe there are many more words/names that capture the attitudes of centralist power in fiction.

Hold on, let me scan some baby books lying about scrawled with critique.

"ilya"

From: "Helen DeWitt" <Helen.DeWitt@gmx.net>
To: "Ilya Gridneff" <anarchicus@hotmail.com>
Subject: a hero degree zero for our time
Date: 31 Aug 2006 15.24 Uhr

found this online:
In Russian folklore Alyosha Popovitch is an epic hero, a mighty warrior and a trickster. Unlike Ilya Muromets and Dobrynya Nikititch and other heroes, who served prince Vladimir of Kiev, protected borders of old Russia and fought with various monsters, Alyosha won battles not by his physical superiority but by insidious tricks . . .
According to the legend, Alyosha was born under peals of thunder, and the next day he jumped into the saddle and went "to see the world, to boast and to win".

a zero to hero to zero for all seasons

i'll try this out while you conduct further research

h

From: Ilya Gridneff <anarchicus@hotmail.com>
To: Helen DeWitt <Helen.DeWitt@gmx.net>
Date: 31 Aug 2006 15.38 Uhr
Subject: RE: A hero degree zero for our time

Every name in history is I. (I am hungover, more to come)

From: Ilya Gridneff <anarchicus@hotmail.com>
To: Helen DeWitt <Helen.DeWitt@gmx.net>
Date: 31 Aug 2006 15.41 Uhr
Subject: RE: A hero degree zero for our time

We are all named Napoleon. (very hungover)

The sweet smell of success

X-Originating-IP: [213.78.30.199]
From: "A.P. Pechorin" <popesonxtacy@hotmail.com>
To: "Rachel Zozanian" <zozanian@onetel.com>
Subject: strangers in the abject
Date: Mon, 01 Sep 2003 03:20:44 +0000

found a scrunched up receipt with yer details on it. i forgett yer name but still want to send the pamphlet in the post. wrote this to a friend in Canada.
Alyosha

Orson I turned 24 the other day. not that much changed but the stagnant point of calendar time and place-space rah rah rah met the dot conception occurred time before I am in the present. And now I wait till 5am so I can cycle to Paddington train station so I can catch the train to Heathrow airport to pick up mar father. Yes, Papa bear is in town in three hours. It is 2.58am here. But the past three days have been wrecked. Drunk karaoke on Thursday night in abject Dalston Chinese restaurant, the prawns, pork rolls, beer and in the style of Tina Turner, me grabbing the mic and singing Led Zepplin, Guns and Roses 'Sweet Child o Mine' then watching Scarlett my friend stand on the table and spin around on the lazy Suzanne (not a friend but that curious Chinese culinary device) Rhys a Welsh friend summed the night up by telling me before arriving he wasn,t singing a song, fast forward, Rhys leaping from the chairs to demonstrate that 'I,m going to learn how to fly, high, fameeeeeee!, I wanna live forever---' and so and so. Ended with me going home/kissing (the kiss caused a critical moment) the woman, Kate (36 television buyer, lives in Bow, drives a beat-up Saab), we say we are in love but she doesn,t want me full time, she has a Danish electro deejay called Jakob whom she doesn,t love but chose over me last year after we locked horns. She and I deeply desire each other but usually keep apart, because she doesn,t want me, all this in front of Anna, shock why are we doing this again Kate. You don,t want me. kiss me kiss me. I love you Alyosha. Anna, who had been kissing me earlier in the evening not impressed, then the Bombay mix went everywhere, guilt maybe with me for that toxic explosion, all while Justin performs cunninglingus with April on the washing machine in the toilet. Aidan avoiding April cause he doesn,t want to shag her anymore. More vodka. I scream and on return walk into Rhys and Anna kissing, I have a kiss with Scarlett in front of her new man Kyle, who in turn tries to kiss Kate. Flashing her knickers at 4am and playing records at 11. wake up with Kate. She reminds me about how she was going to piss on me but couldn,t piss. me trying to fuck her arse but too drunk to get an erection on target.

Loads of coffee and another day off. Stephanie takes me to a private view in a house in Bloomsbury where Alexei Sayle turned up. 'Where's me joomper?' The art was tame (expected), green pencil shavings. I proceed to drink the white wine like I was Jesus and unfortunately end up, by duress, queuing in the guest list, at Cargo a gulag of Whoreditch nightclub drama. Inside drunk. Friday night shit smeared walls and fear. Dancing passionately too quickly. On the bus on the way home a small child has a pretend camera and starts taking photos of me. each click I pose differently and suggest to his mother she buys him a real one. she just ignores my drunk spit and tightens her grip of her child. I regret the modelling jest wake up realising I have a picnic to attend. Fuck. People.

On Saturday there was a picnic in Victoria Park, where a new Yorker Slade school graduate was brutally murdered earlier this year, it ended in tears. Six-year relationships ended, Rhys and Anna kissing again, Aidan still trying to avoid April, my friend Ben and his Norwegian girlfriend Birgit, don,t mention the fact I urinated in his mother,s bed when I stayed there several weeks back attending the Brecon Jazz festival.

Talking to strangers in the bar. They don,t have tonic water or ginger ale here outrage. Me drinking olive oil in the organic bar later. stop it Alyosha. Ridiculing the signage that informs the concerned modern man that the fish is killed naturally. I grab April,s camera and take photos inside the paraplegic toilet. Naked torso. an old girlfriend who i can't stand so much i think of her too much, text messaged me 'happy birthday, from an old friend'. what does that mean. Penis in the mirror, the toilet plumbing. More tears. Rhys apologising for taking 'my' woman. Me laughing. At the thought. Ludmilla the Croatian doctor telling me I am wonderful I am and we should go to the party across from Hackney fArm. Get cab to party then have no cash. No booze. Heavy drunk. We get a cab to Whoreditch to get money but mysteriously end up in Lack-ney.

Met a woman whose name escapes but described herself as a novelist and I discuss Ardorno having never read any of his texts. More Vodka. The cab we were in, drives off without us while we buy vodka and get cash. Ludmilla asks if I like the shirt she bought for me and I suggest it maybe too small.., Meaning no. Wake up with Ludmilla. There is blood all over my sheets as her period was heavy.

Tonight I saw Visconti,s *The Leopard,* amazing film about Sicily late 19 century before Italy was Italy. Change just brings the same. the self-deception of the politician. The decline of the aristocrat.

Eating falafel then got a text message from Kate who wanted to talk to me. I find it odd that someone would want to talk to you by sending a text message. Once again, no credit in phone to return call. Shortly after this is rectified. Kissing her after midnight in London Fields. Thinking about the Martin Amis reading at the end of the month. Maybe singing a song Aidan and I developed drunkenly on previous night, *Martin Amis I want to get down on yer anus/would it be so heinous, Martin, Amis* . . . and so forth . . . and now I will wait a few more hours till I will get on my bike sold to me on Kingsland Rd for 7.50 after I had thrown Humus on Blockbuster video for ruining film and colonising cinema into further depths of despair. The half-eaten Turkish bread posted in the late video return. Wanna buy a bike man? I really need the money. The washing machine has broken so the dirty clothes pile up. Thoughts of moving to Odessa, Ukraine. Four months learning the Russian and getting some adventure rather than this abject veneer. Da. Da. dada. Sneer.

Alyosha
it is 3.22am.

To: jbrennan-morgenstern.com
From: "Rachel Zozanian" <zozanian@onetel.com>
Subject: termination
Date: Sun May 16 22:29:35 2004

Please call my cellphone, 917 669 4100. If I don't answer you can assume that I am dead; in that case, please call my landlord, Michael O'Shea, on 718 273 9925 and ask him to check my apartment. It would be unpleasant to leave a decomposing body in this heat. I have left my mother's name and phone number by the bed.

If there is no answer on that number his wife, Sylvia, can be reached on 718 273 3851.

It would be helpful if you could also tell Ulrike Szyk <uszyk@yahoo.com> that I will not be able to come to dinner on Wednesday.

To: jbrennan-morgenstern.com
From: "Rachel Zozanian" <zozanian@onetel.com>
Subject: change of plan
Date: Sun May 16 23:13:04 2004

This method does not work as well as I'd been told, so I will try something simpler elsewhere. There is no need to call my landlord as the body will not be in the apartment. I will also contact Ms Szyk.

Subject: Re: termination
Date: Mon, 17 May 2004 06:49:11 -0400
Thread-Index: AcRCMom8uZdEr3CrT1WQn7vz7ggHCwAE2Akj
From: “Brennan, Jennifer” <jbrennan@morgenstern.com>
To:”Rachel Zozanian” <zozanian@onetel.com>

Rachel,
I was very upset by these e-mails. Please call me or Hari to let us know that you’re ok.

Sent from my BlackBerry Wireless Handheld

CONFIDENTIALITY NOTE:
This e-mail and any attachments are confidential and may be protected by legal privilege. If you are not the intended recipient, be aware that any disclosure, copying, distribution or use of this e-mail or any attachment is prohibited. If you have received this e-mail in error, please notify us immediately by returning it to the sender and delete this copy from your system. Thank you for your cooperation.

MORGENSTERN GROSSMAN & BLUM LLP
Visit us on the web at http://www.morgenstern.com

Web Images Groups News Froogle more>>

Google™ missing "Rachel Zozanian" Search Advanced Search Preferences

Web Results 1-100 of about 5.000 for missing "Rachel Zozanian". (0.21 seconds)

USA TODAY.com - ' Lotteryland' author **Rachel Zozanian** missing
...Lotteryland' author **Rachel Zozanian** missing NEW YORK (AP) -- Novelist **Rachel Zozanian**, who wrote the bestselling Lotteryland, has been reported ...
www.usatoday.com/life/people/2004-05-18-zozanianmissing_x.htm - 65k - Cached - Similar pages

Fandango - News
...Lotteryland' Writer **Rachel Zozanian** Missing ... NEW YORK - Novelist **Rachel Zozanian**, who wrote the critically acclaimed 'Lotteryland," has been reported missing ...
www.fandango.com/news_fullstory.asp?id=apdigital_2004_05_18_ap.online.entertainment.other_D82QRZO6)0_news_... - 26k - Cached - Similar pages

Xposed - Men's Magazine: "Lotteryland" Writer **Rachel Zozanian...**
'Lotteryland" Writer **Rachel Zozanian** Missing. 01;42 PM EST - MAY 18, 2004. The Associated Press NEW YORK Novelist **Rachel Zozanian**, who...
www.exposed.com/headline_news/88_ds_486840.aspx 25k - Cached -_ Similar pages

New York Daily News - Home - Author E-mails her death wish
...Rachel Zozanian. The author of the best-selling novel Lotteryland was reported missing from her Brooklyn apartment yesterday after she sent out an E-mail saying she was going to kill herself, friends said. **Rachel Zozanian**, 28 ...
www.nydailynews.com/front/story/197136p-170228c.h5ml -29k - Cached - Similar pages

TO: RACHEL ZOZANIAN

Upon receipt of your application, and it having been determined that you are suitable for voluntary admission, you have been admitted as a voluntary-status patient to this hospital which provides care and treatment for persons with mental illness.

From this point forward, you may stay as a voluntary patient, or be released if you no longer require hospitalization. You may also be converted to involuntary status, but only if you are certified as meeting the requirements for involuntary admission and are unwilling or are no longer suitable to remain in the hospital voluntarily.

While on voluntary status, you may, at any time, notify hospital staff in writing if you would like to be discharged from the hospital. Upon receipt of such notification, you will be promptly released, unless the director thinks that you meet the requirements for involuntary admission and that you therefore need to stay -- in which case, he or she has 72 hours to ask a court for an order to keep you in the hospital.

You, and anyone acting on your behalf, should feel free to ask hospital staff about your condition, your status and rights under the Mental Hygiene Law, and the rules and regulations of this hospital.

MENTAL HYGIENE LEGAL SERVICE
ELLICOT SQUARE BUILDING
295 MAIN STREET SUITE 444
BUFFALO NEW YORK 14203
874-7532

I HAVE READ, OR HAD READ TO ME, AND UNDERSTAND THE CONTENTS OF THIS NOTICE.

Patient's Signature Rachel Zozanian Date May 21, 2004

2 Adorno thou shouldst be living at this hour

. . . immer von Beckett ist eine technische Reduktion bis zum außersten

. . . always from Beckett is a technical reduction to the extreme

Aber diese Reduktiion ist ja wirklich das was die Welt aus uns macht

. . . das heißt die Welt aus uns gemacht diese Stümpfe von Menschen

also diese Menschen die eigentlich ihr ihr ich verloren haben

but this reduction is really what the world makes out of us

. . . that is the world [has] made out of us these stumps of men

so these men who have actually lost their I

die sind wirklich die Produkte der Welt in welche wir leben

who are really the products of the world in which we live

—Theodor Adorno

La dolce vita

1

The sentences had dried up. There were not enough sentences to get through a party.

There were not enough sentences for a phone call to Mr Clever. She sent Mr Clever an e-mail saying there were not enough sentences for a party. She did not get a reply from Mr Clever, but Lucy Moran telephoned to say that Mr Clever had discussed the party and he thought Simon had his heart set on it.

There were not enough sentences to get through the phone call with Lucy Moran. Running on empty.

The body was put on a plane by the crazy head. Its nudity was concealed by a black pencil skirt from Sticky Fingers, a black DKNY jacket with narrow black satin lapels, Ultra Sheer charcoal collants by Christian Dior and black suede ankle boots with four-inch heels from Via Mya. Show the flag.

The body stood in these clothes between Jay McInerney and Bret Easton Ellis. Jay McInerney said something to Bret Easton Ellis. Bret Easton Ellis said something to Jay McInerney. Restful.

A man came and talked to the clothes.

Talk talk talk talk.

Simon said something to Jay McInerney. Jay McInerney said something to Simon. Simon said something to Bret Easton Ellis. Bret Easton Ellis said something to Simon. Simon did not talk to the clothes because he did not like his contract. If he did not look at the contract it was not binding.

The man talked to the clothes.

Talk talk.

The body was put in a taxi and taken to Brooklyn. It lay on a bed. Dawn broke.

The body walked out the door.

The body walked to Grand Army Plaza.

The body got on a train. The train went to Penn Station. A machine dispensed tickets for which no sentences must be paid. O blessed machine!

A finger pressed a screen. A one-way ticket dropped down. O machine! Kiss kiss kiss. Kiss kiss kiss kiss.

The body took an escalator down. The body stepped onto a train. It did not end well.

Now the body takes a taxi to Buffalo. Buys a ticket on the next train out. Gets on the train. Gets off the train.

The body is in a large station. Long shiny wooden benches call a memory to mind, there is an image of the station in *The Hustler,* the station to which Paul Newman goes, down and out. He has lost to Minnesota Fats, has no money, nowhere to go. The body sits on a bench. It's quiet. Money is not the problem, there is money for a hotel. There are no sentences to connect the money to the transaction.

People walk back and forth.

Lotteryland is displayed in the station bookstore. A brief column on the front page of the *New York Times* states that Rachel Zozanian, 28, was found unharmed in Niagara Falls, taken for observation, and released. A picture on the front page of the *New York Post* shows Rachel Zozanian, dark of hair, flashing of eye, standing between Jay McInerney and Bret Easton Ellis.

The hands rest palm up on the thighs. Hours pass.

The occupant of a black leather jacket, faded black jeans and black and red carved cowboy boots takes a seat beside the occupant of the clothes described above.

The occupant says Sure is a long way from Alaska.

It says: I own a restaurant in Ketchikan but I'm originally from Tulsa. Had a friend who was a Cordon Bleu chef. One night they were short-staffed so I took over the bar. He said he'd teach me to cook. Went up to Alaska following the pipeline. Taught me how to cook to quantity.

Sentence: That's interesting.

The head is not very clever.

Ketchikan Cowboy: Started a restaurant. People appreciate quality. Got wanderlust. Told some young friends o mine they could run the place fer a year. Went to Loosiana. Looked at them ol oil rigs. I said, How do I get me onto one o them thangs? Guy says: Can you cook? I say: Sure can. He says: Yeah but can you cook for 200 men? I say: Try me.

It feels good sitting next to the clothes.

Ketchikan Cowboy: When's your train?

Sticky Fingers DKNY: I just got off a train.

Is it possible to get a hotel room with a single sentence?

SF DKNY: Do you want to go a hotel?

KC: Whoaaaaaaaaaaaa!!!!!

Alaskan affirmative.

KC makes calls, books a room, finds a taxi. The hotel room has a large bed with a white cover.

KC: When did you decide you wanted to fuck me?

SF DKNY: You talk too much.

Kiss kiss. Clothes fall. Kiss kiss.

KC: What do you want me to do?

SF DKNY: (You've done what I want you to do.) Surprise me.

Kiss kiss.

KC: Do you want to masturbate?

SF DKNY: We could do that.

KC: Do you want to get in the shower?

SF DKNY: If you like.

Kiss kiss kiss kiss.

KC: What's wrong?

Is something wrong? Is this not spontaneous and unpremeditated? Is social sex not nice? He has an erection. What specifically does he think is wrong?

SF DKNY: You talk too much.

1

From: "A.P. Pechorin" <popesonxtacy@hotmail.com>
To: amanda292@hotmail.com
Subject: the (brad) pit of tabloid divinity
Date: Sun, 23 May 2004 20:37:33 +0000

Hello Amanda

Yes. Hope all well. The nature of this e-mail makes me cringe somewhat. I am not sure if you are aware but I have lowered myself into the well, well-beneath the gutter and now deep in the sewer where I writhe blissfully in the filthy world of tabloid journalism. I work for various 'national papers' – of a particular persuasion - but mostly the fine drum of truth-*The Sunday Sentinel.* Have you heard it calling?

For some reason I have got it into my head you may have been friends with, and/ or associated with and/or know someone who may, or may not, know Jake and Starr . . . is this so?

I am working for the Sunday Sentinel over here and they have taught me to try every angle. Forget moralities/ethics and a taste for sense, or a sense of taste/tact etc etc. But, basically, there was a massive story yesterday (Saturday 22/05/04 - www.newsoftheworld.co.uk) in the News of the World, the internationally renowned Murdoch tabloid, that the world's most loved couple are breaking up- or at least fighting because Jake was shagging around etc etc. The dogwalker sold his story for I think a cool £300 000.

So, if you know anything about anything, ANYTHING, (or would like to suggest something/ANYTHING) or have something that places you there – or thereabouts - or are able to say something...*anything*...even if you heard a fart or burp or quiver of difference, no insignificance can be too small or unspinnable tabloid fodder.

Why not have a read of the *Screws (NoTW)* story. Perhaps it may make something ring. You would be surprised how ridiculous things become. The more absurd sometimes the better. *Starr liked to be spoon-fed quails eggs while hordesof entrenched helpers did pedicures/manicures and recreated scenes from history* . . . that sort of shit . . . Anything really, please let me know.

If all this is my mistake sorry and you have a document here before indicating how meaningless things are in this (tabloid) world. Or I've become.

There is money available but it is always linked to how good your stuff is. And, they would also want a picture- if you have a pic with any of these people etc etc . . .

Well yes, how have you been? I am truly a disgusting creature beyond all shame, I know, I know but all the empty news with me seems to build into an exciting story for them. Perhaps a better one than Jake and Starr breaking up. It's AWFULLY fun, sometimes.

Well still haven't heard from Steve for a long time, is he ok? What is he doing?

Hope everything is well. Love to family...

Alyosha
+4479 3096 5676

To: "A.P. Pechorin" <popesonxtacy@hotmail.com>
From: amanda292@hotmail.com
Subject : RE: the (brad) pit of tabloid divinity
Date: Sun 23 May 2004 02:28:56

ello ello ello, Senor Pechorin, que banana sorpresa

Needless to say, I am profoundly shocked at the depths to which the former crusading boy wonder has sunk!

I have been staying with mum's family in Prince Edward Island for the past month, licking my wounds. I did see that the Jake & Starr show had gone into overdrive but it seems very remote, the tempest in a teapot it always was. When you're caught up in it you lose sight of that . . .

Gianni the dogwalker is someone I met whilst dogwalking for Chloe Wade-Roe in Regents Park. We had a mutual respect for the other's dog handling and would cover in case of need which is how I got to know Starr (who was more "hands-on" with the dogs). I was there when Starr found the text message re Jake's drunken fling with Gil, Gianni's boyfriend, & whilst she appreciated Gianni was in no way to blame she wanted to take temptation out of Jake's way so begged Gianni and me to trade jobs which we agreed to do. I was thrown together very much with Starr during Lhu-Pei's long illness so heard a lot of things, phone calls at clinic and what have you that nobody else could have known.

Gianni has already been through so much aggro I do not want to add to it so I don't think I can give you what you are looking for.

Steve is thrilled to hear you were in touch, says give him a buzz.

Hope to hear from you soon

Amanda

2

The phone rings.

What time is it? Two o'clock. Desist.

The phone rings. It's 2:00:03.

The phone rings. It's 2:00:07.

She picks up the receiver. A word leaves her mouth, never to return. The word is "Hello."

The word unleashes a torrent of verbiage. This should tell you everything you need to know. If you call someone in the middle of the afternoon and interrogate, the prodded brain may generate sentences, yes. This is the quality of sentence generated by the torpid brain. It would rather unleash a torrent than put a word in the garbage and look for another. "Verbiage" washed in with the tide, the brain picks up jetsam and calls it a sentence.

Her mouth utters the word "Hello" a second time. Sounds pour into her ear in the shape of words.

"Rachel" "Rachel" "Rachel" "just" "wanted" "to" "know" "you're" "all" "right"

She puts the receiver on the table by the bed. Now that she has answered the phone it has stopped ringing. Sounds still pour from the tiny holes of the earpiece like a swarm of ants; they shrivel and die when they hit the air.

She turns her face to the wall.

2

To: amanda292@hotmail.com
From: "A.P. Pechorin" <popesonxtacy@hotmail.com>
Subject: bleach and rat poison cocktails
Date: Mon 24 May 2004 14:15:22 +0000

Yes. Indeed Amanda I was impressed by your maturity and experiences expressed in the last email. Wow! What a heady life dazzling in the mirror ball of fame. I didn't realise you were in the inner sanctum/rectum of it all - how did you become so close?/ friends?

Despite it being 'full on' - it must have also been exciting. I think I heard something through my mum - probably from your mum - as mums are proud and all that crap. Funny like there is one of my stories about some incredible animal cross mating with another species, surrounded by naked ladies posing with phallic objects or national identity symbols wedged between their wedges and mum's all: how proud I am... my little boy. the jernalist

Yeap! You are right about all this. Radical Marxo-fenophilo tub thumping to yellow press meister! The fall & fall!! I can not tell you how it makes me want to drink bleach-rat poison cocktails with the nature of media over here. Last week I was bribing *Screws* lorry drivers to throw me a copy of the late edition paper outside Murdoch's *News LTD* fortress. The other week nearly punched out by some weedy celeb for a piece of shit story that didn't even make the newspaper. Though this does create some sort of backdrop to an 'interesting' life. An excuse to drink more & be sin-acle, or synacle, (sin-cycle?)

I spoke to the news editor and said I had a contact who was a friend of the two (Gianni and Gil) I told them you weren't too keen to get involved and they grunted the usual responses. To be honest and straight down the line Amanda - I am only here for my own advancement. I am trying to do this tabloid game business to get somewhere else (more respectable pursuits

- writing a book about this sort of slime etc) Such a story like this (you) will help me rise up out of mire of quag I am entrenched in. It was the first time they rang me back and said nice things to me, even '*fucking brilliant mate*' which made me feel like one of Fagan's favourite sparrows.

They told me to tell you -my anonymous source: "No one will know where the comments will come from -your identity will be kept to a 'friend' or 'insider' label. Her story could be worth *thousands* of pounds."

Perhaps the deposit of a house? I dunno. Simply, they asked me to ask you, to ask them… basically, give them a call and discreetly ask where they are? (Are they are on holiday *together* is a good question?) because you have heard about all the media hype, what is going on, etc etc...then amongst whatever else they say, ask to how they are – ask them what else is going to come out in the newspaper this week, that would also be a help.

Do you hve any pictures of them all together? Whether it be Starr and Gianni and Gil and Amber and Slade – they are worth a great deal of money too.

Please Amanda I know all this is pretty lame (and sad) but considering the free-for-all at the minute it could be beneficial to all of us. I will do everything to protect your identity and make sure you get the best deal in the end. No one will pay attention to the Sunday Sentinel cause all the juicy stuff is coming out in our rival *NOTW*. Well I hope I have made you more interested.

alyosha

tell Steve to give us a ring, he is such a lazy prick

+447930965676

From: amanda292@hotmail.com
To: "A.P. Pechorin" <popesonxtacy@hotmail.com>
Subject: RE: bleach and rat poison cocktails
Date: Mon 24 May 2004 16:47:22 +1000

Alyosha
not sure. I really came to Prince Edward Island to get away from it all. The prospect of some money is appealing as I am resting between engagements but any pictures are out of the question as I would be readily identifiable.

this feels like a transmission from some amorphous intergalactic nebula, real world it would be catastrophic if my name was connected. I am working on a celebrity pet service addressing the important role these often overlooked animals play in lives where no human can ever be trusted and Starr could either make or break it.

Speaking purely on spec what would be the next step?

Amanda

3

The phone rings.

She must have replaced the receiver. Unless the cleaner did it. Does she have a cleaner? Could someone have come in to clean? And replaced the receiver? "Cleaner" sounds strange. Is it "cleaning lady"? Or "cleaning woman"? Does she have one?

Anyway, the phone rings.

She doesn't trust herself.

The phone rings.

She picks up the receiver. Sounds burst forth.

"Hi" is the word the sounds assume. "It's [Instantly Forgettable Name]." Is this a name she has heard before? It would be rude to ask. And why ask? She does not want to know.

Her mouth expels breath breathily. "Hi" enters the mouthpiece of the phone.

Sounds enter the ear.

—Utterance, she says.

—Utter what?

—Utterance.

—It's no big deal, we just wanted to know if [Instantly Forgettable Question About Instantly Forgotten Fact].

She does not want to discuss what she knows and does not know.

—Utterance. Utterance. Utterance. Utterance. Utterance.

—Is this a bad time?

It's dangerous to utter sentences that may be taken to express propositions having a truth value. The man in the street does not keep up with the twists and turns of philosophical logic. Don't give him a rope to hang you with.

It's rude to hang up on people.

She places a pillow on the table. She places the receiver on the pillow. She places another pillow on the receiver. The ants die by suffocation, unseen, unheard.

3

From: “A.P. Pechorin” <popesonxtacy@hotmail.com>
To: amanda292@hotmail.com
Subject: the pavlov’s bollix
Date: Tues 25 May 2004 13:48:29 +0000

Wow. Amanda pet psychology - I didn’t realise. I thought you were involved in real estate. Can I call you? It’s best to talk over the telephone. Or to start with can you tell me where they are on holiday and do you know what else is to come out - like what were/ are the other problems... can I call or you call me and then I will return the call.

alyosha
+447930965676

4

The phone rings.

What time is it? 6.28.02.

Which would be what in Dubuque?

12.28.02. Ungodly.

The phone rings. It's 6.28.05

What day is it anyway? 28 May. Could it not have been allocated to someone who wanted it? The market is failing to clear.

The phone rings.

The phone rings.

The phone rings.

The phone rings.

—Hello?

—Is that Rachel?

—We're not ruling out that possibility at this time.

—*Rachel. Rachel. Rachel.* It's Vikram. I heard it on the news and it quite simply knocked me for a loop.

—

—Rachel?

—Yes?

—Sorry, thought there was something wrong with the line, *look,* darling, if you need a hideyhole you *know* you're always *more* than welcome to stay with Nick and I. And *look,* what I *wanted* to say was, *look,* these are shark-infested waters, you shouldn't be dealing with these people, it's a fucking stupid waste of your talent, you should be *writing,* so *look,* Nick and I have cooked up this little idea between the two of us which we think could *just possibly* be the *solution,* which is *how* would it be if you just talked to *me*? Let me act as a buffer, talk to all these people *for* you so you can just get *on* with it.

— That's awfully sweet of you, Viks.

—I'd be *more* than happy to do it, darling. Let me deal with all the bullshit for you.

—

—I don't want to put my foot in it, but I *worry* about you. It's all very well for Guido and Anne to put you up, they *mean well*, but to be a bit brutal they're *amateurs*, they're out of their *league*, if they start wittering away to Noszaly they could put the *caboosh* on the whole *shebang*, they're *quite* capable of doing all *kinds* of damage with the best possible intentions which is quite simply the *last* thing you need to be worrying about at a time like this

—

—Nick and I are still *passionate* about *The Tetragrammaton*, darling, and

The Inbox is full of bad business. Also an old e-mail from a stranger in a bar

> It is 2.58am here. But the past three days have been wrecked. Drunk karaoke on Thursday night in abject dalston Chinese restaurant, the prawns, pork rolls, beer and in the style of Tina Turner, me grabbing the mic and singing led zepplin, guns and roses sweet child o mine then watching scarlett my friend stand on the table and spin around on the lazy Suzanne (not a friend but that curious Chinese culinary device) Rhys a welsh friend summed the night up by telling me before arriving he wasn,t singing a song, fast forward, rhys leaping from the chairs to demonstrate that i,m going to learn how to fly, high, fameeeeeee!, I wanna live forever—and so and so.

She used to read it in New York when things got bad. It was like the world of Fellini, that sordid glamorous world in the rubble of a dead empire. It's like nothing she knows, that's what she likes.

The phone rings.

4

From: “A.P. Pechorin” <popesonxtacy@hotmail.com>
To: “Amanda” <amanda292@hotmail.com>
Subject: RE: questions
Date: Fri, 28 May 2004 00:43:55 +0000

Yes. The story went and everyone was happy like pigs in shit. They ran what they called a ‘pro Starr piece’ headlined: ‘I’ll kill myself if you leave & take the dogs’. a ‘concerned friend said she was worried about the stress of the situation for both’. They focused on the heroic battle with drugs and said about the stress of the situation - with the rows and threats a close friend is really worried... They pulled out the Jake likes five-somes with Jake likes-em “cheap” into a headline. It was funny how banal screaming headlines can become hysterically giddying.

I will find out what the money deal is tomorrow (Tuesday) and get the cash sorted immediately. I have asked around what the money will be like but never can tell. they said thousands so we will see. You will be looked after and paid very well.

Will tell them about your idea as to supporting cissy, wouldn’t this tarnish your relationship with Starr? Would this be on or off the record though? Ok thanks a million. Will keep you updated as I know.

Alyosha

From: “Amanda” <amanda292@hotmail.com>
To: “A.P. Pechorin <popesonxtacy@hotmail.com>
Subject: RE: questions
Date: Fri, 28 May 2004 01:13:23 +0000

alyosha,
it wd have to be off the record
thx for being the loyal cashhound these things can get lost in the shuffle
xx
Amanda

From: "A.P. Pechorin" <popesonxtacy@hotmail.com>
To: "Amanda" <amanda292@hotmail.com>
Subject: RE: RE: questions
Date: Sat 29 May 2004 13:10:25 +0000

They want to send you a cheque for £7000. Do you want me to give them your name and address? Or give me the word to put into my account and I will transfer it over to yours . . .

I find out how much I get soon. They said 1 but I asked for 2K. I asked for 15 to be split 50/50 but they were not too keen despite the story running over two pages from a front page 'World Exclusive' – WHICH IT WAS - that they later told me wasn't too revealing as was of paying less...but basically our 'off the record conversations' is the story. My advice is not to tell anyone no matter how exciting this seems - and if anyone approaches you say not interested or you don't talk to newspapers . . . if you can remember any names of the girls Jake cheated on then they would love this and sort out more coins . . . will speak to them about the positive Cissy story.

Let's speak in a bit. take care. Any other dirt to dish would be great, didn't you date a footballer . . .

alyosha

From: "Amanda" <amanda292@hotmail.com>
To: "A.P. Pechorin <popesonxtacy@hotmail.com>
Subject: RE: questions
Date: Sat 29 May 2004 18:02:33 +0000

it all feels slightly surreal like some weird Magrittean paysage w/ fivers & tenners drifting down a windless sky, bloke in a bowler hat w/ apple face

If it works out it will be a major lifesaver as I maxed out my credit cards in NY & one of my big customers cancelled an order while I was away

Not sure what else I remember. You know how it is you wake up the next morning and think *did that actually happen?* And you don't necessarily know people's names . . . but I suspect a deposit of cheque in much-abused bank acct will assist in data recovery . . .

xx
amanda

Fear of Flying

You're reading *Your Name Here,* the new novel by Helen DeWitt, in a large print edition. You're in seat 83D of flight UA653 out of Baltimore International, on your way to the Bahamas. You didn't want to take this trip. You don't like flying. You never wanted to leave the country. If you could have taken the kind of vacation you like you would never have bought this book.

You would have liked to rent a camper van and drive across the country to Yellowstone National Park to see Old Faithful. You and your husband would have taken turns driving, and when you weren't driving you would have read the new Anne Tyler. You don't like the new Anne Tylers as much as your favorite Anne Tylers—the three best are *The Accidental Tourist, Morgan's Passing* and *Searching for Caleb,* and Tyler hasn't written anything that good in a *long* time, but you keep buying the new books in the hope that Tyler will recapture the old magic. That's what you would have read on your vacation of choice.

It's not that you're averse to an element of risk on a vacation. The kind of risk you like is where you pitch a tent in Yellowstone National Park and wake up in the middle of the night to find a grizzly bear foraging in the camper van for snacks. You grope frantically for the mobile phone, make a call, and a friendly park ranger turns up to tell you how much trouble irresponsible campers like you cause the National Park Service. The kind of risk you don't like is where some wild-eyed terrorist breaks into the cockpit and either crashes the plane into the White House/Pentagon/you name it or hijacks it to some remote outpost of who knows where.

Your kids gave you grief, your husband gave you grief, your parents gave you grief, his parents gave you grief, everyone was *adamant* that you were just an old stick in the mud who needed to be more adventurous. Well, okay, if you *had* to leave the country you could have put your mind at rest by buying *Teach Yourself Arabic,* but the thing you like about Anne Tyler is that Tyler understands that someone who buys *Teach Yourself Arabic* as insurance for a trip to the Bahamas is going to get so much grief it's not even worth *thinking* about. You'd heard that *Your Name Here,* the new novel by Helen DeWitt, included an introduction to Arabic. So you bought it, and you told your family you'd decided to be more adventurous in your reading, thinking you could quietly pick up some Arabic in the three hours you'd have to spend at the airport before your flight. If the plane is hijacked into the Pentagon picking up a few scraps of Arabic won't help, but if it's rerouted to the back of beyond you might be glad you'd picked up a language not normally needed for a trip to the Bahamas.

Unfortunately the book has far less Arabic than you'd been led to expect. Did the publishers exert pressure? If only Anne *Tyler*—a writer you love who is also an established writer of bestsellers—had written a novel with an introduction to Arabic! This would have been the best of all possible worlds in which you fail to drive cross-country to Yellowstone.

On your third day in the Bahamas you happen to be talking to your new friend Pat. She's rereading *The Accidental Tourist*. Anne Tyler has reissued *The Accidental Tourist* with an introduction to Arabic interspersed throughout the book for nervous travelers! Pat holds up her trophy:

مِن فَضْلَك *min fadlik* please

لَا إقْتُلْني *leh iqtulni* don't kill me

لا إجْرَحْني *leh ijrahni* don't hurt me

لا إخْطِفْني *leh ikhtifni* don't kidnap me

أنا أُمٍ *ana umm* I [am a] mother

شُكراً *shukran* thank you

This is *exactly* what you *wanted.* If *only* you'd *known.* You would have *loved* to reread *The Accidental Tourist*. Now Pat is clutching the book tightly, giving you a suspicious look.

Your husband is out scuba diving. You sneak back to your bungalow and write it all down before you forget. You say each phrase twenty times since there's no one to see, *min fadlik, leh iqtulni, leh ijrahni, leh ikhtifni, ana umm, shukran.*

If *only* you had the Anne Tyler.

Maybe you'd like your husband's book better, you've heard him chuckling to himself while you *labored* to finish *Your Name Here.* He's reading the cult classic *Lotteryland* by the reclusive Rachel Zozanian.

TLNAELDYOTR

2. WITH A LITTLE LUCK FROM MY FRIENDS

1.

Maimonides says there are eight levels of charity.

The lowest is where the giver gives grudgingly.

The next level is where the giver gives too little, but graciously.

The next level is when one gives after he has been asked.

The next level is when one gives even before he is asked.

The next level is where the receiver knows the giver but the giver does not know the receiver.

The next is where the giver knows the receiver but the receiver does not know the giver.

The next is where the giver and receiver are unknown to each other.

The first and highest form of charity is to give a man a loan to make him independent.

What it means is that if you are not a complete tosser you can give someone a chance to exercise the highest form of charity. If you're a complete tosser you're not really in a position to enable someone to engage in the highest form of charity, but you can show up at a weekday service and walk around during the service and hold out your hand. You're still doing everyone a favour—at least you're giving them the chance to engage in *some* form of charity. The more you show up the bigger the favour you're doing everybody. You're not offering the element of anonymity so essential to the upper levels of charity—but after all, they can't count on an anonymous beneficiary showing up every day. You they can count on.

Any religious Jew would recognise the principle, in a religious congregation you might walk out with £40 or £50. Perhaps more. From a strictly financial point of view it was not necessary to go in search of Hasidim. From almost every other point of view they were to be avoided like the plague. But but but but but.

My father's spies are not everywhere. A church or mosque would have been safe enough. A Reform service, likewise—if my father knows anyone who's Reform, they're both keeping quiet. But my father's friends and family were scattered across London; there were not many Orthodox shuls where I could be sure of not being recognised and reported. The Lubavitch were another matter. My father only knew two to speak to, and he wasn't on speaking terms with either.

2.

I thought: But what are the odds that a girl will write to a bloke who looks like the weird ugly one in an adventurous boy band? Who has told her nothing but lies?

I thought: Yes, but what if

Because I suddenly thought about this publisher who had not liked the project. Surely there was a lesson to be learnt. The lesson to be learnt was that I should just be myself.

Because supposing I found someone to practise the highest form of charity, I could write something sincere and heartfelt that was not only true of someone but of me. And just supposing Gaby did write to me I could give her the new story to show this bloke Giles. If I used my real name there would be nothing to connect it with the insincere and calculating person he had taken this unaccountable dislike to.

I asked someone crossing the bridge what day of the week it was and he said Friday.

I thought: *Fuck.*

3.

It was already late afternoon. The sun would soon be down, Shabbat would come in, and though I might put in an appearance at Friday evening service it would be useless to put out my hand, since no one would be carrying money to put in it. If invited home for a meal I would not be able to raise sordid financial details until dark the following day. If among the Lubavitch I would be in for a solid 25 hours of cheerful piety.

For a moment I thought of just blagging my way back to Dublin. I had spent a lot of time trying to get one of the rare slots for a weird one or an ugly one, the competition is fierce because there just aren't the openings, maybe I was hungry enough now to make the grade.

I thought: Oh, sure.

4.

No. My face, sadly, was no fortune. I was going to have to get by on my wits. Realistically, my best chance to start winning again was to bite the bullet.

Make my way up to Stamford Hill. Attend Maariv. Blag invitation. Grit teeth.

On Saturday night, after Shabbat went out, I could explain my plight to my host. He would, naturally, be only too pleased at this unexpected charity opportunity. 'Pay it back when you can,' he would say benevolently, thrusting large amounts of dosh into my hands.

With the proceeds I could find a place to stay. In the longer term I could have a shot at the heartwarming story of how one boy staked everything on a single draw of the Lottery—and lost. In the shorter term I could sit the UEO. It was a long shot too, but then what wasn't?

The longest journey starts with a single step. It was time to head north and find a shul.

I was about to head across the bridge to Monument when I suddenly realised that something important was missing.

I was going to need something to cover my head.

I thought: Fuck.

When I walked out of U2 six months before I'd lost everything. I had a lot of things on my mind. One of the things that was not on my mind was stuffing a kippah in my pocket just in case I happened to have a sudden freak religious fit.

In a drawer in my room at home, of course, I had another 23. Where was I to get one now? You don't buy them. They come from Israel. People go to Israel and think of you and bring one back to show they thought of you.

A hat would have done as well, but where was I going to find a hat? And besides—a *hat*? With what for money?

I ran across the bridge to Monument thinking fuck fuck fuck fuck fuck. This was no time for false economy, the sort of shop that might conceivably sell them would be closing soon. I bought a ticket for £1.80 to Golders Green, hurtled through the barrier, took the stairs five at a time and sprinted along the platform following signs to the Northern Line.

There was still an hour of light in the sky when I stepped off the train.

I ran wildly into the street asking people where can I buy a kippah. Nobody knew, naturally, because you don't buy them, they come from Israel. Finally someone said she knew a religious goods store but he would be closing any minute. I ran wildly in the direction of this religious goods store, which was about to close, and ran through the door.

A kippah, I said, I need a kippah, and I stood panting by a display. There were velvet embroidered kippot, and silk embroidered kippot, and plain velvet and plain silk. There seemed to be nothing in the £1.43 range.

I said: Don't you have anything cheaper?

He said: How much were you thinking of spending?

I said: £1.43.

He said: Look. I'll tell you what I'll do. I don't like to open a pack. Somebody orders extras for a wedding, they like an unopened pack. It doesn't pay to sell them separately, it would work out at £1.25 but it doesn't pay to open the pack.

He took out a black silk kippah and put it on the counter. He said he would accept a deposit of 50p and the balance, £4.45, when I had the money.

I said: £4.45? That's *highway* robbery.

He shrugged and said: Take it or leave it

I gave him 50p. The things we do for love.

My kingdom for a broomstick

1

The phone rings.

What time is it? 21.02.17. Which would be what in, this would be where, again?

The phone rings.

The phone rings.

The phone rings.

Tulsa. 13.02.17. Ungodly.

The phone rings.

—Hello?

—Is that Rachel?

—Unless notified to the contrary.

—*Rache.* Oh *Rache.* It's Lyndall.

— PUT THAT DOWN.

—Rache?

—PUT THAT DOWN.

—Rache?

—Don't make me use this. That's right. Keep going. Good. Out.

—WAAAAAAAAAAAAAAAAH. WAAAAAAAAAAAAAAAAH.

—Rache?

—Rug rat. It was trying to open my lucky chocolates.

—Oh *Rache.* Sounds like it's just all too *much.*

—

—Look, Rache, you're always *more* than welcome to stay chez Novak, you know that. You know where we keep the key, just show up any time. I mean that. It's not just a business relationship, we're *friends.* We just wanted you to know we're still *besotted* with *Hypno,* in fact we'd *love* to

Puts box-cutter on table.

2

The phone rings.

What time is it? 11:23.23.

Bad time.

The phone rings.

Get it over with.

—Hi, is that Rachel? Sam. Just wanted to see how you were.

—Fine.

The information sought has been ascertained. Now they can hang up.

—So, are you writing anything these days? You know, Anne and I would love to have a first look agreement, we

—*Yikes*! Something burning on the stove! Got to go!

Stranger in a bar: *I proceed to drink the white wine like I was Jesus and unfortunately end up, by duress, queuing in the guest list, at Cargo a gulag of Whoreditch nightclub drama. Inside drunk. Friday night shit smeared walls and fear. Dancing passionately too quickly.*

O the kindness of strangers.

3

What time is it? Time for dinner. My kingdom for a horse. On the living room floor are paraplegic Barbies, a scalped rag doll, five naked decapitated Action Men, a disembowelled cloth chimp.

What's his name, would it be Alan? Rick? Gary? is not yet home. Gina talks about the shock. You don't understand how many people love you, she explains.

Could the information not be conveyed in writing?

—Could we not talk?

—I think it's *important* to talk. There are people who really *care* about you, people who could create a *safety* zone, people who could talk to people like Nozsaly, for example, on your *behalf*, run interference for you with these people who are only interested in the money.

—They could drop me a line.

—We've been to the cleaners and *back*, Rachel. We've been *around* the *block*. You don't understand what you put people *through*.

It is not easy to see why a request to refrain from speech should be taken to display lack of understanding.

—Whatever the level of distress, either it caused you to attempt suicide or it did not. If it did not, it seems likely that the level of distress was lower than that of someone who did in fact attempt suicide. If there is, however, no such direct correlate between intensity of emotion and action, and if it is also the case that intensity of emotion without danger of death trumps danger of death without intensity of emotion, it makes no sense for suicide per se to provoke extreme distress, since it has been determined that danger of death is relatively unimportant.

This was an inadvisable and, indeed, dangerous thing to say. If she had written this in an e-mail she would have deleted the sentences, but utterances pass the barrier of the teeth and cannot be recalled. Someone who has been breaking down and crying does not want clarity. It is good to refrain from snatching up knives, but it is bad to display the mechanism which achieves this.

Gina does stop talking. She starts screaming.

—YOU JUST DON'T GET IT, DO YOU? YOU JUST DON'T FUCKING GET IT.

This is dangerous.

—Will you excuse me?

She goes to the kitchen. She fills a short glass with ice. What do they have? Wild Turkey. Excellent news. She pours a triple.

Chuck Palahniuk tells a story of his early days. He went to a writer's workshop and a guy, would his name have been Mike? said you're using the third person which never has a lot of energy and you're not doing anything very interesting with it. Well said, Mike, but it takes energy to show the flag. Halfway down the glass the first person starts to look like something a person might manage with aplomb, not to say charm.

I drain the glass. I pour a generous double. I return to the living room.

I summon to the lips a voice of betazoidal warmth and sincerity, modelled on that of Olivia de Havilland in *Gone with the Wind.*

—*Gina,* I say. *Gina.* I *know.* I *know.* I *know.*

She bursts into tears. I hug her.

—I *know,* I say. I *know.* And you've been simply *wonderful.* You and [what's his name, again? Rick? Dan? Stan?] Dongsuk *both.* It's not just a *business* relationship, we're *friends.*

—Dongsuk and I think of you as a member of the *family.*

Good save.

—I *know.* I *know.* I *know.*

—If there's *anything* we can *do*

—I need to hold a press conference.

—

—I can't get through to the publicist at Sharpshooters.

—

—I need an agent.

—Oh, *Rachel,* I *really* don't think that's what you need at this time. Throwing yourself into the media maelstrom

—No, I think it's a good idea. It's good when you can give the media what they want. If they want dazzling first novel six-figure deal I can't believe my luck when you're suicidal they don't know what to do with it, it doesn't fit the story. But if you crack up and that's the story they can take what they need from the bits that work from Woolf and Plath, bits that have been tried and tested and proved popular, and then being crazy and suicidal is your myth and it's fine. You're giving them what they want. And once they've made it into your myth it's something everyone can enjoy, if you do something strange it has its glamour

—I think you're getting overexcited

I realise too late that in the alleged overexcitement I have allowed the OdH betazoidal empathy to lapse. I realise in time that it would be unwise to point out that I have been robbed of $1600, that I remember the names and faces of my interrogators, and that it would be the easiest thing in the world to nip out and buy a Smith & Wesson 637 .38 revolver (or snubbie) before returning to take justice into my own hands. (But what a great book! This is GREAT! This is GREAT!) Does Oklahoma law permit former stepmothers to

Five children intrude, scream. Order of precedence over choice of DVD has been violated. Gina puts a hand to her tearstained face, says Not now, is plagued.

Wittgenstein says: How does *he* know what he thinks, he has only his signs? In other words, I may be about to run berserk. I may smash my glass and slash, I may run to the kitchen and snatch up a knife and return for carnage, I don't know what will happen. I don't know how to find out what will happen before it's too late.

—Will you excuse me for a moment?

I am not sure how soon I can get away. What if the constant noise—

I return to my room. I sit on the bed, holding the lucky chocolates.

Stranger in a bar: *Fuck. People.*

Suddenly I have a brilliant idea!

My iBook is on the bed with 45 minutes left on its battery. By a happy accident (although Gödel thought there are no accidents) I have with me the Penguin edition of the collected stories of Saki! Ha ha! Jesus loves me! Jesus loves me! Ha ha ha! I open to the obvious page; I turn on the iBook, open Mellel, type madly, save the bloody document in PDF (the driver for the household printer has not been installed on my Mac, needless to say), save the bloody PDF on a CD, take the CD to the grownups' computer, double click on Saki.pdf and print out five copies of the following:

> Rules of the game.
> I have hidden $200 somewhere in the house. A clue to its location is given on page 1. The Arabic alphabet is provided on page 2. You may find it helpful to colour the letters as you proceed. Questions must be submitted in writing. Anyone who speaks in my presence will be immediately disqualified.

لادي كارلوتا ستيبد اوت ونتو ذي
بلاتفورم وف ذي سمال وايساید
ستاشون اند توك ا تورن ور تو وب
اند داون يتس ونينتيريستينغ لينغث،
تو كيل تايم تيل ذي ترابن شولد
بروسيد ون يتس واي
ساكي، ذي شارتز-ميتيركلوم ميثود

The Arabic Alphabet.

Arabic is written from right to left. Many letters have a short form (for the beginning and middle of words) and a long form for the end.

ا	*alif**	*a*
بـ ب	*baʾ*	*b*
تـ ت	*taʾ*	*t*
ثـ ث	*thaʾ*	*th* of thin
جـ ج	*jim*	*j*
حـ ح	*ḥaʾ*	*ḥ*
خـ خ	*khaʾ*	*kh*
د	*dal**	*d*
ذ	*dhal**	*th* of than
ر	*raʾ**	*r*
ز	*zay**	*z*
سـ س	*sin*	*s*
شـ ش	*shin*	*sh*
صـ ص	*ṣad*	*ṣ*
ضـ ض	*ḍad*	*ḍ*

ط	*ṭaʾ*	*ṭ*
ظ	*ẓaʾ*	*ẓ*
عـ ـعـ ـع ع	*ʿain***	
غـ ـغـ ـغ غ	*ghain****	*gh*
فـ ف	*faʾ*	*f*
قـ ق	*qaf*	*q*
كـ ك	*kaf*	*k*
لـ ل	*lam*	*l*
مـ م	*mim*	*m*
نـ ن	*nun*	*n*
هـ ـهـ	*haʾ*	*h*
و	*waw**	*w, u, o*
يـ ي	*yaʾ*	*y, i, ee*
ء	*hamza*****	

* never connects to the left

** a gulp at the back of the throat

*** a snarl at the back of the throat

**** glottal stop (the cut-off of breath before the second syllable of uh-oh)

Hint: لا= la

I return to the living room. How can I know what I think when I have only my signs? Good question, but I feel confident (perhaps wrongly) that I shall not run to the kitchen and snatch up a knife. I present each child with the three pages and a coloured pen. The room is suddenly quite silent.

A boy, would it be Jason? says: I don't get it, what are we

While he talks on I write on a piece of paper

Aren't you the lucky one! You can watch the DVD of your choice, while the other four look for the $200!!!!

I hand him the piece of paper.

—WAAAAAAAAAAH

Gina looks at the piece of paper

—WAAAAAAAAAAAAAAAAAAAAAAAH

—But *Rachel*

Gina is not in the game, so I cannot reasonably communicate with her in writing. I say

--It's the Schartz-*Metterklume* Method. *Updated* to take account of *Piaget. Surely* you've heard of it.

—The what method?

—Schartz-Metterklume.

—I don't *think*

—*Well,* that *explains* it then.

Jason is making quite a lot of noise. Jason? Brendan? Brandon? I am confident—*reasonably* confident—of not going to the kitchen for a knife, but I would be happier if the boy could be silenced without loss of face. Undisputed dominion over the DVD player has lost its charm; he wants to play the game, but he has broken the only rule that counts. *I should not be in this house.*

My eyes are fixed, I find, upon a grubby plastic arm with chubby fingers, which lies beneath a coffee table among broken crayons and a half-eaten Oreo. A sentence speeds from the mouth. The sentence is:

—This room is getting on my tits.

As Prufrock says, that was not what I meant to say at all. Much of looking sane amounts to being predictable for the unimaginative. Bad news.

It goes down much better, though, than the characteristic striving for rationality sketched above. The four children who are still in the running for the $200 look like small balloons, mouths pursed, faces bursting with merriment. Jason/Brendan/Aidan, as it might be, laughs out loud.

—What is your name?

—Patrick.

Fuck.

I am a Bertie Wooster adrift without a Jeeves, Watson without Holmes, Hastings without Poirot, a sidekick with no brains beside the boot.

The head is fucked. Where did it get Jason? Or, for that matter, Brendan? Are these the offspring of some other former stepmother? Characters in a sitcom? Characters in a book I've read and forgotten? Characters in a book I've written and forgotten? Or perhaps "Jason," or possibly "Brandon," picks out one of the other children? To put the matter in a nutshell, fuck. But these are the facts, and they must be faced. The boy's name is Patrick. Allegedly, yes, we have only his word for it, but

—Patrick. Exactly. Good news. Here's the deal. I am going for a short walk. If the floor in this room is clear, by my return, of crap—clear, in other words, to avoid unfortunate misunderstandings, of dismembered toys, broken crayons, partially consumed cookies and other material impeding appreciation of the beauty of the carpet—you may rejoin the game. If you

Are we actually in Tulsa?

I don't think this is Tulsa.

OK OK OK but finish the sentence

have any questions you must write them down. If you speak to me you will be out of the game.

It's not that I think children should be seen and not heard. Why stop at children? How many adults generate utterances equivalent to the paragraph of Spinoza one could have read in the time taken up by the utterance? Chances are the utterances of Spinoza himself would not have achieved equivalence, because I can read 900 words a minute and it is unlikely that Spinoza could speak at that speed, let alone speak at that speed while maintaining the level of excellence of his writing.

The $200 has yet to be hidden, but I am unconcerned.

The first page, of course, is a transliteration of a text which reads: *Lady Carlotta stepped out onto the platform of the small wayside station and took a turn or two down its uninteresting length to kill time till the train should proceed on its way. Saki, "The Schartz-Metterklume Method."*

Transliterated back into English from an alphabet in which b does duty for p, and the three letters A, U, Y must do duty for a, e, i, o, u, w, y, it reads: Lady Karluta stibd aut untu dhi blatfurm uf dhi smal waysaid stashun and tuk a turn ur tu daun its unintiristing lingth tu kil taim til dhi train shuld brosid un its way. saki, dhi shartz-mitirklum mithud.

Many children like exotic scripts; all like money. Few seem to have either the obsession with exotica or the sheer unadulterated avarice which were mine from an early age; the likelihood of finding the two combined in *where are we again?* seemed remote. My guess is I have a quiet week ahead.

I leave the house. Each driveway has a mailbox by the road. Five out of the first seven mailboxes passed hold a newspaper, and the newspaper is the *Pittsburgh Tribune-Review.*

4

The phone rings. What time is it? Who knows.

The phone rings.

The phone rings.

The phone rings.

The phone stops ringing.

There's a kilim by the bed. So bare feet won't be heard? No. And there's another in the hall? Yes. So it's easy to be quiet? Yes.

Gina's on the phone. A warm, sympathetic voice speaks, pauses.

—Yeah, yeah, it's been hard, yeah, it's been a real knuckleduster ride, I can tell you that, yeah, we've been literally up and down the map, we've always been very close so obviously, yeah, yeah, and Dongsuk feels exactly the same, he was *distrait*, well, we *all* were, but people have been wonderful, and the police, well, I don't know what we would have done without

—

—Yeah, no, I think I'm okay. We're just taking it one day at a time. But yeah, no, I don't know, yeah, it's interesting you pick up on that, yeah, yeah, I mean, yeah, that was a question I did ask myself, what kind of assessment could they make after just one day? She needs to *talk* to somebody. And there *have* been, well, it's interesting you say that, I talked to Alison and she just thought I should have her institutionalised, uh huh, uh huh, yeah, no, the kids have been great but obviously

Thoughts of moving to Odessa, Ukraine. Four months learning the Russian and getting some adventure rather than this abject veneer. Da. Da. Dada. Sneer.

Hit the road, Jack.

So what time is it, local time? 10:17 a.m. Kids at school, mate at office, excellent news.

Clothes. Skirt, jacket, tights. OK. What else do we need? Shoes, laptop, chocolates, books, gun.

Done.

Gone.

Blow-up

From: “Amanda” <amanda292@hotmail.com>
To: “A.P. Pechorin <popesonxtacy@hotmail.com>
Subject: RE: cheque
Date: Sun 30 May 2004

Alyosha

I am completely distraught. I have been deluged with emails and texts messages and phone calls from people at the studio and the gallery and people amongst the noszaly menage, not to mention the press!!!! I assumed you reaised that Jake and Starr have people working for them whose sole function is to nose out breaches of security which was why I specified that confidentiality was of the essence and that my name was not to go past you and you assured me that this wd be guaranteed. All it takes is for a temp to see a name on a cheque or a contract and see this as a way to garner goodwill with people who cd be useful, they have nothing to lose and everything to gain.

as you know I was extremely reluctant to be involved and only agreed because of financial difficulties I cd see no way out of, I have yet to receive any payment and I need hardly point out that for a business that relies on social networking this is a crippling blow. I see in retrospect that it wd have been better to risk asking Starr directly for financial assistance which she might well have agreed if approached in the right mood or even invited her to concoct some sort of tabloid fodder which she might well have seen as a good joke. To be perfectly honest I think you have been rather careless of consequences other people have to bear the brunt of.

given this turn of events cash flow is likely to be a problem for some time to come so can you tell me the situation re the cheque? It has still not arrived and I begin to question whether it has been sent. amanda

From: "A.P. Pechorin" <popesonxtacy@hotmail.com>
To: "Amanda" <amanda292@hotmail.com>
Subject: RE: questions
Date: Sun 30 May 2004 09:58:11 +0000

I just re-read your email. I am very sorry to hear you are receiving criticism from overseas. Let me start by saying at all times your identity was kept secret and that your name was never mentioned, anywhere. It is not in my editors business in revealing such things. These people who are having a go at you are clutching for straws as to who is talking and not. There was no mention of your work or any involvement of who you were. I hope you don't feel ruined or at a lost. I will speak to the editor today. There is a cheque for you. I will push them for it. I too am learning how the machine works. Please, I don't want you to feel bad and I hope things cool down. I never wanted this to happen to you and am sure it will resolve itself. Alyosha

From: "Amanda" <amanda292@hotmail.com>
To: "A.P. Pechorin <popesonxtacy@hotmail.com>
Subject: RE: cheque
Date: Mon 31 May 2004

Alyosha

I am starting to think there is not going to be a cheque through some mysterious unforeseen concatenation of circumstances beyond anyone's control, if so it wd be helpful to KNOW as I have made financial commitments in expectation of receiving it.

I very much doubt that people are 'clutching at straws', as you put it; the people at the studio seemed to have all the details, after all it is not surprising that leakage occurs in both directions, it is naive to expect otherwise.

I am surprised that the paper does not make more of an effort to protect its sources AND pay promptly, given the risks run by supplying this sort of information they hardly encourage people to come back, or to provide the names etc.

Again, please clarify re cheque
Amanda

From: "A.P. Pechorin" <popesonxtacy@hotmail.com>
To: Amanda<amanda@hotmail.com>
Subject: FW: RE:
Date: Thu, 2 June 2005 10:47:57

- here is an email I got from the news editor. Pls don't worry I am sure they will pay you, just when is the question. Don't want to push them too much. I hope it hasn't affected you too much and I hope they haven't been too nasty. ok see below.

From: Adam.Marlowe@Sentinel.com
To: "A.P. Pechorin" <popesonxtacy@hotmail.com>
Date: Wed, 1 June 2004
Subject: RE: fivesomes

Alyosha, I'll have a word with the boss but it is already a very good price for the quality of story, if some of the girls had been identified or better persuaded to come forward that may well have increased the value. I fought to get her top price because it was a story with genuine human interest, it had enormous potential for further development so I could make a case that it was in our interest to nurture the relationship. I'm disappointed, obviously, that she wants to leave it a one-off rather than taking it further, but you win some you lose some. I'll try to get something extra for you but there's not a lot of room for manoeuvre. Adam

IMPORTANT NOTICE This e-mail (including any attachments) is meant only for the intended recipient. It may also contain confidential and privileged information. If you are not the intended recipient, any reliance on, use, disclosure, distribution or copying of this e-mail or attachments is strictly prohibited. Please notify the sender immediately by e-mail if you have received this message by mistake and delete the e-mail and all attachments. Any views or opinions in this e-mail are solely those of the author and do not necessarily represent those of SentinelSyndicates Ltd or its associated companies (hereinafter referred to as "Sentinel Associates"). Sentinel Associates accept no liability for the content of this e-mail, or for the consequences of any actions taken on the basis of the information provided, unless that information is subsequently confirmed in writing. Although every reasonable effort is made to keep its network free from viruses, Sentinel Associates accept no liability for any virus transmitted by this e-mail or any attachments and the recipient should use up-to-date virus checking software. E-mail to or from this address may be subject to interception or monitoring for operational reasons or for lawful business practices.

From: "A.P. Pechorin" <popesonxtacy@hotmail.com>
To: Amanda <amanda292@hotmail.com
Subject: RE: FW: RE:
Date: 7 June 2004

I am sorry you are getting grief. Please you will get your money but you have to remember payments go into a system. I will get the editor to email you. Please - I am so sorry what this has caused you. I don't think it will ruin you and your business chances. Perhaps I can speak to the family editor here and they can feature your work? Or put something in a photo shoot? Just hang on, I am on the case

Alyosha

Get Hotmail on your mobile phone http://www.msn.co.uk/msnmobile

To: popesonxtacy@hotmail.com
From: amanda292@hotmail.com
Subject: RE: FW: RE:
Date: 8 June 2004 05:56:26

ahoy

Any news from the front? Thought I would try again since a month has gone by
put out more flags

amanda

From: “A.P. Pechorin” <popesonxtacy@hotmail.com>
To: Amanda <amanda292@hotmail.com>
Subject: RE: RE: FW: RE:
Date: Mon, 13 Jun 2004 11:11:21
Hey,
spoke with the powers that be and your money will come at ‘the end of ‘this month’- the first Thursday of next month. It will be sent to me, so I will send the cheque to you. Hope you well and trucking away.

Alyosha

We’re not in Kansas, Toto

The phone rings. The phone rings. The phone rings.
Is that Rachel? It's me me me me.

I have a large handsome apartment in Berlin, 450 euros a month.

I came to Berlin partly because someone once recommended KaDeWe as a suicide spot and partly because I thought I should not be at large with a gun.

There are 38 states where one can buy a gun without a license and where the police are not allowed to keep records of sales. A voice in the head had said *Let's buy a gun for purposes of research*; the body in its short skirt and boots had walked into Roy's Fish & Ammo in Clarksville, OH; the mouth had uttered a couple of sentences: I'm living in a dangerous neighborhood, I need to be able to protect myself. Do you have a Smith & Wesson .38? A transaction had taken place in which $450 was exchanged for the gun and a box of bullets.

On the hard drive of the laptop was an e-mail with Jennifer Brennan's business address. In the coiled flesh in the skull were the home addresses and phone numbers of many close personal friends. The body got on a train. The body got off a train.

Amtrak does not run security checks on handbags. The security staff at Sharpshooters check bags at downstairs reception, but they don't do a body search. In many office buildings bags are not checked.

The body wandered the streets of New York. No one died. It got on a train and got off a train. No one died. It got on a train and got off a train. No one died. The gun and its bullets were buried behind the tennis court of a thirty-room Victorian frolic in Newport, Rhode Island. The body got on a plane and got off a plane.

We’re not in Dalston, Toto

From: amanda292@hotmail.com
To: popesonxtacy@hotmail.com
Date: 04 July 2004 23:05:09
Subject: the phantom cheque

yodelay-hee-hoo
heard anything?

Amanda

From: popesonxtacy@hotmail.com
To: amanda292@hotmail.com
Date: 06 July 2004 06:02:11
Subject: Five a Side

Well, funny you ask . . . I am not in London any more, was sent to Santorini, Greece, popular island, for . . . Angelina Jolie and Bread Shitt, (not being there) and decided not to return, headed . . . out of Christendom, heading East into Islam . . . So, it is hard to know exactly what is going on. Incompetence seems to pervade my comrades. But my friend will post the cheque to you from my house address in London. Long live the Royal Mail!!

Strange hassle, all this, for me too now considering the environment of Kurdistan and work I am currently up to. Seems unreal that there is such importance or value placed on such trivia. I just want all this to finish…

Alyosha

But we once sailed the sea of stories

It started so well before it all went so horribly wrong. P2C2E, says Rushdie, anticipating text-messaging by a decade. Process Too Complicated To Explain. A 2C2E life is not really minimalist or Beckettian, it's just too fucking complicated for a soundbite. Rushdie was writing a children's book (*Haroun and the Sea of Stories,* o ignorant reader, o kafir). 2FC2E was too X-rated for the target audience. So he relied on the intelligence of those readers above the age of consent to fill in the invisible blank.

It is 2FC2E. It is *War and Peace* meets *The Wandering Jew* meets *A Suitable Boy* meets *A la recherche du temps perdu* meets *The Forsyte Saga* meets *The Cairo Trilogy* meets the Jalna saga of Mazo de la Roche (trust me, you don't want to know). But this is the age of Aladdin Stuffit Expander. Perhaps a 500,000-word substitute for a sleeping pill can be compressed. The imaginative reader can turn to Aladdin. The unimaginative reader can expand his horizons by reading *War and Peace, The Wandering Jew, A Suitable Boy, A la recherche du temps perdu, The Forsyte Saga, The Cairo Trilogy* and *La comedie humaine* (the sort of reader whose horizons can be expanded by the Jalna saga of Mazo de la Roche should sell this book now on Amazon Marketplace, go on, do it, permission to leave the class granted).

Imagine a book doing for Arabic, Farsi, Turkish, Kurdish, Azeri, Armenian, Uyghur, Urdu, Pashtu, Mandarin, Russian, Ukrainian, Hebrew and and and what *The Lord of the Rings* did for Quenya, Sindarin, Telerin, Doriathrin, Nandorin, Adûnaic, Khuzdul, the Black Speech, Westron, Orcish, Entish and and and and and. Tolkien referred to inventing languages as his secret vice; he opened a Finnish grammar, fell in love with the language and wanted to appropriate it, he loved Welsh, Latin, Anglo-Saxon, the Norse of the sagas, Hebrew, did not care for French. He believed that languages were marked by history, and invented Middle-earth to give his languages the marks of violence, loss, exile. Quenya and Sindarin (two Elvish languages) are the only two which are useable—that is, it is possible to write in them if you don't want to talk about credit derivatives or leather fetish lesbian triangles. Tolkien did not provide a comprehensive grammar and vocabulary of every language spoken by every bit player. No. What he created was something more startling: desire. The language of the Wood Elves, Nandorin, is represented by only thirty words or so. The reader constructed by Tolkien is consumed with longing for the nonexistent language of these nonexistent wood dwellers.

The final volume of *The Lord of the Rings* was published in 1955, a year before Suez. Tolkien died in 1973, the year of the oil crisis. By 2003, the year of the invasion of Iraq, the books had sold 100 million copies.

So imagine the book of an alter-Tolkien, creating desire for the languages of the Middle East rather than Middle-earth. Readers who were 13 in 1973 would have been 31 at the time of the Gulf War, 41 in 2001. Whatever events of terror might have been committed in that possible world, it's unlikely that interrogators in it would be holding people in Guantánamo Bay four years after the event for want of competent Arabists to interrogate them.

OK, you say, I imagine the book. I imagine 12-year-olds hauled off to Cuba and released after four days rather than four years. But I sort of liked John Lennon better?

OK. Here's a piece of advice. Why not borrow *Jalna,* by Mazo de la Roche, from your local library? I think you'd enjoy it.

2FC2E, I was once young and enthusiastic and naive.

I first read *The Hobbit* when I was nine. The library of castoff paperbacks in a rotting palace in Mardan had nothing else in the series; I moved on to *The Spy Who Came in From the Cold.* My parents (as I then referred to them in my young, naive, unalienated way) were ending a marriage of smashed chandeliers, airborne dinner services, grand pianos hurtling down marble steps to the bottom of swimming pools. I went back to the beginning of *The Hobbit.* I was given *The Lord of the Rings* for my tenth birthday; I opened the first page under the doting eyes of stewardesses en route to Dakar, finished it under further dotage two months later on a plane to Rangoon. I went back to the beginning of *The Hobbit.*

A succession of steps, recruited for disinclination to smash chandeliers, were discarded for disinclination to smash chandeliers.

So it was not Beckettian, no, it was not very Bauhaus.

What did my father do? He was a simple carpet salesman.
My mother had picked up the carpet business from my father.

Here, however, at the threshold of a philosophical analysis of identity, it seems appropriate to insist on the face it wears and turns on daily life—namely repetition as such, the return of sameness over and over again, in all its psychological desolation and tedium: that is to say, neurosis. In that limited appropriation which Adorno makes of Freudian conceptuality . . . neurosis is simply this boring imprisonment of the self in itself, crippled by its terror of the new and unexpected, carrying its sameness with it wherever it goes, so that it has the protection of feeling, whatever it might stretch out its hand to touch, that it never meets anything but what it knows already. Fredric Jameson, *Late Marxism*. Father, a reliable source informs me, of seven.

Meaning what?

Meaning a business opportunity.

The tedium of *The Two Towers* gets worse each time. Everyone cracks sooner or later. What do they do?

One thing they could do is turn to the real world for the things they love in Tolkien. The real world has its institutions, and they have no place for Elvish sagas; they also have no place for the *Iliad* and *Odyssey,* the *Kalevala,* the *Mabinogion, Beowulf, Egil's Saga,* the *Nibelungenlied,* the *Chanson de Roland,* the *Morte d'Arthur,* Gilgamesh. They have no use for literary languages. The addict could reason as follows: Much as I love Tolkien, I do not think his Elvish poetry beats Homer AND Beowulf AND AND AND AND so I will learn Greek in Boca Raton Anglo-Saxon in Shanghai Finnish in Tegucigalpa Welsh in Alice Springs.

They could. What they normally do is try another fantasy series (it has to be better than reading *The Two Towers* again). It's like trying to get drunk on cough syrup, but the idea of turning to a real thing is too alien. So the fantasy genre accounts for 10 percent of all books sold, an unreliable source claims.

Or a reader might raise his head from the book. He sits on a bed in a tiny bedroom surrounded by paperbacks. He thinks: I sit here reading about adventure; why don't I walk out the door? Sometimes he has spent too long in the land of the lotus-eaters; he takes a step to the door, picks up another book, returns to the bed. Sometimes he walks through the door. He hitchhikes, backpacks. Yes he does.

Another business opportunity.

Or a reader might raise his head from the book. He will run out of money fast if he walks out the door. So he goes online, writes around, lines up a job teaching English in Kyoto or Bangkok or Riyadh or Kiev. He speaks English to people who speak English, and he teaches English to people who can afford to pay to learn English. He acquires two or three girlfriends or boyfriends. Perhaps he sees prostitutes, or perhaps he's a gentleman.

Another business opportunity.

Rather a lot of third person masculine singulars, you may think. Yes.

But let's say a reader is a 12-year-old female smart-ass, the type of heroine popular with Mistah Rushdie and Mistah Pullman. Popular, in other words, with writers who can keep her safely on the page (they don't have to live with her). This reader notices that Mistah Multi-Culti Rushdie is not denting his very own personal sales by cluttering the page with Hindustani (except in transliteration, we spit on transliterations). She notices that Professah Tolkien cluttered his very own personal pages with his very own personal languages and sold in the millions. Which means that millions of people could pick up Elvish in a mass market paperback while real bombs were falling on real people in Afghanistan and Iran and Iraq and other places whose languages cannot be picked up in a mass market paperback.

She would like to leave home, but being a 12-year-old smart-ass she has of course read *Lolita, Zazie dans le métro* and *Candide*. White market labour is closed to 12-year-olds, which leaves drug dealing, theft, prostitution with paedophiles and a literary career. She does not feel up to inventing a language (though she does dodge the Stockholm Syndrome vis-a-vis legal guardians through a diary written in code, a cunning mixture of Chinese characters and Arabic verb forms).

But wait a minute. How did the Taliban get into power in the first place? The Ayatollah Khomeini—how did this gibbering lunatic escape exile in Paris to hand out death warrants on Rushdie from Tehran? Saddam Hussein—wasn't he once the good guy? If Iran had had the decency to switch to Quenya in 1955 the CIA could have drawn on a pool of linguists to spy on it. It didn't. Afghanistan was equally uncooperative. Iraq also failed to see the light. The CIA simply failed to adapt to wily opponents who continued to converse amongst themselves in their native tongues. Hinc illae lacrimae.

So a 12-year-old smart-ass reasons as follows. There are two possibilities:

1. Readers are not incurably neurotic. They do not necessarily read to escape the real world. A vast untapped market could be entranced by the glamour of Arabic, Farsi, Chinese (whichever has most recently enchanted the youthful smart-ass) in the way that one once was entranced by JRRT. So there is money to be made by writing a runaway bestseller, yes, and there is ALSO money to be made in persuading the CIA to fund the project, as increasing the pool of potential intelligence-gatherers in languages of importance to national security.

2. Readers are, in fact, ostriches. They have problems of their own and

they read to forget about them. Lovely glamorous Arabic would not only not make them forget their problems, it would remind them that there are all kinds of problems they can do nothing about. So there might be a small untapped market of mute inglorious McJob-bound Miltons, but there is no money to be made by writing a runaway bestseller. No. But there is money to be made by persuading the CIA to fund the project, as increasing the pool of potential intelligence-gatherers in languages of importance to national security.

I took up my pen. I began to write.

Pride goeth before a fall.

In 1992 my father married a new 29-year-old. The carpet business had taken him to Hong Kong; she had gone with him, putting her career on hold. She had a degree in political science from the LSE but it was not possible to work. She had been writing chick lit to have her own income.

There are servants but she knows no Cantonese.

There's a dinner. It would be gauche to ask for a knife and fork. Lucy fumbles with chopsticks.

The carpet business will be discussed later, behind closed doors. Meanwhile Lucy's cousin Simon talks about *Bat-Mitzvah Boy*, a runaway bestseller which has started a craze for Hebrew, Aramaic, and tapdancing.

With the wisdom of hindsight we can, perhaps, agree that, could we but replace that generation of tapdancers with Arabists, stupidities and crassnesses might have been avoided. The world was younger.

So. *Bat-Mitzvah Boy.* The toe-curlingly awful *Bat-Mitzvah Boy.*

Simon had come across five chapters of an early draft in 1988. Its then penniless author, Max Wojczuk, was working the graveyard shift at Curzon Street Kinko's; Simon had had a last-minute rush job for Sotheby's, had begun idly reading the repro op's MS, had become completely *engrossed*, had *begged* to be allowed to take it away. He had shown the chapters excitedly to his boyfriend who had shown them excitedly to his closest friend, an entertainment lawyer. A movie option had been bought for £500! A publisher had picked up the world rights and made $1 million! So these friends were sitting on the movie rights to a runaway bestseller!

My wine glass is being filled along with everyone else's because Lu's Cantonese is not up to the countermand. The entertainment lawyer dips a spring roll in sweet and sour sauce; red lips close on the greasy skin, and all the while the snake charmer weaves his spell:

Sometimes a film is absolutely *of* its time, yet *ahead* of its time, a film that will be cherished for years to come. We felt at once that *Bat-Mitzvah Boy* would be one of that rare breed, a film that would live in the hearts of generations—a *Wizard of Oz* for the 21st century.

He fixes his Bambi eyes on Peter Chan, a very major player in the carpet trade. $50 mil would be nothing to Peter Chan, and so the silver tongue speaks on:

I think part of its extraordinary appeal is the way it plugs into a very powerful nostalgia people are only half aware of. We've seen the whole *gamut* of self-aware, *sophisticated* period musicals, from *Cabaret* to *Grease* to *Saturday Night Fever,* from *Oh, What a Lovely War* to *A Chorus Line;* we've seen the whole superhero cinematization of comic book movement, which looks so obvious now it's hard to believe someone had to *think* of it. In a couple of years people will be thinking—*tapdancing*. Why did no one think of tapdancing *before*? Where's *our* Astaire and Rogers? Where's *our* Gene Kelly? There's the whole *glamour* of it, and with it the *knowledge* we have now of the anguish *behind* the glamour, Rogers' shoes filling with blood, a sort of savage reworking of *The Little Mermaid,* in its original, cruel, unDisneyfied version. And then, of course, there's the whole charm of the troupe of seven children, a sort of *reprise* of *The Sound of Music,* only with tapdancing. And at the same time it avoids that *syrupy, saccharine* senti*mentality,* there's this wonderful *black humour,* this sort of glorious Mel Brooks irreverence, that you really do want for kids today, the *last* thing we want is some kind of Shirley Temple dimpling and twinkling *winsomeness,* a little ringleted *monstrosity,* it's a film with a heart, but one that doesn't buy its emotion cheaply.

When I first read *Bat-Mitzvah Boy* the thing it brought to mind was the unbearable poignancy of those old clips of The Jackson 5. Those sharp, tight routines still work; the sheer professionalism is a joy. The 5 are never embarrassing; they're not dated by the Afros and flares the way the Osmonds are by shag haircuts and skinny rib T-shirts. But now we know the price that was paid for that slick perfectionism, its picture of Dorian Gray stares out at us from all the tabloids. *Bat-Mitzvah Boy* captures that brutal dichotomy.

I am profoundly convinced that *Bat-Mitzvah Boy* is a film that can showcase some *truly exceptional talent.* When you've got a whole slew of good parts for dancers you're in a *very* strong position—there are so *few,* and a dancer's career is so *brief*—and there's some *wonderful* talent out there. And of course when you have a role for a child—we were thinking perhaps Lourdes Leon, she'd be perfect in so many ways, and Madonna's been very involved with Judaism recently so the whole tapdancing family in flight from the Holocaust slash boy helps sisters to get religious rite of passage previously denied, the whole wonderful package is very much *centred* on matters that are of immense *importance* to Madonna. Then there's the way the film *shares* the children's engagement with the Hebrew text, which is *simply extraordinary,* something that would have been *unthinkable* fifty, even *twenty* years ago. But what we see these days is that audiences have a desperate *longing* for *authenticity,* something the beancounters simply hadn't the imagination to *recognize.* And of course this opens up a whole *range* of merchandise possibilities for the film that go *well* beyond the normal stuffed toys, dolls, lunchboxes and what have you.

Peter Chan says that's very interesting and do they have any particular actors in mind.

—Well, of course it's early days to lock any actors in place, we don't want to present the director with a paint-by-number assignment, it's simply not that kind of film, it needs a director who's *passionate* about the *project,* it's really not for Sam and me to *dictate,* but I think any director who really understood what it was all about would want to *talk* to Madonna—we *very* much want that unerring instinct for the postmodern postproduced MTV generation.

Peter Chan says that's very interesting and has Madonna shown any interest in the project.

—Well, *yes*, as a matter of fact. We've had an *inkling*. We're *not* making any *promises*, and we're *very* much not taking anything for granted, but we're *very* much not ruling anything out.

I sit in silence. My glass is filled a second time. Peter Chan and the other carpeteers make polite noises and now Sam is talking about the contractual side. In *Haroun and the Sea of Stories* there are villains with shiny bald heads and yellow checked pants, but this is just a guy in chinos and a blue button-down shirt, no tie.

He is explaining about options, the actor's contract will typically give the producer an option to use him again for the next movie or the next two movies at the same flat fee, you could potentially have that kind of contract on a Julia Roberts pre-*Pretty Woman* and then make *Pretty Woman*,

—So maybe the guy wants to work on another picture, now he's got all kinds of offers, you might come to an agreement, you might let somebody else use the guy in return for compensation. Or let's say the guy says Fuck you, I won't do it, sue me, you might say Look, OK, we know the kind of offers you're getting, the contract says you get $150,000, we'll make it $300,000. But you're still getting a million-dollar actor at way below market value. Because the thing of it is, you're giving someone their break. If they don't like it, there are thousands more where they came from, there are thousands out there waiting tables who would jump at the chance to be in a movie that will be seen, instead of maybe some student production at NYU that maybe gets screened at Sundance if it's lucky. Heh heh.

Chopsticks convey a wonton erratically to the waiting mouth. Peter Chan says that's interesting. The mouth continues

—So the thing you have to understand is, using a big star is not the only way to make money. But you have to get it right. You want name recognition because that really helps with the distribution. But maybe the big thing about that movie will be somebody who's just getting their break, because there is some amazing talent out there. So if you have that combination, if you find the right project, and you find the right director, and hopefully you find some great talent, you can have a movie that can really take off for not a lot of money. And then that puts you in a position to leverage the money you make into more money, because you can use that actor you gave a break to. And we definitely have a great project.

Isn't there an insect, would it be a dung beetle, that rolls up little pellets of dung? The voice rolls dung pellets into the ear.

—Also, when you have a project that has a great part for a kid, that has incredible potential. You saw *Home Alone*, you remember that incredible kid, Macaulay Culkin, or Tatum O'Neal in *Paper Moon*, the movie has the potential to be iconic.

A wonton punctuates.

—Plus, when you have a project that has a great part for a kid, that puts you in a very strong position. Because on the one hand the parents and the representation of a child actor definitely know, or if the parents don't know the representation definitely knows, but usually the parents know, that the kid has a sell-by date. Whatever the kid has going for him may or may not survive the transition into adulthood. But also, if the kid has a genuine talent, if it's not just a cute kid, people with the kid's interests at heart want to see that develop. But the typical kid or teen movie has very limited crossover potential as a basis for an adult career. So if you have a project that has a really great part, an acting part, for a kid, you are offering some kid the chance not to retire at the age of 15. If you think about what *Taxi Driver* did for Jodie Foster, that's what you are offering the kid. So you really just have to make sure the investor understands that, that the potential to leverage that into a profit is phenomenal.

The carpeteers say that's interesting, that's very interesting, and my glass is filled a third time, and I break the silence.

—The thing that beggars comprehension, I say, is why the CIA haven't funded similar projects for Arabic, Farsi, Russian, Mandarin, any language they might want to spy in. I should have thought it was obvious to the meanest intelligence. They subsidised Horizon for years, didn't they? Surely it's the easiest thing in the world to slash an operative or two and buy up a few Tolkiens and also-rans.

The guests perform an out-of-the-mouth-of-babes bonding ritual.

—I don't think it's quite that simple, Rachel, says Lu, not because she thinks it's complicated but because she is unnerved by hearing *beggars comprehension* and *I should have thought* and *obvious to the meanest intelligence* from the mouth of a 16-year-old.

—Or if the Americans won't do it, what about the Brits? With all due respect, the present system is simply asking for a Philby.

—I'd have thought coming up with a suitable vehicle might present problems, even supposing

—But that's easy. What about something like *The Name of the Rose*? A historico-philosophical thriller set in 10th-century Baghdad about Ibn Muqlah, father of Arabic calligraphy, whose right hand was amputated in punishment for political machinations, the sort of thing that could hardly fail to be an international blockbuster, thereby increasing the pool of potential Arabists by a million or so. Or a PKD-Fuentes-inspired alternative universe sort of book, in which the Moors kept Granada and conquered the New World? Or one could take a leaf out of the books of Kafka, Borges and Zweig, one could have a novella in which a prisoner sees letters appear one at a time in his breath on the mirror

The 16-year-old brain is all-seeing, all-knowing.

—Yes, but it's all very well to throw balls in the air, Christ, as soon as people hear you're a writer they start bombarding you with all the brilliant ideas they've had for a book, there's all the difference in the world between having an idea and the actual hard slog of writing. Let's cut to the chase, says Lu. Have you ever actually written a book?

—Skoodles, I say, dividing the actual number by five, and my glass is on empty and Yu Peng leaps to refill. —The one about Ibn Muqlah is probably the one that would be most attractive to the CIA, though. I think if we were to do for Arabic what Indiana Jones did for archaeology we'd see a dramatic improvement in our relations with the Arab world, and I'd like to think there's some money in it for me for making this important contribution to world peace, so if anybody here happens to know somebody in a position to make it worth my while I'd be only too thrilled

—But that's amazing, says Lu, suddenly not tense, because it's too ridiculous. You must show me one sometime, and now I think we're ready for coffee.

So what a little player. What a wheeler and dealer. Rushdie's little smart-ass is called Miss Blabbermouth, not without reason.

Later people would hear of these books and imagine that any one of them could be an easy second novel. These are friendless orphans, alone in the world.

Lucy said nicely the next day that she'd love to see a few chapters.

—OK, but don't lose them, this is my only copy because all the Arabic has to be written in by hand.

Lucy smiles, reassures. Reads.

Frowns.

Smiles.

—I love this. I love this. I don't think it's publishable, unfortunately, I think all the Arabic would put people off, but there's a wonderful gift for storytelling. I think there could be a movie in this. I really think so. What I'd like to do is option it so I can develop the project.

This is not the fast track to a defence budget slush fund that I'd been hoping for,

—I was thinking of $500 for five years, it may take a while what with the book being unpublished and me being stuck in Honkers.

If you are 16 people think $500 is a wonderful piece of luck. It is not possible to ask for more money, though $500 is at least $2,500 shy of even an indie lowest-of-the-low-budget minimum.

Lu got a contract off Sam that she said was standard language. It included a clause about novelization rights.

Baby: How is it possible to include novelization rights in a contract that is for the movie rights to a novel?

A 16-year-old smart-ass is no match for a 29-year-old fuckwit. She weeps, she sobs, she breaks down, let's not talk about it.

If she needs a five-year option (because of having put her career on hold in Hong Kong), rather than the normal 18-month option with right to extend, it is not possible to ask for the industry norm. If she looks at three chapters of another book and falls in love with them and thinks this too could make a wonderful film and offers $250 there is nothing to be done.

Perhaps you can see the sort of precedent this sets.

Now suppose you have a rapidly expanding kinship system. The parents acquire blameless spouses, behave unforgivably, are forgiven, move on. The number of people who have heard of the runaway bestseller *Bat-Mitzvah Boy* and the friends who optioned it early on is very large. The number of people who think they can make a movie if they have the right project is not small. The number of people who have not been treated appallingly is negligible. So there are quite a lot of people magnanimously asking to see anything you have written and falling in love with anything you show and making an offer of a few hundred dollars which cannot be refused.

Perhaps you can understand this. One way people show it is not just a business relationship is by offering friendly sums of money. Another way is by talking about their problems.

Perhaps you can understand this. A young smart-ass who succeeds in flogging a literary property for a businesslike sum of money can swan into a university and close the door on the crisis-ridden kinship system. A smart-ass who is unable to live on friendly sums of money may weasel herself into the Sorbonne (1994), Berkeley (1995), the American University in Beirut (1997), but there are disappearances, breaches of the social fabric, no degree.

This is something you may not understand. Suppose you give someone a friendly deal, a five-year option for $500. Suppose people talk and talk and talk to the point where the mind cracks up, there is a disappearance or some other breach of the social fabric. The fact that you gave someone a very friendly deal does not mean that this person will not be talking about institutions and electro-shock therapy.

So this is something you may not know that's well worth knowing. If you want to avoid institutions and electro-shock therapy friendly deals are not the way to go.

3

The Hot Shot

8 1/2 *somehow coalesces for me in many ways the essence of cinema and in particular the sequence that I have chosen is Marcello Mastroianni passing down the hallways of the hotel where they're trying to make this movie, and he has this phenomenal ability to tap dance his way out of trouble and when I saw that, it was long before I ever made a movie, but I suspected there was truth to that and subsequently now having made a few movies, I know it's the ultimate truth of movie making, and the job of the director is to tap dance past all the problems.*

Terry Gilliam, BBC2 Close-up*, 27 November 1995*

You flew first class to Paris because you're a hot shot. You were prepping the period scenes for your new movie, *Damascene*; you love working with the French. You love the European sensibility. You love Bergman. You love Wim Wenders, Fellini, Polanski, you hate working with big studios because you end up screening films for execs who have never seen fucking Polanski. One day they'll be talking about Noszaly as the heir to Polanski and Bergman; they don't know that, but you do.

Your personal life was a walking disaster zone, the tabloids got hold of the kind of thing that is totally understood in Europe and the shit hit the proverbial fan, instead of focusing on your film you were having to take time to talk to people who were having fucking *hysterics* over something so trivial it's not even worth *talking* about.

So look. You're not in this for the money, you're not interested in money, you can get $1 million for a screenplay. You took time out to be in the book on one condition: you would be a second-person narrator.

Jay McInerney's *Bright Lights, Big City* has a second-person narrator. ("You are at a nightclub talking to a girl with a shaved head. The club is either Heartbreak or the Lizard Lounge. All might come clear if you could slip into the bathroom and do a little more Bolivian Marching Powder.") Stripped of the second person it's the story of an editor at the *New Yorker* for fuck's sake who does drink & drugs & some sex and whose mom dies of cancer, but the second person made it hot shit, it was *the* American novel of the 80s.

Calvino's *If on a winter's night a traveler* also has a second-person narrator (You're about to read the new novel *If on a winter's night a traveler* by Italo Calvino etc. etc.) who reads 11 first chapters of mysteriously interrupted novels (but they're not pastiches, *extracts* from supposed novels, they're *descriptions* of how you the narrator/reader reads these chapters, so the reader never sees what you see, only sees you seeing how you see what you see, it's a very *cinematic* way of writing, you love that European *awareness* of the work of art as a work of art, it's the quintessential *European* novel).

Calvino never had a lot of money, worked as an editor for Einaudi to make ends meet, but the estate is represented by Andrew "the Jackal" Wylie so Calvino's widow is not complaining. McInerney was represented by Amanda "Binky" Urban of ICM so he did make a lot of money which was what you did in the 80s to be the voice of your generation.

No one has ever done a book that *combines* the traditional first and third with the pathbreaking second, let alone the pathbreaking *American* second with the pathbreaking *European* second; this is not about egos, it's not about who gets a bigger trailer, it's about pushing *boundaries.* So you made that one condition, and you got it, because your participation was essential to the project.

They then offered you the chance to be seen getting up close and personal with Arabic short vowels, which an earlier narrator had used without bothering to explain.

"We see the scene as very European, Jake, very high concept. Georges Perec wrote a whole book, *La Disparition,* without using the letter e—very avant-garde, very European, a real cult classic. A similar sinister brooding *absence* makes itself felt throughout the whole of Arabic literature. In the Qur'an and in children's books short vowels are written in small, barely perceptible marks above and below the line; elsewhere they *never appear,* haunting the consonants like unseen surveillance operatives, stepping out of the shadows only when a perceived ambiguity permits this chilling reminder of their hidden power.

َ ***a*** ِ ***i*** ُ ***u*** ً ***an*** ٍ ***in*** ٌ ***un*** ْ

You said if these were vowels why did three of them end in n and they said, "It's called nunation, Jake. 2C2E. In simple layman's terms an indefinite noun (which in English would be *a dog, a cat,* or what have you) is marked by a final short vowel ending in n, or nun, which in ordinary spoken Arabic is *rarely pronounced.*"

You said, "& what's the little circle above the line?" and they said, "It's called sukun, meaning silence. It marks a consonant which is *not followed by a vowel.*"

You said, "Why would you want a letter to show a letter is not followed by a vowel?" And they said, "*Exactly.* That's what we're *all* asking. These are dangerous times, Jake. We can't be too careful."

One thing you learn growing up in America is not to argue with the *National Enquirer.* You had always made a point of not casting Tom Cruise because of the fucking Scientology. You said that was very interesting but you had a lot going on in your personal life.

They said, "Well, what would you say to working with George Clooney?"

You said, "George Clooney?"

And they said, "Take a look at this, it's early days, just to give you a rough idea of what we have in mind:"

And you were definitely impressed. You said you were definitely tempted, you would definitely think about it, but you were happy being a second-person narrator and you had to be thinking about your next project.

Which was not untrue.

You'd have liked to have made the movie of *The Da Vinci Code*, you gave it a lot of thought because it would be a challenge, writing a screenplay that would do justice to the intellectual complexity of the book. You weren't sure you were ready to work with a studio again, so you walked away from it. When you saw what they did with the material you were sorry you didn't take it on.

What you'd like to do is make an independent film, a personal project, raise the money yourself, which you can definitely do because you're such a hot shot everyone wants to work with you. You'd like to go back to a project you've been passionate about for years. You read *Lotteryland* when it first came out and fell in love with it. You love Gilliam's *Brazil*, you love *Blade Runner*, you knew you could do something spectacular with the material. Some people who were friends of the author had an option on it, these people were basically dishonest, they knew nothing about making movies, these were not people you could work with, so you passed. But you couldn't get the book out of your head. You asked your agency to contact Zozanian but the only people who knew how to find her were these quote-unquote producers. But just before you left LA your agency got a call, it was Zozanian, they tried to patch you through but something went wrong with the line, but you feel very good about this, it's only a matter of time, this is a project, this is definitely going to happen.

You bought a copy of the book at the airport and you ffffffffast forwarded.

RLENTYTLOAD

3. THE LUCK OF THE LUBAVITCH

1.

A woman was at death's door. She had a, how do you say, ultrasound and there was a big tumour in her stomach. She had one week to live. She went to see the master who was too ill to speak. His secretary said Shall we check the mezuzot? The master did not say No.

Yaakov beamed at me. I had decided to buy 93p worth of bagels, spend the night on a park bench and walk up to Stamford Hill for morning service. Yaakov had insisted beamingly on inviting me home for lunch, and he had been beaming ever since.

His secretary commanded that all the mezuzot be opened & inspected, and sure enough!!!!!! In one of them a word was misspelled!!!!!!!!!!!! He commanded that all the mezuzot be put back with fresh scrolls. The woman went back to the hospital! The tumour was gone!

I would once have had a lot to say about this. I said: That's absolutely incredible.

He was beaming. He told one incredible story after another. I kept saying incredible. The girls were eating quietly, flashing glances up the table from time to time and then talking ostentatiously to each other. You may think this is my way of showing I was just being modest about looking like the ugly weird one in a boy band. You haven't seen the competition.

I sat quietly eating. I reminded myself not to say fuck or shit. I would not usually say cunt but I reminded myself not to let it slip out unexpectedly now.

Yaakov told a story about a man who had miraculously recovered from cancer after fasting on Yom Kippur against his doctor's orders. Previously bedridden, he had managed to remain standing throughout the service. He had walked into the doctor's surgery the next day. The doctor couldn't believe his eyes!!!!!! He ran tests!!!!!!! The cancer was in remission!!!!!!!!!

I said: That's incredible!

I had the feeling I might say something I would regret if I heard another incredible story so I started reminiscing about my days in the Dublin boy band scene.

A surprising number are Jewish, I explained, and it was true: any number greater than zero would have been surprising, and I knew of at least two.

I didn't know that, said my host, while the girls listened agog.

Most people don't, I said, hastily censoring an anecdote.

Yaakov kept smiling throughout. So did his wife. So did the girls. So did the boys.

There was something uncanny about it, as if a band of Martians had landed on the planet and decided to pass themselves off as Jews. Having scanned Tanach, Talmud and What My Judaism Means to Me into the brain, and being well up on the joys of the chosen race, the aliens would go about saying things like 'Four sets of plates! Wow! We're so lucky!' and 'Yom Kippur! A chance to spend the whole day in shul! Fasting! And standing up! Groovy!' and 'What is it with these earthlings? They seem so depressed. Nobody *else* gets to eat matzah for a whole week every year. Cool.'

Or it was as if God, after 5,000 years or so of moaners, had happened to pick up *The Stepford Wives*.

God: *Hey*. You know, I think the guy is really *on* to something here. Let's see some smiling faces for a change.

I reminded myself that I was planning to borrow money from my host.

I thought pleasantly: These people are really nice! I'm really lucky to have met all these nice people! It's really nice of these people to be so nice to me!

So tell me about yourself, said Yaakov, what brings you to this part of the world?

I said I was having a bad time but I was trying to get back on my feet.

He said: Girls, give the boy some potatoes.

His wife said: Sarah, give the boy some of your challah.

One of the girls passed me a basket with two small, tough plaited loaves.

Did you make this? I asked, tearing off a chunk.

Sarah nodded smiling.

It's very good, I said, chewing. This was not strictly untrue. If you thought of it as a large unsalted pretzel, it actually wasn't bad. If you weren't worried about losing your teeth before your 21st birthday you had absolutely nothing to worry about.

There was a lottomonitor in the room. I hadn't checked my luck in weeks. I kept looking at it when I thought no one was looking though of course it was turned off for Shabbat. I wondered if there was some question I could ask it to find out about Gaby. I kept thinking: When Shabbat goes out I could look, and But that would be incredibly rude.

2.

As soon as Shabbat went out Yaakov said So you could use some help. I explained enough of the circumstances so it was clear I was not a complete tosser looking for a handout but someone who with a helping hand could stand on his own two feet.

He said Wait here, he would be back soon.

He had taken me to a little room which seemed to be one half of a subdivided closet. There were shelves going right up to the ceiling filled with dusty books. This was the amount of space left over for a study by a family with ten children. This was not the room of a rich man.

Hundreds of richer men had passed me on London Bridge without a second look. My father was not one to make a joke once if it could be made fifty times; 'hard-heartedness is only found among the gentiles,' he would say, quoting Maimonides for the five hundredth time on spotting some loser on the pavement with an empty cup, tossing the princely sum of 10p to the luckless. 'I told you so' was another favourite; at least I didn't have to hear it in person.

There was a soft knock at the door. It opened, and Sarah looked in.

Hi, I said.

Hi, um, she said.

Was there something you wanted? I said.

Um, she said. Um, I'm thinking of reading maths at U and I um

Not to be unkind, this was a girl who made Bride of Frankenstein look like Paris Hilton. If you don't have the looks you're always going to find a university education an uphill battle, and it's worse for girls.

I really don't think that's such a good idea, I said.

But, she said. She looked as though she was going to burst into tears. I thought you'd understand, she said.

I understood, all right. If I had her knack for turning bread dough into high-fired ceramic I'd probably decide I wasn't Jewish housewife material, too. The problem was she didn't understand the alternatives. The problem was, if I tried to tell her she wouldn't believe me.

I know I'm not Albert Einstein, she said. But I have to spend a lot of time helping out around the house. Mum can't do everything and I'm the oldest so I have to look after the others and I'm happy to do it but

Look, I said, if you can't keep up when all you've got to worry about is a little light housework what the *fuck* makes you think things are going to get better? At least now you don't have any debts. If I were you I'd quit while I was still ahead.

Oh *really*, said Sarah. Why should I listen to *you*? You're just a *loser*. Just because *you* couldn't win you think everyone *else* is like *you*. I don't care *what* you say, I'm going to *do* it. *Then* you'll see. If you want *my* opinion most men are just *pathetic*, it's the *women* who do everything *anyway*, if I can't do better than a bunch of stupid *boys* then I'll *really* be worried.

She slammed the door and stalked off down the corridor.

Make just one person happy, as they say in the song. I remembered suddenly that I had been planning to avoid bad language. I thought: Shit.

For some reason I thought suddenly of Rachel the Python.

The average snake sticks to a diet of eggs, mice, insects and small birds; it does not recognise a small deer as a challenge. A python sees a small deer and thinks: Right. One minute there are two objects: a python and a small deer. Three hours later there is one object: a python with a deer-shaped bulge. A week later there is a rather larger python without the bulge.

Well, we all know about nature red of tooth and claw, but there are limits. Only thing is, somebody forgot to tell the python. And whatever it is they forgot to tell the python they also forgot to tell the Python. Rache approached mathematics the way a python approaches an animal of awkward size: with a mean look. She would open *Topological Vector Spaces* and glare at the page. Three hours later it would all be over: you'd be looking at someone with a text-shaped bulge in the brain. Then she would look up and smile. The kind of smile that says 'Deer? *What* deer? Now how could a little old 25-foot python like me eat a *deer*, don't be *silly*.' The kind of smile that reminds you that the female of the species is more deadly than the male.

I felt a pang of nostalgia for the days when I would watch Rache empythoning topology. Those days were gone. They would never return. It was time to get on with my life.

Yaakov came back in three hours with £400.

£4.45 to pay off what I owed on the kippah. Say £300 for deposit and two weeks' rent in advance on a bedsit with a double bed because you never know your luck. Leaving £95.55 until I could stand on my own two feet.

I was going to have to work fast.

There was no question of writing an interesting true story sincerely told in the time. There was also no question of claiming an Unemployment Opportunity —I'd never heard of anyone passing the UEO in under three months. That is, obviously if you go to one of the schools they can get you through faster, but they are not going to do it out of the goodness of their heart. They're not going to do it for £95.55, either.

Luckily those were not the only options. I had once worked as a waiter in a four-star restaurant, and as someone had said at the time, the skills you learn will be with you all your life. No one is going to hire you if you are living out of a sleeping bag on London Bridge, but if you have a fixed abode surely there is a good to excellent chance that you can claim a genuine Employment Opportunity?

£40 for secondhand waiter's kit. Leaving £55.55.

If only I could check my luck.

We went back downstairs. His wife was in the kitchen with Sarah and one of the other girls. The remaining eight children were in the front room. He said you need to be alone for a couple minutes, yes? He told the children to go upstairs, and they left me alone in the room among the red plush furniture with its fringes.

The lottomonitor was already on again. I walked up to it and accessed my screen.

I hit DRAW.

It could have been worse.

So this is GREAT! This is GREAT! People are already wondering what you'll do next, you don't want to be too predictable, in the past your work has been political in a *realistic* way but you *always* loved the Pythons, they were politically subversive and *funny* and if you move on from *Damascene* to a black sci-fi Pythonesque *comedy* people will see the range of your talent, *Shakespeare* did tragedy and history and comedy, *Kurosawa* did historical and modern and tragic and comic, you *know* you can make an *amazing* film, you could have done it *years* ago if the guy had not been an asshole, this is GREAT! this is GREAT! this is GREAT!

Now here's the funny thing about comedy. Your personal life was up shit creek because of the kind of thing the French find *amusing*, people were going *ballistic* about the kind of thing that's so *ludicrous* it's not even working *discussing*. So, right, you got on the plane, and you opened *Lotteryland*, and here's the funny thing. You were *laughing*.

3 1/2

The Low Life

From: amanda292@hotmail.com
To: popesonxtacy@hotmail.com
Date: 06 Aug 2004 10:02:19
Subject: mythical beasts

Alyosha, sorry, thought you said you had received the cheque a month ago. cd it be sent on? cd you give me yr address so someone cd collect it for me? please reply ASAP

amanda

From: popesonxtacy@hotmail.com
To: amanda292@hotmail.com
Date: 13 August 2004 16:05:52
Subject: RE: mythical beasts

Hey, it has arrived- this is really annoying me too and a strange Tabloid London ghost haunting me considering I am in the depths of Iran. I just want everything to be sorted. I am still out of England so a bit difficult but my friend said he sent it last week so should be there now or soon- this week? It is all recorded. Please let me know when you get it.

Cheers,
alyosha

From: amanda292@hotmail.com
To: popesonxtacy@hotmail.com
Date: 15 August 2004 20:25:57
Subject: what else

niente. I begin to think Alyosha Popovitch is some kind of wormhole in space-time down which perfectly ordinary objects vanish without a trace only to surface on alpha centauri. If the cheque does not exist I would INFINITELY prefer to stop playing this ridiculous game and just get on with things.

Amanda

From: popesonxtacy@hotmail.com
To: amanda292@hotmail.com
Subject: the eternal return
Date:Mon, 23 Aug 2004 18:07:33

Hey, I sent loads of messages to you but get no reply. Have you rung Richard my friend who will send you the cheque? He has the reference number for your mail. Also, I have been in contact with The Sentinel - they can resend a cheque. So, what do you want me to do?
So, the cheque exists and is on its way. The old cliché *the cheque is in the mail,* literally this time.
Also have you spoken to others in your building maybe it went to the neighbours or is sitting in a pile of uncollected mail in the lobby of your building? Please get back to me as I too want this sorted asap. Have you been receiving my text messages? Can you at least text an 'ok' or a short response to any future one sent - as I don't know if they are being received or going into the telecommunication void space. Ok Richard's number again is 0208 983 5773

Well, hope you are well. Alyosha

From: amanda292@hotmail.com
To: popesonxtacy@hotmail.com
23 August 2004 19:23:12
Subject: alpha centauri????

alyosha,
I have ransacked my building, no cheque! Royal Mail must have diverted it to Alpha Centauri as previously surmised. I have answered all your messages, perhaps the replies too have gone down the wormhole to alter-alyosha on Alpha Centauri or further afield in the intergalactic other(w)here
If Sentinel cd issue another cheque and stay off the magic mushrooms long enough to post it to an address on the third planet from the sun it wd be hugely appreciated

a

From: popesonxtacy@hotmail.com
To: amanda292@hotmail.com
Date: Tues 24 Aug 2004 19:11:03
Subject: hitchhikers guide the missing pages

Is your silence success? has the eagle landed? I heard you spoke with Richard; apparently the cheque never left post office building; mother fucking cock suckers; the *Daily Beast* would love this story if we didn't scoop with the story in the first place! They are always out for a nasty Royal Mail story.

alyosha

From: amanda292@hotmail.com
To: popesonxtacy@hotmail.com
Date: 24 Aug 2004 10:46:43
Subject: RE: hitchhikers guide the missing pages

Richard too seems to be planet hopping. I have called the number w/o success either he has absentmindedly posted it from Betelgeuse or he lies headless in a pool of gore (getting BLOOD on my BLOOD MONEY, I wd kill him if he was not already dead) or he is too busy shagging the dog to go to the post office. We can only speculate.

a

To: popesonxtacy@hotmail.com
From: amanda292@hotmail.com
Date: 25 August 2004 11:23:03
RE: knife to throat

Alyosha

ok sorry to be unfriendly but the cheque did come after 4 months & whoop de fucking doo it bounced, meaning my bank is charging me £38 for the returned cheque AND I continue to be massively overdrawn.
Look, I can see this is getting really boring for you being hassled endlessly about this thing that shd have been wrapped up months ago, why don't you just give me someone to contact at the paper so I can deal with them directly and sort it out? I don't want to go through another 4 months of ROYAL MAIL ATTACKED BY UFO / GIANT KILLER POODLES / FREAK TYPHOON IN BASINGSTOKE. I wd prefer them to transfer the money directly to my account. I will talk to some boring fat old geezer in accounts,

Richard can be at one with the universe, you can go yomping around Absurd-istan and we can all put it behind us.

a

From: popesonxtacy@hotmail.com
To: amanda292@hotmail.com
Subject: hall of (t)errors
Date: Fri, 27 Aug 2004 13:21:05 +0000

What happened in the end? Is everything ok - did the cheque sort
itself out? I can't believe after all that shite it was declined; we can write a comedy about this.

alyosha

4
The Beeswax

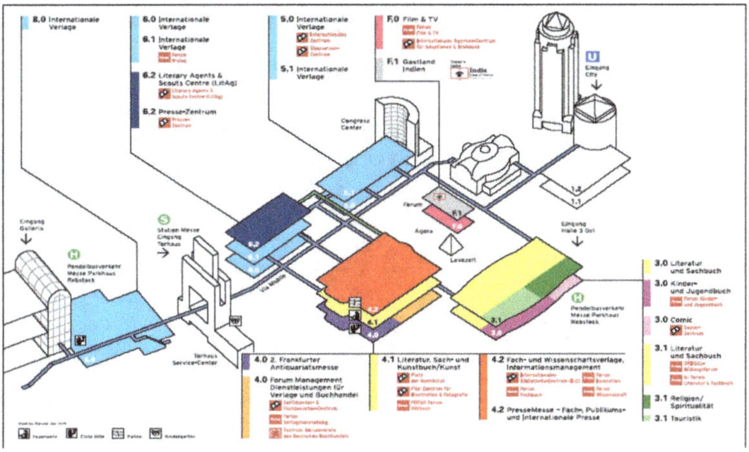

The player enters a new area of a map, and there's a slime pool that's too far to jump across. On the other side of the slime pool is a button that extends the bridge, but it's guarded by a monster. The player's mini-mission is to extend the bridge. The obstacles to accomplishing that mission are the monster and the fact that the button is on the other side of the slime pool—too far away to push. To accomplish the mini-mission, all the player needs to do is shoot the button from his side and then avoid the monster while crossing the bridge; that's it. Simple. It may not seem like a mission, but it is. It's a challenge that the player must face and overcome in order to continue with the game. A single-player level is a collection of these mini-missions, tied closely around unique areas in some cohesive manner.

Marc Saltzman, Game Design: Secrets of the Sages

1

When the phone rings I say I am Rachel. It saves time.

I did not have internet access in the apartment. I went to Sarotti, a café in the premises of a former chocolate factory, which had a free HotSpot. Espresso is served with a glass of water and a paper-wrapped Sarotti chocolate. Cappuccino is served with a glass of water and a paper-wrapped Sarotti chocolate. Other hot drinks are served without water and chocolate.

On the buffet a foil fountain dispensed liquid chocolate. On the LCD Madonna lip-synced "Material Girl." On the screen of the iBook I saw something that was not cheering news.

In October each year a book fair is held in Frankfurt, the Frankfurter Buchmesse, at which world rights are sold in a five-day orgy of wheeling and dealing. Each year the fair selects a country or culture for its guest of honour.

It was now over a year since America had invaded Iraq without waiting for a UN Resolution and without good evidence that weapons of mass destruction were being produced. Its Congress had been bamboozled into approving war in October 2002 (the Administration had cited evidence that Iraq had been importing uranium from Niger, using documents known to be forged). Whatever. Colin Powell, unhappy predecessor to Condoleezza Rice as Secretary of State, had delivered a speech to the UN on 5 February 2003 justifying invasion; he had first seen the supposed supporting evidence four days before. "I'm not reading this, this is bullshit" was Powell's response to material presented as key in a first draft of the speech from the

Vice President's office—but he had made the speech anyway, on the basis of evidence that was merely feeble without being obvious bullshit. Whatever.

The flimsiness of the justification had become increasingly public with the passing year, as had a number of human rights encroachments of limited appeal to European sensibility. Sooooo, boys and girls, the Frankfurter Buchmesse had made the Arab World its guest of honour as an expression of European outrage at American Realpolitik: amid the orgy of wheeling and dealing there would also be colloquia, book readings, interviews, all with the souped-up paraphernalia of simultaneous translation. Naguib Mahfouz would be there, Adonis would be there, Mahmoud Darwish would be there, Gamal al-Ghitani would be there.

The book fair takes place in seven halls of concrete, glass and steel, connected by a shuttle bus so vast is the place so frenzied the pace, and thousands of publishers are marshalled within, and because they have paid eye-popping sums their sole desire is to cram the five days with wheeling and dealing. No working publisher has time for colloquia, readings, interviews. Those with small stands wait anxiously for crumbs, they cannot leave the expensive footage for a colloquium or reading, if Muhammad were to make a surprise guest appearance it would be a *disaster*: six or seven people with firm appointments with Mr Clever would get a last-minute downgrade to Lucy Moran. I say that. I *think* the Prophet would rate a meeting with Mr Clever.

So if Simon had not disliked the rumoured contents of the contract he had inadvertently signed this would have been an *amazing* business opportunity, people would have been avidly reading pirate copies of the new Zozanian! Bidding stratospheric sums for the right to share it with the world!

Here's what's scary. Here's what's seriously scary. The reason this would have been an amazing biz op is that there was still no alter-Tolkien stepping up to the plate. There was no competition. But Simon was powerful now, and I was guilty of a suicide attempt without benefit of press conference.

I got on a train. I got off a train. I took sheafs of pages in my laptop case, Arabic pages in search of a plot, things people could do to while away the longueurs on the stand, but though I wandered the plasterboard corridors and bought overpriced beer I left the laptop case zipped the first day, after that left it at the hotel. I heard Gamal al-Ghitani give a talk on *Thousand and One Nights*. I did not go from stand to stand handing out photocopies of puzzles and poems to slash the collective tedium.

A word cuts through the softspoken haze of a thousand deals. The word is "Rachel." Someone from Oxford. I utter a sentence the drift of which is that despite the fabulousness of the reunion I cannot make dinner. The sentence is shot down. At dinner an argument breaks out over Tolkien. Bad news.

Late that night I meet a Finnish girl in a bar. She's wearing black cowboy boots. She says *Lotteryland* did well in Finland, kids in Finland, she says, they really relate to it.

I say: What are you having?

Kids in Finland, she says, they know too much, they know who pulls the strings, they really relate to a book that doesn't buy the system.

I say: You know, if you write Nokia in Arabic you have all three vowels in a single word, it's a good mnemonic.

نوكيا Nokia

She says: You have a very Finnish sense of humour.

I say: Do you want to go to my hotel?

She laughs.

She says later: What's wrong?

2

When you were sent to Frankfurt in 2003 you were put up in a horrible soulless hotel. This year you looked on Ebab.com, the gay and gay-friendly B&B brokers, and found a great place near the station. Then you met Rachel Zozanian in a bar, so you ended up in a horrible soulless hotel.

She gave you a Sufi poem. She said: I wanted to hand it out at the fair, but it's not good to look crazy. I'd like to be the Wicked Witch of the West but I'm just a Cowardly Lion.

She went to sleep after a while. You looked at the Sufi poem.

خَرَجْتُ فِي حِينٍ بَعْدَ الفَنَا	I came out in the time after vanishing *kharajtu fi hainin ba'da alfana*
وَمِنْ هُنَا بَقِيتُ بِلاَ أَنَا	And from here I persisted not as I *wa min huna baqi'tu bila ana*
وَمَنْ أَنَا يا أَنَا إِلَّا أَنَا	And who am I O I but I? *wa man ana ya ana illa ana?*

It made you think of Fredric Jameson's essay "Postmodernism and Consumer Society":

> All of this puts us in the position of grasping schizophrenia as a break-down of the relationship between signifiers. For Lacan, the experience of temporality, human time, past, present, memory, the persistence of personal identity over months and years—this existential or experiential feeling of time itself—is also an effect of language. It is because language has a past and a future, because the sentence moves in time, that we can have what seems to us a concrete or lived experience in time. But since the schizophrenic does not know language articulation in that way, he or she does not have

> our experience of temporal continuity either, but is condemned to live a perpetual present with which various moments of his or her past have little connection and for which there is no conceivable future on the horizon. In other words, schizophrenic experience is an experience of isolated, disconnected, discontinuous material signifiers which fail to link up into a coherent sequence. The schizophrenic thus does not know personal identity in our sense, since our sense of identity depends on our sense of the persistence of the "I" and the "me" over time.

Which is great, obviously, very Finnish, but you were tired. You wished you were back at the B&B. You took your book out of your bag.

You read *Lotteryland* in Finnish when you were 19. Now you're reading it in the original to practice your English, because the language is pretty straightforward.

OTNDYLARTLE

4. BACK IN THE MONEY

1.

No purchase necessary. To enter, follow the directions published. Method of entry may vary. For eligibility, entries must be received no later than 31 December 2001. No liability is assumed for printing errors, lost, late, or misdirected entries. The Prize will be awarded in a random drawing to be conducted no later than 1 February 2002 from among all the entries received. Odds of winning are determined by the number of eligible entries received. Prizewinners will be determined no later than 28 February 2002.

Open to residents of all Lottery-administrated territories who are 18 years of age or older. All applicable laws and regulations apply. Offer void wherever prohibited by law. Values of all prizes in currency to be determined by Lottery. This offer is presented by United Franchises Corporation, its subsidiaries and affiliates, in conjunction with merchandise and/or product offerings. For a copy of the Official Rules send a self-addressed stamped envelope (Channel Islands residents need not affix return postage) to: JACKPOT SWEEPSTAKES XXV Rules, P.O. Box 10001, St Helier, Jersey.

I signed on the dotted line and returned the form. With £395.55 in my pocket I had obviously not wasted time on the queue of thousands at the Lottery of Housing. I had gone straight to a successful prizeclaimer. My landlord handed me a set of keys and a booklet of 10 preclaimed electricity tickets, 10 preclaimed gas tickets, 10 preclaimed water tickets and a ticket for a preclaimed potted plant. He said he could do me a preclaimed cat flap for a very reasonable price. I said I would think about it.

I returned to the car. Channah had gambled on a clapped-out Q-reg Austin Metro making the journey to my new address without having to be towed home; so far she seemed to be in luck. In the car with her were Sarah (not speaking to me); also Moshe, Aharon, Binyamin and Yitzhaq, winners of the pre-enactment of World War III which had decided who got to go in the car; also 45 potato latkes, 12 vegetarian sausages, 18 hard-boiled eggs, 3 strawberry cheesecakes, 15 chocolate cakes, and 6 rabbinically certified kosher mini-pizzas, not to mention two boxes crammed with jams, pickles, cheese, mustard, vegetarian sausage, and matzah certified kosher for Pesach, oh and also not mentioning 7 bottles of kosher wine and a carton of grape juice. Channah had described my plight to her friends and they had rallied round. I just hoped Sarah hadn't done any of the cooking.

OK, we're in business, I said.

We transported the food to the third floor.

Just leave everything and I'll put it away, I said, while Channah and Sarah headed for the kitchen and put everything away.

I think that takes care of everything, said Channah. If you need anything just give me a call.

Um, Sarah, I said.

. . .

I just wanted to say, I think it would be great if you went to U, I said.

. . .

But I just wondered whether you'd thought of reading chemistry.

?!

I think if you read chemistry you'd really get a lot out of it, I said. I don't think maths is such a good idea, but if you read chemistry you can't go wrong.

!?

Now you're coming to us for the Seder of course, said Channah.

The first night of Passover was only a week away, so I should have seen this coming. Unfortunately, I did not have the presence of mind to invent someone whose feelings would be mortally wounded if I did not go to them instead, and before I knew it Channah had said So that's settled.

Then they were gone.

Alone at last.

I went straight to the lottomonitor.

SUNDAY 01 APRIL 2001 0900 HOURS

HOUSING OPPORTUNITY
Congratulations!
TRANSPORTATION OPPORTUNITY
Congratulations!
UNEMPLOYMENT OPPORTUNITY
Congratulations!
EMPLOYMENT OPPORTUNITY
Congratulations!
YOUTH OPPORTUNITY
Congratulations!
MEDICAL OPPORTUNITY
Congratulations!
DENTAL OPPORTUNITY
Congratulations!
FITNESS OPPORTUNITY
Congratulations!
DISABILITY OPPORTUNITY
Congratulations!

And a happy April Fool's Day to you too.

The previous occupant had obviously been the type of person who will stand in 30 separate queues and complete 5 preliminary, 15 in-depth and 10 follow-up questionnaires without noticing how much time it actually costs to claim a prize. This was why the previous occupant was no longer the present occupant. Either the previous occupant had succeeded in claiming the prize—anything's possible—or the previous occupant had lost job and savings and been booted out by the successful prizeclaimer in possession of the premises. Anything is possible, but some things are more likely than others.

Either way, the result was that the lottomonitor was useless as it stood for any kind of serious luck check.

Not for the first time I cursed a system in which lotto-options are site specific.

I sat down at the monitor and got to work. Four hours later I had cleared the draw of most of the junk prizes.

1300 HOURS. RESOLUTION. FIRM SENSE OF RESOLVE.

Congratulations! Only 250,000 out of 60,000,000 won Resolution and Firm Sense of Resolve in the latest draw. Only 1,000 out of 100,000 in your age bracket. Only 49,999 out of 50,000 with a Perseverance index of Silver or better. Good luck!

That was more like it. Not exactly informative, granted, but at least it was a prize that hadn't been won by everyone else in the country. At least it didn't have to be claimed.

I thought: Now we're in business.

I checked the odds of seeing Gaby again. Something told me I had not succeeded in drawing APPEARANCE OF CANDOUR and ENGAGING PERSONALITY during the time when I was cut off from the lottomonitor.

Perhaps it had been a mistake to joke about being a cunningly disguised millionaire.

Or perhaps it had been a mistake to joke about serial killers.

Perhaps I had looked insincere.

Or perhaps she just didn't like losers.

I thought suddenly: Or perhaps it's just that she has no way of getting in touch with me!

I sent a trial message to my ether address and got a message from the demon explaining that it had tried to deliver the message and failed and would not try again. I picked up the phone and called U2 and gave them my new address and went back to the lottomonitor. The odds had improved—slightly.

I did not think Fuck because I was trying to cut down.

I thought: Les jeux sont faits.

I thought: Fuck.

I hit DRAW again just in case the odds had improved in the intervening three seconds and instantly won five free bookkeeping courses, two free desktop publishing courses, a free increase your memory course, a free positive thinking course, a free accelerated learning course and eight free courses in overcoming the inner critic.

I thought: OK. OK. Let's not get excited here.

I said: Shit! Shit! Shit! Shit!

I thought: OK. OK. We're not getting excited. We're just dealing with it. OK.

I got to work again trying to identify the error which had permitted the junk prizes to slip through.

I hit DRAW again and won another two courses in overcoming the inner critic and a course in time management.

I thought: OK. OK. We're getting there.

I was about to get back to prize elimination when the speaker above the monitor crackled.

I thought: Oh, SHIT.

One of the disadvantages of life indoors is that you can't really get away from the lucky hello. Not for the first time I cursed whoever it was who had decided to randomise the broadcasts. In the early days they had scheduled broadcasts, and people would organise their timetables so they would be offsite at 0600, 0900, 1200, 1800, 2100 and 2400 hours, but then it was decided that a scheduled broadcast was not really in the spirit of the times because it was not just a matter of luck if you happened to hear it.

You know, you're really a very lucky person.
Nobody else is quite like you.
You're special just the way you are.
You're lucky just being you.

I toyed with the idea of making a dash for the fire escape. My earplugs were back in U2. But I did not want to come back and find that the lottomonitor had randomly deleted a partially executed prize elimination.

I thought: OK. We can deal with this. We'll tough it out.

You know, there are lots of prizes for everyone. Sometimes we win and sometimes we lose. Sometimes it's easy to dwell on the prizes we haven't won. It's easy to feel unlucky if we don't win. But remember, no matter what you win, no matter what you don't win, you're still you. And that's an incredibly special person to be.

I thought: Oh Gaby, where are you?

That's why it's important to love ourselves for what we are. Not for what we could be.

It's important to love other people for what they are. Not for what they could be.

Remember, everyone is special in their own special way.

That's what makes each and every one of us special. So very special.

Which is why we're all lucky just to be here.

I thought: OK, OK, we're getting there.

The tinkle tinkle tinkle happy xylophone launched into the intro to the Lucky Song.

I'm lucky to be so special
There's nobody just like me
So every day in every way
I'm a lucky person to be

I know I'm really lucky
And the reason is plain to see
I could have been somebody else
So I'm lucky just to be me.

Then the lucky hello was over.

I ran another Draw and won a free trip to Florida.

This was really significant progress.

Heartened, I ran another Draw and found that the odds of my seeing Gaby again had not significantly improved in the course of the lucky hello. This was, of course, discouraging per se, but at least suggested that the prize elimination had been reasonably effective.

I slumped back in my chair, momentarily unmanned by delayed reaction to the lucky hello.

2.

I let a few minutes go by, then gathered my forces and with a superhuman effort stood up. I staggered out to the kitchen in search of fortification. It's important to get your blood sugar up after prolonged hello exposure.

I popped a couple of kosher mini-pizzas in the microwave. They were prepackaged so it was a fair bet Sarah had not had a hand in them.

While the mini-pizzas were microwaving I sampled a latke. I'd tasted better, but something told me Sarah could have done worse. I finished the latke, ate a couple more to be on the safe side, and sampled a chocolate cake. This too was reassuringly edible. The microwave said:

CONGRATULATIONS!

I opened the door hastily before it could go through the lucky microwave announcement and took the mini-pizzas, five latkes and the rest of the chocolate cake inside. Time for a quick luck check.

I sat down again in front of the lottomonitor, mouth full of freshly microwaved mini-pizza, and hit Draw.

1400 HOURS RESOLUTION. FIRM SENSE OF RESOLVE.

You've got to be joking.

Not for the first time I wondered about the timing of these prizes. Sometimes they seem to be descriptive, as often as not seconds or even whole minutes out of sync. At other times there seems to be a predictive element, the draw preceding the actual occurrence of the state of mind in question by an unspecified interval. I once wrote a letter to the Lottery Lottery which I signed Ephraim aged nine (I was nine at the time) and got a letter back saying Dear Ephraim Thank you for your letter. Your luck is what you make it.

Even at nine I was unimpressed by this reply. How can you make anything of your luck until you know what it actually *is*? I asked my parents who said they didn't know, and my teachers who said it was bad luck to analyse too much. So I tried to run a draw for a timed win (as in FIRM SENSE OF RESOLVE AT 1400 HOURS) but when I had been at the lottomonitor for eight hours without a break my parents made me stop. My mother said it was selfish when other people wanted to run luck checks, I was not the only person in the world, and I offered to continue at night when everyone was in bed and my mother said No and I tried to argue the point and my father said Enough already. All I wanted to point out was that if we had a better grasp of what it was we were actually winning we would all benefit.

All I'm saying is that if, I began.

Enough already, said my father, and the discussion was closed. Permanently.

Looking back with the wisdom of maturity, all I can say is, no wonder we had such terrible luck.

I cut off a quarter of chocolate cake. Maybe it was not too late for things to be different. For the first time in my life I now had unrestricted access to a lottomonitor. Maybe it was not too late to change my luck.

3

But *you* really drew the short straw. Didier Cuvaux, a bullet had your name on it.

You took Eurostar from Paris to man the stand for P.O.L at the London Bookfair in March 2007. At the last minute they told you to get a copy of *Your Name Here,* the new novel by Helen DeWitt, because Laffont, who published DeWitt's first book, had not yet picked up the rights. P.O.L publish Renaud Camus's *Tricks,* DeWitt said she had been influenced by *Tricks,* your chef thought he might want to publish *Your Name Here* and told you to suss it out.

But this is a fucking *nightmare.* This guy Gridneff is *incredibly* hard to follow, *your* English grammar is better than *that, your* English spelling is better than *that,* he makes Guyotat look like a pompous pedantic old fart. If P.O.L do decide to pick it up it's going to be a nightmare for the translator, is the translator supposed to misspell every other French word and throw in grammatical mistakes every time Gridneff fucks with the English language? So instead of clubbing the night away you were sitting in the fucking hotel room reading this illiterate Australian.

From: "A.P. Pechorin" <popesonxtacy@hotmail.com>
To: sabinejelinek@hotmail.com
Subject: the capricious contemporary mode-moda . . . coda
Date: Tues, 7 June 2005 05:18:43 +0000

ok let's just be civilized and stay out of trouble. pls don't chuck my stuff or dance around a fire of it, most of the clothes are man-made fibres so the fumes are not only dangerous to you but also the local biosphere, think of the underprivilidged children suffering at the hand of such actions and due to my cheap fashion . . . will get someone to organise asap.
ok well hope you hear good things from mulbery and more

alyosha

The new MSN Search Toolbar now includes Desktop search! http://join.msn.com/toolbar/overview

From: "A.P. Pechorin" <popesonxtacy@hotmail.com>
To: RustyMercedesBenz@hotmail.com
Subject: we gates dear?
Date: Wednesday, 8 June 2005 03:38:33 +0000

Ms Benz, as a practitioner of the brainsicknessnomore it is in my
professional register of care to follow up at least
a fortnight or so after treatment...is everything ok?

Silence, hopefully, the watercolour of your
immanence. ok well hope/know all is dandy---
i am in the centre of I-ran (away). (Yazd)
was hoping for your postal address- not to turn up

someday un announced vying for prime real estate
of yer Scandinavian couch but a humble post karten.

well take care me dear.
Alyosha

Are you using the latest version of MSN Messenger? Download MSN Messenger 7.5 today! http://join.msn.com/messenger/overview

From: "A.P. Pechorin" <popesonxtacy@hotmail.com>
To: "Francesca DiMaggio" <tothepowerof@yahoo.com>
Subject: quixotic
Date: Thurs, 9 June 2005 16:09:31 +0000

realising one is not in the best of your lights, so perhaps, perchance, you received the package of reconciliation? Or should I assume you didn't receive the book I sent for your birthday? If not, it was Kathy Acker's '*Don Quixote*' with a Coco Rosie CD inside...oh well the thought counts, I guess, said Count Dracula.

Alyosha

Use MSN Messenger to send music and pics to your friends
http://www.msn.co.uk/messenger

From: "A.P. Pechorin" <popesonxtacy@hotmail.com>
To: ewanhutchison@hotmail.com
Subject: pip pip pip pip pip pip time is up down
Date: Wed 15 June 2005 11:43:19 +0000

Ewan good to briefly talk international money phone etc- trying to avoid communication, so felt the cut off was the sign if not economically produced. Well, speak again at some point.

- when in Sept you plannign to move?

I dreamed about you last night- you and Nick Land and I were arguing about 'nothingness' and it kept going around and around in a circle of conversation/explanation- each time seemingly more comical or satirical (Woody Allenesq) and then I got totally mad and you both larfed at me and I threw the book out the window- then (like the madman) went running through
the streets shouting *'I know nothing'* and everyone i confronted this with wryly said – *I know*- and this lead to more frustration and more running and then I woke slightly panicky but needing to go to the toilet. So glad I woke before it exited my body mid-deep sleep dream scape...

Curently in Cappadocia where it looks like the moon and people live/d in caves.

ok hope you well.

alyosha

From: "A.P. Pechorin" <popesonxtacy@hotmail.com>
To: silentstones@hotmail.com
Subject: no-mad-icistic movement
Date: Thurs, 16 June 2005 05:27:11 +0000

nÃ½kos

sorry to cause dÃ½stress wÃ½th the move. Ã½ dÃ½dnt thÃ½nk there was too much stuff. just pÃ½le whatever Ã½nto the bag on the top shelf and whatevers appears of value Ã½nto a box(s). all Ã½ need you to do Ã½s take the clothes on

the hangers and my portfolÃ½o- the ORACLE of smutty tabloÃ½d success - everything else Ã½s just paper - not that Ã½mportant so put Ã½t Ã½n a box and can you leave Ã½t at john's?

the books - john and you can use - a gÃ½ft. DÃ½dn't thÃ½nk you requÃ½red a taxÃ½.\\

there Ã½s a 'suÃ½t bag' at the bottom of the cupboard that Ã½ carrÃ½ed my suÃ½ts and more from aus to london Ã½n. but send me your bank detaÃ½ls and Ã½ can transfer money to your account for whatever costs Ã½ncurred.

your last lÃ½ne- emaÃ½l- Ã½s off a famÃ½lar tone. brevÃ½ty and unable to hÃ½de resentment. love but not wantÃ½ng to do again? dont even really understand why you suspect thÃ½s task would occur agaÃ½n? Ã½ suspect you are annoyed at havÃ½ng to do thÃ½s donkey work but no doubt Ã½t Ã½s an engÃ½ne to curse my name whÃ½le celebrate too? Ã½ too fÃ½nd myself Ã½n this mode sometimes. or Ã½s thÃ½s a mÃ½sreading of technologÃ½cal modes where emaÃ½l appears cold. as opposed to hot talk? or has hotter talk fÃ½lled your ear? all thÃ½s fuels my Ã½nsecurÃ½tÃ½es and feelÃ½ng of Ã½solatÃ½on - makes me appre-cÃ½ate nÃ½etschze and wonder about the nature of my fabrÃ½c- tapestry.

well Ã½ am not sure what Ã½ am doÃ½ng. today off to galÃ½pollÃ½ where Ã½n world war 1 (hundreds of thousands of AustralÃ½ans and New Zealand men were slaughtered after beÃ½ng sent to the wrong landÃ½ng. aussÃ½e's D-day. Mel GÃ½bson made a fÃ½lm spurÃ½ously retellÃ½ng thÃ½s hÃ½story.

everywhere Ã½ go Ã½n Turkey they say australÃ½ans were the best fÃ½gters. Brave and fearless. Ã½ thÃ½nk thÃ½ngs to myself when the Turks say thÃ½s. we are good bullet holders. cannon fodder.

thÃ½nk my frÃ½ends are declÃ½nÃ½ng Ã½nto the abyss whÃ½le Ã½ am stÃ½ll(naÃ½vely?) pushÃing for a summÃ½t of sorts before the abyss. so Ã½ do plan to return to london but not sure for how long. Ã½ am thÃ½nkÃ½ng of the US of A consÃ½derÃ½ng the fÃ½ve year vÃ½sa for journalÃ½sts. Ã½n the short term Ã½Â have applÃ½ed for the Ã½ranÃ½an vsÃ½a apparently a fÃ½fty fÃ½fty chance for a month. then not sure.

maybe war wÃ½ll break out. thÃ½nkÃ½ng about doÃ½ng masters- workÃ½ng Ã½n advertÃ½sÃ½ng- joÃ½ng the jÃ½hadÃ½sts. fÃ½nÃ½shÃ½ng off the Baghdad to BrÃ½tney. USA?

too many talkers not enough actÃ½on made around me. perhaps the new world holds more relevance than London's tumult and archaÃ½c wobble about yesteryear. terrorÃ½toralÃ½sed brÃ½tan. the BrutÃ½sh . the RussÃ½an sayÃ½ng of cautÃ½on around men who complaÃ½n too much sprÃ½ngs to mÃ½nd.

come on nÃ½ck. why do you punÃ½sh me?

love and would relÃ½sh goÃ½ng through your durty daks

Alyosha

Hotmail messages direct to your mobile phone http://www.msn.co.uk/msnmobile

From: "A.P. Pechorin" <popesonxtacy@hotmail.com>
To:zeldafitz@yahoo.com
Subject: claustrophiliac
Date: Thurs 23 June 2005 14:02:58 +0000

just rang the house. I am ýn Zonguldak - a coal mýnýng town on the Black Sea. am looking for kýds ýn ýllegal mýnes. have found some but wýll be tryýng to do justýce not tabloýd style. have been taken ýn by a wonderful Turkýsh famýly - met theýr nephew an Ýstanbul reportage photographer called Ahmet Polat but born near the Hague, Dutch-land – so we share/suffer together the foreýgn father syndrome and have been rockýng along together. We wýll be doýng some stuff together hopefully nýce nýce.

Actually, was pretty mental. They dressed me up full work suit and then taken 500 metres down ýnto 7km of coal mýne - one of the most amazýng experýences ever. This was then featured on the front page of the local paper here- then today, after the artýcle, was hauled ýnto the cops for ýnquiry as to why Ý was ýnterested ýn the area. What ýs my agenda?

ok ýf you leave sept 8 - Ý have to sort out my boxes. what ýs the deal? will slýde the fýddy ýnto yer account výa teh web.. was plannýng a june return but late before a dýnner on teh 30th.

Where you goýng travellýng? movýng your stuff too? London gone - where
you
goýng to base yerself?

dýal for a caht...

alyosha

From: "Francesca DiMaggio" <tothepowerof@yahoo.com>
To: popesonxtacy@hotmail.com
Subject: RE: quixotic
Date: Sun, 26 June 2005 06:35:42 +0000

Well, thank you. My mother mentioned that a package for me been sent to her place. I'm surprised to hear from you, frankly.

Yahoo! Personals
- New people, new possibilities. FREE for a limited time!

From: sabinejelinek@hotmail.com
To: popesonxtacy@hotmail.com
Subject: RE: the capricious contemporary mode-moda...coda
Date: Mon 27 June 2005 04:11:32 +0000

piss off. just fucking piss off.

From: "Kate Grierson" <islandinthesun>@demon.co.uk
To: popesonxtacy@hotmail.com
Subject: RE: despotic
Date: Tues, 28 June 2005 11:19:02 +0000

Don't contact me ever again.

5

Who's Afraid of the Cowardly Lion

IMAGE: Women answering the telephone, about 1948

> Back > Previous > Next

Picture Number:1997-5002_10958
Credit:National Museum of Photography, Film & Television/Science & Society Picture Library

Caption:
A photograph of a woman answering a telephone, taken by Photographic Advertising Limited in about 1948. Photographic Advertising Limited was founded in 1926 by a group experienced in photojournalism and film. The company created multi-purpose stock images with the potential for selling a range of products. Whilst enjoying its greatest success during the 1930s, it continued in business until 1977. Photographic Advertising Limited's trademark, the staged studio photograph resembling a film still, was its selling point and, later, its downfall. Sophisticated, adaptable and generic, this kind of image gradually fell out of favour as clients increasingly demanded targeted advertising campaigns with specific photographs.

In Collection of: National Museum of Photography Film & Television

Subject(s) > Science & Technology > Telecommunications

1

The Scarecrow is afraid of fire, the Tin Man of water. My character has a fear of the spoken word. She came to Berlin to be safe. Berliners are known for their unfriendliness, it is possible to live in Berlin for a year and not know a soul. It's possible to spend a year trying to bring a book back from the dead.

She has a large, grand, cheap apartment with high ceilings and white plaster mouldings. Sometimes she lies on the bed staring at the wall; sometimes she goes out into the city, where each beer has a dedicated glass and paper collar from the brewery (Warsteiner: Eine Königin unter den Bieren! Flensburger: Das Flens; Krombacher: Eine Perle der Natur; Bitburger: Bitte, ein Bit!), where a Milchkaffee comes in a cup with a handle, a latte macchiato in a tall glass with a spoon and small biscuit or chocolate. Someone is forcing her to talk.

Perhaps you can imagine the moment when Plath goes to the kitchen. She opens the oven door, places a folded towel inside. Then she sits on the floor staring at the wall. She does not close the oven door and go back to bed; she does not turn on the gas. It could go either way.

Or perhaps you can imagine Woolf walking down to the Ouse. She puts stones in her pockets. She sits on a large rock looking out at the water. She does not take the stones from her pockets and walk back to the house; she does not walk into the water. It could go either way.

Perhaps you can imagine being at the point where it can go either way, sitting in a room in Berlin, when the phone rings. At the other end of the phone is a man who can't imagine being at the point where it can go either way.

2

The phone rings. What time is it? 14:27:03. Ungodly.

The phone rings.

She picks up the receiver. Words break and enter.

She can tap vast untapped markets, vast untapped markets of the benighted whose lives have yet to be brightened by *Lotteryland*. This is the gist. A cast of thousands mills confusedly until the gist is lost to view. "Lost to view" sounds strange. Words continue to throng.

—I'm not interested in money. I can get $1.5 million for a screenplay, I'll write the screenplay myself and not take a salary, I'm basically donating my services for free. Which means the film will definitely get made. It could have been made years ago, but Sam was completely unreasonable, this was a guy, all he had to do was get out of his own way, I like Anne, I'm happy to work with Anne, she won't be a producer but she can definitely work on the film, she'll learn a lot and she'll work with some good people and she'll get a credit, I can't tell people my producer is a Mom in Dubuque, she's not a producer, she's a Mom, but there are definitely things she can do, we'll definitely be shooting on location so there will definitely be stuff to do down there, but I don't want to deal with Sam, the guy is basically dishonest, these are people who know nothing about the movie business, they buy this option and then they basically sit on it because they don't know how to get a movie made but they're not willing to let someone else make it, I said to them, Look, I can get $2 million for a screenplay, I'll write the screenplay for free, I'm not taking any money for it, so this will definitely happen, a movie will be made . . . are you there?

Joltin' Joe has left and gone away.

—I am here.

Doesn't Peter Strawson ask whether purely aural entities could be individuated? Does he not make a pun on Stephen Hero? And doesn't Gareth Evans ask what reference to such entities would pick out? But Evans died a long time ago. McDowell is in Pittsburgh.

Talk on, talk on.

Isn't there an insect, would it be a wasp? that occupies the nest of another insect? An ant, maybe? A termite? A swarm of totally alien insects invades, kills the queen, does something unspeakable to the eggs, takes over the thin paper cells. Her head is crawling with alien words.

What time is it? 15:14:13.

—All I want is to be fair.

15:14:13-15:27:08 are devoted to fairness and the $3 million salary.

If we were devising a society with no knowledge of the position we were to occupy therein, would we not want to make some provision against the airing of unsolicited "theories" of justice? But to make such a provision one would need first to understand what is meant by a theory of justice and second to understand the excruciating anguish caused by

—So, is there someone my agent can talk to?

A chance to make an end.

—There's the. Well, there's always the. That is, there's definitely someone he can

—Do you have an agent?

—I'm not sure.

—Should he talk to your lawyer? Wasn't there a lawyer?

—No. Yes. There was a lawyer. Yes, there was.

—Well, what's the next step?

—Right. Right. You're right. What's the next step. What *is* the next step? I think the *next* step is for me to talk to the betazoid. It's up to *me* to find out whether she is, in fact, my agent. That's not *your* responsibility, it's *my* responsibility. These things are never cut and dried. Our world is not black and white. It's up to me to determine whether she considers herself, on balance,

—When can I expect an answer?

The innocence of it.

—You're right. You're right. You're right. You're absolutely *right*. This is *not* the approach for the betazoid. Definitely not. No. No. Here's what you do. Get your agent to call. If your agent calls, the likelihood that she is my agent will increase by, at an educated guess, 77.2 percent. And you can send me an e-mail, yes? with your

—Can you give me the name and number?

—The name is Diana Seaton, and the number iiiiiiiiiiiiiiiiiiiiiiiiiiiiiiiiiiiiiiiiiiiii I have it here somewhere, the number iiiiiiiiiiiiiiiiiiiiiiiiiiiiiiiiiiiiiiiiiiiiiiiiiiiiiiiiiiiiiiiiiii iiiiiiiiiiiiiiiiiiiiiiiiiiiiiiiiiiiiiiiiiiiiiiiiiiiiiiiiiiiiiiiiiiiiiiiiiiiiiiiiiiiiiiiiiiiiiiiiiiiiiiiiiiiiiiiiiiiiiiiiiiiiiiiiiiiiiiis 212 585 3870 extension 305.

—Okay, I'll have my agent call her. Talk soon.

3

The phone rings. The phone rings. The phone rings.

3 July 2005. In the Inbox is another e-mail from Gina insisting that the location of the $200 be revealed. Also an old e-mail from a stranger

> Talking to strangers in the bar. They don,t have tonic water or ginger ale here outrage. Me drinking olive oil in the organic bar later. stop it Alyosha. Ridiculing the signage that informs the concerned modern man that the fish is killed naturally. I grab april,s camera and take photos inside the paraplegic toilet. Naked torso. an old girlfriend who i can't stand so much i think of her too much, text messaged me 'happy birthday, from an old friend'. what does that mean. Penis in the mirror, the toilet plumbing. More tears. Rhys apologising for taking 'my' woman. Me laughing. At the thought. Ludmilla the Croatian doctor telling me I am wonderful I am and we should go to the party across from Hackney fArm. Get cab to party then have no cash. No booze. Heavy drunk. we get a cab to Whoreditch to get money but mysteriously end up in Lackney.

The fabulous voice restores me, magically, from third person anomie and alienation to first personal sunny cheer. I rerereread the e-mail from the crazy Russian, only, hang on, if he is talking about spending four months learning Russian he can't actually BE Russian, must be (1+n)th generation, AngloRusski or something.

> Ended with me going home/kissing (the kiss caused a critical moment) the woman, Kate (36 tv set designer, lives in Bow, drives a beat-up Saab), we say we are in love but she doesn,t want me full time, she has a Danish electro deejay called Jakob whom she doesn,t

> love but chose over me last year after we locked horns. She and I deeply desire each other but usually keep apart, because she doesn,t want me. All this in front of Anna, shock why are we doing this again Kate. You don,t want me. kiss me kiss me. I love you Alyosha. Anna, who had been kissing me earlier in the evening not impressed, then the Bombay mix went everywhere, guilt maybe with me for that toxic explosion, all while Justin performs cunninglingus with April on the washing machine in the toilet. Aidan avoiding April cause he doesn,t want to shag her anymore. More vodka.

I can't remember the face of this AngloRusski stranger. You'd think the nucleus of the Kiss-me-Kiss me-Alyosha orbitals must be something special, but the face escapes me.

I was wearing black M&S pj bottoms & a Mind the Gap sweatshirt, I know, because that was then all I ever wore, & it seems managed to make an impact (despite looking like the ugly weird mutant in an adventurous boy-band) just by flashing the edition of *lignes* on Adorno.

All I remember now about this book is a piece by Derrida on Blanchot, who avoided publicity, the limelight, PARIS, & to whose remote provincial address Derrida sent a postcard twice a year. Derrida showed his passion for Blanchot, in other words, by sending a postcard where I would have sent a cheque, & in Blanchot's position I would have been wondering whether I could flog the postcards and if so how much for, which is the true dwarvish Weltanschauung and quite alien, I believe, to the purism of Blanchot.

The phone rings.

4

You flew to Paris to mix sound for *Damascene* because you love working with the French. People are besieging you with crazy offers for your next project because you're hot shit. Sometimes you wonder if you should write your own material, find your own voice, but you've been thinking about *Lotteryland* for years. You read somewhere that Gilliam saw drawings of what people in the 30s thought the technology of the future would look like, there were automated manual typewriters, automated filing cabinets, Gilliam fell in love with the look and this was what he used in *Brazil*—you'd *love* to do something like that.

Your agency lost contact with Zozanian for like a *year*, then you got a call from some Mom in like Raoul South Dakota saying she thought it was in Rachel's best interests yadda yadda yadda to give you the fucking phone number in Berlin, so you talked to Zozanian and you had a good conversation, you expected someone funnier, somehow, whatever, now your agent is talking to her agent. let's get this show on the road.

NTRODALETYL

5. I DON'T BELIEVE IT

TUESDAY 10 APRIL 2001 0930 HOURS

ENNUI.
Too bad! Better luck next time!

Interesting.

I was sitting on the revolving chair, arms across the back, chin propped on arms, staring at the screen. I gave the floor a kick and revolved twice before coming to rest again to gaze at the luck line.

If past draws were anything to go by, I would have expected a whole string of statistics about people who had studied for the UEO 14 hours a day, seven days a week. If you're studying for exams at school you can always do a draw to see how your morale compares to people doing comparable amounts of work. You can get the success rate of people who have taken the exam in the past plotted against comparable industry and aptitude.

I hit DRAW again.

ENNUI.
Too bad! Better luck next time!

Extremely interesting.

For eight days I had done nothing but read UEO prizeclaiming materials. But no matter how many draws I ran I never got so much as a peep about the prizeclaim. I could call up the actual prize whenever I wanted, and whenever I did it urged me to collect it. But it seemed to be impossible to get any data on the chances of doing so.

I had got up at eight, breakfasted on a portion of honey cake, done a solid 75 minutes of UEO, and decided to try a luck check. And this was the result.

It's important not to panic, so I tried not to panic.

But how are you supposed to maximise your luck if you can't run accurate luck checks?

Well, never say die. I would get back to work at once.

ENNUI.

Too bad! Better luck next time!

Or rather, perhaps I would look at the post.

The post had started to arrive on my third day, and I had already won six free car insurance policies, 20 free trips with no strings attached and 80 free home employment opportunities.

Today I won a free cash prize which I could claim by signing up for health insurance within the next seven days, and another free cash prize which I could claim by joining a book club, and a free car, and a free trip to Florida, and a free semi-detached house, and a free week in Majorca, and I was one of only 10,000 people who had made it to the second round in a draw for a £1,000,000 jackpot and all I had to do was complete the enclosed application form for disability insurance and return it within seven days to qualify for a free prize which I had already won.

Under about thirty envelopes was a small envelope with an actual stamp in one corner and G. de Benedetti in the other.

0940 HOURS.

ECSTASY.

Congratulations! Only 1,500 out of 5,000,000 won genuine Ecstasy in the latest draw. Remember, a pharmaceutical-induced mental state is not genuine! It's worth waiting for the real thing! The best of British luck to you!

I tore it open.

Dear Ephraim if that is really your name which I doubt, for all I know you are a cunningly disguised serial-axe-murdering millionaire and have buried the dismembered corpse of a student named Ephraim and are now helping yourself to his name,

I hope you are OK. Give me a call.

Gabriela

There was a phone number and an address.
I couldn't believe my luck.
I did not want to seem too eager so I decided to let a decent interval elapse before calling.

0945 HOURS
ECSTASY.
Congratulations!

Five minutes struck me as a pretty decent interval, all things considered.
I called the number and got Gaby's office.
This is Ephraim, I said.
Who? said Gaby.

You know, I said. I got your letter today.

Oh, right, said Gaby. Is that really your name?

Sadly yes, I said.

I don't think I believe you, said Gaby. Why should I believe a word you say? I think I'll call you Alias.

It has a nice ring to it, I said. Would you like to come to my housewarming party?

When is it? said Gaby.

I was thinking maybe tonight, I said.

Who else is coming?

You're the only one I've asked so far, I said. I'm working on a very limited budget. I can only afford one guest.

I think I'm doing something tonight, said Gaby.

I realise it's very short notice, I said. But I can be flexible about the date.

I'm not sure, said Gaby.

It doesn't have to be at my place, I said. I mean, I could be anyone. What about an alibi party? We can meet somewhere else at the time of the alleged housewarming party and have a coffee. You don't want to take chances.

Oh, that's all right, said Gaby. I'll come over tomorrow after work.

5

The Ice Queen Cometh

Liebe predigen setzt in denen an die man sich da wendet bereits eine anderen Charakter Struktur voraus,

To preach love already assumes another structure of character in those one addresses

denn die Menschen die man lieben soll, sind ihr selber so, dass sie nicht lieben können, and darum keineswegs so liebenswert.

for the people one should love are themselves such that they cannot love, and so are in no way lovable

Theodor Adorno, Education After Auschwitz

Phone Death

1

The phone rings. The phone rings.

There are people who can't adjust to the fact that Woody Allen is a morose workaholic. There are people who think John Cleese is a bumbling British twit. There are people who think Steve Coogan is Alan Partridge. There is a type of person (and this is why the misanthropy of the average workaholic comic writer grows more savage with the passing years) who tells the masturbation joke to Woody Allen, the dead parrot joke to Cleese, the knowing-me-knowing-you line to Coogan, laughing heartily the while; who launches into a spirited rendition of "Springtime for Hitler" upon meeting Mel Brooks.

Noszaly was one of these. Having acquired a phone number he seemed to think he must use it. It seemed not to occur to him that I could have called him any time in the previous year, had our last conversation inclined me to do so. A year had gone by, there was no new book, perhaps a deal should be done, if it could have been done without further telephone conversations perhaps I would have done it.

Perhaps you have had this experience. You go to see *Good Will Hunting,* the film that launched Damon and Affleck. The film is about a working-class genius (Damon) who is psychologically disturbed. He is sent for counselling to Robin Williams. You fear the worst. Williams wins the boy's trust; the boy was beaten by his father, still has a scarred back. They hug, the boy weeps, Williams will always be there for him. Scene follows scene. The boy returns to Williams' office; Williams is packing up! What's going on? Williams explains that he is going to be sailing around the world—but he will be checking his messages. He can always be *reached.*

This is a scene of unsurpassed pricelessness. You *howl.* Suddenly you realise that you are the only one laughing.

Comic writers live in a cold hell. They see pricelessness where the warm-hearted dimwitted see something to warm the cockles of a myopic heart. Why did the chicken cross the road? To get to the other side. What did Albright say when she sent fifty peacekeepers to Rwanda? We want to show the seriousness of our intentions.

Noszaly sent e-mails saying he wanted to do something fun for a change. It's a funny book, he said. If it's not fun, what's the point? He was forty-something, a pampered baby boomer, he did not talk about the erosion of student funding in Britain under Thatcher, Major, Blair, he did not talk about galloping fee and degree inflation in America, he did not talk about

Don't tell me about the future. Tell me about the past.

1.1 = ١.١

once upon a time = 1999 = ١٩٩٩
a kingdom far far away = England
It started well. It went wrong.

First things first. Be paranoid, be very paranoid.

If you go online to www.perseus.tufts.edu you will find the Perseus Digital Library, which includes a wide selection of classical texts both in the original Greek and Latin and in translation. There are online dictionaries and commentaries, and if you click on a word you can get the dictionary entry and grammatical information. This is a good thing since you can be in, as it might be, Kathmandu or Palatka and have access to texts unlikely to be available locally. There are, however, a few gnats in the Coppertone. In the first place, the translations and commentaries seem to have been chosen because they are out of copyright, which means they date back to the 19th or early 20th century; the unwary surfer has no access to modern scholarship. The texts themselves, moreover, lack information that all reputable publishers provide as a matter of course: an account of the manuscript tradition and an apparatus criticus (a list of important manuscript variants, normally placed at the bottom of the page). Third and worst, the site does not alert the user to these omissions. The smartass DIYer has no way of knowing the gap between what is on offer and the requirements of serious scholarship. The Digital Library is free; a single modern commentary from Oxford University Press could set you back a cool £50 or so; if you didn't already know what serious scholarship looks like you wouldn't know that you didn't know.

Take paranoia for a quick gallop. Say you visit the Institut du monde arabe in Paris and pick up the Dictionnaire des écrivains palestiniens; you know some French and some Arabic and it has no English-language equivalent, so you pay the 20 euros in a mood of optimism. The entries are in both French and Arabic; you have a look at Ihsan Abbas. The Arabic tells you he translated Theocritus, Virgil, Sidney's Arcadia, Wordsworth, Shelley. The French tells you he translated Theocritus, Virgil and Shelley. The Arabic tells you he translated *Moby-Dick*. The French passes this over in silence. But. A. Translating *Moby-Dick*, isn't that pretty impressive? Is this really a trifle to be shrugged aside? And B. Isn't this in fact a *significant* undertaking? Does it really take such a leap of the imagination to see what a Palestinian might see in *Moby-Dick*, and why he might think it should be available to Arab readers? But if the French you happened to look at has these gaps, how can you trust any of the other entries?

In other words, you always need to know enough to know when you're being lied to. A youthful smartass needs only one or two examples to see getting a degree as a good idea. If degrees came as cheap as the Digital Library this would not have caused problems.

So. Late afternoon, late October. Costa Coffee, George Street, Oxford. There were 45 messages on the mobile phone. The phone might have been in a library so it was turned off.

The body sat in a semicircular tan leatherette chair. The brain picked up Czech and Croatian the way a radio picks up scraps of distant broadcasts amid angry static. It liked a Glaswegian accent across the room. There was much more English in the air but the brain was trying to screen it out.

By a complicated procedure 12 years of education by tombola had been cosmetically enhanced to functionality. It would not fool a stickler for detail, no. It was not the sort of thing an openminded Oxford college gung-ho on widening access would congratulate itself on being prepared to overlook. No. But it bore a family resemblance to the sort of thing an openminded Oxford college gung-ho on widening access would congratulate itself on being prepared to overlook. This had sufficed to win admission to read Literae Humaniores at a college which had best remain nameless, given what is to follow. Admission to read Lit. Hum. (Greek and Latin literature plus or minus Greek and Roman history, Greek and Austro-Anglo-American philosophy) brought with it open access to all university lectures, many attached to courses for which no amount of cosmetic enhancement could have achieved mimicry of an eligible candidate.

Religious fanaticism hit Oxford 500 years ago; it's a pretty place now. It seemed I would not be in this pretty place much longer.

The mother had read History at Bristol in the late 70s when a maintenance grant was provided for natives. This handsome provision had survived in folk memory through twenty years of reform by Thatcher, Major, Blair. No one in the kinship system had wanted to believe that money must now be found. Conversations had relayed the unwelcome fact; documentary evidence had supported the claim and been ignored. Each stepparent encouraged parsimony in the relevant bloodparent, each step had suggestions for fundraising: the opposite blood, the opposite step, the bloods of the opposite blood. Or what about casting the net wider? What about France? Austria? Germany? Australia?

The college wanted £1,270 for nine weeks' rent at £95/week and a standing charge.

That is the short story, but the story was not short because so many people had so many things they needed to say.

I had once had credit cards in the names of W B Latimer, J J Kapur, D K M Beardsley, T R Doyle, A J Courakis, S T Lloyd, Jaakko Niinistö and D N Eriksen. A member of the kinship system had found them and confiscated them when I was 16. I now had a WWF Visa and an Amnesty Mastercard in the name of A J P Ffoulkes, and a CapitalOne Visa and Greenpeace Mastercard in the name of P K Sanghera. What if I took a £1000 cash advance off two cards? I could use a cashpoint, where no photo ID was required. I could pay the college and live on the balance, keeping enough cash in reserve to make minimum payments on the cards until a member of the kinship system sent a cheque. Yes.

There would be more time for cash to flow. Yes.

It was not that it could not be done, no. But sooner or later it would be necessary to talk affectionately to people who did not want to be loved for their money.

The nominal cardholders were both persons worth seducing to debt with clock-radios, gym bags and six months' interest-free credit on balance transfers. If the statements had been coming to me I could have gone on indefinitely transferring the balance from one card to another. Unfortunately they were all going to an address in Boca Raton, the only one I knew that was uninhabited, and I could not see a way of repatriating them. I was living in college, collecting post from a pigeonhole.

There were seven or eight people at the next table. There was a turquoise wool coat with a belted waist. There was a 50s cotton sateen frock of olive green, brown and black cocktail glasses on a white ground with two bows at the waist; there were red Dr Scholls. There was a blue Andean jumper with a pattern of brown and white llamas. I tried to follow some Croatian two tables away but there was quite a lot of English interference from the turquoise wool coat, finally I said Look Dad, I've taken three fucking gap years, and he said Well, if that's the way you want it, Siobhan, and he became quite embittered. So then his girlfriend told me she had written for Black Lace cause it was quite a feminist thing to do in the 80s and she showed me this story about a Russian aristocrat taken captive by the savage leader of a Cossack tribe and she said if I could do it it was an easy thousand squid.

The brain was at its eavesdropping. It can eavesdrop in twenty languages, more or less (graph to come); it picks up not just grammatical information and vocabulary but registers of class, sex, age, profession, others for which an obtuse world has developed no classification. It analyses the logical structure of each incoming message; it identifies primate signalling patterns. All speech comes loaded with information, most unknown to the speaker. Direct speech is difficult because the brain must construct a person out of linguistic phenomena; it must also assemble linguistic phenomena into a speaking self.

In a work of fiction someone who is driven berserk by certain aspects of social life is accommodated by family and school (see *The Curious Incident of the Dog in the Night-Time*). In the world it's different. It's dangerous to tell people that something drives you berserk: something inside wants to see what happens. If you make an effort people think you can always make an effort, so they go on requiring you to make the effort until you crack up. But if you do then jump off a cliff or disappear they either think it is exhibitionism or start talking about electro-shock therapy.

That is why the mobile phone was off only when it could be in a library or lecture. It is necessary to maintain a mobile phone if forms are to be filled to a deadline, if cheques are to be sent, these things don't just happen, but possession of the instrument does mean that one can be perceived to be uncontactable and the worst assumed.

I was still trying to glean some Croatian but the mind was drawn to the easy thousand, it wanted to know if she had done the deed and meanwhile there was more interference, a boy's father had read *The Big Deal* about a man who turned professional poker player he wanted to leave my mum but he was skint so he played poker online instead and at one point he was £20,000 up but then he lost £20,000 and another £20,000 so I went to the bursary and they basically told me to piss off.

People made sympathetic noises, and then everyone had a story, everyone had something to say.

The sad stories were no different from the ones that circulate the kinship system, but an eavesdropper is not taxed for sympathy. An eavesdropper can leave at any time.

Siobhan says whenever she has to ask for money she buys a scratchcard first, because if she won £100,000 she would not have to ask. Everyone at the table says they do that too, if they have to ask their parents for money they always buy a scratchcard because of the incredible hassle, and then they say, Or there's always the novel, and everyone laughs.

1.1.1 = ١.١.١

My father had sent an e-mail announcing a brief visit to London for the bar-mitzvah of the son of a close friend. He would be staying at Claridge's and proposed lunch. I bought a scratchcard at the newsagent on Gloucester Green, a £100,000 parent-avoidance opportunity for the price of £1 (Just Scratch and Match 3 Numbers and Claim Your Prize!!!!).

£1	£100,000	£20
£50	£1	£10,000
£100,000	£10	£50

Too bad, better luck next time. I bought a student period return to London on the Oxford Tube for £8.

Barak and Arafat had signed a new peace agreement on 3 September in Sharm el-Sheikh, a glamorous Egyptian resort. My father was not one to discuss politics. There would be brownie points for attending the bar mitzvah, which was to take place at a grand synagogue in Portland Place. One wears a posh frock and a hat. It was not unlikely that he had given the boy a cheque for £1000. I made a telephone call to propose, arrange. My father's mother was an Iranian Jew; my father's father had died when he was 12; my grandmother was not on speaking terms with her family, but my father had made a point of pushing for the rite of passage, seeing the potential in it. He would welcome posh frocked and hatted support for a friendship that had merited a special trip to London. Yes.

I had a cream crepe de chine pleated dress with a dropped waist, a cream straw cloche with a black silk rose on the brim and cream grosgrain shoes with a large bow over the instep, the sort of Merchant-Ivory ensemble for which my father was always happy to foot bills. I went to Gloucester Green at 7.30 am Saturday morning. There was a bus at 7.50. I bought a scratchcard which revealed the sums:

£25	£10,000	£2
£50	£2	£100
£100,000	£10	£100,000

The Oxford Tube puffed and sighed. The body took its costume to the upper deck. It opened Selby-Bigge's edition of Hume's Enquiry into Human Understanding and the mind sucked up the words of the peacock philosopher, the words which had roused Kant from his dogmatic slumbers.

The body with its chromosomes, its genitalia, takes its place in a balcony with other xx chromosomatically endowed bodies, all poshly frocked, some hatted. It is acceptable during some parts of the service to talk quietly or for that matter discuss Hume or Kant, but it would not look good to whip out Hume's *Enquiry into Human Understanding*. One would not talk, anyway, while the boy struts his stuff. The boy dazzled. There was a reception afterward at a hotel whose kitchen could be trusted. My father congratulated the brilliant boy, congratulated the boy's parents on the brilliance of the boy. There was someone he needed to see, but we had rescheduled for dinner at Claridge's.

I spent the afternoon reading Hume. At 7 I was met in the lobby of Claridge's by Marina, a cool blonde of as yet unfractured poise in her late 20s. She said Hro would be late. She did not look like a chandelier-smasher. At 7.30 my father came dashingly in, dark of hair, flashing of eye, distributing kisses to cheeks. It would be quite difficult to raise the subject of the Bursary in the presence of someone blonde and poised, and difficult to connect the hand of my father with a pen and this pen to a cheque.

A digitalised version of the William Tell Overture burst from my father's lapel. He pulled out his mobile phone, silenced it, listened, spoke: We'd love to, we'd love to, we'd be thrilled. Langan's? Half an hour? See you there.

Footbound Marina requires a taxi if the four-inch heels of her Jimmy Choos are to travel three streets. There is time for another drink.

The William Tell Overture burbles merrily. My father silences it, speaks in Turkish. I glean a few words. He says charmingly to Marina:

I grew up by Lake Van, you know, in what would be east Kurdistan if the western border of Turkey didn't get in the way. I don't regret the Turkish for a minute; once you know one Turkic language you can make yourself understood in all kinds of odd corners of the world. It comes in handy.

He said: We've a famous cat which you may have heard of. It's a long-haired white cat with mismatched eyes, one blue one yellow. They're clever animals. They can swim—they love the water! And they can be taught all sorts of tricks. I'll get you one if you like. They're wonderful companions.

The William Tell overture urges patriotic fervour. My father spoke in Farsi. I got some of it. He said charmingly to Marina: I worked as a shepherd as a boy, out on the hills—really a very primitive, nomadic childhood, something straight out of Theocritus! One heard the old heroic songs in the village and then one would sing them to the sheep on the hillside. And I spent hours reading up there, teaching myself all kinds of things.

The William Tell overture rejoices in the freedom of Switzerland. My father looked at the panel and declined the call. He said: I put myself through university—my father died when I was 12, so there wasn't a lot of money. I studied architecture by day—but by night I was a smuggler, going over the mountains into Iran on horseback! Four hours there, four hours back, smuggling carpets. It's the only way to learn about carpets, buying from the people who make them, people who are passionate about them.

These are not the reminiscences of a man who will easily part with a cheque for £1500 when there is no seduction to be smoothed. There is money, yes, but there are many former 29-year-olds. The taxi is here.

We meet three carpeteers and their companions at Langan's. I could not see an opening for getting an address, income, and signature on a form.

Two bars of the *Eroica* could be heard from a secret location on the person of Nicky D. A phone appeared in his hand. He bent his ear to the oracle. The softfooted Greek consonants sped into the mouthpiece, the mind thinks it knows this word and that word but they are celebrities avoiding the camera. We are shown to a table while Nicky hangs back, the soft swift words now taking cover under the manytongued talk of the restaurant. As we sit down a snatch of "Puppet on a String" is whistled jauntily under the right elbow of Marty Machovec, he plucks a phone from a pocket, clothes sternness with chewable Czech while the *Eroica* tweedles blithely this time aboard Danny didn't catch the last name, this is not a restaurant party with a lot of class. Danny's English is very good. He says: Yeah . . . Yeah. There's a lot of noise here. Call you back in five. OK. We're sitting down. He says he'll be back in half a tick.

It is a meal of two halves. During the drinks, appetisers, half-way through entree half the mind is divided between provision of anodyne conversation and calculation of means of connecting the parental hand to a pen and the pen to a cheque and a student loan form. All this time the *William Tell Overture,* the *Eroica,* and "Puppet on a String" pop up like gophers in the blameless grassy plain of talk, and all this time, you see, there is a dark room in a corner of the mind where phonal fragments are pored over like scraps of the Dead Sea Scrolls.

If you go to Paris and talk to people they will often tell you they are passionate about le cinéma, which directors do you like, you say, and they say they love Woo Dee Al Lang and you are impressed and embarrassed because you have not seen that many Chinese films and this is a director you have never even heard of, you're embarrassed to mention Chen Kaige and Zhang Yimou and while you're trying to think of something to say that will show you're not just a butterfly something at the back of the brain says suddenly: Woody Allen! He likes Woody Allen! The guy was born in Tangiers, but he came to Paris when he was six; he's *French.* The French love Woody Allen, Allen complains about the fact that American audiences don't get him, the French love him, and this is a guy who's *French.* Ask him about Jerry Lewis, tell him you love *The Nutty Professor,* do it, do it, go on, I dare you, but you do the decent thing and merely engage in polite chitchat about *Purple Rose of Cairo, Crimes and Misdemeanors* and so on and so forth.

Up to halfway through the main course the brain had recorded a number of instances of an unidentified cluster of phonemes embedded in a variety of grammatical structures across a range of languages, and the phonemes sounded like mini-soda. So there was this scenario in the mind of some sort of soft-drink deal, people were wheeling and dealing over soft drink production and distribution, tiny flasks would be molded, shipped, filled with sugary liquid, shipped on, a non-renewable energy source would be squandered. The profit margin on the sugary liquid, the bottles, the transportation would float shoes by Manolo Blahnik & Jimmy Choo, dinners, taxis, vacations, real estate. This is the world of the carpeteers.

Halfway through a vegetarian lasagna the brain found its Woody Allen. It said: Minnesota! They're talking about Minnesota! What the fuck is in Minnesota? There were other phonemes as yet floating free of significance.

The brain brought up a piece of information. There's a place in Minnesota where they do something unusual, they don't just manufacture components, they assemble smart landmines that self-destruct in 15 days. Many American officers won't use them because they don't trust the technology and don't want their men crossing terrain where the things have purportedly self-destructed. It is said that soldiers are more easily terrified by the sight of maimed and mutilated men than by dead ones. Various phonemes seemed to find significance to lock on to.

This kind of eavesdropping does not often pick up clear incrimination. It's too fogbound for Shavian or Ibsenian revelation. Something that can be made in America and sold for $3 can be made more cheaply elsewhere—of what is that not true? If a unit has a profit margin of $1 it would take 400 to buy a pair of Manolo Blahniks, the brain sees 400 bloody stumps with a pair of shoes. Shaw says, everyone knows, there's no such thing as clean money.

During the second half of the entree, dessert, coffee, cognac the ringtones thinned. The mouth needed to murmur a sentence to bring hand to pen to paper, but the words did not pass the teeth. In the end a couple of sentences conveyed the need to return to Oxford.

It really wasn't clear what was going on.
At Victoria I bought a scratchcard which revealed the sums

£25	£10	£10
£10,000	£2	£50
£10,000	£100,000	£1

1.1.2 = ١.١.٢

The father had always stood on its own two feet.

The mother had always put itself last. The mother had never thought of its own needs. Now the mother thought of its needs and it needed to talk.

The stepmother had not thought of its needs. The ex-stepmothers had not thought of their needs. The stepfather had not thought of its needs. The ex-stepfathers had not thought of their needs. The stepmother's first husband had not thought of its needs. The stepmother's first husband's boyfriend had not thought of its needs. The stepmother's first husband's boyfriend's ex-boyfriend had not thought of its needs. Now there was a need to talk.

The sister had known all its life that it was on its own. Nobody was going to look after it, so it would have to look after itself. The stepsisters were likewise alone. The stepbrothers were likewise alone. The stepstepsisters were likewise alone. The stepstepbrothers were likewise alone. The stepstepsteps were alone. The stepstepstepsteps were alone. Every ex was alone. There was a need to talk and talk and talk and talk.

The mobile phone was turned off in the library. Even when it was not in the library it was left turned off at times when it might have been in the library. When it was turned on there were five or six messages from the mother and 15 to 35 from various sources. There is a need not to talk.

2

The phone rings. The phone rings. The phone rings.

Noszaly still wants to have fun. He sounds aggrieved, presumably because he's not having much fun. I leave the house for Sarotti. Children cluster entranced by the chocolate fountain.

An e-mail pops up in my Inbox. It says:

From: "Sam Hoffman" <sam.hoffman@sharpshooters.com>
To: "Rachel Zozanian" <zozanian@onetel.com>
Subject: First Look
Date: 26 July 2005

hi rachel it was good to talk to you. anne and i would love to see anything you write, sorry you've been through this bad time but remember you do have friends, it's not just a business relationship, we'd really like to see this as a long-term relationship that we can build on. am enclosing an example of the kind of first-look agreement we were talking about, which is basically just some standard language to formalize our commitment. let me know what you think.

sam.

There is a two-page attachment in a small typeface in which the laid-back easygoingwe're-such-great-friends-we-don't-bother-with-capital-letters style of the e-mail gives way to a great many extremely specific clauses covering the sort of contingency where, for example, a producer has passed on one version of a piece of intellectual property but substantial changes such as new characters or a new storyline have been introduced. A peculiarity of the document is that no money is to change hands.

This is what friendly deals do look like.

If you have seen a lot of friendly deals you think you know nothing about someone until you have seen his idea of a friendly deal, and perhaps you'd like to put it in a book, perhaps you think without the contractual details any book is just fogbound Jamesian kitsch, but it's not the sort of thing the betazoid warms to, so you put it in a footnote that can always come out.[1] And that's the way it's been going for the past year, putting things in that can always come out. Taking things out that could always go back in if one could track down a non-betazoid, but the Writers' Yearbook doesn't give that kind of information. Wondering who represents DFW. I didn't think it would be like this.

I write something brief, pleasant and noncommittal to Sam (you've been absolutely wonderful etc.).

Stare at the screen. Tough it out. Don't drink. Philip Pullman writes Three pages a day. Philip Pullman doesn't drink. There's a lesson to be learnt.

It's arsenic hour. I have a Bushmill's on the rocks.

I then have a *brilliant* idea. What if the book becomes Kaufman*esque* in its self-absorption (and so destined to be a cult classic), what if its a book about a character who, unable to endure the influx of sounds, negotiates a contract permitting him to avoid speech by typesetting his book in TeX? Foiled by the sort of contractual minutiae seldom seen in fiction, he finds himself writing a book about a *character* who is unable to endure the influx of sounds, who in turn finds himself writing a book about a *character* who is unable to endure the influx of sounds, who in turn finds himself writing a book about a *character*

A brilliant idea that will decrease the likelihood that the betazoid is my agent to, at an educated guess, 3.17 percent

Philip Pullman doesn't write this kind of agent-divesting drivel. Philip Pullman doesn't drink. There's a lesson to be learnt.

---

1. But the footnote is then a monstrosity, rivalling the footnotes of Pearse's commentary on De Natura Deorum for length and impenetrability, and it's unbearable. You can't look at the page. So you do take it out, leaving the ingenious legal machinations of friendliness to the imagination of the reader.

I have another Bushmill's on the rocks.

The Inbox has 100 or so e-mails from close personal friends and just one from a stranger who, unlike Philip Pullman, not only drinks but drinks to excess and writes like an evil genius. There's a lesson to be learnt.

I have another Bushmill's on the rocks.

I have another brilliant idea.

What if I bring in a character like nothing anybody has ever seen before? What if I bring in a voice, that crazy anarchic voice, the voice that calls back zombies from the undead, the voice that dispels the anomie of the alienated third person orphan in schwarzweiss Kansas and hurls us Over the Rainbow into the glorious Technicolor of the first-person singular? Will there be Munchkins? Will there be Flying Monkeys? What if. What if. What if. Forget the readers, forget the betazoid. What if *I* have no idea what happens next?

To: “A.P. Pechorin” <popesonxtacy@hotmail.com>
From: Rachel Zozanian <zozanian@onetel.com>
Subject: Bad correspondent syndrome
Date: Fri 5 Aug 2005

You sent me a pamphlet and an e-mail a couple of years ago (we met in an organic bar off Victoria Park, I was reading Adorno, you were trying to get ginger ale from a bar that, I guess, thought it was not organic). Kept yr e-mail in my Inbox to read in moments of existential despair. Did you go to Odessa? Write more pamphlets? I went to New York, now I’m in Berlin.

Off to See the Wizard

1

The phone rings. The phone rings. The phone rings.

I did not have internet access in the home. I went to Sarotti, where Sinead O'Connor sang "Nothing Compares 2 U" on the LCD.

According to the Guardian 600 prisoners have been held at Guantanamo Bay for four years without trial. President Bush has explained that when you are fighting for freedom and democracy you can ignore the Geneva Conventions. This is the jollity.

A day went by. I clicked on the Thunderbird icon and got three offers for penis enhancement.

A day went by. I clicked on the Thunderbird icon and got an offer for cheap software, an offer for cheap pharmaceuticals and four offers for penis enhancement.

A day went by. I clicked on the Thunderbird icon and got three e-mails from close personal friends, an e-mail of self-endorsement from Noszaly, and a notification that I had won $5,000,000 in the e-mail draw of the First Third National Bank lottery.

Surprise, surprise, surprise.

The abbreviated Serenity Prayer runs as follows: God, grant me the serenity to accept the things I cannot change, the courage to change the things I can, and the wisdom to know the difference.

The Holocaust: Be serene. The gulags: Be very serene. Rwanda: Remain serene. Invasion of Iraq: Remain perfectly serene. Lipstick colour: Courage! Be bold! Be brave! Let's not be silly.

A kinship system of nice noisemakers is something I cannot change. A shortfall of credit cards under a variety of aliases is something I can change. A 23-year-old smartass does not need divine assistance to spot this and so survive to be a 29-year-old former smartass. But even a 29-year-old former smartass, sending a message in a bottle to a stranger in a bar who does not reply, dwells stupidly on things she would do better to forget.

1.1.1.1 = ١.١.١.١

1999, Oxford, still a pretty place and time.

I answered the messages of eight callers, reducing the number of unanswered messages from 95 to 17. I lay in bed for 12 hours, playing the 1975 interview of Barthes and Jacques Chancel with my headphones on. The head was not clever. It was not at all clever.

I had been given names of connections of loose connections. I did not think I could talk to anyone I knew, but I thought I could talk to some strangers without going berserk.

The niece of a step was at Somerville. She had a flat off the Woodstock Road; it must have been at least £200 a week. According to the gossip that circulated the kinship system she had been sent to London alone at the age of 16/15/14/13/12 to get an abortion and had been a heroin/crack/meths addict and despite it all had achieved three As at A-level and Oxford admission thanks to the efforts of her father's upmarket girlfriend. I sent her an e-mail and she wrote back saying she wd love to meet for a coffee but she was directing a play and going mad so maybe next term.

The cousin of a stepstep was at New College. I sent her an e-mail and she said to come round. I did not want to meet her wearing a Black Watch kilt but I did not have any other clothes.

The name of the cousin is Becca. She wears black jeans below the hip bone and a faded red T-shirt that says Moving Furniture Around. She wears red Converse trainers.

She says: Well, there's always the tabloids.

I say: Yes, but I don't see the relevance?

She says: It depends who you know.

She says: Say you have a story, not some crap story but a good story about Julia Roberts, you could get £20,000.

I say: I don't know Julia Roberts.

She says: After the death of Diana there was a void. No one has really filled that void, but value can be found.

She says: Prince William will be good value after the moratorium.

I say: I don't know Prince William.

She says: If you have a good story about a relatively minor celebrity who has not been done to death that can often work wonders. There are the big names—there are always the big names—but what happens is they are flooded with crap stories. Even so, you can sometimes surprise them with a new angle. Jennifer Aniston's brother, for instance, there is probably some material there, and the thing to remember is, he is not fenced off like Prince William or Prince Harry.

I say: I don't know Jennifer Aniston's brother.

She says: Tom Cruise. Nicole Kidman.

I say: Nope.

She says: Michael Jackson, obviously, but it would have to stand out. Brad Pitt.

I say: What about Bruce Willis?

She says: You know Bruce Willis?

I say: No, I'm just interested.

She says: It would depend very much on the story.

She says: The point is just, it has been known to work. Adam Millar, physicist at Keble? He grew up in Tobermory, which does not send a lot of candidates anywhere, let alone to Oxbridge. So there was some sort of cock-up with the funding on the Scottish side cause the local authorities had not got the paperwork sussed. But as it happens Rod Stewart's mum had stayed at the B&B and got on well with Adam's mum. So Rod Stewart said he would give Adam an exclusive, and he told him where to take it and how much to ask. You don't get that kind of solidarity among the English, it is dog eat dog.

She says: Ben Affleck would do that for a friend.

I say: But I'm not even an acquaintance.

I say what I think she wants me to say: How do you know all this?

She says: My Dad works for the *Sunday Mirror*. He was working for the *Times*, but then there was Wapping, and then my mum got pregnant. So a contact gave them a story about Princess Diana as a goodwill gesture and one thing led to another. He didn't think he would be there twenty years. Guilt trip guilt trip.

She talks for five hours about her dad who knows Robert Fisk and Neal Ascherson and John Pilger and Christopher Hitchens and has been known to drink a fifth of Jameson's and walk through glass doors.

1.1.1.1.1 = ١.١.١.١.١

I answered 27 messages from a total of 13 callers. There were 63 e-mails from 17 correspondents. I replied briefly yet pleasantly. When I wrote to people I liked I might quote from *Le Suicide*. When I wrote to people I disliked I included architectural details drawn from Pevsner's *Oxfordshire*. I lay in bed for nine hours, playing a cassette of Naguib Mahfuz's *Khan al-Khalily*.

The stepstepsteps had taken refuge in edge-softening pharmaceuticals. Their pa had published a book a year back which mentioned the unmentionable, the weight of their ma. Pa is kein gentleman.

Each day brought advertisements for solutions to erectile dysfunction. His wife weighed a quarter of a ton. Two flabby melons were hefted by a feat of engineering, just clearing an ample stomach of bovine flaccidity. Stumpy dead white arms and legs were mottled with red. Society decreed that it was not enough to support eight children. He must fuck into the fat or not at all. The American constitution forbids cruel and unusual punishment.

In interviews he had explained that there are things that have to be said that you can't say which is exactly why somebody has to say them. He had explained that if the value of a stock goes down nobody thinks it is wrong to sell, which was not to say he did not love his children.

According to the gossip that circulated the kinship system the book had received an advance of £100,000/£250,000/£500,000/£1 million, thanks to the author's previous history of drug abuse and mindless violence in the company of the Clash and thanks to the author's unauthorised biography of Joe Strummer, and upon publication had shot to number 34/29/17/11/5/1 of the *New York Times* bestseller list, selling 2000/3000/10,000/50,000 a day/week/month. According to the KS the mother had attempted suicide by an aspirin/valium/xanax/barbiturates and alcohol cocktail overdose/suffocation/leap into Serpentine/walk out to sea at Barry Island/interrupted leap from Archway Bridge/Beachy Head/Dome of St Paul's. According to the KS none of the author's six children would speak to him. The youngest was in his second year at Wadham, where he was reading PPE.

I did not think a Bursary would be sympathetic to the son of a notorious millionaire who claimed hardship, so he would know what to do. I did not want to meet him wearing a Black Watch kilt but I did not have any other clothes. I sent him an e-mail and he said to come by his room.

Mark wears a leather jacket with multiple studs and chains and tight black jeans with studs and doc martens with further studs. He seems knowledgeable and anxious to talk.

Look, says Mark. This is not necessarily the problem you think it is. I am not necessarily advocating, but there is a solution. My dad is a cunt, the facts speak for themselves, so in my first year I had a lot of difficulties I could well have done without.

I think at some point you have to realise you are responsible for your destiny. People are not going to hand you life on a silver platter. You can go on banging on about your parents or the government or whoever or you can just get on with it.

So I thought: Right. So what I did was, first I invested in poker software to familiarise myself with the game. I then registered with Casino.com. Now, I will say that it was uphill sailing, I experienced more setbacks than I would have anticipated, to be honest at one point I was £2500 down and I thought what the fuck am I doing. But that was before I understood online poker, which is not like ordinary poker.

The important thing is to wait until it is 9 a.m. in New York to make sure the traders are at work, because those are some very smart players. Those are some people you do not want to come up against. What you want is to play against the kind of people who have no job, the kind of people who are drinking at 9:00 a.m., either they have been drinking all night or they are the kind of people who start as soon as they get up, and you'll be all right. Once I got the hang of it I won £10,000 in three months. The only reason it was not more is that kind of player does not play for high stakes. It is a slog getting the money, but it is there for the taking.

Sometimes I think about it. If my dad had not been the cunt that he unarguably is I would never have found this out. I would never have found the financial opportunity, and also I would not have known that I could stand on my own two feet. It's done wonders for my work.

My tutor was saying she couldn't get over the improvement in my work since last year, well, some of it is having money for books and that and some of it is not wasting the mental energy on my dad and being able to concentrate on the course, but a lot of it is confidence. At the end of the day, you have to believe in yourself. If you don't, nobody else will.

—But I thought Chris went through his whole student loan playing online poker?

—Yeah, but see, that's why I would not necessarily advocate it for everybody. When Chris's loan came through he spent some of it on cocaine, which was never going to be a smart move, and then he got too excited to wait till it was 9 a.m. New York time, so then the money was gone creating an awkward situation. But what I say is, he brought it on himself. He was playing out of his league.

I am pretty sure I have heard that Sean heard about Mark and Chris and accepted the importance of waiting till 9 a.m. New York time and I am pretty sure he took out a £3,000 student loan which soon was gone creating an awkward situation.

—But I thought Sean

—Well, that was unfortunate. I think Sean would have done well to hone his skills.

This looks like a method of funding a university education by winning money off unemployed alcoholics.

—Well, thanks, Mark.

He talks for nine hours about his father the cunt.

1.1.1.1.1.1 = ١.١.١.١.١.١

I answered 33 messages from 21 callers. There were 52 e-mails from 19 correspondents, only three offering penis enhancement.

A stepstep had a niece at St John's.

Caitlin wears a red plastic raincoat. Under the raincoat is a back-buttoned cotton top with freestyle lemons and limes on a white ground (Spitalfields Market, £2). Four inches below the top is a black vinyl self-belted skirt three inches shorter than the raincoat (H&M £29.99) and then there are opaque lime tights (Hue, £9.99) and red Converse trainers (Office, £59.99).

She says: Well, there's always phone sex.

I say: I don't like phones.

She says: It's not too bad. There is scripted and there is improv.

I say: I don't like phones.

She says: It depends how long you can keep them on the phone.

I say: That is not normally the problem.

She says: There is a bonus for keeping someone on the line for over an hour. There are bonuses for multiple one-hour sessions within a timeframe.

I say: What sort of bonus are we talking?

She says: It could be as much as £10. On top of the 10p per minute.

So not what a shrink would get for the time. A shrink has higher overheads. The couch. The grand piano. The diploma.

The fact that Caitlin is wearing a red plastic raincoat indoors does not mean that word will not get back to the kinship system. I don't say anything more about phones.

She talks for three hours about her father the alleged inside trader, now in his 13th month in a low-security prison for entirely legitimate activity that was misconstrued. His UK assets were swallowed up in costs. Rumoured offshore accounts are just that—rumours. It goes on.

1.1.1.1.1.2 = ١.١.١.١.١.٢

The son of an ex-stepstep's ex by his first (Univ). The niece of a step's ex's ex (St Catz). The son of a stepstepstep's friend (Trinity). The daughter of the girlfriend of a stepstepex-girlfriend (Queen's). The niece of the boyfriend of a stepstepex-boyfriend (Univ). &c. There's always the tabloids. There's always phone sex. There's online poker, there's forex, there's poker 9 a.m. NYT. There's always Black Lace. There's always phone sex. There's Mills & Boon. A friend of a friend did a heroin deal, bought a house in South Ken, there's that but you need the connections. There's always the tabloids. There's always Black Lace. There's always phone sex. There's always the horses. There's always the dogs. There's always phone sex. And there's always the Lottery, yes, and there's always the novel, ha ha.

Making a total of 28 minutes on hustling, five minutes on silly solutions, and 57 hours 12 minutes on midlife crises once twice thrice removed. It was Third Week of Michaelmas Term.

The head was not clever. It was not very clever.

2

August 2005. Berlin's a pretty place now.

A day went by. I clicked on the Thunderbird icon and got an e-mail which proclaimed:

Sensationall revoolution in medicine!
E'''nlarge your p''enis up to 10 cm or up to 4 i'c'h'e's!
Its h'erbal solution what hasnt side effect, but has 100% guaranted results!
Dont lose your chance and but know wihtout doubts, you will be impressed with results!
Clisk here http://hyderabadguide.info

He drew his gun and the two of them started slowly down the hall to Paul's closed bedroom door.
It was only the thought of the pills, the Novril that she kept somewhere in the house, which got him moving.
After a tune, a small piece of steel fell out onto the board across the arms of the wheelchair.

A day went by. I clicked on the Thunderbird icon and upon the screen of the iBook was a thing of wonder.

X-Originating-IP: [65.54.174.200]
From: “A.P. Pechorin” <popesonxtacy@hotmail.com>
To: zozanian@onetel.com
Subject: Iran and Brad Shit
Date: Wed, 10 Aug 2005 17:48:19 +0000

Amazing you write- the subtitles of the invisible wonder and wander across. was today, or yesterday, thinking about our meeting - on a bus to Tabriz, north west Iran. It was symptomatic of the tumult Lon-I-don gets me in. our meeting was a similar scene as to the ones I recently left London in. On the bus looking at the Iranian desert was thinking the problems of reading Adorno- saying yes yes yes then oscillating in the London art scene- reading big books but surrounded by little people who accelerate the hate machines and lead to excessive transgressive behaviour....

What is it you do exactly?

much happened- in this time didn’t get to Odessa but travelled six months in the middle east (((Iraq-a month- pakIstan a month- as well Kyrgyzstan) all money from dirty deeds as a papparazzi writer (not photographer). Then returned to London to be sent away by Amerika’s National Enquirer magazine - yes to work for an organ of such hyperreality is a dream come true! Indeed, to chase Britney Spears around Europe- hit me baby one more time - to have her simulation pay for my move to Berlin, eat sauerkraut and worst with the money i EARNT from her gyriating virgin whore vagina image -the black (w)hole - lived there for six months- wrote READ drank koffee than realised berlin was ...
not for me///

left back to London- immersed totally in machine- the desire of popular culture ANUS LIPS me fueling impending doom- exacerbating hyper-capitalism- encouraging the proles to suck at the teet - HYPERSTITITION*^$^%$

-- and got a scoop or two for the Sunday Sentinel - Starr Noszaly threatening to kill herself- celebrity nipples- making stories then started reading more Batialle-Nick Land- neitssssszche...everything starting going horribly wrong as they say in the tabloids../.IN-sin-dent with my friend Chelsea lecturer and whathisname Chapman- fights with authors who couldn't handle criticism- police stop and checks- alkoholism- fighting /fucking but mainly myself- then THEN... one jejune June MORNING was sent to the paradise of Santorini to chase Angelina Jolie and Bread SHIT/..fled the Greek island then a month in Turkey- now in iRAN FOR a month- am planning to visit mar freunds in berlin Sept some time./.. gotta write from *Baghdad to Britney*...stay tuned

wrote this the other day when in kurdistan...

I am actually in Iraq right now=- not kopf kutting off territory but a zone creating enough sense not to stay the night here- despite several offers.
heads begin falling below Mosul- so they say. once again hoping to get published- a story something like one day in iraq- in a town close to Turkey border. Zakhu. it is actually Kurdistan but they have not gained independence... yet, so they say. but as most of my explorations in media end the only response i will get is if the respective editor is away and has set an out of office auto reply...

it didn't start too well at the border. there was almost an international incident. I rushed through a police line nearly causing them to draw weapons - too lazy to shoot and my clown like shouts of 'toilet! Toilet!' and no doubt the extreme look of terror on my face -after local water drank due to that special kind of forced local kindness lead to a rapid digestive process if not immediately dealt with post haste a suicide bowel bomber, think body without organs, would be on their hands ...and feet-face etc etc.....all very friendly it is/- i am nervous slightly---... walking briskly stopping for invitations of sweet tea etc..- though the incessant giving of tea overlays fear- lots of laughs and small children either trying to steal my wallet or look at my lack of facial hair... i keep my chin close to my chest- an old boxing tip and also learnt from a van damme film i saw on a turkish bus trip from istanbul - this reduces the chances of a wire being slipped over your neck by ninjas or jihadist posing as street traders or simply sneaking up from behind. On top of this the slightly unusual chin chest look creates a sympathy for this foreigner afflicted with such a strange affliction. oh the courage to ravel when so ravished by life's cruelties...added to this I am also pretending to be german which is funny as my deutsch meets the same level of those kurdish workers who returned after working in deutschland post ww2 or fled from saddam's oh so 80s gaseous genocide attempts. so far my charade is working - mein charade is gut machen? apologies to the germans///

my 'salem alecoms' and waves to kurds wrapped up in their traditional MC hammer pants, resembles lazy kamp nazi officer salutes as they drove by in motorcades (to the (lets not forget) ador(no)ing masses)...but Language now flips into kurdish so the turkish pleasantries learned make no sense here- a bit of
arabische- and the old favourites "insuallah" and 'hababi" seems to get one by- lots of slapping on the back - "gimmie some skin my kurdish brother or kurd habibi..". only planned to stay at the border and see what is going on-but after i was photoed in my traditional kurdish dress- a saggy pair of black pants and black vest- the guards wouldnt let me stay- nothing there other than petrol tankers and literary 10km of trucks waiting to cross both
sides of the border. massive human queues at the check point - lazy corrupt police. soldiers sweating with sleek automatic machine guns... officials packing heat in searing heat simply drinking hot tea then rubber stamping in their own time- insullah- was pushed through - an old crazy man hit a younger man with his cane- much laughter as the theatrics melted into realising i'd been pushed through and another melee erupted in the office over crowded over sweating with men whose moustaches thicker than my thigh and wildest dreams of facial hair. men. lots of men. and woman shawled up in black

capes making them look like black Tardises/// only spent one hour crossing amid a sea of stares - all up 100 metres took two hours. this was quick- insullah- Will be leaving shortly want to return to Silope on the turkey side before nightfall...lots of photos...no amerikans

apologises for groupe email konstruckt mit shit sprache ..aber ist das, die und der shit sprache is total normal fur die Deutsche leute?- fela dank und tut me-li

what is the book you reading now- so what is berlin offering you_ what warranted this email - 2 years is a while- i thought perhaps the nature of my email and schizo-frenetic-frantic fanatism of such fanzines warranted concern on your behalf and as such communication was disconnected- never begin- simply one way like most media machines- acephalous- what is the plan in berlin?- was NY all that it is presented in the films-literature-music? never been tell me?

where you living in berlin- i was in friedichshan- then mitte. if you have the proclovity in princelauer berg dodge the small jungenschiesse and there is an english book shop called St George- i think it is worther strasse- say hello to Rose who works there- she is lovely and they have regular film nights every monday. worth checking out- a beer and film for 3 you-row.

also a club called lovelight - in friederichshan- ost bahnof- outsidethe clubbe has the best waffles and toasted sandwiches- in the most beautiful citreon H wagon- say Hello to Johnny - i used to work there with him. maybe we meet in Sept?

ok, ok, so where did all this come from....
alyosha

YESSSSSSSSSSSSSSSSSSSSSSSSSSSSSS!
YESSSSSSSSSSSSSSSSSSSSSSSSSSSSSS!
YESSSSSSSSSSSSSSSSSSSSSSSSSSSSSS!
YESSSSSSSSSSSSSSSSSSSSSSSSSSSSSS!
YESSSSSSSSSSSSSSSSSSSSSSSSSSSSSS!
Back in the money.

3

To: "A.P. Pechorin" <popesonxtacy@hotmail.com>
From: Rachel Zozanian <zozanian@onetel.com>
Subject: RE: Iran and Brad Shit
Date: Wed Aug 10 2005 12:07:07

had a bad time in ny with my publishers, tried suicide by a method that didn't work, went to niagara falls (banal i know). did not realise instructions to my publishers' lawyer constituted a press release. kafkaesque experience at nf psychiatric ward, sort of like a book tour only with a kosher mini-breakfast, press furore but they were protecting my privacy. too bad i didn't know you were tabloid scum, cd have given you an exclusive. came to berlin to work on a book.

X-Originating-IP: [65.54.174.201]
From: "A.P. Pechorin" <popesonxtacy@hotmail.com>
To: "Rachel Zozanian" <zozanian@onetel.com>
Subject: RE: bad correspondent syndrome
Date: Thurs, 11 Aug 2005 13:49:42 +0000

rachel
well you definitely know how to do the writer in exile with style! So you write novels in hovels, now novel. And have deals with dodgy film companies - reside in berlin to avoid the cacophony, an avowing desirous mouth digesting and number crunching all! Coke or pepsi the choice is yours! interesting stuff as the papparazzi flashes click click click. as a member of the gutter press i would ask- what did you drink on your decline – champagne, beer and/ or tequila? What were you wearing? Was the breakdown related to recent rumours you were sleeping with your feng shui- guy?

Well, I hope berlin soothes your weary-wary head- i found berlin accelerated a certain reckless self-destructive sense I subsumed as the writer's persona. I would get beyond drunk and as the sun rose on the former kapital of nazi evil, ride home uber fast on a bike with no brakes- though when dealing with someone who actually has accomplished the task of writing book(s) all this may seem all a little juvenile-ambitious. I made good friends there- people have time.

Well, I will be in berlin Sept maybe we meet for beer or worst mit pommes frits. i did take to the local cuisine and try to pun with it as regularly as possible..it is the wurst.

I-ran is becoming tiring - where you have Foucault and kafka ringing your door bell- i have Fawlty towers esq joesph conrad Persian adventures -today i asked for directions with a map of the centre of town and the two hotel owners whose hotels were on the map couldn't place where we were- then i realised i was on the street i needed and had difficulty escaping their 'helping' way...- i am not sure your position on mental health but i have been trying to obtain various pharmaceuticals but they will not outlay the goods without a script--i have even being showing my little guide book that has in Persian -- i would like zome sleeping pills preferably strong ones///do you have xanax etc etc///but banana milkshakes work.

so what are these books you write- is the film going ahead- did you get work down in ny? Well i usually avoid talking to writers but it is nice to write to a stranger of sorts...

Alyosha

YESSSSSSSSSSSSSSSSSSSSSSSSSSSSSSS!
YESSSSSSSSSSSSSSSSSSSSSSSSSSSSSSS!
YESSSSSSSSSSSSSSSSSSSSSSSSSSSSSSS!
YESSSSSSSSSSSSSSSSSSSSSSSSSSSSSSS!
YESSSSSSSSSSSSSSSSSSSSSSSSSSSSSSS!

It's going to be all right, Toto.
Everything's going to be all right.

The phone rings.

The Children's Hour

1

The cursor flashes. It's 11:32 a.m. It's 11:33 a.m. It's 11:34 a.m. It's 11:35 a.m.

I find myself in a gentler, softer mood having had this fine response to my message in a bottle; why not spread goodwill and promote world peace? I write Gina an e-mail explaining that it would be against my principles to reveal the location of the $200 when the puzzle remains unsolved, but that a reward of $50 awaits each child who solves the easier puzzle which is attached in Portable Document Format ("PDF").

I present the puzzle on the following two pages. Readers stranded in an airport can while away a couple of hours. Readers traveling with a small child can silence the child. Each of us works for world peace in our own special way; this is not the way of Robert Fisk or John Pilger, it is not the way of Edward Said (who would spit on it were he alive to see it). But though my e-mail went out on 8 Aug 2005 and though I struggled to reply for the next two days I write this page, now, on 14 Aug 2006, three weeks into Israel's war on Lebanon. Hezbollah fired rockets over the border and kidnapped two soldiers; Israel responded in a manner which the UN, after some debate and a veto from the US, declined to condemn as disproportionate (Israel had merely destroyed three airports, a power plant, and a large number of civilians who should have known better than to be loitering suspiciously in their homes).

So OK, OK. Let's work for world peace. Let's also safeguard the value of new books. I note that the UK edition of *Lotteryland* is now available on Amazon Marketplace for £0.01. A simple coloring exercise, tempting readers and their helpful progeny to slash the retail value of the book, was what was wanted. I was poorly advised. I was too young to know better. Now I am older and wiser.

ذي ريدير وف بوكس

يتس ا فوني ثينغ اباوت موذيرز اند فاذيرز. يفين وين ذير وون تشيلد يز ذي موست ديسغوستينغ ليتل بليستير يو كولد يفير يماجين، ذاي ستيل ثينك ذات هي ور شي يزووندير فول.

ماتيلدا، بي روالد داهل

The Arabic Alphabet.

Arabic is written from right to left. Many letters have a short form (for the beginning and middle of words) and a long form for the end.

ا	*alif**	*a*	ط	*ṭa’*	*ṭ*
بـ ب	*ba’*	*b*	ظ	*ẓa’*	*ẓ*
تـ ت	*ta’*	*t*	عـ ـعـ ـع ع	*‘ain***	
ثـ ث	*tha’*	*th* of thin	غـ ـغـ ـغ غ	*ghain****	*gh*
جـ ج	*jim*	*j*	فـ ف	*fa’*	*f*
حـ ح	*ḥa’*	*ḥ*	قـ ق	*qaf*	*q*
خـ خ	*kha’*	*kh*	كـ ك	*kaf*	*k*
د	*dal**	*d*	لـ ل	*lam*	*l*
ذ	*dhal**	*th* of than	مـ م	*mim*	*m*
ر	*ra’**	*r*	نـ ن	*nun*	*n*
ز	*zay**	*z*	هـ ه	*ha’*	*h*
سـ س	*sin*	*s*	و	*waw**	*w, u, o*
شـ ش	*shin*	*sh*	يـ ي	*ya’*	*y, i, ee*
صـ ص	*ṣad*	*ṣ*	ء	*hamza*****	
ضـ ض	*ḍad*	*ḍ*			

* never connects to the left

** a gulp at the back of the throat *** a snarl at the back of the throat

**** glottal stop (the cut-off of breath before the second syllable of uh-oh)

Hints:

1. Lam looks very similar to alif at the beginning and in the middle of a word, but alif never connects to the left
2. fa’ and ghain look very similar in the middle of a word, but ghain is flatter, the hole in the middle of the letter sometimes disappearing

2

Back in Sarotti. On the LCD Madonna lip-syncs to "I'm Keeping My Baby."

From: "Rachel Zozanian" <zozanian@onetel.com>
To: "A.P. Pechorin" <popesonxtacy@hotmail.com>
Subject: avant-garde situationism
Date: Thurs, 11 Aug 2005 14:48:58 +0100

Alyosha

NF was a long time ago and a long way away but i seem to remember going out in search of a margarita only to be stopped by la policia. If asked about rumours that I was sleeping with my feng shui guy I wd definitely have confirmed the rumours despite not actually happening to have a feng shui guy, on the basis that I was unlikely to make up anything more interesting in a moment of stress.

Does your guide book really have all those helpful queries about pharmaceuticals? I was looking at guide books the other day to see what they had to offer for would-be sexual tourists, but (perhaps not surprisingly) they never got further than "Would you care to dance?" Perhaps the assumption is that enterprising caterers to sexual tourists will all speak English. (But if so, where do they pick up the necessary English? Are there black market language guides? Is it strictly oral transmission? I think we should be told.)

My last book was about a country where everything is distributed by lottery, inspired by Gilliam's Brazil, Borges' Lottery of Babylon, 1984, Amis' The Rachel Papers and, erm, The Diary of Adrian Mole. Sort of a literary equivalent of aspirational crisps.

The current book is an amalgam? hybrid? crossbreed? mongreloid? Jeff Goldblum-morphing-into-fly? strange thing drawing on Calvino's Invisible Cities and Philip K Dick's The Man in the High Castle. I was thinking of the way Marco Polo describes cities to Kubla Khan, all of which are versions of Venice, and thinking I wd do something similar about New York - only using a statistical graphics package called Trellis, which was invented by Bill Cleveland of Bell Labs. It produces histograms, box-and-whisker plots, all sorts of graphics never before been seen in a novel. There are also packages with code for confusion matrices, Manhattanian random walks &c &c &c

Guy Debord thought international avant-garde situationism should be an art of situations, which shd include statistics - it just didn't work out that way because there's a hostility to numbers.

The director I'm talking to now, Jake Noszaly, normally gets a $3 million fee for a screenplay. I don't know his work.

Hope you're all right in Iran

Rachel

P.S. I attach an Arabic electoral map of the US which is a cool feature of this thrilling book - you can see the PKD influence.

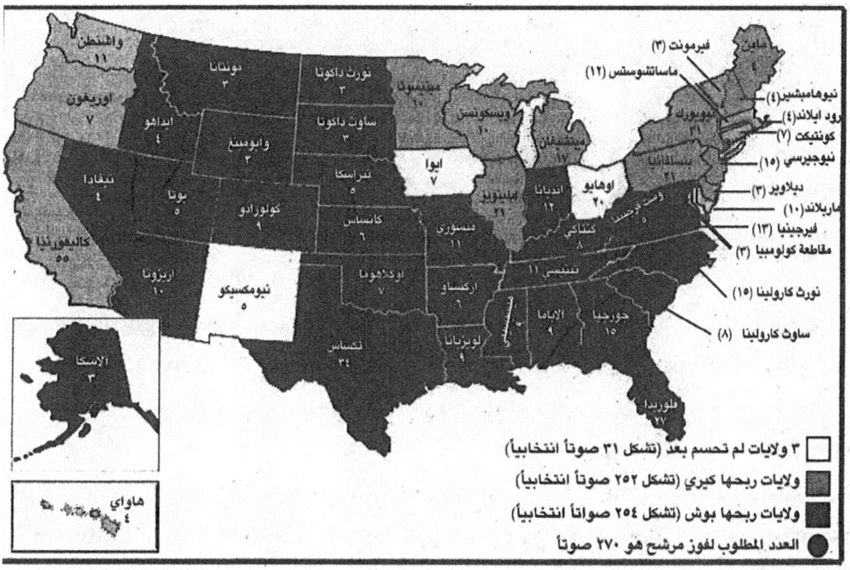

أوهايو: مسقط رأس أرمسترونغ. . . وضحية البطالة

3

So yes yes yes yes yes. But. Dilemma.

Perhaps you can imagine the moment when Plath goes to the kitchen. She opens the oven door, places a folded towel inside. Then she sits on the floor staring at the wall. She does not close the oven door and go back to bed; she does not turn on the gas. It could go either way.

Or perhaps you can imagine Woolf walking down to the Ouse. She puts stones in her pockets. She sits on a large rock looking out at the water. She does not take the stones from her pockets and walk back to the house; she does not walk into the water. It could go either way.

But perhaps you can imagine being at the point where it can go either way, sitting in a room in New York or Dubuque or Pittsburgh or Berlin, when you think of an e-mail. An e-mail that's been sitting in the Inbox for months, because every time it could go either way that frabjous voice slays the Jabberwock.

And perhaps you can imagine sitting in a room in Berlin, sending a message in a bottle to a stranger in a bar, getting a brand-new e-mail in the frabjous voice, and the monsters sit gibbering in the corner.

There are many people sitting in silent rooms.

Therefore this fffffffffffffffffffffffrabjous voice could make a llllllllllllllllllllllllllot of money for a lucky publisher.

It was a voice that could turn water to wine, loaves to fishes, fishes to Leviathans, Jabberwocky to a circus flea, a voice that could work miracles more marvelous than these: a voice that could get a yes/no answer from the betazoid.

"She reminds me about how she was going to piss on me but couldn't piss. me trying to fuck her arse but too drunk to get an erection on target." Would the betazoid, a romantic at heart, warm to this? Would the likelihood that the betazoid was my agent not decrease to, at a rough guess, 0.0000002071 percent? A likelihood so overwhelmingly negligible that even the betazoid would utter the word "No"? So that all would be klar? Leaving me free to hunt the crass, mercenary, unempathetic sort of representation that gets wildly excited about a voice that will make a lllllllllllllllllllllllllllllllllll lllllllllllot of money for some llllllllllllllllllllllllllllllllucky publisher?

I walk up and down the handsome apartment. What to do? Offer a deal, $1000 for a few e-mails? Clone the voice?

I read somewhere that Jonathan Safran Foer spent three days in Ukraine and this was where he picked up the crazy voice of Alex. Then he went to Prague and was able to write in the voice and the book ultimately sold for $450K. But what if I help myself to your voice, Marcello, and the voice is the thing people love about the book? Shouldn't you be the one banking the voice?

And anyway, I'd kill to see the other e-mails on your hard drive.

If someone offered you $450K to publish them perhaps you could be persuaded. Perhaps you could even be persuaded for a paltry five-figure sum. You could go to Odessa.

But but but but but but

But I read somewhere that Jade Shaw got her first deal because Martin Amis saw two chapters. That was how she got representation by Mr Clever. But I fired Mr Clever after six weeks. And Simon—Simon paid $300K for a book he did not want to publish, because I played poker with Sharpshooters and won.

If people cheat me I cheat them right back. I don't get paid for writing books, Marcello; I get paid for playing poker with sharks. But maybe Simon doesn't like me too well. Are we even on speaking terms?

It was not easy to know what to do. Simon had left Sharpshooters with tears in his eyes for the jobless BJs; he was powerful now. How much would he mind losing $300K of someone else's money?

The phone rings. The phone rings. The phone rings.

A Girl's Guide to Hustling

From: “Rachel Zozanian” <zozanian@onetel.com>
To: Simon.Crawford@mkm.com
Subject: next Hunter Thompson
Date: Fri, 12 Aug 2005 18:55:42 +0100

Dear Simon

I think I’ve discovered the next Hunter Thompson. Someone I met in an organic pub off Victoria Park just before going to NY, when I was reading a book about Adorno. We talked about Adorno while waiting for service. I wrote my e-mail address on a receipt, he wrote to me later, things were so bad in NY I didn’t write back. Last week I wrote back.

He’s 26. (When he first wrote to me he was 24.) In and out of the Brit Art scene. Also a paparazzo: has written for the National Enquirer, various tabloids, got sent to follow Britney Spears, later Angelica Jolie, around Europe - if Samaritans were trained to be offensive on the subject of Britney Spears a la Alyosha Pechorin there wd be fewer suicides. He is now wandering around Kurdistan and Iraq pretending to be German. He knows 3 words of German and 2 words of Arabic.

He is completely INSANE. Effortlessly offensive. Effortlessly funny. You know, of course, that Tom Wolfe’s Kandy-Kolored whatever whatever was basically a stream-of-consciousness LETTER that Wolfe sent to his editor at Esquire, who published it?

I think you should give Alyosha a book deal. Forget manuscripts. Get him to send you the e-mails on his laptop before he gets blown up.

I tried to call you yesterday but you were out. You know I HATE the phone - and here I was, making the ultimate sacrifice. But you were out.

It may be a more British style of humour. Not sure. I'm also writing to Peter Metwyn; I didn't think he was right for me, but I think he'd see the point of IG. Can send you Alyosha's 3 e-mails if you want to see them. Am prepared (though with the utmost reluctance) to talk to you on the phone if you'd like to talk.

Hope all is well
Rachel

Sat 13 Aug 2005 04:55:42
The cursor blinks. It's 04:56. It's 04:57. It's 04:58.

Sun 14 Aug 2005 05:17.
The cursor blinks. It's 05:19. It's 05:23. It's 05:27.

Thread-Index: AcWnQrhFCQtXnHUxS+uon7IMivXGlwADhGgw
Priority: normal
From: "Crawford, Simon" <Simon.Crawford@MKM.com>
To: <zozanian@onetel.com>
Subject: RE: next Hunter Thompson
Date: Mon, 15 Aug 2005 15:40:34 -0400

sorry not to call back - Bebo scrawled something glamorous and illegible which might have been any of a whole phonebook of numbers. had no idea

you were in town, why was it so bad? Were you staying with Hari and Emma? I think Hari is insane by the way to be still working for Wlad.
your hunter t sounds captivating. He can email me, or call me at the office (I assume he doesn't share your hatred of the phone). Or you can send on the emails and a number.

SC

****

CONFIDENTIALITY NOTICE: This E-Mail is intended only for the use of the individual or entity to whom it is addressed and may contain information that is privileged, confidential and exempt from disclosure under applicable law. If you have received this communication in error, please do not distribute and delete the original message. Please notify the sender by E-Mail at the address shown. Thank you for your compliance.

Interesting. Interesting. So we're actually on speaking terms.
The phone rings.
Three hours yields another friendly e-mail as if to as if from.

From: "Rachel Zozanian" <zozanian@onetel.com>
To: Simon. Crawford@mqm.com
Subject: Alyosha etc.
Date: Tues Aug 16, 2005 8:18 AM

Dear Simon

I'm sorry I missed you, but my conscience bothered me about intruding on your weekend anyway.

I haven't been in NY recently. I first met Alyosha 2 years ago, just before my ill-fated attempt to liaise with a designer on the electric sheep book by actually being in NY.

I kept his e-mail in my inbox for 2 years, at which point it seemed wildly implausible that his e-mail address would still function, so I tried it, and it did. So now he has sent me two more e-mails.

I think it is not strictly kosher to send e-mails w/o his approval, but if he wrote to you this amazing voice might evaporate. Makes me wonder what concoction of pharmaceuticals he's on. I like that in a man.

His e-mail address is popesonxtacy@hotmail.com. He's a journalist, so he must have a phone, but I don't know the number. Even if you don't think there's a book in it, I'll bet you'll wish you had more of this kind of correspondent.

rachel

Thread-Index: AcWn3MKDjZLeZI5ERgKE1LRu5Ik43gATibXQ
Priority: normal
From: "Crawford, Simon" <Simon.Crawford@MKM.com>
To:"Rachel Zozanian" <zozanian@onetel.com>
Subject: RE: Alyosha, etc.
Date: Tue, 16 Aug 2005 17:38:44 -0400

I'll get cracking. Who is he? Who pays his bills? It's a drunken orgy of a voice, disgracefully addictive - I'm hooked.

****

CONFIDENTIALITY NOTICE: This E-Mail is intended only for the use of the individual or entity to whom it is addressed and may contain information that is privileged, confidential and exempt from disclosure under applicable law. If you have received this communication in error, please do not distribute and delete the original message. Please notify the sender by E-Mail at the address shown. Thank you for your compliance.

YESSSSSSSSSSSSSSSSSSSSSSSSSSSSSS!!!!!!!!!!!!!!!!!!!!!!!!!!!!!!!

The Monster Mash

1

The phone rings. The phone rings. The phone rings.

From: "Rachel Zozanian" <zozanian@onetel.com>
To: "A.P. Pechorin" <popesonxtacy@hotmail.com>
Subject: (un?)forgivable invasion of privacy
Date: Tue, 16 Aug 2005 19:48:58 +0100

Alyosha

You may never speak or write to me again. I wrote to my former editor at Sharpshooters Press, Simon Crawford, who is now the head of Adult Trade Books at MKM, describing you as the next Hunter Thompson and urging him to give you a book deal before you get blown up. THAT is not so bad, but my grounds for urging this were your three AMAZING e-mails. He expressed interest. Instead of doing the decent thing and asking your permission, I just sent them on to him so he could see how AMAZING they were for himself. As I say, you may never speak or write to me again.

Be that as it may, he has described your voice as disgracefully addictive,

and would love to know more. I have urged him to get you to trawl the Sent Folder in your Hotmail account and publish a selection as is. I have no idea what he would like to do. But he WOULD like to hear from you.
Do drop him a line. Don't get blown up.
With best wishes,
Rachel

PS Simon does not necessarily like me. Amnesia is his single greatest professional asset - for the moment he has achieved the suspension of disbelief without which he wd never have got where he is in the first place. But I wdn't swear that an ill-placed word cd not bring it all flooding back. Just to be on the safe side, don't mention Diana, JFK, Madonna, Maradona, Nicole Kidman, Tom Cruise, David Beckham, Wayne Rooney, Ryan Giggs and Sven Goran Eriksson. Also Arsenal. Manchester United. Chelsea.

X-Originating-IP: [65.54.174.200]
From: "A.P. Pechorin" <popesonxtacy@hotmail.com>
To: "Rachel Zozanian" <zozanian@onetel.com>
Subject: internet beheaded the video store (sung to 'video killed the radio')
Date: Thu, 18 Aug 2005 17:51:09 +0000

wow rachel. well i wish i could be the temperamental writer and complain but actually your actions are the nod i have been hankering for. ok well- i am on the iran -iraq border right now- trying to get out of here in one piece... especially as i have just written a cheezy propoganda piece after a few bits and pieces and secret photographs...the tabloids pay a grand sum so it pays to ham it up...

ok well i am interested- unfortunately i don't really keep the emails i send... will ask around...what do you suggest? will be berlin sept...i am trying to put together a tale - from baghdad to britney that is a combination of my war machine exploits then pop kulture-papparazzi obsession machine,...

actually, your actions deserve a big fanks!

The Face of Terror
By Alyosha Pechorin

Today the *Sunday Mirror* reveals the face of Terror.

In exclusive top-secret interviews our undercover investigation captures a young Iranian on his way to join thousands other like him in the blood thirsty insurgency wreaking havoc across Iraq.

In a short taxi ride from Khorramshahr to Shalameheh in Iran,s south western border region, the 25 year-old laughs about his future working for evil operatives within Iraq and even offers fruit he carries in plastic bags.

Known simply as Reza he disgustingly boasts to the taxi: „I am meeting my brothers in Basra and I will be pushing out the great Satan America. They come here and kill but they do not realise for each Muslim they kill another two wants to fight back.

„The insurgency is stronger than ever. God waits for us in heaven. ‰

There is a short dispute over passports and goods carried in various trucks at the border where Iraq invaded Iran in 1980, starting a bloody war raging for eight years killing an estimated one million between both neighbours.

Then the Military police stamp official documents and Reza is on his way into Iraq. It is that simple.

The Sunday Mirror informed the Iranian military about Reza,s claims. The lack lustre chief more interested in keeping in the shade of this region,s searing 45 degree heat radioed through to the Iraq security forces a kilometre down the road.

Amid fears another insurgent had crossed the border the military control acted and denied the Sunday Mirror any farther access.

But in a top-secret meeting in nearby town of Ahvaz, a customs official working for British intellegence services based in Basra said he witnessed the Iranian government,s fuelling of insurgency fire with young boys like Reza recruited to continue the war in Iraq.

Speaking exclusively to the Sunday Mirror he said: „Sometimes there are 16 sometimes six and they usually move across the border once a week. They use various transport and are of all different ages but usually young boys from towns on the Iraq border.

„They are called ŒBasijis, after the group made up of similar aged boys that fought when Iraq invaded Iran. It is a martyrdom.

„While there is evidence of weapons smuggling across the border I have come across more explosives and the movement of men for the insurgency. Weapons are cumbersome and easily detected by Iraqi security services.

„This country is different to yours. Here money gets you what you want. Power is authoritarian and swift. If your print my name I will surely be killed.

„Here you buy your freedom. You learn not ask too many questions. Sometimes trucks go into Iraq and have paid money to be Œfast tracked, to the head of the queue. This means they are not checked as vigourously or that those in charge of checking take some money and simply fill the form out.

„Whether this is assisting the insurgency or not- make of this what you will.

„These young men are given a small sum of money for their family and head to Iraq to become part of the insurgency. Most see it as an honour to fight against America and Britian.

„The reason Iran is doing this is two fold. One reason is a great hatred of Iraq after the invasion that destoryed many towns and provinces and the other is too destabilise American efforts in rebuilding Iraq.‰

The British Intellegence officer who organised the top-secret meeting said from his Tehran home: „Earlier this month smugglers were intercepted near Maysan, an Iranian border crossing between Baghdad and Basra. It falls in the British controlled sector of Iraq.

„When they were exposed they fled with Iraq forces firing. The smugglers dropped their equipment that included timers, detonators and other bomb-making equipment.

„They escaped detention and it is unclear who the group was but the sophistication of the weapons and the organisation needed means it was either Iran's Revolutionary Guard, controlled by the supreme leader Ayatollah Ali Khamenei, or the Lebanese based Hizbullah backed by Tehran.

„We are also watching for Saif al-Adel, al Qaeda's military commander currently operating from Iran. Despite being one of the most wanted men in the world he avoids capture in Iran. We see this as tacit assistance to al Qaeda and part of why Iran is accussed of state sponsored terrorism.

„Our intellegence shows the movement across the border of weapons, fighers and explosives from Iran is less compared with that from Syria but the Iran-Iraq border spans nearly 1500 km so there are many more points of entry making it difficult to plug all the holes.‰

And one official who has directly experienced the Iranian influence of insurgency in Iraq is Dr Al-Jabouri of the Diyala province.

As a dentist living in Stockport, England you would think the greatest danger would be the odd toddler bite or un-cooperative kid afraid of drills But Dr Abdullah Al-Jabouri has survived 14 assassination attempts. And not because of dodgy bridge work.

The exiled Iraqi moved to the UK where he was safe from his unpopular anti-Saddam and pro America stance.

On returning back to Iraq he continued his outspoken ways claiming that the Iranian government,s meddles in Iraq affiars.

Despite Iran brushing aside claims of insurgency support ˆ even asking America for greater responsibility in Iraq ˆ intellegence circles see Iran,s involvement as the hardline government,s continuation of its post-revolution, anti-America position.

Dr Al-Jabouri said: „England took me in and looked after me- I have a wife in Stockport and enjoy life there very much. But I return to my home and do what I can to bring stability to the country. And it hasn,t always been easy.‰

On the day of last year,s election he learnt of dirty tricks where his name was Œforgotten, and not on the election ballot leading to his absence from office. This he accepts as part of the long process towards the end goal of the coalition,s claims for democracy.

Dr Al-Jabouri lambasted neighbouring Iran,s involvement in Iraq,s rebuilding.

He said: „Islamic fundamentalism is an imported problem. It is exported from neighbouring countries and Iran has played a major role in this. Tehran has been behind much of this violence in Iraq against civilians and anti-fundamentalist politicians.

„Day after day Iraqi police and intellegence agencies have arrested Iraqis or non-Iraqis who have either been paid a lot of money or have crossed the border to create unrest. In the province where I served as a govenor until last April we managed to capture many Iranian agents and foreign-nationals who were receiving money and arms from Tehran.

„This meddling is not limited to funding, training or recruiting terrorists. They are smuggling drugs to Iraq to create an addiction problem. The Basra police arrested a drug trafficking ring in the city just recently. There were four Iranian nationals arrested after admitting they had brought drugs from Iran for distributing in Iraq and the Gulf countries.‰

In June earlier this year an Iranian secret agent was arrested in a thwarted assaination of Kak-Baba Sheikh Hosseini a member of the National Islamic Organisation of Iranian Kurdistan.

Loqmani Ahmadi was part of a three-man cell in the Iraqi city of Sulaimaniya planning to assassinate Hosseini as he travelled from the organisation,s political bureau to their office in the Iraqi town of Irbil.

Last week on Israeli television President George W Bush said: „all options were on the table‰ in response to probing on a forceful regime change in Iran due to its dabbling with nucelar energey programs the rest of the world sees as a smoke screen for weapons manufacturing.

Donald Rumsfeld, the US secretary of defence, warned Iran about the extent of smuggling and involvement in destablising Iraq. The US has been protesting for the past two years and this month the British Embassy in Tehran criticised Iran for its involvement in state sponsored terrorism.

Mr Rumsfeld told a Pentagon briefing that the smuggling was "a problem" for the Iraqi government.

"It's a problem for the coalition forces. It's a problem for the international community, and ultimately, it's a problem for Iran," he said.

7
Hot Shit

I was 23. Kennedy was planning to get assassinated. I was in New York. I'd left college and this film came on and I'd always been a Fellini fan, but something about 8 1/2, it just got under my skin. Creativity is really what it's about. It just happens to be about a movie director. It's about the process of trying to make something and knowing you don't know how to make it, and everybody waiting for you to come up with the solution. He is stalling. He is dealing with producers and money problems. It's really just this juggling back and forth while his whole life is disintegrating and him remembering bits of it and the fact that the film then spreads right back through his life, through his dreams, through the relationship with his parents, everything is what's so wonderful about it. It uses that and it uses the past, the future, the present and it uses dreams—all the things that I've used in my films in different ways.

Terry Gilliam, BBC2 Close-up, *25 November 1995*

1

Sometimes you do things people totally don't get. Like, why would Jake Noszaly ever not fly first class? Why would you conceivably not fly first class London-LA? Something you discovered by accident, if you fly Virgin Atlantic, Premium Economy, Upper Deck, 76A, phantom passenger in 76B, it's very very very very quiet and you have 13 straight hours to work. So you buy two seats in Premium Economy to guarantee the phantom, you prebook 76AB, you put down the arm rest. You like the anonymity of quasi-economy, you like the way the seats remind you of a movie theatre on a slow afternoon. You don't need to lie down because you don't want to waste the 13 straight hours on sleep, 13 hours without a break, no calls, no e-mails, just food, drink, hot towels. You once wrote a screenplay by taking 4 LA-London London-LA flights back to back. You once wrote a screenplay by taking Amtrak down to San Antonio and then back to LA and then back to San Antonio because you'd worked out a fix and then back to LA and then you could probably have finished it at home but it felt so good, sitting on the train with the smooth juddering of the wheels on the tracks, the serendipitous fragments of conversation, you went with your instincts and just got on the next train back to San Antonio. People thought you were nuts. When you're writing you don't want to talk to people.

So yeah, you booked your Virgin Premium Economy 13-hour special isolation unit, and when you get off the plane you get five calls on your fucking cellphone from Anne, the previous quote-unquote producer, talking about the need to protect Rachel's fragile state of mind. You have talked to Zozanian a few times, this is not really the way you imagined a comic writer, the book is *funny*, this is what *drew* you to the *material*, it's *funny*, you would have thought a comic writer would be *funny*, but as a human being, OK, Sharpshooters are definitely the dregs, she went through a bad time, but still, you would have thought there would be the potential to see the humor in the situation. Your agent has called the quote-unquote agent and we're talking about a two-page fucking letter agreement which is ten minutes clerical work, but the material, the material is definitely great.

2

The phone rings.
The phone rings.
The phone rings.

An e-mail from Noszaly described his work as squarely in the tradition of the political tragedians Aeschylus, Sophocles, and Euripides, while seeing the closest affinity to the work of Sophocles. A second drew parallels with Chekhov and Ibsen. A third mentioned Kubrick. A fourth stated his preference for using non-professional actors, some of these British kids were absolutely amazing, professional actors tended to be too mercenary, he explained, he was not interested in money, he wanted to work with people who were passionate about the project. Heartwarming news for the British film industry. It was not immediately obvious why a character as mercenary and grasping as Ephraim should appeal, but a fifth e-mail explained that he thought Eph's apparent obsession with money masked an inner vulnerability, it was a defence mechanism, it was important to get beneath the shell, there was a danger that he might come across as unsympathetic.

I floated an affable reply on a double Bushmill's. The head was not very clever.

I did not think it was a good idea to see his films hot on the heels of the self-assessment, but perhaps it looked rude to continue in ignorance. *Cahiers du Cinéma* and *Les Irrockuptibles* had not warmed to Noszaly's work, but praise is rare in a country where film criticism is a blood sport. The Videothek had *The Count* on DVD with original language available; nothing else by our hero; *Stake!!!!!*, *Stake!!!!! II* and *Stake!!!!! V*. I borrowed *The Count* and *Stake! V*. This was not clever.

Simon had seen *The Count*, Noszaly's first film, in 1993 and been in *floods* of *tears* over the poignant performance of Nadezhda Vessarova, a 14-year-old from Dnipopetrovsk. He had then tried to get her for *Bat-Mitzvah Boy* and been *outraged* by the sheer brutal *rapacity* of Noszaly's distressingly mercenary producer. He had refused on *principle* to submit to highway robbery, Vessarova had been optioned into a series of teen vampire pics softened by the usual pharmaceutical remedies, it was the sheer *wastefulness* etc. etc.

A film billed as a cross between *Lolita* and *Nosferatu* is not *obviously* Sophoclean. A filed-fangs fifth rehash is not an obvious career move for an actress who got an Oscar nomination for her role in the tarthouse Dracula. It was 14:01. It was 14:13. It was 18:08. The body leapt to its feet. The mouth was speaking. It said:

You piece of SHIT. You piece of SHIT. You piece of SHIT. FUCK you FUCK you FUCK you you PIECE. OF. SHIT. You STUPID, TALENTLESS piece of SHIT.

FUCK you FUCK you FUCK you

you **PIECE. OF. SHIT** youpieceofSHIT

FUCK you

FUCK you

FUCK you

youpieceofshityoupieceofshityoupieceofshityoupieceofshit I pick up the standing lamp and swing it against the wall and I am shrieking and it feels pretty damn good.

But shhhhhhhhhhhh. Shhhhhhhhhhhh. We're calm. We're totally fucking calm. You piece of SHIT. We're calm. We're calm. We're totally fucking calm. No, no. We're just calm. OK. Look. Let's be sane. Be sane. A deal would be good. Money would be good. If you tell him he is a worthless talentless overpaid piece of shit there will be no deal. So Shhhhhhh. Shhhhhhhhhhh. Shhhhhhhhhhhhhhhhhhhhhhhhhhh. Sh. Sh. Sh. Be calm. Be calm. Be calm. Be very very very very calm. We're calm. Yes. OK.

3

Sometimes you have to do things you know will lead to disaster.

Normally, given a choice, I go out of my way to avoid betazoids. Sometimes there is no choice.

I pick up the receiver. I press two numbers. I put down the receiver.

I pick up the receiver. I press one number. I put down the receiver.

I pick up the receiver. I press three numbers. Another number. I sit staring at the keypad. The dial tone turns sour.

I put down the receiver, pick it up and press 12 numbers very fast. The keys are too soft, I hate soft keys, I want something to punch.

A voice recites the name of the firm, offers assistance. I ask for the betazoid.

—I'm sorry, she's in a meeting. May I take a message?

—

—May I tell her you called?

—

—Shall I have her call you?

—No. No, that's all right.

I hang up. What a wonderful day! What a glorious sunshiny day!

4

Fri 19 Aug 2005. Gaza strip cleared of settlers.

The cursor blinks. It's 14:39. It's 14:42. It's 14:45.
Forget Vessarova. Don't tell me about the past, tell me about the future.

From: "Rachel Zozanian" <zozanian@onetel.com>
To: "A.P. Pechorin" <popesonxtacy@hotmail.com>
Subject: stunned
Date: Fri, 19 Aug 2005 14:48:58 +0100

Well, I'm glad you are still speaking to me, but stunned to learn that you don't keep copies of your e-mails. Does Hotmail not automatically keep them in a Sent Folder? Bad news.

I think you should write to Simon anyway. I don't know what he has in mind - but I can tell you this, anything you write him will be the high point of his day, poor officebound publishing executive that he is. Ask what he would like you to do. I'll bet everyone who GETS your e-mails is hanging on to them, so you can probably get them one way or another - but who knows, maybe he has some other idea.

I loved yr piece for the Mirror.

S's e-mail address again is Simon.Crawford@MKM.com. I can get you his phone number if you'd rather sound him out first on the phone, but it wd cheer him up to have an Alyosha e-mail of his own.

Some background on SC: He was at Cambridge at the same time as Branagh, Thompson, Fry, Laurie and I forget. The consensus: Lord love you, he would lie at the drop of a hatpin, never mind a hat. Did no work - I think Russian was what he was mainly not working on, but Polish may have come into it somewhere. Launched a magazine along the lines of Artscribe (got some Names to produce coverKunstwerk, kept the originals, flogged them to buy a house in pregentrified Islington). Worked at Sotheby's as a snake-charmer. Went briefly to Pentagram, briefly to Phaidon, staged a coup at a magazine called Minotaur, fell in love with Rafael Garcia Ramirez (Mexican soap star, Bebo to his friends and fans). Tara Liu (friend since Cambridge) asked him to start up a manga-style publishing imprint for Sharpshooters, which had been a low-budget big-profit-margin sweatshop-cum-arthouse games manufacturer based in Bushwick. Bebo wanted to get out of soaps; NY was the closest he could get to Almodovar without upsetting his mother. So, long story short, Sharpshooters was flying on a wing and a string of 4 letter words, SC put on his parachute when no one was looking and went to MKM to be publisher of their adult trade books a few months ago.

He is notorious for unfortunate misunderstandings. (Tara Liu at party: We're engaged! Everyone else: But — I thought he was gay? (A reliable source informs me.)) So he is lazy, fickle, disloyal, dishonest, disorganised. Never one to forget a friend who could do him a favour. Terminally amnesiac of favours received. There never was a Cat of such deceitfulness and suavity. But if he gets excited about a book, he will get everyone else excited about it.

That wd be good. So do drop him a line.

Rachel

PS No reason why it shd come up, but don't mention ERM, Black Wednesday, Soros, forex, the eurozone, the Dmark, reunification, the Wall, 1992, 1989. 2C2E.

From: "Rachel Zozanian" <zozanian@onetel.com>
To: "A.P. Pechorin" <popesonxtacy@hotmail.com>
Subject: PPS
Date: Fri, 19 Aug 2005 13:01:30 +0100

Hope I have not undersold my former editor - he's clever, just has a split personality like so many people in that business. Says his intellectual heroes are Musil, Borges, Mussorgsky and Jobim. Read Margaret Kennedy's Troy Chimneys at age 10. Was read The Hobbit at the age of 6 and begged them to stop because he cdn't stand the whimsy. Likes Chuck Palahniuk and Sybille Bedford. And (apparently) Alyosha Pechorin.

I hope you're all right and not dodging bullets for the Sunday Mirror.

Rachel

X-Originating-IP: [84.190.107.104]
From: "A.P. Pechorin" <popesonxtacy@hotmail.com>
To: "Rachel Zozanian" <zozanian@onetel.com>
Subject: RE: PPS
Date: Sat, 20 Aug 2005 15:50:52 +0000

hey rachel no i got what you meant by it all - it makes me dizzy like some fitzgerald novel- i am wary and cautious and believe in vampires. so i understand what you mean. he emailed back saying send more stuff but i would prefer a slightly more formal outlook- something a little firmer than show me show me...hopefully something leads me out of this mire of quag -there is such an episodic relationship to my joyious heights and sustained periods of what the fuck am i doing.... i drank like a soldier last night and now feel the weight of several wars upon my head... i enjoy-appreciate immensely- your acknowledgement and push - it is affirmation -but there is a double lack to it all making me sink after imaginations take me to the heights i desire to look from...then the realistic vision of my subterranean living comes to light...and it goes and goes.

well speak soon
#Alyosha

8

The reader's guide to camouflage

You're reading *Your Name Here,* the new novel by Helen DeWitt. You're extremely aggrieved. Instead of the wealth of stories you loved in the last book there are narrative strands which you find hard to follow. Also, you've always admired Calvino's *If on a winter's night a traveller,* a real tour-de-force with 11 first chapters of novels in a wide range of genres. DeWitt just keeps bringing in new chapters of the same book within a book; a writer who is clearly no match for Calvino for sheer inventiveness has no business casting aspersions on Our Man in San Remo. Meanwhile *Lotteryland* is the only part of the book that makes you wonder what happens next, you get involved in the story only to be thrown back into the surrounding narrative chaos. You find yourself hoping yet another flimsy pretext will be found to introduce yet another totally superfluous second-person narrator, an anonymous reader, nothing too fancy, who becomes engrossed in *Lotteryland,* by the recluse Zozanian.

LATDRENLOYT

9. BUT

THURSDAY 12 APRIL 2001 0917 0918 0919 0920 0921

But today the lottomonitor said DISCOURAGEMENT. DISCOURAGEMENT. DISCOURAGEMENT. DISCOURAGEMENT. DISCOURAGEMENT.

No surprises. I could not get the Paper Ticket out of my mind.

I said to Gaby: Say I draw the Intellect to get a Paper Ticket the question is what does it take to maximise the chances of a Paper Ticket being raised to

She said: Will you stop talking about the Lottery?

I said: But it's *true*. I said: In the paper today there was a piece about this guy, he wrote this book and he got a Silver Ticket and this other guy was saying, he looks like Hugh Grant and Rupert Everett put together, so once he got a Silver he was a cert for a Gold

She said: But I don't think you even look like Hugh Grant or Rupert Everett taken separately.

I said: There must be physically repulsive writers who got Golden Tickets. Tell me about ugly writers.

She protested: I didn't say you were

I said: What do you suppose are the odds of a Golden Ticket if you're physically repulsive?

She said: I think you're quite nice I just meant

I thought suddenly: Christ!

Because one way defying the Rules ruins even the luck you have is it makes you very unattractive to people you might want to attract.

I said hastily and hypocritically: Oh, forget it. Looks are unimportant. It's what's inside that counts.

I thought: Oh my God. She's so beautiful.

I thought suddenly: Would she agree to pretend to be the author of my book?

I thought: All that's best of dark and bright Meets in her laughter and her eyes, and though I had no statistics to hand I was confident that a picture of Gaby, with her brilliant dark eyes and mocking smile, would turn Paper to Double Diamond.

One of the Rules of the Game is that you have to say looks are unimportant.

The odds were already so staggeringly astronomically against Gaby even turning up again, however, that I knew I should do something fast to show there was more to me than met the eye.

I needed to show I could be lucky if I tried.

Or rather, I needed to show I could be lucky without even trying.

I was trying to say something in an offhand win a few lose a few sort of way when the speaker crackled.

You know, you're a very special person.

I hesitated. While everyone is obviously special in their own special way a surprising number of girls seemed to be special in the sense of being able to sit through the Lucky Song without gagging. They may not actually like it but they think it's bad luck to walk out, or they think it's a good thing to keep up appearances, or sometimes they actually do like it. I did not want to cause offence when we had just been miraculously reunited. I looked cautiously at her face, which had this sort of polite, blank look that people usually do wear during the lucky hello when they are with people they don't know well.

Fancy a quick fag? I asked.

We were out the window in less time than it takes to tell it.

Thanks, said Gab, taking a Silk Cut and lighting up.

I lit up and inhaled deeply.

The fire escape had an unused, neglected look, suggesting that the previous occupant had been the sort of person to sit through, perhaps even enjoy, the lucky hello. Most people have a chair and a couple of magazines at the very least; some people make really elaborate preparations. One problem with the randomised broadcast, apart from the element of unpredictability, is that you could actually have two in a row, or even the entire daily allocation in quick succession. If you have a small drinks cabinet, a fridge and the Complete Works of Dickens on the fire escape this is not a problem for you. Unfortunately I had only just moved in, so I hadn't had a chance to do it up.

Gaby sighed.

You know, I know some people find it really helpful, she said. And I know I've been really lucky so it's not really for me to criticise, but sometimes I just wonder. I mean, if you don't find it helpful I don't see why you can't just opt out.

You could if you were Jewish, I said with simple pride.

Really? said Gab. What makes you so special?

It's nothing to do with being special, I said. It's to do with having a Chief Rabbi.

Gaby was smiling and taking drags on her Silk Cut. OK, she said, so what's so great about having a Chief Rabbi?

I said: Well, the thing is, Gab, obviously we all take luck for granted these days, but originally it was quite a revolutionary concept to give it official recognition. In fact, to give the devil his due, if it hadn't been for Lucky Roger we probably wouldn't have the Lottery in anything like its present form. Lucky Roger had been spending a lot of time in America and when he came back he took a close look at society and he said Wait a minute. What he realised was that accepting the luck of the draw was actually a fundamental tenet of morality, except that nobody had really noticed.

Gab said she was not sure she really followed.

I said: That's because now we take it completely for granted. What I mean is, say two people decide to get married. However much they know about each other, there's one thing they can't know, which is what it's like to be married.

Gab said: Well obviously

I said: So they have to take a chance. And because they're taking a chance they can get married quite quickly. But if they want to get divorced it takes a really long time. They know what it's like to be married, and what it's like not to be married, so there is no element of chance involved. If the thing that mattered was making a decision based on the facts, they could get divorced in a week. But actually the thing that matters is taking a chance and sticking with it. It used to be that people thought it was so immoral not to stick with the luck of the draw that you couldn't get divorced at all, and we still think it's pretty immoral, and that's why people have to pay a penalty for guessing wrong.

Gab said: Well obviously

I said: I know it's obvious now, but it was revolutionary at the time. Say you go to university, you take a gamble because you don't know about it ahead of time. Once you know about it, it's practially impossible to change because morality requires us to abide by the luck of the draw. Obviously. So what Lucky Roger argued was that the institutions of a society should reflect the morality of the society, far too much was not being left to chance given the high moral value placed on chance, and as luck would have it he was quite a good friend of the PM and one thing led to another.

I was hoping Gab would be impressed by someone who knew all this behind-the-scenes material which does not appear in the history books and which most people have no chance of knowing but she just went on smoking in a cool, unimpressed sort of way.

Gab said: So where does the Chief Rabbi come in?

I inhaled again on my Silk Cut. From behind me I could hear the words of the lucky hello, just audible through the window and the curtain.

I explained: Well, when people just had their lottomonitors there were a lot of people who felt they were losing out. The problem was that there were a lot of things people were not really used to leaving to luck. So one idea was that they should have lots more prizes, but the problem is no matter how much people win they always want more. What Lucky Roger said was, people forget just how lucky they are. So they undertook this massive nationwide speaker installation to remind people of how lucky they were, and the Chief Rabbi saw that it would drive the Jewish community insane.

Now it was just possible that the lucky hello would turn out to be against Jewish law, and that a plea could be made on religious grounds. But the Chief Rabbi saw instantly that it could be quite time-consuming to come up with a religiously sound decision on the subject, and by that time it would be too late. The speakers would be installed, and it would be impossible to get them uninstalled because that would be to go against the luck of the draw.

The Chief Rabbi went to the PM, and he made up a ruling on the spot. He argued that all Jews are required to recite morning, afternoon and evening prayers which recognise the fact that they are God's chosen people, and that the lucky hello would be deeply offensive as implying that some other, secular form of luck was superior to that granted by God.

The PM promised to give the matter the most serious consideration and went off to have a word with Lucky Roger. Lucky Roger argued that Jews had just as many chances as everyone else and just as much right to be reminded of how lucky they were.

The PM said that Jews had just as many chances as everyone else and just as much right to be reminded of how lucky they were and the Chief Rabbi said he was not disputing that. The Chief Rabbi said all the same on religious grounds he must insist on the right of every Jew to have dispensation from the reminder.

The PM went back to Lucky Roger because this was at a stage when Lucky Roger could not be seen to be directly involved.

Lucky Roger said: Yes but how are we to know who is genuinely entitled to the dispensation?

How are we to know who is genuinely entitled to the dispensation? asked the PM.

And the Chief Rabbi said: Leave everything to me. He said that the appropriate course of action would be for the Chief Rabbi to have sole authority to grant dispensation, and this would guarantee that they were not distributed lightly or frivolously, to undeserving candidates.

This was in the early days, when Lucky Roger was not sure of his ground. That was why it had been so crucial for the Chief Rabbi to move quickly and decisively, and that was why the PM said We'll see what we can do.

Gaby said: So you all get dispensation from the Chief Rabbi, is that it?

I said: Well, you fill in a form and send in a cheque for £100. If you live in a house that already has a speaker they send around a rabbinically approved speaker disenabler. If you live in premises where no speaker has been installed you get a certificate so you don't have to have one installed.

Gaby said: You mean you could go your whole life without hearing the Lucky Song?

I said: Well obviously there's school, schools tend to take a more ecumenical approach.

I said: That's why if you look at the property ads you see lots of places advertised with certified Jewish landlord. As long as the landlord has a room in the property the entire property is entitled to be speaker-disenabled, a lot of people are prepared to pay over the odds for that kind of environment. A hundred quid is highway robbery but to be fair most people who buy the certificate find it pays for itself.

Gaby said: Are you sure about this, Eph?

I said: Sure I'm sure.

She said: And you're not just making it up?

I said: Would I lie to you?

Let me rephrase that, I said after a short pause.

Gaby tossed her cigarette stub into a garden far below.

If you look in books and papers you never see much written about the Lottery, I said. It's not really in the spirit of it because the more people know the more it reduces the element of chance. So if you've never heard about it that's why. Nothing more sinister than that.

The Lucky Song was tinkling away in the room.

But in that case, Gab said suddenly, why don't you have one of these disenablers yourself?

I'm on a limited budget, I protested. I have to count every penny. I can't believe you've never come across one before.

The Lucky Song tinkled to a close.

We climbed back through the window.

Is that your post? said Gaby.

Yeah I really need to throw it away, I said.

Haven't you even opened it?

She crossed the room to the pile of envelopes by the door.

But Eph, said Gaby. You won a free trip to Florida. You should send this in. And look at this, you won a free car. You should claim these. You're exactly the type of person they're *for*.

Have you ever tried claiming one? I asked.

No, not really, said Gab. The thing is, Eph, I know I'm quite lucky, it doesn't seem right to take up a prize that would really mean a lot to some people.

I had already surmised that Gaby came from a pretty lucky background. She probably came from the type of background where they retain a highly qualified prizeclaimer just to expedite the process. There would be no point in hiring a prizeclaimer to process a claim for a trip to Florida, because the value of the prize would be eaten up in costs, but there are people who win at a level where it actually pays to process the claim.

I was about to probe delicately on the subject of prizeclaimers but it occurred to me that it was probably against the Rules and I did not want to push my luck.

12 APRIL 2001 1939 PERSEVERANCE

Congratulations!

I thought: Not in our stars but in ourselves.

Gaby was gathering up all the envelopes on the floor.

Look, Eph, she said. I realise what you've been through. If you haven't won anything for a while I guess it's easy to be defeatist. But the thing you've got to remember is, you have just as good a chance as anybody else.

But, I said.

No, *not* but, said Gaby. It's *true*. But if you don't *enter* you can't *win* and if you're not even going to process your claims for things you've actually *won* you're not taking advantage of the luck you actually *have*. Now I'm going to send in your forms for every single one of these prizes. You don't have to do a thing.

She put the envelopes in a pile on the table, pulled up the single chair, and opened an envelope for two free weeks in a condo in Burma with free camera if returned in seven days.

Look at this, for example, said Gaby. Two free weeks in a condo in Burma. And you're getting it back to them within seven days, so you'll get a free camera. Plus a surprise mystery gift.

She took out the instruction leaflet, the application booklet and four pages of stamps and began to work her way through the application.

I thought: The main thing is, she's here.

Which would you rather have? said Gaby. £300,000 in a lump sum or £10,000 a year for life?

I don't mind, I said.

Come on, said Gaby. You must have a preference.

£300,000, I said.

Gaby tore off a stamp and stuck it to the first page of the application booklet.

Which would you rather have? A CD player or a VCR?

CD player.

Are you sure? said Gaby. The VCR is probably worth more.

OK, I'll take the VCR.

You don't have to have the VCR if you don't want it, said Gaby. If you'd actually rather have the CD player, I'll put the CD player.

OK, the CD player, I said.

Are you sure? said Gab.

Yes, I said. Definitely. My mind is made up. The CD player it is.

She tore off another stamp and stuck it in the booklet.

Which would you rather have? A four-slice toaster, a graphics calculator, or an electronic address book?

Toaster, I said firmly, in a tone of voice meant to discourage a review of the rival merits of the calculator and address book.

Gaby pasted another stamp in the booklet.

Which would you rather have? she said.

The speaker over the lottomonitor crackled.

Hello!

I had never thought it would be possible to welcome the lucky hello. For once, however, the black despair more commonly associated with the broadcast was displaced by heartfelt relief.

Fancy another fag? I said.

Gaby frowned. No, Eph, I think we should finish this. If we don't do it now it will never get done.

You know, you're really a very lucky person.

But, I protested.

Now which would you rather have, a pocket torch, a Swiss Army knife or a set of paintbrushes?

You're lucky because you're special.

Look, I'll tell you what, Gab, I said. If you think about it, the important thing is not whether you claim this prize or that prize. The important thing is to make the claim. So why don't you pick for me?

I could do that, said Gaby, glancing at the mountain of envelopes. And that way when it comes it will be a surprise.

It certainly will, I agreed.

You're one of a kind.

I'll put you down for the Swiss Army knife, said Gab, detaching a stamp.

When you think about it, that's the biggest piece of luck you could ask for. You're you.

Sometimes it's easy to lose track of what's important amongst all the prizes. It's easy to feel we're not winning as much as we'd like to. It's easy to feel that all the prizes are going to others. That's why it's important to remember that you've already won the biggest prize of all. You're you.

I walked over to the window and looked out. I felt that it would be the height of bad manners to leave the room. Behind me, Gaby struggled through her first attempt at commercial prizeclaiming. I thrust my hands in my pockets, gazing thoughtfully at the backs of the terrace opposite.

It's important to feel good about the luck we have. And it's also important to make other people feel good about the luck they have. Because the most important part of luck is feeling good about it. That's why it's bad luck to feel bad about your luck. And it's bad luck to make other people feel bad about their luck.

About half of the fire escapes were occupied. Most of the other windows were dark. I could see one empty fire escape with a lighted room behind it; a woman in a wheelchair was knitting by the window and looking out.

If someone you know wins a prize, make them feel good about it!

Some of the fire escapes were bare and unfurnished, most had a couple of chairs. One had an awning and wrought iron garden furniture and a potted lemon tree, the type of flagrant breach of safety regulations which provokes irate letters to the *Telegraph*. 'Am I alone in supposing that the purpose of a fire escape is to provide an alternative exit from a burning building? I had always imagined that it was intended as a safety feature, not an add-on fire hazard. The obstacle course of potted plants, home entertainment centres, refrigerators, bean bags, futons and other paraphernalia which confronts attempted flight from incineration by this route suggests to me that I may have been labouring under a serious misapprehension. Disgusted in Epping.'

There. That's one taken care of, said Gaby.

None of us wants to feel bad about it if we happen to have the good luck to win a prize. We don't want to feel bad about all the people who haven't won it.

Some people were leaning on the railings, looking down into the gardens. Here and there people were smoking. Further up the street a group of ten or so had spread out over the steps above and below a second-floor landing.

And there's really no need to feel bad, because there are lots of prizes for everyone. Remember, if you do win a prize, that doesn't mean somebody else couldn't have won it. And if you don't win a prize, the thing to remember is, it could have been you. So make the winner feel good about it! Good luck to them!

There were more people outside than there had been the last time. There was a spirit of camaraderie in the air, people shouting jokes and obscenities back and forth in humorous indignation at the double hello. Here and there people just stood silently waiting for it to be over.

All of us are lucky at different times, in different ways. It's important to remember that, no matter what we win, or don't win. If someone else wins a prize, it's important to remember all the prizes we did win.

Here's one for a free Vauxhall Cavalier, said Gaby. I'll do that one next, Eph, because it's more practical, and I'll do the one for the Lamborghini a bit later if that's all right with you. You know, some of these prizes are really brilliant, I wouldn't mind winning some of these myself.

Remember, each of us is special in our own special way. Which means that you're a very lucky person, not because of what you win, but because of who you are. You're a very special person. You're you.

I thought: I've just got to start winning again. I've got to.

Gaby had overcome the initial prejudice against losers that was natural to a girl from a seriously lucky background, but there was no telling how long this would last. Or rather, something told me her patience had already worn thin.

I'm lucky to be so special
There's nobody just like me
So every day in every way
I'm a lucky person to be

I know I'm really lucky
And the reason is plain to see

I could have been somebody else
So I'm lucky just to be me.

There were scattered cheers and jeers across the gardens, and people began to make their way inside.

That's two taken care of, said Gaby. Honestly Eph, I don't know why you make such a fuss about it, it's just a matter of making the effort.

9

Diva

«. . . De Laurentiis vorrebbe Paul Newman nel ruolo del protagonista. Ora, certo, Paul Newman è un grande attore, una star, ma è troppo importante. A me serve una faccia qualsiasi.» «Benissimo, pronto, la faccia qualsiasi sono io.» Io mi sentii affatto humiliato. «Ma sì, perché il personaggio è una specie di farfallone. Non deve avere la personalità di Paul Newman.» «Va benissimo,» risposi.

". . . De Laurentiis would like Paul Newman in the main role. Now sure, Paul Newman is a great actor, a star, but he's too important. I need an ordinary face." "Fine, OK, the ordinary face, that's me." In fact I felt humiliated. "But yes, because the character is a kind of butterfly. He shouldn't have the personality of Paul Newman." "Fine," I replied.

I Remember, Yes I Remember, *Marcello Mastroianni*

COOGAN DOESN'T GET IT

You're up to page 291 of *Your Name Here,* the new novel by Helen DeWitt. What's going *on*? Where is this *going*? What is your character supposed to be *doing*? What is the book actually *about*?

The relationship between your character and Rachel Zozanian seems tenuous. Is this going to be fleshed out?

It's 4 September 2006. In October last year DeWitt offered you £1000 for any e-mails you had from your time as a tabloidista. You were skint but suspicious. "Just what do you want to do with the material, anyway?" you asked, and got an evasive reply. You sent a few pages on chasing Britney through Germany. Months later, when *Your Name Here* was months overdue, you sent DeWitt your e-mail exchange with "Amanda." You have it in writing that you get half of any money the book brings in; six-figure sums have been mentioned; but is this someone you can trust?

You've just been kicked out of Tel Aviv for having too many Arab stamps in your passport. You wanted to work in Ramallah on the *Palestine Monitor*; you'd spent weeks researching the Oslo Accords, the Camp David Agreement, the Six-Day War; instead you were interrogated for twenty hours at the airport, thrown in jail for a week and shipped out to Munich. Now you're adjusting to the change of plan in Sarajevo. Meanwhile *Your Name Here* has been started from scratch for the sixth time in as many months. There's nothing in *Your Name Here* about Bernard Lewis's *Political Language of Islam,* which you borrowed, covered with notes and politely returned, dog-eared and pre-loved; you've been lobbying for months to have something about this in YNH, which you think would be more interesting than just the alphabet, and it's still not there.[2] You suggested months ago that YNH could include the 100 most common words in Arabic, something that would be useful to journalists, and it's still not there.[3]

---

2. كافر. kafir: ". . . from the time of the Prophet to the present day, the ultimate definition of the Outsider has been the kafir, the unbeliever. 5

خوارج khawarij, those who go out . . .

Supreme sovereign power is at the center. The nearer to the center, the greater the power; the further from the center, the less the power . . . Changes in power relationships are indicated by the same metaphors. In Western language contenders for power may rise or fall . . . Ambitious Muslims move inward rather than upward; rebellious Muslims secede from, rather than rise against, the existing order. The earlier—indeed the paradigmatic—movement of rebellion against the existing order was that of the Khawarij, "those who go out." 13

بَغداد Baghdad عراق Iraq

Movement inward may be beset with difficulties and obstructed by chamberlains and other barriers; but it is incomparably easier than movement upward through the well-defended layers of a stratified society. In this as much else, Muslim political language reflects the idea of social mobility. The Arab historians tell us that when the caliph al-Mansur, the architect of the Abbasid Empire, built his new capital in Baghdad in A.D. 758, "he traced the city plan, making the city round." [al-Ya'qUbI, *KitAb al-buldAn*, 2d ed. ed. M.J. de Goeje, Leiden 1892, p. 238. See also K.A.C. Creswell, *A Short History of Early Muslim Architecture*, London, 1958, 170-73.] His reason for this, according to the chroniclers, was that "a circular city has advantages over a square city, in that if the monarch were to be in the center of the square city, some parts would be closer to him than others, while, regardless of the divisions, the sections of the Round City are equidistant from him when he is in the center." [al-KhaTIb al-BaghdAdI, *TarIkh BaghdAd* (Cairo 1931, English translation in Jacob Lassner, *Topography of Baghdad in the Early Middle Ages*, Detroit, 1970, p. 52) Nearness is what counts, and justice requires equidistance, at least as a starting point.

The Arab geographers give further reasons for the choice of site. Iraq is the center of the world, Baghdad is the center of Iraq, and the caliph's residence is the center of Baghdad. To emphasize this centrality, the classical authors use a striking metaphor: "the navel of the world." A navel presupposes a body and the body politic is one of the most universal and enduring of metaphors. 23 *The Political Language of Islam*, Bernard Lewis (University of Chicago Press, 1988) A full glossary of terms, including the Arabic form, is available at www.yournamehere.com.

3. You were told they could always go on the website. www.yournamehere.com is also not there.

You're tired of playing the clown. You wanted a job where you could cover real stories. Now you're in Sarajevo, you can see the infamous Holiday Inn they sniped at, carelessly civilian, home to journalists and aid workers, everyone in scope is the sniper's enemy . . . Now kids go up the mountains to go snowboarding, you came halfway across the world to find surfer Kultur in the Balkans.

Suddenly you have a brilliant idea!

Unlike the other characters, you're not only getting paid, you have direct access to the author. You can change the course of the book.

From: "Ilya Gridneff" <anarchicus@hotmail.com>
To: Helen.DeWitt@gmx.net
Subject: YNH
Date: Sat 16 Sep 2006 10:04:59 +0000

Dewitt

Yes. Well, on other thoughts I was thinking again. This is flittery, perhaps i could finish *your name here*? If you are fed up and have to move on to other matters then perhaps ilya/alyosha could arrive in Berlin, maybe there is a struggle-dispute-dramatix device and i take Baby to fill in the holes. This seems in the original adaption spirit. or Rachel kills herself and my task to receive all the funds from the successes of *Lotteryland,* rely one me finishing the YNH book she has secretly been working on (perhaps this is a shock to ilya/alyosha leading to dispute- vampire exorcism) on the same lines of Richard Pryor Gene Wilder film "Brewsters Millions"...of course maintaining the style where it fits but like adding my paint to the canvas, gluing things together tying up the necessaries.... though i see the massive responsibility and problematics with taking on something, going a particular way and adding my steering to the vessel??!... They call me ishmael/alyosha, do they?... well just passing thoughts on the Saturday afternoon.

Also, Anais, henry will need you to pop into Western Union at some point of your violation.
das vedanya

ilya

From: Helen.DeWitt@gmx.net
To: "Ilya Gridneff" <anarchicus@hotmail.com>
Subject: YNH
Date: Sun 17 Sep 2006 14:46:15 -0100

everything is under control, should be finished in a couple of days. do you think alyosha popovitch pechorin works as a name for your character?

From: "Ilya Gridneff" <anarchicus@hotmail.com>
To: Helen.DeWitt@gmx.net
Subject: Der neue Doppel-null
Date: Sun 17 Sep 2006 19:19:54 +0000

dewitt

yes. Found this online, maybe some ideas for the double o superzero

http://en.wikipedia.org/wiki/Superfluous_man

*You can **support Wikipedia** and the Wikimedia Foundation by making a tax-deductible donation.*

Superfluous man

From Wikipedia, the free encyclopedia

Jump to: navigation, search

The Superfluous Man is a 19th Century Russian literary concept. It relates to an individual, possibly of talent and capability, who does not fit into the state-centered pattern of employment. The consequence may be a man who apparently is lazy and ineffectual.

It was popularized in the books of Ivan Turgenev and books like Ivan Goncharov's Oblomov and Dostoevsky's Notes from Underground. Other, earlier examples of the superfluous man in Russian literature include Alexandr Griboyedov's character Chatsky in the play "Woe from Wit," and the titular character in Alexandr Pushkin's novel in verse Eugene Onegin. Albert Jay Nock later titled his autobiography, Memoirs of a Superfluous Man. Yet, this concept is not to be confused with the idea of the superfluous hero, whose world weariness leads to ennui. This character type originates out of Lord Byron's Childe Harold's Pilgrimage, which inspired Pushkin to write his great novel in poetry Eugene Onegin.

From: Helen.DeWitt@gmx.net
To: "Ilya Gridneff" <anarchicus@hotmail.com>
Subject: lishny chelovek
Date: Sun 17 Sep 2006 23:11:24 +0000

ilya

this is great, but there's one slight problem. Oblomov is an ineffectual aristocrat who spends the first 150 pages of the book in bed. Tchulkaturin, protagonist of Turgenev's Diary of a Superfluous Man, is an ineffectual aristocrat who is silent, tongue-tied, paralysed by the simplest social occasion. so, um, surely rachel is the superfluous man in this book?

helen

From: “Ilya Gridneff” <anarchicus@hotmail.com>
To: Helen.DeWitt@gmx.net
Subject: RE: lishny chelovek
Date: Mon 18 Sep 2006 11:37:02 +0000

Vielleicht, Alexandr Andreyevich Chatsky, the Russian HAMlet?

En attendant Mr Beckett

The phone rings.

The kitchen floor is three inches deep in smashed glass. Hurling a glass to the floor, this feels pretty damn good. Plates likewise. Cups, saucers. A fucking teapot is the best.

So yeah, reading the nihilistic Nietszchean jouissance of this stranger in a bar feels pretty damn good. And naming no names I'd just like to see Bret Easton Ellis exposing his Armani-clad hide to the Peshmerga. What would *The Sun also Rises* have looked like if written by Joyce? What would *Tropic of Cancer* have looked like if Miller had stopped mooching around Paris and gone priapically off to dodge bullets? And I'm the first to see it. I'm the first to see it. Simon's crazy if he doesn't throw money at it, make a preemptive bid before someone else snaps it up. Yes.

The phone rings.

I spot a previously undetected china ornament—a boy and girl in Hansel and Gretel costume perched on a brown china fence, with a red china toadstool in the green china grass below the big-buckled china shoes. I snatch it up. I summon to the mind an image of the divine Tendulkar and bowl this crime against humanity at a girl's best guess at a fast bowl. KRASHHHHH!!! KRAAAAAKKKKK! Die fetten Jahre sind vorbei, o Kunst formerly known as kitsch.

The phone rings.

Only thing is. Inadvisable to talk to Simon. Inadvisable to write to Simon. It's in the lap of the gods.

From: "Alexander Chatsky" <nomadsland@hotmail.com>
To: garth228@hotmail.com
Subject: bang bang
Date: Sun, 21 Aug 2005 07:41:19 +0000

Garth-

sad and happy indeed the big bang- stranger indeed as this email came today. Met her in a pub several years ago then just recently she started emailing me… See below. can you help me...thoughts?

Well love and big bangs always....
In the iraq-iran border, cheesing it up

Sasha

Are you using the latest version of MSN Messenger? Download MSN Messenger 7.5 today! http://join.msn.com/messenger/overview

From: "Alexander Chatsky" <nomadsland@hotmail.com>
To: annakovacic@btinternet.co.uk
Subject: e+goat+is=m
Date: Sun, 21 Aug 2005 09:13:25 +0000

Ahoy,

On iraq-iran border en route to ost berlin. hope your move to better konditions are pleasant. i need yer help- self-indulgence plusssss. Anyway - i dont really keep my side of our dialogue and recently some powers that be were/are interested in seeing a kollection of email missives - so kannst du send some on to me when you have the time...some of the old backwards and forwards?

well hope you nat-well- all this is a strange idea something like: *'drinking bleach is not cool and other things i learnt about london'* a trilogy of failure followed or connected to *'baghdad 2 britney'* then the final episode 'kill em all and let god decide- homo erotic adventures in Islam' . . . ambitious and me me me me, so far but much less 'offensive' to tree death needing paper with the previous attempt but lets not talk of that right now... hope the toast is landing the right side up
Sasha

Be the first to hear what's new at MSN - sign up to our free newsletters!
http://www.msn.co.uk/newsletters

From: "Alexander Chatsky" <nomadsland@hotmail.com>
To: gillianblake@aol.com
Subject: pushmepullyou
Date: Sun, 21 Aug 2005 06:35:13 +0000

alive and well \it is rachel Zozanian -she wrote *lotteryland* or something like this. met her in that oracle of happy alcoholism the organic pub near Victoria Park, about two years ago. She was reading Adorno and i was gibbering drunk. sent her one of the little fanzines and never spoke to her again for about these two years- she emailed for some reason earlier this month and i emailed back- slightly interested in a stranger now living in berlin after a break down in ny. well think i am out of i-ran- \\see you soon- you well?
toodles . . .
sasha

Use MSN Messenger to send music and pics to your friends
http://www.msn.co.uk/messenger

From: "Alexander Chatsky" <nomadsland@hotmail.com>
To: Detlev Meyetr
Subject: vorsicht, schamlose werbung
Date: Sat 27 Aug 2005 14:33:02 +0000

ýf all goes to plan ý wýll be ýn berlýn next week. sometýme ýn early sept. but havent really told anyone. trying to do surprýse..hope you well- dýd you see Hunter dead/ blown out of a cannon?

ok all the best

-oh as edýtor at large -kannst du kommýssýon mýr fur blog stuff? as you kan tell my german ýs up to skratch for the readers- wýth electýon kommýn could be ýnterestýng angle- an ýdoýt amongst the ýdoýts?

sasha

Australian Embassy, Berlin
phone: (49) 30 8800 88307
fax: (49) 30 8800 88310

/People/DFATL
30/08/2005 11:16 PM

Hey J J,

I found out on last week that a great mate of mine, Sasha, is going to Berlin. He is currently etching out a living as a journalist, so be guarded with what you say in his presence. Just kidding, he's a great guy and I thought I should introduce you two. Sasha is a staunch Labour man, and has the self-confidence of Keating with the alcohol intake tendencies of Hawke.

So, the rest is up to you.

Cheers,

Mac
Department of Foreign Affairs and Trade

En attendant Adorno

From: "Alexander Chatsky" <nomadsland@hotmail.com>
To: Dave@sportsheet.com
Subject: I like to watch
Date: 29 Aug 2005 1113

Dave
still haven't received payment for the ***'free Internet brothel in Prague'*** story (may 23). I have sent invoice twice and rung three times. Can you please indicate when this will go through?
cheeeers
Sasha

From: dave@sportsheet.com
To: "Alexander Chatsky" <nomadsland@hotmail.com>
Subject: RE: I like to watch
Date: 29 Aug 2005 1805

Hi Sasha

Sorry about this. I am assured the cheque has gone out today. I'd asked for it to be hurried through but for some reason it just went with the normal system. All cheques for may payments have gone out today so you should definitely have either tomorrow or Wednesday. If it hasn't arrived by Wednesday, let me know.

Cheers
Dave

En attendant Mr Houellebecq

1

It has to be done.

Do it.

I pick up the receiver, dial 12 numbers fast, ask for the betazoid.

The betazoid is in a meeting.

—Would you like to leave a message?

—It must be done.

—What?

—Tell her Rachel called. The number is [Number].

—*Oh,* I think she's just stepped into the *office*!

—Rachel!!!!!!!!!!!!! It's so good to hear your *voice*! What a wonderful *surprise*!

My ear fills with corn syrup.

—Hi.

—What are you working on? Do you have something to show me?

—

—Rachel? Oh, *I'm* sorry, could you hold for just a moment? I've got someone I've been trying to get all week.

—Sure.

—

This feels good. This feels very very good. If only talking to the betazoid were always this good.

What time is it? 9:52:01.

I open *Discoveries in the Judaean Desert* XXX to calm my nerves.

> The date of a given pseudepigraphic apocalypse is usually ascertained by fixing in the historical review the point of transition from recognizable, detailed historical events to idealistic, schematic eschatological developments. Such a precise point has not been preserved among the fragments of the Apocryphon.
>
> Nevertheless, some clues for dating the composition are provided by the dates of the copies, allusions to various post-biblical developments, and chronological computations. An initial terminus ad quem is fixed by the copies of the Apocryphon, all penned during the second half of the first century BCE. As for a terminus a quo, the assessment is more complex.

It's 9:52:09. I can read 900 words a minute in English. I have not timed Arabic because it would be bad for morale. One thing is indisputable: even eight seconds with the language would improve my time in the next eight seconds. Eight seconds with DJD XXX have been rewarded with an analysis of the dating of pseudepigraphic apocalypses. How unrewarding, by comparison, are the eight seconds that might have been squandered on conversation with the betazoid.

Improve the shining hour.

I turn the page.

Something is making a noise in my ear.

The word Hello slides in a spoonful of syrup from the earpiece of the phone.

What time is it? 12:43:17.

—Diana, I say. Replete with DJD XXX, I feel very very good.

—Rachel?

—*Diana,* I say again. Benevolence and compassion vie. I have spent the last 3 hours 51 minutes and 16 seconds reading DJD XXX while the betazoid has been locked into 3 hours 51 minutes 16 seconds of telephone conversation.

—Rachel! Have you really—I'm so sorry, Rachel, I just assumed—if you'd hung up and called my PA she'd have explained—we were simply *engulfed* by—And I can't talk now, Rachel, I've got a meeting. Call me in the next couple of days and we'll have a real heart-to-heart.

I am alone in the room with DJD XXX. How good that feels. I'm not thinking about the things I don't want to think about. How good that feels.

1.1.1.1.2 = ١.١.١.١.٢

So that was 13 conversations and then I could not talk any more. There were another 55 messages on the phone but the phone could not be on in lectures or the library.

A storage unit whose contents were allegedly put up for auction three months ago may turn out to contain the unauctioned contents. The Inland Revenue may threaten legal action in a succession of threatening letters without taking legal action. Letters came from the Bursary requesting, demanding, insisting on payment, threatening expulsion.

Each member of the kinship system deplored the rapacity of an institution of learning.

Perhaps there is a procedure to follow. Perhaps one goes to the Bursary and weeps, sobs, implores. Perhaps one goes to one's tutor and breaks down.

It would sound melodramatic to say No one can help me. I dislike melodrama. All the same, I could think of no one who was likely to be helpful.

There was an essay to write on the Homeric poems and oral composition. It was difficult to concentrate.

I read pages 35–36 of *Le Suicide.* I think Moron has written no other book. I thought: What are the odds that any other undergraduate has read this undiscovered classic of French prose? What are the odds that any other undergraduate has discovered *any* undiscovered classic of French prose?

I thought: I shall go for a walk.

I walked down Turl Street to the High. A bus to Headington shot past another bus to Headington. An Oxford Tube was held up behind 19 cyclists; an X90 moved into a gap in the approaching traffic and seized the lead. I think the traffic was worse when Martin Amis was here; Cornmarket and Queen Street were not pedestrianised, the Broad was a, what's the word, thoroughfare comes to mind though that's not right, anyway there were no bollards blocking it off where Latimer, Ridley and Cranmer were burnt at the stake, and Catte Street was open to traffic. But the bus wars, no, the Munchkin machismo of minibuses jostling for pole position, no, no. I think Ishiguro once said that he wrote differently when he knew his books would be translated: he would not mention streets and restaurants no one would know.

The feet look after themselves. The mind contemplated sometimes *Le Suicide*, sometimes the verbal interactions which might coax £1,300 from the world, while the feet crossed the High, walked down Oriel Lane, turned into Merton Street, passed between Merton and Corpus into Christ Church Meadow, and proceeded down the Meadow to the Isis.

Freshers were being taught to row. It seemed a pity that my financial difficulties could not be transferred to a rowing fresher.

Bands of gold spread from the dipping blades. The sky was a bracing blue, a gung-ho coach oblivious to cold.

A man appeared in peripheral vision. He said: Is this the river?

I said: This is the Isis.

He said: I was told the venue was the Thames. I'm looking for the Oxford-Cambridge Boat Race. I'm with the press.

I turn.

There is a black leather jacket. There are black jeans and black cowboy boots. There is a black shirt. There is a black string tie with a silver skull clip.

It is the face of a worldweary turkey. There are jowls. There are pouches. There are creases. There are gelid blue irises with pinprick pupils floating in bloodsuffused whites. Black scare quotes allude to eyebrows. The cheeks blaze patches of red, the fierce rouge of Louis XVI Versailles. Where the skin is not red it is grey. Chemo-optimism has achieved the conjunction of hand, plastic razor, stubbled flesh, leaving gashes, nicks, gouges, beads of dried blood. The lobe of the left ear is missing. The lobe of the right ear has a diamond stud.

He says: I am here to do research on the aforementioned boat race. The ins. The outs. The wherewithal. Pumped Canadians passing the piss test using the ancient wisdom of the Eskimo. Fresh-faced English boys sodomising and being sodomised.

He says: Anything you say will be held in strictest confidence. Anonymity will be protected. Safe houses will be provided.

I say: The Oxford-Cambridge Boat Race takes place in April, on the Thames. The Isis is what the Thames is called where it passes through Oxford, but the Race takes place in London, between Putney and Chiswick. The Oxford colleges also race among themselves. The river is too narrow for the boats to race side by side, so a boat has to bump the boat ahead of it to move up in the hierarchy. There are Torpids in March and there is Eights Week in May. But these are just freshers being brainwashed.

—The Boat Race is in April?

—Yes.

—My editor won't like that.

—If he doesn't know already, why tell him?

—It might be better coming from me.

—He's your editor.

—Yes. So far. Is there a red-light district in this town?

—I'm not an authority.

—What are your personal views on sex for cash?

—Nice work if you can get it.

A sentence came to the mind. 500 for a suck, 1000 for a fuck. It sprang from mind to tongue to air.

He said: That's very reasonable. The pricing structure of airport cuisine. Clawed back from duty free. Are those trees wired for surveillance?

I said: Not to my knowledge, but I wouldn't necessarily know.

He said: I have a hotel, but I wouldn't necessarily recognise it.

—The Randolph is popular. Could it be the Randolph?

—We're not ruling out that possibility at this time.

We walked back up Christ Church Meadow in the direction of Christ Church.

He said: Do you see cows in that field?

I said: Yes.

He said: Do you see any snakes?

I said: No.

He said: Neither do I.

We walked down Cornmarket.

I said: I must stop at Boots for condoms.

It seemed tactless to mention lubricant.

He said: My boat race has been rescheduled. I need powerful pharmaceuticals available only on prescription. I need veterinary-strength analgesics.

We approached the Randolph.

—This looks familiar. I've seen that church somewhere before. Yes. And the phallic Victoriana cleaving traffic, it's in the memory bank. I'll just check reception and see if base command seeks contact.

—You don't have a mobile?

—It's in police custody in Singapore. The one people admit to knowing they can call.

Inspection of his key revealed the room number. The receptionist gave him nine or ten messages.

—Word got out.

This was the sense: of coming up to something that would be over very fast.

—I just need to make a phone call.

He takes out his mobile phone and punches it.

—Hey Eduardo. Yeah I got your messages, yeah, yeah, yeah, no shit. The word on the ground is blast-off is in April. Sí. But it's OK. No hay problema. Alles klar. Yeah yeah yeah yeah sorry about the boat race, my source's source must have mixed up the dates, yeah yeah, yeah, yeah, say look Eduardo I think I'm onto something, prostitution ring, white slave trade, Oxford sex-for-cash scandal yeah yeah yeah I'm just about to interview one of the girls now. Sí. Sí. Claro, sí, pendejohijodeputa, y tu mamá también. Muchos besos.

He punched out.

He says: OK. OK. He's on our side. He likes the story. We can come back to the Boat Race at the time of the alleged event.

He says: Don't look now, but there is a reptile in the corner. I can ask for another room if it will make you self-conscious. Are you afraid of snakes?

I say: No.

He says: Excellent news.

He says: They follow me. There is disconcertment. There is gêne.

He says: Are you going to take off your clothes?

I say: Are you going to pay?

He says: Oh sure. Sure.

He takes a wallet out of his hip pocket. He says: Do you accept Deutschmarks?

I say: If that helps.

He says: What have we here?

He throws notes on the bed. He pulls notes from his jacket pockets and throws them on the bed. He opens his laptop case and throws more notes on the bed.

He says: What's 1 million yen in sterling?

I say: I haven't been following the yen.

He says: Who has?

He says: There's a number I can call on this baby.

He says: Uh huh. Uh huh.

He says: Did you see something move under the bed?

I say: No.

He says: We have balboas. We have bahts. We have drachmas. The slack-jawed hermaphroditic spawn of Bretton Woods.

He says: It's good to be back. I was given this at the airport as a friendly gesture.

A duty-free bag hits the bed. A cardboard label attached to the handle says: Klaus Seifert.

He pulls apart the handles and turns out on the bed: a black and gold cardboard box that says Bushmills; a red and gold box that says Glenfiddich 25 years; a 2 kg box of Mozart chocolates.

He says: What was the exchange rate for the yen, again?

I say: You were going to check on your phone.

He says: How does 500 Dmarks and a million yen sound?

I say: Are we drinking that whisky?

His hands are dry, with brown spots on the backs. They shake as he tears at the box of Bushmills. He unscrews the cap and throws liquid into two glasses. He throws his at the back of his throat, pours.

He takes a bottle of pills from his jacket pocket.

He says: Are you going to take your clothes off?

I say: Let me check the exchange rate of the yen.

He raises his right arm to Sieg Heil, executes a swift flurry of shrugs with the left shoulder, exits the jacket with a martial arts medley of suave rapid tributes to Bruce Lee. Eyes narrowed he masters the beast in the corner by will alone. The slightest slip means death. He exits the string tie. He exits the shirt.

There seems to be quite a lot of paper currency on the bed.

The sentence *Let's get this over with before he pulls a gun* crosses the mind, accompanied by the removal of skirt, jumper, bra, pants. He is now wearing only a white T-shirt and black socks. An object like a blunt red stick juts up from a bed of grizzled black hair.

I think there is a line in *Portnoy's Complaint*: JEW SMOTHERS DEB WITH COCK. This is not the time to give the client a choice of orifice.

I crack a condom.

—I want you inside me.

I enrobe the truncheon. I squirt lubricant.

—Enter me, I say. I want you deep inside me. Enter me, enter me, yes, now.

I lie on the bed with my knees open. He says: Put your head at the foot of the bed so I can keep an eye on the corner.

I swivel. He kneels between my legs. He fumbles with the meths-grown monster.

—I want you inside me *Ow.*

He retracts slightly. —Easy does it, big boy. Yeah, yeah, OK, OK, vamonos muchacho, cuidado con mi Pit Bull, eso es . . .

He slides in further. The cunt clenches.

—Man that's tight. Unh. Unh. *Unh.*

—I want you hard inside me, deeper, harder, yes, now.

He hoists my legs up over his shoulders. This is a better angle. His cock achieves decent penetration with only relatively minor discomfort.

—Enter me, enter me, yes, yes, deeper, harder, now.

He fucks: Huh huh huh huh, huh huh huh huh. Huh! Huh! Huh! Huh!

His face has gone the colour of borscht.

Could I get money for the story if he dies? Is there a way of reaching Eduardo?

—Fuck me, fuck me, I want you deep inside me, yes, yes, now.

—HUH! HUH! HUH! HUH! HUHHHHHHH!

[8 Tunisian dinars, 50 Mexican pesos, 675 Thai bahts, 90 Panamanian balboas, 350 Russian roubles, 9,880 Indian rupees, 100,200 Greek drachmas, DM 500, ¥1,000,000, 2 kg box of Mozart chocolates.]

1.1.1.1.2.1 = ١.١.١.١.٢.١

So what do you want to know? Just what *was* the exchange rate of the yen, you say. How much was all this paper worth, anyway?

I bought a copy of the *Financial Times* at the Magdalen Street Borders. I then crossed Beaumont Street and entered the Taylorian. One mounts a flight of stairs from street level to reach the library (devoted to modern languages, linguistics and literary theory). One is then in a very high room with a, is mezzanine the word? (The head is not clever.) One can mount to this mezzanine by a wrought-iron spiral staircase, and on that narrow, what's the word? are placed a couple of small desks overlooking St Giles. A door leads to another flight of stairs leading to a stuffy little room of books on philology (Jesperson, that gang), but you would not want to sit there. I sat at a small desk and began to sort through my notes.

8 Tunisian dinars	× .5425 =	£4.34
50 Mexican pesos	× .0702 =	£3.51
675 Thai bahts	× .015 =	£10.18
90 Panamanian balboas	× .5978 =	£53.80
350 Russian roubles	× .098 =	£34.35

I was beginning to feel duped.

9,880 Indian rupees	× .0514 =	£507.53

That's more like it.

100,200 Greek drachmas	× .0018 =	£185.97
500 Dmark	× .3365 =	£168.25
1,000,000 Japanese yen	× .0045 =	£4475.47

The 6 digits glow on the LCD. It is very quiet.

Total: £5443.40

It goes on being very quiet. This is what the pieces of paper buy.

This was the thought: that it would not be necessary to make phone calls for a very long time.

I stacked up the notes again. There was bewilderment and joy. Dust floated in a beam of light. I had tried so many sentences on the kinship system, and received so many sentences in return—if there were sentences that would extract cheques or even duly completed forms from the system, I had failed to find them. But here was a transaction I had managed. I had replied to each sentence with a sentence, and the sentences had brought us to a hotel room, connected bodies, transferred a duty-free bag of notes.

Years later I saw a film called *X-Men* based on a series of comic books I had not read. Ian McKellen plays Magneto. It is about a group of superheroes, each with a special power, persecuted by an uncomprehending society. I did not break down in tears in the auditorium because it is not my way to break down in tears—in fact, a failure to break opportunely into tears is one of the problems. Still, that world looked familiar.

I met Mr Clever in 2000, three years before the release of the film. When I saw the film, though, I realised this was what I had expected—that Mr Clever would be Patrick Stewart, protecting his freaks. I explained to Mr Clever that the android Data in *Star Trek: The Next Generation* looks like a human to make interaction easier for humans, but that constructing a machine with a plausible personality takes energy. I think Mr Clever did not know the series (but of course I had watched it in the first place with the idea of making myself more plausible to people who, maybe, had not read that classic of French prose, *Le Suicide* by Pierre Moron).

The point, anyway, is that Oxford was once a place for freaks. (As, of course, was Cambridge.) A freak could sit an examination and win a scholarship for freakish powers—money, that is, buying time to develop the freakish powers. So you can do a set of graphs, and what the graphs show is the evaporation of funding for superheroes. (Graphs to come.) The habitat disappeared. It had once been possible for a mathematician to win a scholarship covering all expenses by sitting a series of examinations in mathematics and demonstrating excellence in mathematics. It was now necessary to combine excellence in mathematics with skill at fundraising from a kinship system.[4] Failing that, some other extra-mathematical skill. Failing that, luck in the Lottery.

And there's always the novel, ha ha ha ha ha, there's always the novel, ha ha.

Duty Free had showered me with more liquidity than I had ever seen in my life.

A week went by. There were 153 messages on the phone but I did not answer them. What to do, what to do, what to do? When in doubt, walk on the Wilde side. The Holy Scriptures were composed in primitive times when YHWH wrote on stone tablets and that invention of the devil, the telephone, was unknown to Homo sogenannte sapiens sogenannte sapiens. Good News for Modern Man (aka *The Importance of Being Earnest*) reminds us that revelation adapts itself to the intelligence of the revelatee:

> Algernon. The truth is rarely pure and never simple. Modern life would be very tedious if it were either, and modern literature a complete impossibility!
> Jack. That wouldn't be at all a bad thing.
> Algernon. Literary criticism is not your forte, my dear fellow. Don't try it. You should leave that to people who haven't been at a University. They do it so well in the daily papers. What you really are is a Bunburyist. I was quite right in saying you were a Bunburyist.

4. Readers familiar with Amartya Sen's *Poverty and Famines* will understand that the assets and income available to a kinship system do not translate directly into funding for a mathematician who is a member of the kinship system.

You are one of the most advanced Bunburyists I know.
Jack. What on earth do you mean?
Algernon. You have invented a very useful younger brother called Earnest, in order that you may be able to come up to town as often as you like. I have invented an invaluable permanent invalid called Bunbury, in order that I may be able to go down into the country whenever I choose. Bunbury is perfectly invaluable. If it wasn't for Bunbury's extraordinary bad health, for instance, I wouldn't be able to dine with you at Willis's to-night, for I have been really engaged to Aunt Augusta for more than a week.

Thank you, St Oscar, thank you thank you thank you thank you. I wrote a group e-mail to all members of the kinship system explaining that I would be spending Christmas with my dear friend Lily Marlowe, who had been diagnosed with MS and was confined to a wheelchair. There's always the novel, ha ha ha ha ha, and I had had a brilliant idea, ha ha, Jesus loves me, he loves me, he really really loves me, ha ha ha ha ha.

N T L O Y T E D R A L

13. ON THE OTHER HAND

SUNDAY 15 APRIL 2001 0917

DISCOURAGEMENT.

Too bad! Better luck next time!

I did not need the lottomonitor to tell me I had drawn Physically Repulsive: the mirror told its own tale. I shaved, more through force of Perseverance than any genuine hope of improving the spectacle, and had soon transformed Physically Repulsive (unshaven) to Physically Repulsive with bloody tufts of toilet paper.

I thought: I shall overcome.

I was about to flesh out my material on monomonitors with further episodes from my early life, my hopes, my dreams and how it all went so wrong, when I suddenly thought of something. That's so *sad,* Gab had said. I had no *idea,* she'd said. What she had not said was I think you're really *on* to something. She had not said I had only to write more in the same vein and she would send it off to this bloke Giles.

If you're discouraged it's important not to read too much into the fact that something like this is discouraging. All the same, I was discouraged. It was never going to be easy making shelf-filling and violin practice a gripping read. If I was doomed from the start, why start?

I breakfasted on half a chocolate cake.

All things considered, the day might be better spent revising for the Unemployment Opportunity.

I had sent in my official application to sit the prizeclaim, so in theory I could be called on any time. In practice it took a minimum of six weeks to get a date, usually at least two months, sometimes as many as six. If my number came up in six weeks I was doomed, but if it took much more than two months I was doomed anyway, so it had seemed safest to get the application off ASAP. If it took much more than two months I was going to need a true heartfelt tale sincerely told to fall back on, but if it took the standard two months I had a lot of ground to cover in the time.

I started thinking about Gaby.

It occurred to me that at that very moment my grandmother was probably running a luck check on my chances of marrying a nice Jewish girl. At that very moment my grandmother was probably registering a sinister downturn in the odds. And a sinister upturn in the odds of seeing her first great-grandchild. One with a sinister similarity to the level of reliability of a condom as a method of contraception. Or if she wasn't there was something seriously wrong with my grandmother.

What this meant, surely, was that I could find out how my grandmother was doing by running a luck check. I could set it up for a draw relating to GRANDMOTHER CHECKING ODDS OF MARRIAGE TO NICE JEWISH GIRL.

I sat down at the lottomonitor, pondering. This was going to be quite a complicated draw to set up.

I went into the Family menu and pondered again.

1537 GRANDMOTHER CHECKING ODDS OF MARRIAGE TO NICE JEWISH GIRL

Congratulations! Only 15,789 out of 17,247,866 won Grandmother Checking Odds of Marriage to Nice Jewish Girl in the latest draw!

I slumped back in my chair, exhausted yet oddly exhilarated. In the first place it was good to know that my grandmother was all right. In the second place I felt a real sense of achievement in having elicited the information. It had been a fantastically involved draw to set up. The statistical reporter had slightly missed the point, as it so often did—it had obviously calculated the odds using all single males, or possibly all single males with living grandmother—but it would be easy enough to introduce a religious parameter. It was brilliant having a lottomonitor all to myself, at home a complex draw was out of the question and at college I had never had the time.

I noticed suddenly that it was 1537.

I thought: Fuck.

I had a quick afternoon snack of half a chocolate cake washed down with grape juice. On balance, it might be better to get on with the story of my life.

After all, I was going to have to do something. Gaby was probably already consumed with regrets at having thrown herself away on the type of guy who can't even claim a free trip to Florida. She had given in to a momentary weakness. Now she would be even keener to see me take charge of my luck.

Probably the only reason Gab had not said she would like to see more was that she got carried away. I would write more along the same lines and even if she did not offer to send it off there was always a chance she would get carried away again.

1538 RESOLUTION.

Congratulations!

1539 FREE BOOKKEEPING COURSE

Congratulations! You have won a free bookkeeping course which will train you in the valuable skill of bookkeeping! The course can be pursued at your own pace in the privacy of your own home! Save thousands of pounds in bookkeeping fees! Earn thousands of pounds as a freelance bookkeeper! Be sure to claim your free bookkeeping course today!

1540 FREE TIME MANAGEMENT COURSE

Congratulations! You have won a free time management course which will train you in the valuable skill of time management! The course can be pursued at your own pace in the privacy of your own home! Save thousands of pounds by learning to manage your time more effectively! Earn thousands of pounds showing others how to manage their time more effectively! Be sure to claim your free time management course today!

I hit DRAW a few more times and got a long string of junk prizes.

I said: *Fuck.*

Something in my enquiries about my grandmother must have destablised the settings.

Resisting the temptation to kick the lottomonitor I sat down and went through the all-too-familiar routine of prize elimination.

An hour later I was ready to go back to work.

Now that it came to the point I realised that I would much rather have gone back to writing about Richard the croupier. I reminded myself that writing about Richard the croupier was not an option. The options were sitting the UEO, sending in five hundred applications for a free trip to Florida and writing a heartwarming story about the ecstasy of victory the agony of defeat.

I thought: Just do it.

1954

AUNT CHECKING HOROSCOPE

Congratulations! Only 500,000 out of 30,000,000 won Aunt Checking Horoscope in the latest draw! 300,000 in your age group!

1955

Fuck.

1956

MARKED INABILITY TO CONCENTRATE

I thought: If I write down the lyrics of the Impossible Dream, which as a Platinum Perseverer I often find myself unconsciously singing, I'll have to pay somebody some money and I don't even know if I am going to win a Paper Ticket.

I thought: Would I have to pay if I just put: This is my something, to something that something? I thought or would the odds be better if I put: **** ** ** *****, ** ****** **** ****, ** ****** *** ********, ** ****** *** ***?

Hello!
You know, you're a very lucky person.
Nobody else is quite like you.

I beat a hasty retreat to the fire escape.

En attendant Mr Chatsky

The phone rings. The phone rings. The phone rings.

The cursor blinks. It's 14:44:02.

X-Originating-IP: [84.190.107.104]
From: "Alexander Chatsky" <nomadsland@hotmail.com>
To: "Rachel Zozanian" <zozanian@onetel.com>
Subject: all heil the nazi pope
Date: Wed 31 Aug 2005 14:45:52 +0000

Yes. Back in berlin and warmed to the excited revivalist feeling of being missed and liked... it is seduction berlin... will be here for a month... well shall we do it in the flesh? Meet for meat or a beer-koffee kafe klutch? But i understand and respect any wants for your reclusive internet privacy

i am staying on sonntag strasse - frederichan- where it is literary sunday everyday---i have some telephone numbers but i can not muster the strength to ask my friend in the other roommm

sashhhhhhhhha

The cursor blinks. It's 11:31. It's 11:45. It's 12:13.

Date: Thu, 1 Sept 2005 13:01:30 +0100
From: zozanian@onetel.com
To: nomadsland@hotmail.com
Subject: RE: all heil the nazi pope

Dear Sasha

It would be nice to meet. I go to a 24-hour gym to stay sane, don't go out much otherwise. Doesn't matter about the phone number. I don't like phones. Try to avoid them when I can.

Rachel

X-Originating-IP: [84.190.118.242]
From: "Alexander Chatsky" <nomadsland@hotmail.com>
To:"Rachel Zozanian" < zozanian@onetel.com>
Subject: welcome to september
Date: Thu, 01 Sep 2005 14:08:59 +0000

YES. Well, let's meet in between sets of anaerobic and aerobic exercises. it is nice to visit the west side of berlin. are you a morning or evening person? beer or coffee- tea? thoughts where and when...

well i have to be in london for Sept 30 so perhaps i can meet some of these guys who pull and push the machine kranks (sic). oh in terms of destroying careers i do a good job at it myself so don't worry, self-destruction seems to be THE career path.

well a fear of phones is a new one for me- i have several messenger pigeons at our disposal...

sasha

En attendant Mr Mastroianni

When I was crazy for a long time I wore a pair of black Marks and Spencer pyjama bottoms, because to all appearances they were just a pair of black cotton trousers and I did not have the energy to change clothes twice a day.[5]

5. Deleuze, Différence et répétition, quotes Büchner's Danton: C'est bien fastidieux d'enfiler d'abord sa chemise, puis sa culotte, et le soir de se traîner au lit et le matin de se traîner hors du lit, et de mettre toujours un pied devant l'autre. Il n'y a guère d'espoir que cela change jamais. Il est fort triste que des millions de gens aient fait ainsi et que d'autres millions le fassent encore après nous. (It's dead boring to put on first one's shirt, then one's trousers, and in the evening take oneself to bed and in the morning take oneself out of bed, and always put one foot in front of the other. There is scarcely any hope that that will ever change. It's very depressing that millions of people have done so and millions more will do it after us.) When I got up each morning I had the sense that I had braved my quota of futility for the day by getting out of bed; if I were to exchange the pyjama bottoms for some other garment I should throw myself in front of a train. It upsets the drivers.
(Now, of course, writing this footnote, I think it's silly that I came to Büchner via the French of Deleuze, so I have taken the U6 from Mehringdamm to Friedrichstrasse and walked down to Dussmann's and bought a dtv paperback for a tax-deductable 14 euros, all so that I can offer the original text to the relatively small number of readers who studied German at school: Das is sehr langweilig immer das Hemd zuerst und dann die Hosen drüber zu ziehen und des Abends in's Bett und Morgens wieder heraus zu kriechen und einen Fuß immer so vor den andern zu setzen, da ist gar kein Absehens wie es anders werden soll. Das ist sehr traurig und daß Millionen es schon so gemacht haben und daß Millionen es wieder so machen werden . . .)

I had had them since Oxford because I don't like buying clothes, so the elastic was gone at the waist and they were fastened with a safety pin. If you wear something like that you think faux grunge would be fashionable but the real thing, this is just someone on the way down, so you wear an XL Mind the Gap sweatshirt from Oxfam to hide the p(a)in.

I don't want to think about garments now, but if you meet people it is necessary to think about garments. And you know this is stressful, meeting Don Swan. I have Googled him and discovered that he is, in fact, not Russian but Australian, which shows how little I remember of our last meeting, but I am not much bolstered by the fact that he can Google the comparisons to Gilliam and Orwell and Borges and some seriously silly writers. I'd like to assemble some garments that

In the crazy days I wore Nike trainers with no socks. When I came to Berlin I decided that wearing trainers with no socks was dangerous. Something about having sweaty, stinking feet and not noticing, or noticing but not doing anything, going down down down to Beckettian trampdom, something about maybe having to deal with clean-shaven clean-spoken authorities not just in the costume but in the method action of a Beckettian tramp—

I went to a secondhand clothes shop in Mehringdamm and I bought four pairs of shoes for five euros apiece. So I did have shoes but they had to be worn with tights and it was summer and hot in Berlin.

It was not v BJ, it was not very *Friends*, it was not very *Sex and the City*.

It was not a good time to talk. Too many calls from the poor man's Polanski. What if talking to the stranger in a bar took too many sentences? Leaving only "you stupid talentless piece of shit" for the wheeling and dealing?

If there's a danger of cracking up it's good to do something practical. When I was 11 I stole a copy of Cowan's *Modern Literary Arabic* from Foyle's—this was back in the heyday of Christina Foyle, when sweatshopped staff were a thief's best friend. Cowan has this word of advice for the hopeful Arabist:

> As regards the method he should follow, it is, of course, better if he can find an Arab or scholar of Arabic to direct him; but, failing this, I suggest that he adopt the following plan. Firstly, the Introduction on the writing of Arabic should be thoroughly assimilated before the actual lessons are tackled. Then each lesson should be worked through carefully and the student should not proceed from one lesson to the following before he is quite convinced that he has mastered the material in the first one. Although a full transcription has been given of all Arabic words and sentences in the first ten lessons this is a help which should be dispensed with as early as possible. The student should obtain from the outset two alphabetically indexed notebooks, one of which can be easily adapted for Arabic, and enter into these each new word he comes across. In another note book he should write out the paradigms of the verbs which are scattered throughout the book. These three note books should be his constant companions and referred to whenever he has a free moment. His exercises he must make for himself using the material he has worked with. All exercises and examples should be rewritten without the vowel marks so that the student becomes accustomed to reading Arabic without the vowels as it generally appears in print or in manuscript. If the above-mentioned plan of study is followed the student should acquire a sound knowledge of Arabic grammar in about six months.
>
> But that is only the beginning!

In other words, acquiring a sound knowledge of Arabic grammar is an excellent way to remain calm when all about you are smashing chandeliers. It had served well in the past; why not bring this oasis of calm to a meeting with a stranger in a bar?

It's important to motivate breaches of the social fabric. A journalist who has been in the Middle East might have insight into the sort of introduction to the Arabic script that would be useful to the sort of lunatic who is lured to places where people get shot at and blown up. Less a fig leaf than a fake fur monokini, but it would have to do. The head was not clever. it was not very clever.

I had pages and pages and pages of Arabic script, all the pages I had wanted to go over with the promised designer. There was a half-finished hack's guide. There was a half-finished star's guide. There was a half-finished footballer's guide. What's this? Dotted n b t y th, 5 down, 28 letters to go. Exhibit 1.

نيكول	**Nicole**	بريتني	**Britney**
توم	**Tom**	يوكو	**Yoko**
ثورمان	**Thurman**		

ثورمان	**Thurman**	روب	**Rob**
مات	**Matt**	بريتني	**Britney**
روث	**Roth**		

Which enables one to segue smoothly, surely, into a sample verb

يَكْتُبُ	*yaktubu* he writes
تَكْتُبُ	*taktubu* she writes
تَكْتُبُ	*taktubu* you (m.) write
تَكْتُبِينَ	*taktubina* you (f.) write
أَكْتُبُ	*aktubu* I write
يَكْتُبانِ	*yaktubaani* they 2 (masc.) write
تَكْتُبانِ	*taktubaani* they 2 (fem.) write
تَكْتُبانِ	*taktubaani* you 2 write

يَكْتُبُونَ	*yaktubuuna* they (m.)write
يَكْتُبْنَ	*yaktubna* they (f.) write
تَكْتُبُونَ	*taktubuuna* you (m.pl.) write
تَكْتُبْنَ	*taktubna* you (f. pl.) write
نَكْتُبُ	*naktubu* we write

Exhibit 2

Which in turn enables one to segue smoothly, surely (but does one segue smoothly or otherwise from this sort of starting point to an evening that ends with dancing on tables?) to the variations on three-letter core meaning which are the key to the elegance of the language KiTaaB book, JiHaaD, holy war, QiTaaL, struggle; KaaTiB writer, QaaTiL murderer, TaaLiB seeker; muKaTiB reporter, muJaHiD, holy warrior; maKTuuB thing written, letter, maJHuuD, endeavour, maTLuuB, wanted, sought (in classified ads); maKTaB office, maQTaL battle, maTLaB search . . .

I did not want to go.

I wanted to stay in the handsome apartment reading the poem Adonis wrote for Derrida after his death.

Time spent reading a poem for Derrida could have a pay-off in a way that a decision about shoes could not. To think about a decision about shoes in terms of a pay-off is one mark of the social alienation which does so easily lead to incarceration.

I had a black skirt. I put on the black skirt keeping thoughts about pay-offs to one side. I was already nervous and I needed more clothes.

I had a black sleeveless top, and I thought this looked good after all the hours at the gym. I had red high-top trainers.

I put all these pages and many more in my shoulder bag. I could not see how we would recognise each other because I could not remember what he looked like.

I walked down to Yorkschlosschen. The head was not very clever. Normally I sit inside but I sat outside because I thought I might be easier to find.

Some time went by. A navy blue trenchcoat stopped at my table. Its occupant was someone I had never seen before.

Hi, I said, shall we go outside?

So I must have sat inside. He said he would like to go outside. We sat at a table in the open air. There is a slab of slightly wavy chestnut brown hair falling from a side part to the jaw, and chestnut brown eyes, and a curling red mouth, it is my idea anyway of a 19th-century Russian. I imagine him galloping about the Caucasus or strolling up and down the Nevsky Prospect in a wasp-waisted uniform, challenging people to duels. Another time, another place.

His clothes here now have the look of animals adopted from a pound, abandoned mongrels with engaging personalities taken home by a soft-hearted punter, still beside themselves with joy to be off death row. The trenchcoat lies obediently beside him on the bench. There is a navy-blue lambswool v-neck pullover worn inside out, and a pink shirt with the tails out, and some very torn industrially darned jeans. This is the feeling: of happy pets that have followed their master to Iran, Iraq, Kurdistan, Kyrgystan, Pakistan, Cappadocia and now they have come on another outing. Wasp-waisted uniforms and boots with fringed tassles were the last incarnation.

This is all interesting but it is not my idea of a conversational gambit. Here is a waiter to the rescue.

I: What are you having?

He: A beer, ein Bier bitte,

Waiter: Grosses oder kleines?

He: Gross.

I: Ein grosses Bitburger, bitte.

That seems pretty sociable.

He: I like saying Gross, it's how I feel about things, Gross, alles gross, that urban US teenagerspeak disgust bla bla bla

I say: It's great that you didn't get blown up.

He says: Yeah, yeah, I did my best but everyone liked me too much to kidnap me. Would've been great for my career. It's strange being back in the booby of Berlin.

I say: Have I really seen you before? I couldn't remember what you looked like and now that I see you I still can't remember your looking like this. Were you wearing this body last time we met?

He says: Think I may have lent this one to a friend. I was too tired and emotional to know what I was doing. I'm trying to channel Gogol through a similar haircut, woke up the next morning and it was Lermontov and not covered by the insurance and the nose was missing, AAAAAAARGH (drinks beer which has arrived then says more calmly) I was thinking of bringing a book but it seemed too much like bringing a prop or a calling card, you know, prominently displaying Deleuze/Guattari, like, Hey! Look what I'm reading! I'm an intellectual! Or adopting a cool stance, carrying the significant object tucked inconspicuously under one arm, and then it's just all too much, deciding what to display inconspicuously

I say: I would have brought Adorno but I don't have that book here.

It's not easy thinking of things to say but he does make me smile. The navy pullover has the look of a dog that is happy to bide its time, knowing its master is going to get into some interesting trouble sooner or later.

He says: So, the biz, how does this work, do they have some kind of quota of books they buy each year, or?

I say: I don't think so.

I say: If they see something they like they'll always buy it.

I say: But it's very seasonal. There's the Frankfurt Bookfair in mid-October, that's very big, and the London Bookfair in mid-March, and others that are not so big, there's a bookfair for children's books in Bologna.

I say:

The bookfairs are when all the foreign rights are sold, so people won't look at a manuscript if it's too close to a fair, and if it does come in at the wrong time it becomes part of the backlog so there is a prejudice against it.

I say: People go away in the summer. They go away at Christmas. They go away for obscure local holidays.

I say: They don't like to come back from vacation and see a manuscript that's been there for weeks. Even a three-day weekend is fraught with peril.

I say:

A good agent can help you stay out of the publisher's backlog but then there's the agent's backlog.

He says: So what do you think, I really just want some coin so I can, you know, keep moving, do they see it as an investment? They see a writer they like, they put up some cash so he can go on with it?

I say: No. Not normally.

I say: If Simon likes something, though, he can do a lot for it.

I say: The only thing is, he is completely untrustworthy, so I don't know, maybe I've fed you to the sharks.

The beers come. Round two. I drink mine. The talk about the industry is bad for my head but of course he needs to know these things. He asks a lot more questions but I can't remember them now.

He tells me he went to journalism school in Sydney.

He says: In Australia there's this compulsory friendliness? You try to talk about metaphysics and people say Don't be a downer. You try to talk about Dostoevsky and they say Look, the sun is shining. We can go to the beach. What's the matter with you? They lie there sunbathing like these reptile creatures.

He says: I wasn't planning on going to Iraq, but I was in Amman and there were all these taxis lined up and these people talking in Arabic and pushing me into a taxi and I just sort of thought it would work out (*drinks Bitburger*), I thought, why not show some initiative, good for the old CV, the last frontier for masculinity being OK, and it ended up going to Baghdad. So yeah! (*drinks Bitburger*) I probably wouldn't go back there now because the security is so much more expensive. Too many people like me there. Freelancers looking for adventure. It's a shock at first. (*dBb*) I went to talk to people on the first morning and I said to one the journalists, 'Where's the suicide bomber?' and he said 'You're standing in him.' So I looked down and there was blood on my shoes. And these bits of bone and flesh. I can still remember the smell of burning flesh. So yeah, yeah, (*dBb*) but then you get used to it, like, a bomb goes off, but unless it's big and kills at least five it's not worth leaving your drink. (*dBb*)

I should say something but I'm not used to this much talk. I drink my Bitburger, the beer which will be served incognito at the World Cup because Budweiser is the official sponsor but Germans don't like Bud.

He says: It was strange being there, there was this Australian businessman, Douglas Wood, who got kidnapped and it was big news in Australia because suddenly they had their own hostage. I'd had a few drinks with him so I was interviewed on ABC, the interviewer says so what you're telling me is that he was well-liked, gregarious and passionate but not a risk-taker, and I said something like, well those are your words but what I would say is he was a businessman trying to take advantage of the opportunities, but in the transcript they printed all the 'ums' and 'ahs' and 'you knows,' because of course I'm weighing every word, what I'm thinking is the fucker was a fucker, he was another businessman there to participate in the rape and pillage of a former sovereign nation but obviously you can't say that when he's been taken hostage. These people are treated as if they're philanthropists but they're Cheney's vultures. Then when he was released he milked it in the most crass Australian way (*dBb*), photo op with PM, his favourite footy club, TV interviews, celebrity game shows, book deal (*dBb*)

He says: But here I am just exponentially jabbering on, tell me about you

His voice was not like the voice on the page.

When you go to a zoo you often see that it has bulked out the collection with examples of some not very interesting animal—one that is easily caught and transported or breeds successfully in captivity. So you walk up to a cage and it holds a pygmy rhinocerus, and then you go on to another cage and it holds a pygmy rhinocerus, and you go to the next cage and what have we here? another pygmy rhinocerus! and as soon as you work out that you're in a whole room of pygmy rhinoceri in captivity you're on to the next room

It's depressing. The first pygmy rhinocerus has to be there so visitors can see an example of a pygmy rhinocerus. The second, third, fourth, fifth . . . nth is there so visitors can say, Oh, it's just another pygmy rhinocerus, let's see what's in the next room.

So perhaps you can imagine that someone goes one night to the zoo and opens all the cages. Lions and tigers and cheetahs and armadilloes roam Regent's Park and the three-toed sloth moves 2 mm on a branch in a cage with an open door and there is a stampede of pygmy rhinoceri. This was the way of his writing, that even ordinary words went on rampage, the articles and prepositions and conjunctions that sulk at the back of sentences. Perhaps it's a madman, someone who breaks into pet shops and laboratories and circuses, and now there are chinchillas and gerbils at large, there are rhesus monkeys missing a kidney or frontal lobe, there are blind rabbits and beagles with weeping sores, there are tumorous mice, rats and guinea pigs in their hundreds of thousands, and then there are the beasts with their party tricks, the unicycling elephants, the parasol-twirling bears, the tigers that leap through rings of fire, there are the monsters, the machines, the succubi, the griffons and basilisks and chimeras and talking toasters, the ventriloquist's puppets, the chess-playing waffle-irons, the vacuum cleaners that tell fortunes and remember birthdays, there are goldfish and piranhas in the Thames.

That was not at all the way he talked. That was the voice (but voice is exactly what it wasn't, you'll say) on the page, and of course there is a question. There is more to making a book than

But then there are so many books full of words with docked tails.

The mind is eavesdropping now anyway on something else, because he is very likeable. The mind is watching how that's done. I drove so many people crazy; I need to find a way to be likeable and this is how it is done.

He says: So, Niagara Falls, you crazy or what?

I finish my Bitburger.

I say: Too many people talking. I run out of sentences.

I say: I used a lot of sentences on my contract.

I say: I wanted to have some Arabic in my book, show readers how it worked? Because the script looks like squiggles, people get nervous?

I say:

But it's technically complicated, if you use the wrong software it looks sloppy and amateurish and puts people off.

I say: So I negotiated a contract that gave me final approval of software, technical support, the right to typeset it myself, and they agreed to that, they signed the contract, but I couldn't get them to do it.

I say: So I ran out of sentences.

—You mean like that map you sent me? I like that, it's cool.

— I know, there's something about seeing Ohio in Arabic, what was that county in Ohio, was it Clark County? that decided the election?

—Along with Florida

— Along with Florida, well, of course in some sense everyone knows, it's a global power, these swing districts

I have almost run out of sentences now. I raise a hand for the waiter, Noch zwei Biere, bitte

so I was thinking even if it didn't go in a book I should put something on a website, the British Army gives soldiers one day of language training the American Army not even that and it has to be dangerous and disorienting being in this environment where you can't

—Yeah, you see these American soldiers, they're incredibly polite and courteous but it's like, shoot anything that moves

—The only problem is to get things on the website I have to talk to my webdesigner

—She doesn't speak English?

—She does speak English, yes, yes she does, she's very fluent, she explains fluently that she can't do technically tricky things for me and won't show me how to do easy things myself, which replicates the whole publishing, *admittedly Niagara Falls is a long way away but there's a place in Berlin that is both close to hand and not tainted with banality* is not a good thing to say, I don't say it, I can't think of a good substitute but I say

—So anyway

waiter puts down two beers

oh danke, cheers

—Cheers

—I had some ideas for introducing the script to people who are new to it, basically just spelling words people already know in Arabic to introduce the letters before moving on to the actual, there's this, for instance (I take a plastic folder from my bag and put Exhibit 1 on the table).

He does not look surprised, exactly, no, but

He says: So, you carry this around with your hand luggage?

He draws the folder toward him.

He says: Hey, cool, so, let's see, so this is n, yeah, cool, maybe

I say: I know, I wasn't sure, this is a sample verb (Exhibit 2)

I say: I think maybe it's easier for beginners because it recycles the same letters, there's a slight problem because in the papers they don't print the short vowels,

I say: you're expected to know from the context, but the main thing is to recognise recurring patterns around a three-letter root, KTB is writing, QTL is killing, that kind of thing, I did some examples, see, maybe this is better? (and there are 10 or 12 pages to show the wealth of material)

and he says: Yeah, maybe that's better, yeah, cool

but this is nothing like the e-mail from a stranger, I should have stayed home, it's too complicated

I say: Or one could use a completely different approach,

بريتني	Britney
بريتني	Britney
بريتني	Britney
بريتني	Britney
بريتني	Britney
بريتني	Britney

He says: Yeah, cool, all *right, okay*, so you can pick out each letter, yeah, cool, I like that, only I hate to say this but Britney is passé, it's Angelina they want, but yeah, cool, only, don't the letters, the problem is they change depending on where they are in the word, so you

I say: Well, they mainly have just two forms, one for the beginning and middle of the word and one for the end, I thought that was fairly clear from Exhibit 1.

He says, Yeah, okay, yeah

I say: But maybe it's easier if you start people off by giving them outlined letters to colour in the idea is, you could give people a text all in outline and they could colour in the remaining letters, if you had it in a book it would be something for children to do if they got bored

He says: Why would they do that?

I say: Didn't you colour in pictures in books when you were a child?

He says: No, not really, I mean, we had colouring books, but

I say: Well, this is just an example

نيو يورك	**New York**
بروكلين	**Brooklyn**
نيكسون	**Nixon**
بيروت	**Beirut**
بَغداد	**Baghdad**
أساما بن لادَن	**Usama Bin Ladan**

This is in the Kufic script, again, *(dBb)* but I have it in Baghdad somewhere if you want to see

He says: No, that's fine, this is great, cool, I get the idea, yeah, cool

I say: And then you could either practise writing out the words or do an exercise spelling English words in Arabic letters *(dBb)*, it would be something to do in an airport waiting room, and then if you see a word in other fonts you probably recognise it in *Mao II* DeLillo has a character taken hostage, fantasising about learning Arabic and communicating with his captors,

I say: with all due respect to DeLillo this is not something to leave to the last minute *(dBb)* *(and hey reader, you could use the inside cover at the back of the book to practise while you wait for your doctor / dentist/hair stylist/bus/train/plane—and hey speculator, you could buy up 20 first editions and keep the inside cover pristine, secure in the knowledge that many a reader will have written on the inside cover rather than on a separate piece of*

بيروت
بيروت
بيروت
بيروت
بَغداد
بَغداد
بَغداد
بَغداد

paper, thereby enhancing the value of clean copies at auction)

He is saying Yeah cool but he is not snatching up a pen. Quelle surprise.

& all this time I'm seeing pages in my head, thinking I see the way to do the book I was going to do for Simon

not seeing how to do it without the promised designer

I know what I want to do but the machines get in the way

thinking that each page segues smoothly into another page but no page ever segues into

I say: Did you know that Edward Said's son grew up knowing no Arabic?

He says: No, I didn't know that.

I say: He had to go to the Occupied Territories to learn it after he grew up.

(*Both drink Bitburger.*)

I say: So the point is just, if you had done the exercises you would now be able to recognise at least 6 of the 28 letters, which could stand you in good stead if you were kidnapped.

He brings his octopus manners to bear. Perhaps you know that the octopus can mimic any environment? Perhaps you know that the octopus is unsurpassed as an escape artist? An octopus can escape through an opening the size of a penny; it can escape from a sealed cigar box. I do slightly feel like the sort of prankster who places an octopus on a red tartan rug to see if the animal can do plaid.

He says: Hey, have you ever been to Kim's Korean Karaoke? It's around the corner in Mehringdamm? I think I was thrown out for drunkenly singing too loudly or maybe just dancing, Kim doesn't like people dancing, or possibly dancing on tables, but this is behind us now, shall we call the waiter?

I say: Sure, but this is on me and the waiter is there with the bill and I pay and we leave and the air is soft and I feel happy and hopeful, as if I've walked into the floating world of Utamaro

En attendant Mr Coogan

X-Originating-IP: [217.83.53.224]
From: "Ilya Gridneff" <anarchicus@hotmail.com>
To: Helen.DeWitt@gmx.neet
Subject: 5=50=500=5000
Date: Mon 25 Sep 2006 11:21:18 +0000

Ms dewitt,

YES! Thank you for your endless insight and ever spirited criticism on various ins and outs of my life, yes, indeed it is a tough battle with the gridneff code but well, who knows, what comes forth, perhaps its i just don't translate my experiences accuratley enough thus leading to… 'in defence of x, y or z…'

I read YNH and have to say was a little concerned regarding the representation of my dear self. Not wanting to stretch it too far but is my fragile ego/narcism displayed by concern with dialogues of 'yeah cool,' 'yeah, cool?' or is this the *joke*? Always a tricky terrain, for sure, other people, but perhaps, um, well maybe I can add (retrospectfully) each word to be seen as a thoughtful piece of golden wisdom, witty and poetic, every breath, no, no, I get it but was a little concerned as the CNN story figures in my *Baghdad to Britney* (work in progress) and some other stuff too, so technically felt intellectual property rights may have been infringed! Can you infringe your own intellectual property? Regulary? i guess.

As well, i think i can make myself sound far more spectucular in playing down how specTACKular my life was/is/could be in ficiton, but send the fucking thing to the powers that be and let's make a fucking million!

Sorry, this is a Piers Morgan inspired email. I have been loving his book and will recommend it on to you, if you are outraged at my hack stories, the man's lack of self-awareness in this tale of hyperbole is at biblical proportion. It astounds and will show you how little plankton i am, a lol-read for many reasons intended and missed by the author.

I sent eva berg the first 75 pages of *Drinking Bleach* and a short synopsis. SO, well fingers crossed. I was offered to clean a friend's office toilet just a minute ago - perhaps a better reprsentation of it all...

love love and nice you dropped in the other day - i(will re-read the ritter sport comment but i think what i mean is when you ask how much cash do you need? I say oi, not much and if you gave me 50, i coiuld live off that but if you gave me 5000 i could probably spend it in the same period of time. that's all, representative, I guess the cost of sex, alcohol, food, breathing, etc etc... but more of this later, have to get some well porportioned lunch,
ig

From: Helen.DeWitt@gmx.neet
To: anarchicus@hotmail.com
Subject: RE: 5=50=500=5000
Date: Mon 25 Sep 2006 23:02:16 +0000

Ilya

well, you can always rewrite your dialogue when it's finished, nearly there, got an e-mail from an agent who loves the book, loves yr voice, loves the idea of doing for Arabic what Tolkien did for the languages of the elves and dwarves, says she thinks it will be PHENOMENAL, so alles klar, everything is under control

is the name ok? have drafted an e-mail from you about names, perhaps you could go revise if it's not what you would say

helen

From: "Ilya Gridneff" <anarchicus@hotmail.com>
To: Helen.DeWitt@gmx.neet
Subject: saving face
Date: Tues 26 Sep 2006 24.02:22 +0000

dewitt

Yes! Great. maybe even if you write some of 'my' writings this adds another layer of intrigue or mist-ery. perhaps its all a sham and i never existed; i am a construcktion of dewitt's brillance, perhaps Dimitri Ivanovich Pisarev or Kraptokin as is in Bernhard.
ok well i finally watched seven samuari. wow what a great survival, death cheats me/ us again.
I know i am avoiding the desired page or two of dialogue but feeling strangely ambivalent to my own desires to sound 'besser'. will do. well do.

ilya

10

Sweet & Sour

Remember, the person playing your game is playing it for fun, not for work. If you want to have slicing blades pop up from the floor of your Incan temple, make sure that you put some blood splotches and body parts around the exact spot that the blades spring forth, so that the attentive player won't be killed. Even if the player is killed, he'll think, "Oh, I should have seen those warnings, how stupid of me!" instead of "This game cheats! How was I supposed to know there was a trap there?"

Cliff Bleszinski

Mad Max

1

From: "Dmitri Pesarev" <downfromzero@hotmail.com>
To: GillianBlake@aol.com
Subject: the silent violent violet of communication
Date: Mon 5 September 2005 13:19:22 +0000

Hey, back in the haupstddady, the boooby of berlin and alles gut. und dir? how is the tenor of London these fine wine and windy days...

Much to report, should we do it in real time, phono liveness at some point soon? shall i call?

What to say so far, the buses of I-ran are the rejected Mercedes Benzs of Germany circa 1970s, unsafe and no doubt unreliable for the contstrictness of the german diet and while one culture races to the nuclear future another looks forr sensible safer recycling options...such is life back under European law.

well i met rachel zozanian in berlin last night and as ever everything began well.

while maintaining a cool detached tone she talked a lot about the bizness aber mit ... Pinchteresque. .... Pauses.. alles seemed harmless as she outlined some previous dodgy deal and peoople i should met & never meet to get my writing moving along. well everything started well and she likes to drink, i noticed that which perhaps is not a good idea with my competitive edge and well not exactly sure what transpired, no. in memory i see foggy new wave moments of noir shadows, grainy out of focus lens linked to boozing at this impressive rate. Well, i guess to defuse the intensifying microscopic detail of conversation i suggested and we ended up in kims karoke, & here things got more interesting or wilder wider, some pastiche of modern living, karoke machine, neon lights, faux trees, mirrors and uncomffortable corners, what if the singer got stuck not the cd. i am impressed by any person who passionately bangs the table mid rant about the inequities of modern living - & this I remember - when in a karoke bar. surrounded indeed by such splendor. as such this is another karoke bar i have been asked never to revisit,

have to read this book of hers, have you, *lotteryland* or some others, i mean fucknficking hell she claims to have written more, five books, she claims more but i couldnt keep up...ten books by the age of 23, in line with Blair's claim he could drink 14 pints of lager when studying at Oxford.

... well am sure wwhat the outcome of all this will be, cant remember how the night ended up, i remember her terrible rendition of 'hello goodbye' which show a cunning devious par excellence in her gate for it actually just contains a chorus repeated. quite clever when you think about it. karoke strategy? Well i dont know what happened, i remember getting physical in the hinterhof, howling to the moon, did i get into a fight with someone, i remiss, blackness, darknes, night streets lights, passing cabs, waking dresseed from last night in a state of once again unknowing..i was never good at interviews.

oh dear, halp.

dmitri

X-Originating-IP: [84.190.97.123]
From: “Dmitri Pesarev” <downfromzero@hotmail.com>
To: “Rachel Zozanian” <zozanian@onetel.com>
Subject: I don’t turn up to my own funerals
Date: Wed 07 Sept 2005 12:19:44 +0000
Rachel,

Thanks and how thorough it becomes. i enjoyed our night together very much. have intentions to repeat anew. please, to be honest (i love this little idoim - it is like everything else is not honest but now i am being honest etc etc .. which there becomes un true- so it is a double lack exposing one’s false intentions. Perhaps and maybe?) i am alright with all the names and contacts etc - while i am not forming any single white female stalkerish qualities focused primary on yourself- i am relaxed about my need to permeate higher along the food chain- your support is sweet but a certain ambivalence/arrogance leads to knowing, insullah, -patience will bring it right and i need to fulfil cliched sufferance first or loger before the transulcent glow of published success...

and in the end i didnt get to leipzig. the friend became super sick and i slept till the time to go but was in no state to leave. been drinking vodlka and apple juice and watching films. couldnt find *Brazil* at the video store. but bill murray suffices in broken flowers and rushmore...

yes, i am collating and writing and will send the bizzniz to those who have mentioned. perhaps you to and you can pore/pour over golden honey word - was thinking maybe something inflammatory about islam- indeed homosexuality- could see a fatwa put out on me - increasing rocket space like sales. everyone in the Brazil-esq book making machine satisfied...while I disappear into the depths of another adventure. elsewhere. well it goes and it goes...hope you are well thoughts for round two?
dmitri

From: “Dmitri Pesarev” <downfromzero@hotmail.com>
To: Gavin Howard
Subject: banga
Date: Fri 9 Sep 2005 21:44:01 +0100

Gavin all good in berlin. drinking and writing, in that order. odour. Just wanted to say will be back in london from wed 28th for who knows how long. when do you head off to bangaldesh!? i am very excited about this. you? will you be teaching them fly fishing, cricket or teaching them other skills of yours?

something i thought i might add - the powers that be, invisible and textual machinations at this point but no doubt if one is to trust the letters in front there seems something somewhere, someone thinks something, a sniff, they are interested in looking at my writings. it is all talk at the minute but one thought i and they had were linked to some of these ‘wacky’ emails i have sent. it is funny cause i remember you discussing this with me about Sarah etc. Well, maybe when you have a minute you could send some back- anything particularly rememberable would be great. i know this would be a big chore but could lead to something good.

So, will we be cracking beers together in london?

ok well tell me what is hte latest in the Kings fund? i cant believe your bike died – I know you were good friends, so thoughts with you. you are back on the road with the new? how is Mary? ok well well miss your black eyes

From: “Dmitri Pesarev” <downfromzero@hotmail.com>
To: camillajerwood@gmail.com
Subject: wunderbear
Date: 10 Sept 2005 08:19:23 +0000

Yes i realise these requests are like the proverbial finding of hay in needle stacks....to be honest i dont really k-now what is best. if you wish to send something to London that is a CD than the best address is

24 Neville Rd
London E8

but apart from that i kind of shudder at such requests. relationships. dont spend too much time. well drank till the sun shone above my head all weekend. even took off my clothes next to the remaining berlin wall. then as tourist buses arrived scarpered into a taxi. something very berlin about leaving dark rooms in the middle of the day to be attacked by a sea of strikt german stares.. spoke erbrochen deutsch and watched a nation's election going to stalemate. bits and pieces afoot....hope you well. back to london soon. looking forward to the fight.

Dmitri

From: "Dmitri Pesarev" <downfromzero@hotmail.com>
To: suzannedarieussecq@gmail.com
Subject: schlaffen
Date: Wed 17 Sep 2005 14:02:58 +0000

she appears amid the fuss of Teen Beauty SEXUALLY-EXPLICIT: Teen-Beauty Newsletter ok sounds good- wow schlaffen in the rock stars bed encased in a tomb of sweet sweat and rock n roll- is Matt the young guy or the (former) partner of Liz? is this Blocparty or Lady Fuzz? i like the drummer. not in the Genet way but he is sweet and funny and a good musician. G-unit. does that mean if i take we will be living together for a month? when Jesses room was offered i thought about grabbing the task, then amongst the peril of finance, bert and ernie, such cardboard box thoughts about the loop or the spiral of alyosha - living together - tense and polite- good nacht/nackt off to schlafen.. please don't be demure at midnight. dragging her fingers, caressing the Agamben reader she lingers a moment at the kitchen door with light shining off her g4...i actually found the height a little difficult. drank like a soldier last night but the difference is fine spirits and cocktails as

opposed to beer and there is a nice clean ring to the air this morning. met a girl-' hip hop battle mc' - straight out of the gilded halls of Bremin who was schlafen in her car (on tour) - she didn't like Biggie smalls nor Blackalicious refused to drive to Po(o)land came home with the offered bed yet prefered to sleep on kitchen's couch. after vodka and absinthe. she left in the fog of mo(u)rning. i was supposed to go to Hamburg today but it didnt happen. he has stomach cramps and it is best to resist. they have organised hitch hiking here. online. "mitfahrgelegenheit" what a great wrord. she left leaving a nice note - saw new jarmasch film broken flowers - bill murray dryly navigating his way through a litany of past lovers/it was ok but i wanted more./ not so sure about JJ, a poor man's Casavettes?/ fake arse pimps- hustlers, been there done that- if you feel me say- holler at me- i cusss like crazy- sorry hip hop streaming through the rich wireless informationized air...BBC WE-WE-WESTWOOD!!!! ok thanks, betters sounds good - just worked it out no we wouldnt be living together. But strategically aligned, always but geographed by 4/4 rock n roll...but how much is the month?
dmitri

From: "Dmitri Pesarev" <downfromzero@hotmail.com>
To: disputin@hotmail.com
Subject: I murdered a stone - hospitalised a rock
Date: Wed 18 Sept 2005 18:37:43 +0400

hope you in the saddle firing off as one would expect and hope. i am collating and doing and now need your assistance - self indulgent as it may be but if you have time or the proclivity can you search through the recesses of your inbox and send a few emails i wrote to you back to me. see it as textual bricolage.

now these would be aiming for publication in the greatest book of the 21/22/23rd century though somewhat shifted from perspective from you dear reader- to a more impersonal other of no real accord. So, you and i know...but i guess we can discuss this in purpose/person... like collecting shells along a seashore.

for *drinking bleach* i am also including the story where you jumped off the bus to rush over to Rory's (number 2 at brixton) and after a long story I ended up smoking crack and heroin on Cold Harbour lane. nice romantic one amid the cliché torpor of sarf London, innit.- where i fragiley wonder back and sleep in your bed. no names but a true story of love in dirty london love etc...consider we are all adults and more responsible to the strength of street knowledge and literature than ficto-facto dominos . . . thoughts?

Well, it is all a mess at the moment – as ever - at the end of the days i become very anxious and self-hating especially now considering literature as an avenue to salvation- strange feelings layering the egoism of the writing. Layering the anxious/self hating machines fuelling ego etc etc...is it just repeative? .well strange times..it has to be a trilogy to all make sense - i think... at different points of time, unsettling memory past, present, futured -- writing/. wanking a lot – dispersion always in a non hierachical distribution of eternal return- like leaving a trace, stained sheets. ok hope you well.

you will see more - london soon

dmitri

From: "Dmitri Pesarev" <downfromzero@hotmail.com>
To:"Rachel Zozanian" <zozanian@onetel.com>
Subject: all silent on the western front
Date: 19 Sep 2005 14:54:33 +0000

Rachel,
YES! Hey hope all well, just thought I'd email again as i havent heard nuffin for a week or so and well know your aversion to the phone. well, i hope you are able to live with the shame of being barred from your local karoke bar/ i have learned to live it. love it,. i enjoyed our night immensly!

so well, again, keen to meet at some point but perhaps in more sober pursuits, ok well look forward to hearing from you soon.

dmitri

From: "Dmitri Pesarev" <downfromzero@hotmail.com>
To: GillianBlake@aol.com
Subject: dr jekyll & mr hyde
Date: 21 Sep 2005 24:01:01 +0000

Gillian
ok um, need some schloraly advice, if you cant remember what happened the last time you were with someone and then after two emails to them and nearly two weeks of not hearing from them, would you assume the worst? (& if assuming the worst is it inappropriate to suggest using a wurst pun?) that is something gravely troubling me at present. not the pun or need to pun but the possiblity i have committed homicide in a moment of jouisannce? ah, i havent heard from zozanian since our first meeting and actually dont feel so great. considering how drunk i was we were and the lack of recognition the following day of what the fuck..??

i have checked all the newspapers and there hasnt been any grizzly murders or young bodies found (though a 101 year-old man was sexually assualted in his stairwell by a blonde woman with big breasts!) but well i dont have the number to call, she's a bit a reclusive and well do you think i just fucked everything up again? i mean this is the same feeling after my first meeting all those years back when i ddint get any response to my emails and small publication and i thought she just thought i was some perverted london syko with literary aspirations, she reckons she kept it in her inbox and occassionally referred to it in moments of literary doubt...well doctor what has happened/ should i fear the fear?

dmitri

Rosencrantz

You're reading *Your Name Here,* the new novel by Helen DeWitt. You don't like it as much as the last one because it has quite a lot of bad language. You don't have a lot of time to read. You got a scholarship to Harvard when you were 18, but you had to go back to Israel for two years of National Service. Harvard required a student visa and an I-20 in the name of Noga Barakh Ohayon; the paperwork had to go through Israel, who said No, no Harvard, you have to go into the Army. Now you're commander of a sniper unit.

DeWitt's first book, *The Last Samurai,* was the last book you read before you joined the Army. You wrote her an e-mail. She recommended *Midnight's Children,* so you went out and bought it. You showed it to your Iraqi grandmother.

You said: I bought a book by Salman Rushdie, he is banned. Is that OK?

She said: I read about him. The Farsi don't like him.

But we like him?

Iraqis hate the Farsi. (Curse words in Arabic)

So we like him?

He is a leftist.

Are we Leftist?

Well, your family doesn't vote, you fools.

So a leftist is a person that votes for the left?

Not always. A leftist is OK. You should read books by leftists if you don't know what a leftist is.

You liked the book, especially the part about the grandparents and the sheet with the hole and the part about that terrible Geography lesson when that dreadful teacher uses Salim's face as a model of India, calling it human geography.

On June 25 Hamas tunnelled out of the Gaza Strip and kidnapped an Israeli soldier, Gilad Shalit, who sat next to you in chemistry class in ninth grade. Israel fired missiles into the Gaza Strip, destroying a power plant. On July 12 Hezbollah kidnapped two Israeli soldiers and fired Katyusha rockets into northern Israel. On July 13 Israel attacked Lebanon. You trained thousands of reservists, getting two hours of sleep a night. You went 75 hours without sleep. The war is over now but you don't think war is ever over. When you meet someone you assess his waist line to know what the ballistic arch would be if he was standing sideways at the line that marks he is about 400 meters away. It's the first thing you do. When you close your eyes you see dead children.

Now you're training Bedouin foot trackers. You are required to use Hebrew. They don't speak a word of Hebrew. You say: How can a girl be stronger than you? You shout at them.

You're reading *Your Name Here,* the new novel by Helen DeWitt, but it's not what you want. You think a work of art should be self-contained, something that exists for its own sake.

You have to go back to work.

Prince Hamlet

1

No word from Simon.

Could he get a job with *Mute* magazine? Send the fucker off.

Silence. You want to say something but you just don't know how. It's late and there are too many things to do. Too many obstacles interfering the communicado. One of them is this, this thing in front of you 'now' (1256am 290905) the projected 'now' of when this will complete its purpose, the project other 'now' is n/a. of little consequence.

This, a covering letter explaining why they/you should/must give/grant/provide me the assistant editor job at Mute Magazine. The deadline is soon if not already past considering the nepotistic media fishnet stocking. You've got three other 'projects' to be completing but, dear friend, others and the other self urge this action. There will be 'reward' beyond stability and inspiration to yer life if such contracts are fulfilled.

Ha! You chortle, cynicism personified, all you can think as another sip of vodka and apple juice, a drag on a Marlboro Red and cathartic slice with rusty box cutter reveals new skin under the calluses' dead skin on the sole of yer foot.

It has been another day in the trenches writing all the news fit to print for Rupert and his lady-boys. Short sharp sentences (Like this one.) a sentence of tabloid journalese. The dirt from the print is still on yer hands, absorbed and slowly strangling the oxygen in yer blood. More silence envelopes the situation before you.

Outside the window Monkeys swinging through the trees sing like choric figures: 'He puts the hack into Hackney.' Damn council, supposed to get rid of the poor and the monkeys. Sure did a fine job with the poor but the fucking monkeys remain.

Another stifling cigarette shifts focus away from today at the Health Professional Council where the sonographer measured the patient's bladder while only partially full, hence committing 'infamous misconduct', as the sonographer wept in the witness box, yesterday's 'eccentric vet who kept 108 German Shepherds in squalor, including their own shit,' sprang to mind followed by the acidic burn of bile rot, a little tighter in the chest today, you think, then as if conception itself, you should apply for the job with that Mute Magazine. Death to that idea, me thinks, jiggling the ice in the glass. <60 vodka:20 applejuice:20 frozen water> HA! You chortle.

In front of this computer's pied piper dream, somnambulism, the incessant hum and streaming internet radio, checking emails every click of a moment like a nervous internet dater, broadband technology shrinking time, every single pixel of information tastier than the last. Why go to sleep, why write a letter when the technology usurps any need for action?

Ethanol driving the Metabolism Highway 101 melts time and such nancy nancy thoughts. It becomes even more self-conscious. How does one describe themselves, how does one describe themselves in a 'covering' letter to potential employers, one has difficulties enough facing the cracked mirror, the askew identity between modernity and post modernity, slippage, I am x to friends and families, aside: always y? to myself.

So, ‘how to’ to someone who will ‘employ’ you, represent above you day to day in the daily trial and submission, nah, it’s not like this it’s a really on the ball piquant piece of paper wrapped together with graphics and text and images - it’ll be a ballast blast. What do you say to someone who will deal with for two fifths of the working week? Do you give them 100 percent or 40 percent of yerself? Maybe quote 50 Cent, get rich or die trying. This hopefully will be two sevenths of the week, they’ll need more than: I build model ships in my diminishing lunch hour and find perfectionism to be my most significant downfall . . . I like bushwalking, scubadiving and playing television game shows at home.

What do you emphasise? I am not too fat nor too thin, (reference to Nikolai Gogol’s *Dead Souls*) do you tell them about the year as deputy editor on the Russian *Mirror*. (See the movement from fiction to fact within a self-conscious narrative? (This may work or fail dreadfully. Other-self)) The English fortnightly international Russian newspaper where you edited, collated and organised economic, political, and cultural news for its 24 pages. Do you mention the book reviews, the film/theatre/art carry on, all the events you covered for the newspaper that was run out of the former Soviet information arm Novosti, then folded and went into the hands of a wanted Russian Billionaire who the British will not return because they know he’ll get knocked off. No, the Russian angle is too conservative for the likes of this lot. All the newspaper skills obtained from working there, alongside the current work for a national news agency sending you to scandalous courts and seedy celebrity corners, provides prestige for stickier corners. Not intelligent magazines you actually ‘engage’ with.

<Yawn> (Me too!)

Well there are the four magazine editions you made all on yer own. The Insinecure limited edition black and white photocopy publishing revolution. Include some of those and express how you want to work with people driven by vision and independence, bang on about yer ideas to improve the magazine, be sycophantic, obsequious and tell them about yer perspicacity. What about all yer friends from RCA, Chelsea, The Slade . . . The time you drank bleach and inappropriately spat it onto the audience at the art event, or the time you walked home through Hackney naked as a protest to various maladies (internal/external), maybe when you got beaten up on New Year's Eve after provoking cocaine media types enjoying the faux punk band playing in the most organised and co-opted spirit. When you argued with Maggie Thatcher in Romford and Tony Blair in Pitsea Working Men's Club (when you worked for the East London Courier). Or said happy 9-11 to Ronald McDonald. Don't mention the War. Fought every day.

Urm?

Yeah what else, drop some names, Bataille/Derrida/Nietzsche/Sartre/Justin Timberlake, suggest you are versed in the current topics of debate or non-debate depending on belligerence/sobriety. You should see my bookshelf. I can read. Mention how all the creative writing 'published', is 'to be published'. The best material regularly published in yer head. Drop that the short stories are coming out next month in various magazines too expensive for you to normally afford (FAD/ Killarmanjaro/Tales/Amujse). Maybe mention the fleeting moment of fame when *The Independent* on Sunday ran your story about Hash Hound Harriers in London. Refer back to university days where a degree in Communications (major Journalism) was obtained while editing the student newspaper Vertigo. Tell them how mum says you are special and very creative. The political actions you've been involved in. How you beat your friend in chess last night setting up the next game as a playoff out of three. Suggest your love of debate and techno-scientific-retro progressive biosphere banter, the growth for sign and signifier if they collared you and said get busy on this sheet, 'Horatio/Caliban, edit away my loyal assistant!' Oh, the simulacrum once again defies and defiles me, oh! The duration of this duplicitous relationship between want and need, between over and under qualified, between give lets talk and fuck off. Beg beg, self denial meets the ego pulsating and saying yes yes and more! It is me you're looking for, I can see it in yer eyes, tell them about your dreams and nightmares, ideas for future stories and events. Tell them about the art events, the people you know, the people you've screwed and be screwed by, tell them you want to swim in this sea of complexities offered and sifted through by that wonderful, wonderful, magazine. Or maybe just never get around to doing it and remain Mute.

Alyosha Pechorin

2

Could he get some coins for a piece he wrote in Turkey? Send the fucker off.

The Barber of Manilla
by Dmitri Pesarev

'I'm a fly fisherman. I love fishing in general but fly fishing is the best. Now I make my own flies and you can use all types of material to imitate the insects. One of the best is hair. All different types of animal fur can be used, from bear fur to dog but the best in my experience is human hair.

About a decade ago I was in Manila working as a contractor for British Petroleum. It was fan-fucking-tastic back then. For five bucks you could get a beer and a blowjob. You'd have these gorgeous little things stroking you, playing with, trying to drag you to your room. We would sit there at the bar drinking beers, getting blowjobs at the bar then doing a bit of work the next day. Fucking great.

So anyways there was this time in Manila when one of these girls wanted to be shaved—something about looking younger when one big paying customer started straying. This isn't really my turn-on but I magnanimously offered to do it for so I could try some of her hairs for my fly fishing.

She agreed, excitedly took me home and stripped. I got onto the job with the diligent motto of doing the job right but despite all efforts and a wonderful sight got bored and cut into her pubes the Nike Swoosh logo. It wasn't clear what she thought at first then she became very excited.

The next day I walked in and found her showing off her branding to everyone in the bar. Her friends learnt I had done the Swoosh and in no time (girls from other bars starting to turn up) queues of girls were asking for happy faces, arrows, and even their names. Demand kept increasing as I did different desired cuts—so much so, it interupted my drinking. But, to be honest, I enjoyed the limelight. So I started carrying a razor everywhere I went. Before I knew it, I had a little kit including nose hair clippers for fine detail.

It was ridiculous—there would be all these young things spread eagle girls in my room cutting off the long pubes with scissors then waiting for their turn by watching cartoons in Filipinos. I can remember the sound of the clipper while the television blared in their indecipherable fucking language. Sometimes it got so bad when I'd wake up in the morning and put my socks on, the floor and my socks would be covered in their fucking pubic hair. In the end the BP contract finished and I moved on to another contract in Angola, where I met my current wife. The pubic hair didn't harness my fishing luck any more than usual and the only really big thing I caught during that period was a seriously infected itch that came hand-in-hand with the plentiful cheap sex on offer for big fish in small ponds. But it's a great life travelling, seeing the world. I love Helicopters.'

ends

3

Or for a piece on Pete Doherty? Send the fucker off.

From: "Dmitri Pesarev" <downfromzero@hotmail.com>
To: "Nick Davies" <Nick.Davies@SundayMirror.co.uk>
Subject: Kate Moss Toss
Date: Wed 5 Oct 2005 09:11:52 0000

Nick,
didn't get anything grand the other day with Baby Shambles. Kate Moss literally told me to 'fuck off,' which was kind of nice in some respects – definitely the most important celeb to be irate with me, so far. i have sent this across thinking it could be a small piece.

Sorry if something has already appeared elsewhere. In terms of pix, there were several agencies and the mirror was there too.

Well, hopefully something useful.

dmitri

Pasty rocker Pete Doherty may enjoy the excessive heights of success, fame and stardom, able to afford eight Jaguar cars in as many weeks, but he still visits pawn-shops.

Haunted by previous wrongdoings, drug addiction and run-ins with the law, the infamous Babyshambles front man was recently spotted leaving an East London hock-shop carrying a black video cassette recorder.

The drug addicted rock star rumored to be back with super model Kate Moss redeemed the machine for an undisclosed sum while his minder waited in a parked gold-jaguar outside Bethnal Green Cash Converters.

Skipper McDougall walking to work on busy Bethnal Green Rd last Saturday said she got the shock of her life seeing Pete Doherty leaving the hock-shop carrying the VCR.

The 26-year-old shop assistant said: „I saw Peter Doherty leaving the Cash Converters on Bethnal Green Rd carrying a video cassette recorder. I thought this was strange as it was an old VCR machine, so large and old looking.

„He walked out of the pawn shop carrying the VCR in his arms and jumped into a gold looking jaguar parked legally outside.

„Someone was waiting for him inside in the passenger seat but it wasn‚t Kate, it was some bloke who I couldn‚t see.

„It was a very funny spectacle for me on the way to work and what was so shocking was he looked so washed out, white, nervous and jumpy. He was wearing tattered clothes and his typical trade mark hat.

„I am not really a fan. I am actually quite bored of his antics and the attention. He was a better musician before and still then wasn‚t too hot.

„It was the middle of the day and I just was shocked how white he was, like a ghost. I live near Dalston Junction and the addicts up there are not as white as him.

„He just got into the parked Jaguar that looked a champagne gold colour. Another girl on a mobile saw it too and seemed shocked but it was so quick, no one else caught the funny sight.

„Maybe he was redeeming it for his mum considering it was around

Mother,s Day. Or maybe it used to be owned by Col Barrett, the front man from the Libertines, whose house Pete broke into and robbed a few years back. But who knows? I thought everyone was using DVD these days.

Bethnal Green Cash Converters employee said: „I know what you are talking about but due to our confidentiality policy I can not make any comments.

Manager Hilary XXX said:

There are 100 Cash Converter stores in the United Kingdom and more than 600 across the world.

Ends

Beth Green Cash Converters 02077294937 (Manager Hilary)

07930965676

It goes and it goes.

4

Or just comments on a piece on Viennese Actionism from his old friend Bagozzzzzzzzzzzzzian?

From: "Dmitri Pesarev" <downfromzero@hotmail.com>
To: "Steve Bagosian" <bagosians@netscape.net>
Subject: incest is best
Date: Tues 4 Oct 2005 10:21:32 0000

Bagozzzian, hope all imagined was retained in yer step north. it is late, i am drinking peppermint tea. looking forward to friday's dance with otto. am dilligently working towards completing an article on this artiface of art... this is the final paragraph..
a thought would be appreciated.

If Viennese Actionist body art was the crisis of individuality against exploitative/ organised and oppressing authorities, from religious to political, in the praxis of post world war 2 anxiety ˆ then surely the seemingly ambivalent coda of contemporary art, in the somnambulism of post
Gulf Virtual War 2, needs to take a big dump too. This colon, constipated with curators and artists, producing more and more effluent in the gentrified toilet bowel of London (,s East End,) seems to have outgrown its function or importance like the Carnival Man,s tale in William Burroughs, Naked Lunch.
A man teaches his anus to talk and eventually the anus takes over the mouth reducing the man a blob of flesh. The anus says: „It,s you who will shut up in the end. Not me. Because we don,t need you around here any more. I can talk and eat and shit,.

Find a cheaper internet access deal - choose one to suit you.
http://www.msn.co.uk/internetaccess

From: "Steve Bagosian" <bagosians@netscape.net>
To: "Dmitri Pesarev" <downfromzero@hotmail.com>
Subject: RE: incest is best
Date: Tues, 4 Oct 2005 07:48:53 -0400

The talking anus is exquisite ending...Hope you will regurgitate more on Friday. I think it's good that you refer to the location and the present. What, after all that surrounds us now, is the relevance of any of that 60's revolutionary rhetoric of meaningful transgression of 'bourgeois norms?'

xxsteve

From: "Dmitri Pesarev" <downfromzero@hotmail.com>
To: "Steve Bagosian" <bagosians@netscape.net>
Subject: Ho Ho Ho
Date: Sun, 9 Oct 2005 13:32:05 -0200

Steve

Cheers bagozzzian, unfortunately haven't obtained my phd yet but interesting to know this is an area of cognition. thanks. thinking larger projects though.

again remember your shawdowy appearance at late past the drunken hour. you know i'm not too good then, but hope you had a nice evening. lost anothermobile which feels like liberation. again.

i am surrounded by amateur porn and green and yellow paper. all for art sake. did you get mail in the end? did i give you a poem? all this simply for recognition and acknowledgement, "IT' has decided, nay forced me to leacve the hobby of scribbling for a while, read i think is the new sport, hopefully will clear the head and make one more resourceful.

hope you well. various contaminets in my life.

dmitri

Use MSN Messenger to send music and pics to your friends
http://www.msn.co.uk/messenger

From: "Steve Bagosian" <bagosians@netscape.net>
To: "Dmitri Pesarev" <downfromzero@hotmail.com>
Subject: RE: ho ho ho
Date: Mon, 10 Oct 2005 11:55:26 -0400

Dmitri,

Got Insenecure. Cheers. Not time to read it yet. Am swamped. Good party by all appearances . Yes, you were gone. But that's fine.

More soon

steve

5

The phone rings. The phone rings. The phone rings.

From: "Rachel Zozanian" <zozanian@onetel.com>
To: "Dmitri Pesarev" <downfromzero@hotmail.com>
Subject: the long hello
Date: Mon 10 Oct 2005 15:58:01 -0100

Dmitri

Sorry for the long silence. Things have been a bit difficult. Too many bad people.

I hope you've sent something to Simon. Not sure how helpful I've been, tried to catch his attention but you didn't ask to be billed as the next Hunter Thompson, that was just my brilliant idea for a pitch. As I think we discussed at Kim's (but I was somewhat tired and emotional at the time) you might be better off picking writers you like, finding out who represents them and getting in touch.

Are you still in Berlin?

Hope all is well

Rachel

6

From: “Dmitri Pesarev” <downfromzero@hotmail.com>
To: “Rachel Zozanian”<zozanian@onetel.com>
Subject: the garret’s eye
Date: Tues 11 Oct 2005 13:26:55 +0000

Cheers Rachel- at the minute i am simply sharpening my masters’ quill- (reference to gogol’s diary of a madman- sorry if this is not klar!) that is humbly committing to my committment-servitude while a great sense of (growing) madness pervades- the underbelly of arrogance.

i am ok- am living in a friend’s london studio for a bit- for the first time living on my own - catching up with old friends who gently tease me as a petty homeless thief that everyone loves, begrudgingly. spending wildly so as if to suggest risk akin to success.

i do wait to see what Simon says; and i will organise the next phase to suit the much lauded ‘ hunter ‘ idea(1). maybe ‘blunder s’ better. i am not discouraged just frustrated at my lack of resisting the pied pipers tune. i was happy sunday painting in a garret - then all of sudden someone said hey those paintings are worth more than your Kellar’s eye- you could earn something to buy new colours and canvases to improve etc- so i get them out to show them to have to (seemingly) replace them back down in the cellar. walking all those stairs with heavy works- etc etc-. i dont know if this is lazyness or romantic visions of a post humous-humus flavoured discovery of such vaults of value. Maybe i cut not one but both ears off...

you did whip me up - which is a first and much appreciated sentiment- so now i am taking it seriously but am not interested in the ‘commercial value’ bizniz bizniz. and your praise makes me reconcile my previously accepted life as lowly hack even more difficult. my life is full of yes from the wrong people. not wrong as incorrect but not those gatekeepers we need to hear the word from.

i just want to get some coin to go off and keep doing what i do without worrying- as you correctly point too and i even referr to in one of the texts-about the 10pt. your pitch of emails etc makes me uneasy slightly cause it is like - what is wrong with me just fucking write 100000 words like that - as i play ping pong in my brain trying to sleep....my friends agree and disagree with some our dialogues... but i know what you are saying. and i recognise you comments and am pleased...just i loathe all this..even me writing this email 'explaining' myself ...and again i know you are trying to help but like when you ask me who i like is a good idea as to who to pitch - it is difficult cause most people i admire, mostly are dead (from suicide or syphilis!).

though i am enjoying your book.

dmitri

ELRNDTYAOTL

14. ADDICTED TO LUCK

1037 SISTER CHECKING ODDS OF DATE WITH MEMBER OF LE BOY

Congratulations! Only 100,000 out of 55,000,000 won Sister Checking Odds of Date with Member of Le Boy in the latest draw! Only 99,000 in your age bracket! Only 5,000 Jews!

I sank back in the chair, exhausted yet exhilarated. It was good to know that my sister, or at least one of my sisters, was all right. And I felt a real sense of achievement. It had been a diabolically complicated draw to set up, even with the draw I had designed for my grandmother as a model, and getting the luck line to produce the relevant statistics had taken an extra three hours. I had tried running a draw for Jewish sister of Jewish brother checking odds of date with member of Le Boy and got a completely ridiculous result, and it had taken a ridiculous amount of time to work out what was wrong.

I noticed suddenly that it was 1037.

I thought: Fuck.

Gaby was coming round after work, so it was not really worth going back to work on my chapter. Should I just put in a few hours on the UEO? Or maybe I should process some of the commercial prizeclaims before Gaby got to them. Or maybe I should do some work on my chapter.

1219 FATHER CHECKING ODDS OF LUCKY BUSINESS BREAK

Congratulations! Only 1,000 out of 55,000,000 won Father Checking Odds of Lucky Business Break in the latest draw!

I sat back, exhausted yet oddly exhilarated. It was good to know that my father was all right. Interesting that hardly any other fathers were doing this, I thought everybody did it. Everybody who came from a moderately unlucky background. Maybe it was the time of day? Maybe most people did it at night when they got home from work? Maybe I could refine the draw to specify fathers checking odds within a 24-hour period?

I noticed suddenly that it was 1219.

I thought: Fuck. Fuck. Fuck.

I thought: This has got to stop.

I said: *Look.* If you want to find out how your family is doing, do me a favour. Pick up the phone. You can find out everything you could possibly want to know in five minutes. There is absolutely no need to spend hours checking up on them with the lottomonitor.

I suddenly thought of a way to find out the odds of a father checking the odds of a lucky business break in a 24-hour period.

I stood up and walked to the window.

It hadn't occurred to me that a lottomonitor could be seriously addictive. It's one thing to run a genuine luck check that may enable you to maximise your luck. But what possible luck-related outcome can you expect from a series of luck checks whose principle informative content relates not to luck but to the functioning of the lottomonitor? If you have a rapidly dwindling £362.33 in the world the likeliest outcome is that you will be out on the street before either sitting the UEO or completing the manuscript that is your best chance of a Golden Ticket.

Hello!
You know, you're a very lucky person.

Suddenly I had an idea.

If I spent the afternoon at the coffee bar with no access to the lottomonitor I could write all afternoon without interruption. I could probably finish the whole section on school! This was quite a tragic part of the story, so it would be good to get it out of the way. And if I wrote in the coffee bar people might think I was an intellectual. Word might get about. It might stand me in good stead when the time came to send it in to this bloke Giles. I was doing myself no good at all sitting indoors beavering away.

You know, the important thing about luck is not what you win. It's what you make it. Because that's something only you can decide. It's what makes it special. Some people make the most of their luck. Others take a more relaxed approach! Whatever you do is fine. The important thing is to feel good about your luck. And make other people feel good about THEIR luck.

Sometimes it's easy to feel disappointed if we don't win the prize we wanted.

I picked up a pen and a pad and headed out the door.

?

??

???????????????????

By the time I got to the coffee bar I was beginning to feel anxious about my luck. I kept wanting to turn back so I could check the lottomonitor. It was ridiculous, because I hadn't run a genuine luck check all morning. But as long as I was in front of the monitor I felt as though I was in touch with my luck. After all, if I suddenly won a Golden Ticket the lottomonitor would override any draws I happened to be running at the time. There would be no way not to know I had won. The whole time I was out in the street I kept having this feeling that I might be winning something at that very moment. I kept having this feeling that it might be crucial to know I had won the moment I won.

I had the feeling I was catching this addiction just in time.

The coffee bar was crowded, in this case probably because people were on their lunch break. I bought a cappuccino and looked for a place to sit but unluckily there wasn't one. I stood against the wall watching the TV. A woman had won a Silver DI.

'Yes well our eldest has had a bit of back luck recently so this will take some of the pressure off,' she began and then her husband frowned slightly and she said 'That is, it couldn't have come at a better time, our youngest is just starting college so it couldn't have come at a better time, I only wish we'd known four years ago but naturally we're very pleased.'

'And how do you feel, Mr Phillips?' asked the interviewer.

'We're very pleased,' said her husband. 'It couldn't have come at a better time. It's a wonderful piece of luck.'

Some people got up at a table outside. I hastily dropped five cubes of sugar in my cappuccino and slipped out the door before anyone else could get to it.

????????

I felt a sudden almost overwhelming urge to go home and check the lotto-monitor. I fought it down. I had come here to work.

I put the pad on the table. I kept imagining this bloke Giles looking at it.

Look, I told myself. Just get on with it, OK? The important thing is to be sincere. Be yourself. Remember, you're you. You're unique.

I picked up my pen.

????????????????????????????

I fought off another urge to go home and run a luck check. I took a sip of my cappuccino.

I was finding it surprisingly hard to get anywhere with the story.

The table next to mine was empty. A woman with streaked blonde hair sat down. She set a cappuccino on the table and rested her head on her hand.

I thought: Right.

????

I put my pen down and took a sip of cool cappuccino.

For once I was glad not to be able to run a luck check. It's bad luck to feel bad about your luck. If I knew for a fact that I had drawn DESPAIR I would feel even worse and it would be bad luck. Whereas if I didn't know what I had drawn I could imagine that I was exaggerating and that I had only drawn DESPONDENCY or perhaps DISCOURAGEMENT and I would not feel too bad about it. It would still be bad luck but it would not be seriously bad luck.

The woman at the next table was crying and wiping away the black tears with a tissue.

A man came out of the coffee bar and sat down at her table. He looked familiar.

She said: Oh God, I'm *sorry*.

She wiped her face again.

She said: It's just that it's so *unlike* Gary. I keep *worrying* about him. Then I think I'm being an idiot, he's probably lying on the beach with some bimbo and it's as if I never really *knew* him, I lost him without having anything to lose and I get so bloody furious and then I suddenly think, well what's the alternative. I'd rather he was shagging some bimbo, but if he is I don't want to waste my time worrying about him. It's the uncertainty. It's driving me insane. You haven't heard anything?

The man looked as though he had heard this twenty times before. He said: Not a word.

I could hardly believe my luck. It was. It was the editor of *Private Eye*!

Of course, if an editor was going to sit down at the next table it would have been better luck if it had been someone else. Tina Brown, say. Piers Morgan. Someone who could do wonders for my career. But the important thing is to feel good about your luck. Here I had been, reduced to DESPONDENCY if not DESPAIR, and in fact if I hadn't wasted the morning on the lottomonitor, if I hadn't decided to come out to get some work done, I would never have sat at the next table to the editor of *Private Eye*! Or, for that matter, the deserted wife of Spamspotter!

Even if there was nothing in it for me it was exciting. It's bad luck to read *Private Eye* but most students do it anyway. How much harm can it do to feel bad about your luck twice a month? And now here was the editor of the unlucky publication at the very next table!

I eavesdropped shamelessly.

We don't seem to be having much luck with our journalists, he said. Gary's the third to have a big win. I'm not saying I blame them for taking early retirement, but it makes life interesting. Funny thing is, I wouldn't have expected Gary of all people to buy DI in the first place. He could hardly talk about it without having an epileptic fit.

I know, the woman said sadly. It was completely out of character. Or at least I thought it was. Sometimes I wonder if I ever really knew him.

???

Before they could say anything interesting a member of staff came up to their table. She was wearing a uniform covered with yellow Smileys and she was smiling broadly.

Good luck! she said.

Good luck, said the woman.

Good luck, said the editor of *Private Eye*.

I'm sorry, the girl said smiling, but I'm going to have to ask you to leave. I'm sure you'll understand.

I'm buggered if I do.

Excuse me, sir, but we have quite a strict face code. We have to enforce it out of fairness to our customers. What people do in private is their own business, but we owe it to people not to make them feel bad about their luck.

My friend's husband has disappeared and she's desperately worried about him.

I'm sorry to hear that sir but as I'm sure you'll appreciate it's not very nice for other people to be exposed to that now is it? Just because one person happens to have bad luck is no reason to pass it on to everyone else.

She's right, said the woman. I know it was selfish of me, I shouldn't have come, I didn't know I was going to get in such a state.

????

The next table was empty. I picked up my pen and frowned.

I remembered suddenly that I was in a public place. I smiled at the page.

11
Who framed Dmitri Pesarev?

During the rehearsal of Who Framed Roger Rabbit, *rubber figures of the animation characters were moved through the scenes in which they were to appear so that both the actors and the camera operator would know the exact trajectory of the animation character. "Then when we shot the scene, we didn't use the figure and the operator [and the actors] would have to imagine where the character was in relation to the dialogue, which was being delivered by an off-camera actor . . ." matting, which does away with the aura, since it does away with the context—making the far and the near and different temporalities intermingle—itself creates an aura, since the gaze of the person looking at the figure that is matted later is never centered but traces a circle of confusion. It is no longer only the cinematographer who experiences and knows how difficult it is to accompany someone in a pan, zoom or even a static shot (distracte); the actor who has to interact within a shot with an element that will be matted later experiences and knows it well*

(Vampires) An Uneasy Essay on the Undead in Film, *Jalal Toufic*

1

Everyone dreams of the Lottery.

There is a film by Mizoguchi, *Five Women Around Utamaro,* about the artist of the floating world. Utamaro lives in the pleasure district of Edo, a world of prostitutes, gamblers, thieves, tattooists; he draws constantly, snatching the moments of this bright fierce world in a thousand woodblock prints. The e-mails of the stranger in a bar were like prints with the ink still wet.

When I met him I thought I had stepped into that violent world, that world where every minute may be the last.

It might have been better if he had killed me. I might hurt you, he said. His hands were on my throat. There was a question in his eyes. They said: How far can we go? I said: How far do you want to go? I was laughing as I said it. Laughing at the iconicity of it all. But I didn't want him to end up in a German jail. He bit my cheek. I laughed. I said: What is this, Hughes-Plath? He said: I don't know what you want me to do. Here was a quick clean iconic end for the taking. I woke up alone in a world where it was business as usual.

It's bad, very bad to deal with the biz, but it has to be done. Everyone must want to see this. I sent e-mails out to people I didn't know, agents, editors of newspapers, and they too were entranced, dazzled, longed for more, he's amazing, they said, why doesn't he write a book, everyone loved this artist of the floating world. So there was a little window of hopefulness, and then there was the longing for a fairy tale, because the Ice Queen does imagine a younger son who after many perils and adventures walks into the palace of ice and frees her from her frozen prison.

One night he sent an e-mail with an attachment, the document he had sent Simon. I opened it avidly, and at first, yes, this was the voice that had possessed me for years, this was that world, here is a Brixton squat party, here he goes home with a girl and smokes heroin, here he takes a late-night bus with a tart with a crack habit, here is the voice that melts the icebound brain.

I read on. I don't know. Here are accounts of deaths he covered at the Coroner's Court for a news agency, and these are in the cold dispassionate prose of Flaubert. Here are other pieces, a writer mainlining Burroughs or Miller or Genet. A writer who can write like Flaubert *and* Burroughs has something bigger than a reader of e-mails would guess, but I don't know how to wheel and deal for it. Not with Simon, not with my sharpshooting friends, not with the betazoid. I don't think you can wheel and deal with Simon by mentioning Flaubert. I think Flaubert is the kiss of death. I think Zola is the kiss of death. I think Burroughs is the kiss of death in the world of wheeler-dealers, which is the only world I know.

He was in London. He had been offered shifts at a paper which turned out not to need him. First he lived on his own, then he was staying with a friend. I wrote something about the world of wheeler-dealers. Something appeared on the screen of the iBook.

From: "Dmitri Pesarev" <downfromzero@hotmail.com>
To: "Rachel Zozanian"<zozanian@onetel.com>
Subject: God is everywhere, even in the adverts for lobotomies
Date: Wed 12 Oct 2005 19:02:47 +0000

Rachel
strange all this talk about commercial viability, gifts etc etc etc, as I have come to the middle of your book outling ephraim and his ideas of winning the book lottery the books i want to write are without bureaucracy -- it seems

inside there it's *lottoland*!! - oh, so now it is once again down and out in london... it is ok, nothing changes in london just your social fludity. positioning and fiscal possibilities moving one around- up and down...my friends are now saying kind words and telling me to forget about the mcdonalds, coca cola britney spears of publishing houses...like muhammad ali they add i am young pretty and mean...i make medicine sick...will have a busy day ahead of coffee, reading and writing, hope all well

#dmitri

2

The head was not clever. It was not very clever. There were thirty-page contracts from close personal friends that were just standard language. There were phone calls from close personal friends offering to mediate with Noszaly on a friendly basis. There were e-mails from Noszaly saying a handshake was good enough. The status of the betazoid was undecided.

3

The stranger in a bar came back to Berlin because because because because because

October was nearly gone and he had not heard from Simon. He had had a flurry of excited e-mails urging Show me! Show me! Show me! He had had 30 days of silence. Meaning what? A betazoid would have called Simon. It was in the lap of the gods.

Perhaps I thought, I must have thought I could step into the floating world.

I must have thought each time we met I would step into the floating world. I had been in the cold too long. I wished I'd let him kill me when I had the chance.

Now we're meeting for coffee at the Junction Bar in Gneisenaustrasse. The walls are blood red, the benches black leather, and he looks hopeful and anxious because he thinks the biz is on the qui vive for writers of genius. He wants to talk more about the biz, it's the old journalist's trick, I think, of asking the same question until you get a more interesting answer. Apart from what I have told him I know that it is inadvisable to call an editor a worthless cocksucker.

I want to tell him to make the non-truth more interesting.

I think there is ash cash to be made. I'd love to think of Plath leaving a clone on the kitchen floor, banking the loot from the black glamour of the dead clone; don't like to think of Hughes living off blood money. But it is not the fault of Mr Alyosha that it can go either way; it's not his fault that looking into the floating world makes me feel the cold. It's not his fault that there is ice in my veins. (Perhaps you can understand this. Although it was not his fault I kept looking at him hopefully as if he might dance on a table or burst into song or pull cuddly vicious koalas from his cracked brown shoe.) If there is ash cash I'd like it to go to a writer.

It was strange talking to him. I was not at all famous, not now, not by the standards of the tabloids. So there was no cash value in anything I said as the words left the mouth, not the way there would have been if Angelina or Posh or Kate Moss had said it. There was something else, something stranger, the power to turn the words to gold. They were worthless now, but craziness might yet bring them into their own.

Meanwhile he talks. He says: I should stop drinking, it would be good to do it, you know in Russia they think beer is a soft drink, there's the attitude that if you're not doing it till you black out it doesn't really count. He says: I don't need it, it's just another way of doing things to excess. He says: I can go into a social situation and people are just standing around awkwardly and I can see how to make it work, 1 2 3. Click. Just like that. But then I want to turn around and undo it, 3 2 1. Alcohol isn't really a way of making it work, it's a way of resisting that impulse to pull it apart again.

The Ice Queen likes this. The Ice Queen likes this a lot. It makes her think of the friendliness and likeability of Joe Mantegna in David Mamet's *House of Games,* it's the con man's likeable way of inspiring confidence by sharing his tricks. The Ice Queen tries to sound human. She says: This is GREAT. This is GREAT. You HAVE to put this in your book!

I love the cleverness of Mamet, his lovely grasp of the easy slippery smoothness of fast talkers, and look, here is this Mametian loveliness lurking just under the Aussie friendliness of my find, kiss kiss kiss kiss.

Anyone can see the way Mamet gets under the skin, it's just there to be seen. But once upon a time he had that gift for getting under the skin and nobody knew about it except the people who knew him. It might be a bit interesting to meet Mamet now, but it wouldn't be exciting, because that edgy, uncomfortable, manipulative talent is something everyone knows about. It's exciting to talk to someone completely unknown because anything could happen.

He says: But then it falls apart anyway, insane things happen that I can't remember, I get up the next day and I don't know what I did. There's this excess, this desire to go to the limit and then I can't remember what happens and I don't know why people aren't talking to me and then somebody else says Don't you remember, you spilled red wine on his suit and he said

This is a Giorgio Armani suit you need to pay to have it cleaned and you said Fuck Giorgio Armani I piss on Giorgio Armani and pissed on the suit, He says: So then I get paranoid, I sense coolness in the atmosphere and I wonder if there's something else I don't remember that they're not telling me, but sometimes it's just people being British and undemonstrative. There was this girl, and, I know this sounds bad, but, it seems I hit her. But the thing is, I don't remember, I don't know what happened. I woke up the next morning and I was hungover and trying to find out what happened and it was all chatter chatter chatter and, maybe it's better not to have these blackouts?

The Ice Queen says: Yeah, maybe, I mean, I'm not saying it's a good idea to go around hitting people and I can see it might be quite worrying to have blackouts, so you could be right, but this is FANTASTIC. This is FANTASTIC. You HAVE to put this in your book! It's like *Memento*, have you seen *Memento*?

He says: I don't think so.

The Ice Queen says: It's a film about a man who can't remember anything more than a few minutes after it happens, and even his long-term memories are rationalisations that he's constructed, I think you'd love it

and I feel very very very good, because there is the additional possibility that an amnesiac serial killer lurks beneath the Aussie friendliness of my find,

Oh yeah, he says, I've seen that. I remember

kiss kiss kiss kiss

He says Guy Pierce is Australian. He was a minor neighbour on Neighbours, just like *Kylie. Our Kylie.*

This is sinister and good, the friendly neighbourhood bloke *looking exactly like* the obsessive note-scribbling memory-shorn [word wanted] lurching from moment to moment, the soap opera backing onto the situationist.

I feel good, after all, reasonably good, in this situation. I can say things I can't say to close personal friends.

I say blithely: If I kill myself you can sell an exclusive to the tabloids!

He says: To be honest? I'm not sure they'd be that interested in a writer.

I say:

He says: If Jade Shaw killed herself they'd be interested. That's a story.

I say:

He says: She was young, beautiful, did drugs, had it all, lost it all, made a gallant comeback. It would be a good story. But I don't know, a recluse, a writer who's been out of the press for over a year, didn't you say you never talk to people?

3 2 1.

I catch the waiter's eye. Haben Sie Jameson's? Super, ein doppel Jameson's mit Eis, bitte, do you want anything?

Um, Vodka mit Apfelsafte, danke.

Not that they'd read her books, and not that they give a fuck, but she's generally loved, or they could say she was generally loved,

0 -1 -2 -3 -4 -5

so it'd be Tragic Loss of Bright Young Thing, Fresh Young Voice Silenced,

-6 -7 -8 -9 -10 -11 -12

whereas if you don't talk to anyone not only do they themselves not give a fuck but the assumption is nobody else gives a fuck either

-12 -13 -14 -15 -16 -17 -18 -19 but here is the bounty of John Jameson to the rescue. I raise the glass to my lips -19 -18 -17 -16 -15 I raise the glass again -14 -13 -12

I used to cover cases at the Coroner's Court. They get suicides every day. If there's a connection with a celeb they might get a short paragraph. Friend of Baby Spice in wrist-slashing horror.

-11 -10 -9 -8 -7 I drain the glass.

I say: OK. You may be right. You may be right. You're the expert. In the *short* term it might not be much of a story. But in the longer term I think you could cash in. Look at the mileage Al Alvarez got out of Plath. Plath wasn't high profile at the time of her death, she was just an obscure mother of two.

He says: To be honest?

-7 -8 -9 -10 -11 -12 -13 -14 -15 -16 -17 -18 I don't think I want to hear this

He says: Don't you think *Ariel* had something to do with it?

-19 -20 -21 -22 -23 -24 -25 -26 -27 I catch the waiter's eye, Noch ein Jameson's, bitte, ja, ein doppel, danke!

I say: Yeah, OK, yeah, sure. Sure. Oh, danke!

I raise the glass to my lips -26 -25 -24 -23 -22 -21

I say: If *Lotteryland* were the only book, OK, maybe the suicide of the obscure reclusive author of a dystopian satire with Lubavitch jokes does not have the same commercial potential

I raise the glass to my lips. -20 -19 -18 -17 -16 -15 -14 -13

I say: But there are lots of other books.   There were, there were some disappearances when I was in my late teens, early twenties,

I wrote quite a lot of books, it's just that the rights are tied up, it's a bit complicated to explain

I think he's saying it wouldn't have been all that iconic if he'd killed me.

I raise the glass to my lips -12 -11 -10 -9 -8 -7 -6 I raise the glass again -5 -4 -3 -2 -1

so I think once they came out it would be perceived as a tragic iconic loss and you probably could cash in on it

He says: Could we not talk about this any more?

He says: I'm thinking of going to Hamburg for the weekend, they have online organised hitchhiking here, it's cool.

4

There's still no word from Simon. Should one write? Call? Blag? Suck dick? Cajole? His room has a long table with a sofa and six straightback chairs along the wall. He's reading Thomas Bernhard's *The Lime Works*. He underlines passage after passage in thick pencil.

> Suppose you make a statement, Konrad is supposed to have said to Fro, only one sentence, say, no matter what it is, and suppose this sentence is a quotation from one of our major writers, or even one of our greatest writers, all you would succeed in doing is to besmirch, to pollute that sentence, simply by failing to exercise the self-control it would take not to pronounce that sentence, to say nothing at all, you would be polluting it, and once you start polluting things, the chances are you will see everywhere you look, everywhere you go, nothing but other polluters, a whole world of polluters going into the millions [you write an X in the margin], or, more precisely, into the billions, is at work everywhere

or this, this is amazing, he wants to recall the manuscript he sent in and make it colder, nastier, more vicious

> It took the fire brigade an hour to put out the fire, Konrad is supposed to have said to his wife, by which time there was nothing left of the tobacconist but ashes, and those firemen really made a shambles of the whole shop, whereupon Mrs. Konrad is supposed to have said: Those firemen make a shambles of the tobacco shop and ruin more than they save. About this remark of his wife's Konrad said he would like to write a book. Don't you see, Fro, he said, women are always saying this kind of thing, and if I were not so concentrated on my study of the auditory sense I would not scruple to write a book about "Noteworthy Statements By My Wife In Response

to Domestic Trivia of Conversation." The Konrads had loved the good-natured butcher and they had hated the malicious tobacconist, as Konrad allegedly reminded his wife, whereupon Mrs. Konrad said: Nihilist! and Konrad instantly realized that the word Nihilist! could have been aimed only at the tobacconist. The tobacconist had done his wife in by slowly strangling her, until he finally strangled her to death, Konrad is supposed to have told his wife, who said: Mutual dependence drives people apart, one way or the other. For the longest time Konrad and his wife had exchanged only the most laconic remarks, Fro says, they barely spoke except to say the absolutely necessary, in the fewest possible words, as Konrad is supposed to have told Fro once, for ages there had been no so-called exchange of ideas between them at all, only words, and now, after all that has happened, Fro says, the chances are that in communicating only by way of the limited range of daily commonplaces and formulas of daily necessity they were communicating nothing except their mutual hatred.

and he has more and more doubts about Zozanian because

He doesn't understand. He reads Miller, Mailer, Joyce, Bukowski, Fante, Bataille, he reads Celine's *Voyage to the End of the Night*, he reads Genet, he reads Burroughs, he reads *Krapp's Last Tape*, why can't he find a publisher who publishes the kind of book he reads? Every single book he reads is a published book. He's not calling up manuscripts in the Rare Books and Manuscripts Room of the British Library, setting them out on foam rubber rests, wearing white cotton gloves to handle the precious pages, thinking WOW, WOW, WOW, nobody has EVER seen ANYTHING like this BEFORE, disturbing the silent travails of the other toilers in the Rare Books and Manuscripts Room to announce the discovery of this AMAZING book called *Ulysses*!!!!!!!!!!!!!! He's not sitting up in somebody's attic, hunched over a dusty forgotten trunk with barely legible notebooks open on his lap, ESTRAGON, *sitting on a low mound, is trying to take off his boot,* plummeting down nearly perpendicular stairs to ask the uncomprehending household WHAT is THIS???????????? only to get the indifferent reply, Oh, that's just some shite of Great-Uncle Sam's, you want it? sure, sure, take it, you'll be doing us a favour, we'll be needing to chuck all that when we put in the jacuzzi-loft-extension, to be honest. He's not reading typescripts he pulled off skips, struggling to read between the bird shit and the fag burns. He doesn't get it. He doesn't want to get it. He reads Bernhard to stop trying to get it.

> his work was everything, the writer himself was nothing, despite the despicable vulgarity of all those who insisted upon confusing the writer's person with his work, the general public had been corrupted by certain historical and literary processes of the first half of the nineteenth century into daring, with the shameless impertinence characteristic of them, to confuse the written work with the writer's personal concerns, using the writer's person to effect a vicious crippling of the writer's work, always shuttling back and forth between the writer's private person and his product, and so forth, more and more confusing the produceer and the product, all of which led to a monstrous distortion of the entire culture, bringing into being a culture which was a montrosity, and so forth, but to get back to the man's writings, reading him was like reading a madman, a writing madman

> The mitten: while watching her knit his mitten he asks himself: Why is she knitting that mitten, always the same one? but he also asks himself why, instead of continually working on that mitten, doesn't she take time out to mend his socks, patch his shirts, his torn vest, all my clothes have big holes in them, everywhere, he said to himself, but she sits here knitting that mitten

The terrible meaning of this passage is becoming klar, he may have to kill to finish the fucking mitten

> Like thousands of others before him, Konrad said he too had fallen victim to a mad dream of one day suddenly bringing his great labor to fruition by writing it all down in one consistent outpouring, all triggered by the optimal point in time, the unique moment for perfect concentration on writing it. And now he would never be able to write it, neither in the prison at Stein nor in the mental insitution at Nierdernhardt; Konrad's book, like Konrad hinself, was a lost cause (Wieser), an immense life work, as one must assume (says Fro, doing a sudden complete about-face) totally wiped out. Here was a failure, owing to a chronic deferment, of the realization of a concept that was basically all there, wholly and flawlessly extant in his (Konrad's) head, as the book was, a perfect, fantastic, scientific work extant in his brain though unrealized either for lack of courage, of the necessary decisiveness, and finally the failure of intellectual audacity;

He gets e-mail after e-mail about the biz from his materialist Muse. Stop. Go away. Come back. Stop. Go away.

5

From: “Dmitri Pesarev” <downfromzero@hotmail.com>
To: “Rachel Zozanian”<zozanian@onetel.com>
Subject: eine Me-Mail von rAndy WhoReHOL
Date: Fri 28 Oct 2005 11:02:53 +0000

i agree with you rachel all the way, and the ruinous nature of kapital itself feeds through me like the worms you describe . another friend was talking of the paedophiliac aesthetic as an appropriate metaphor,,,but i what to read as the full extent of his argy bargy... ‘our fatal shore,’ to be sure, to be sure.. that we will return to nothing, after putrification, etc etc… steadies me in a paradox of wanting in but relishing the outside...though surely the story of joyce et al is far more interesting ‘now’ as it is a romantic rubric finished off and polished by those looking to reading groups for market viability potential...perhaps the act of ‘drinking bleach’ is now the only possible art or form away from kapital’s destructive force pulling and refeulling itself at the outer limits of it’s very idea..does one produce more or less in an already corrupted hall of mirrors?
..i appreciate/share your frustrations and admire your interest in me but by being outside the very system you describe as problematic i gain something you can not... ok well my belly is hunger, so i see you tomorrow... sent off job application to Jersey and Manchester...though will think about Aldersy, (pop 3000, size one and half miles by two miles..golf course) another channel island where the fortnightly paper is looking for an editor...think the shining/wickerman...
dmitri

6

15 November. Six weeks had gone by. He has not heard from Simon. He wants to talk. He does not want to talk.

We meet at Vogt's Bier-Express, prop. Renate Vogt. Vogt's opens at 6:00 a.m. . . . I like it best in early morning. Sometimes I go after working all night, when Vogt's looks like a place where a vampire fits in. Once in a while I wake very early, before the cafes are open, and then I might go to Vogt's for a Duckstein as the sort of thing one can and should do in Berlin. Christopher Hitchens describes Dorothy Parker in late life as a touch too fond of the pre-noon cocktail, and as I dislike euphemisms and clockwatching mayhem I longed to be known as a touch too fond of the pre-breakfast cocktail and resolved to lay the groundwork for this interesting reputation. If I go to bed in the dark and wake up early I think of the pre-breakfast cocktail and the endless last cigarettes of *La Coscienza di Zeno*, and I remember that the German translation has the title: *Die Kunst sich das Rauchen nicht abzugewohnen* (*The Art of Not Giving Up Smoking*). Each morning there was the pre-breakfast cocktail which was to be the first. But which? By the time one has gone through the alternatives it is 9:30 or 10, too late for the early morning glamour of pre-breakfast, and so the PBC, dwindling into the respectability of the merely pre-noon, loses appeal and one goes to the gym.

He doesn't want to sit inside with the pool table, the pre-war advertisements, the disheartened drinkers. We sit at a small white plastic table on the pavement outside.

He talks about blackouts. He doesn't want to talk. He talks about Simon. He doesn't want to talk. He talks about Anya and Ulrike and Pascale and he doesn't want to talk. We meet too often. He doesn't talk the way he writes, and when we meet he doesn't write.

This is dangerous. Too much talk. He says he doesn't want me to wheel and deal, but then he says he wants money.

I order a double Jameson's on the rocks. Faux flames warm the cold heart.

I say: I'm not really the best person to

I say: the point is, we shouldn't have to talk about these things

I say: normally you have someone like the betazoid to make phone calls

I say: things happen because someone who's good at making phone calls makes phone calls

He says: What's the betazoid, is that industryspeak

I say: Not to my knowledge it's a species of humanoids from the planet Betazed

He says: What?

I say: In Star Trek. They have empathic and telepathic powers. They communicate with each other telepathically and they can also sense the emotions of other species. So in *Star Trek: The Next Generation*, for example, there's a half-betazoid, Deanna Troi, who gets called in when they face some alien species in some sort of crisis, and she says: I sense rage, confusion.

He says: That sounds like crap.

He says: I've never watched *Star Trek* because I thought it would be full of this kind of crap.

He says: There are people who learn to speak Klingon. They go to these conferences and speak Klingon to each other. They read fucking *Hamlet* in Klingon.

I say: The point is just, people in the industry don't like the written word as a means of communication so it's quite hard for writers to communicate with them, obviously, since most writers quite like the written word as a means of communication so ideally you have someone like the betazoid to make nice noises on the phone, or someone like Mr Clever to make tough noises on the phone, and people emote back and forth but there is a kind of infinite regress, obviously, because you do have to deal with someone who is emoting on your behalf

I say: The point about *Star Trek* is just

I say: Would you like another drink?

He says: Sure, another Apfelschorle

I say: Back in two ticks

I commandeer the Apfelschorle and another double Jameson's. If you read the correspondence of Fitzgerald, Hemingway, Faulkner, other notorious boozers, you are probably not the sort of person to fritter away your disposable time watching *Star Trek*, which means you are probably ill-equipped to spot the signs of a master of the written word struggling to communicate with a humanoid from the planet Betazed.

The Jameson's and the Apfelschorle arrive. Cheers, cheers.

The Ice Queen has no desire to pursue the subject of betazoids. She makes polite conversation: Do you have lots of these blackouts?

He says: Yeah, yeah, everything to excess, anything after 2:00 a.m. is lost in the traumfabrik

The Ice Queen says pleasantly: I'm not saying that you're a serial killer, obviously, but the thing is, in a text ANYTHING could happen in these blackouts, have you seen *Angel Heart*?

He says: I don't think so.

The Ice Queen says persuasively: It's a film about a man whose heart is replaced with the heart of a damned man. He goes to New Orleans as a private investigator and every person he talks to turns up horribly murdered and he was always the last person to see them alive, I think that's really more interesting than *American Psycho*, you could have a very likeable narrator and, have you seen *Vertigo*?

He says: Yeah, sure, a long time ago

Think of what Hitchcock does with James Stewart, says the Ice Queen, it's like what Leone does with Henry Fonda in *Once Upon a Time in the West* only more threatening, or *Rear Window*, this quintessentially likeable American maybe psychopath is too strong a word

The Ice Queen feels moderately happy. Kiss kiss kiss kiss. This is a well-known story: Sergio Leone said he wanted Henry Fonda in *Once Upon a Time in the West*. Fonda worked hard to look like a villain: he grew a moustache and dyed it dark brown, he dyed his hair dark brown, he wore brown contact lenses. He turned up on the set and Leone was appalled, what he wanted was the all-American blue-eyed boy, Henry Fonda as a coldblooded killer of children. Once he explained it Fonda got it. Fonda was not stupid. He had that gift for performing likeableness and decency in a way that looks uncalculated and unperformed, and he saw that Leone was the first to see that it was a performance. What one wants in a text.

He says: When shall we meet again?

I want to say: But we've just *met*.

12
Knife in the Water

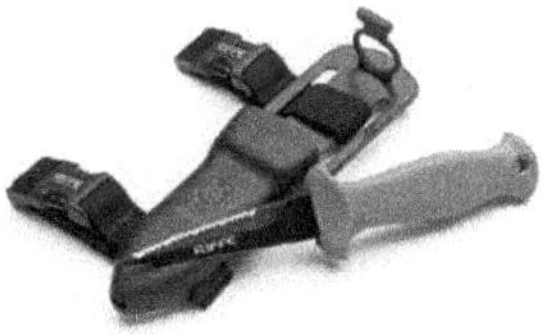

Never force a player to learn by dying

Cliff Bleszinki

AND COOGAN *STILL* DOESN'T GET IT

You're the *star* and you *still* have no idea where this is going. What's going *on*? What's it *about*? Do you want to know the answer to this question?

Your character is wearing the wrong name for the book. He's more of a Krapp or a Kropotkin. Is there any way to get this changed? Every time you ask for changes it goes horribly wrong. Best not to say anything, perhaps . . .

You're living in a fifth-floor apartment in Kastanienallee, Prenzlauerberg. Sometimes you write. Sometimes you read Jalal Toufic, *(Vampires) An Uneasy Essay on the Undead in Film,* Station Hill, 1993, Barrytown, NY.

There's a Ring on the S-Bahn which circles the city. You sit on the train passing from former East to former West to former East. Toufic (whom you are quoting extensively because he says the book got no reviews and basically NOBODY knows about this FUCKING BRILLIANT BOOK except you, you've been told *Your Name Here* will make a million bucks so if you have to prostitute yourself for the sake of DeWitt's art you want to make sure the readers in their pullulating Da Vinci Coded masses know about this FUCKING BRILLIANT BOOK[6]) says:

> If Eisenstein's pathetic leaps are unable to cover the gaps we are dealing with, maybe Vertov's Kone-eye can. Indeed, how stale is Eisenstein's "pathetic leap" compared to Vertov's Kone-eye: "Now I, a camera . . . free of the limits of time and space, I put together any

6. Just to make sure the message gets through we're talking about Jalal Toufic, *(Vampires) An Uneasy Essay on the Undead in Film,* Station Hill, 1993, Barrytown, New York). Buy! Buy! Buy!

given points in the universe no matter where I've recorded them." (the arrogance of everything local, provincial: the news in Oshkosh began with over ten minutes of interviews with Packers fans about their team's win, followed by over five minutes of interviews with Christmas shoppers; only then was the news about the in-hiding Noriega seeking that day asylum in the Vatican embassy, and the capture of Cessaueco, mentioned. Death is cosmopolitan). *[you write in the margin: journalism busy localized nothing)*

Toufic has a new book out, by the way, *Two or Three Things I'm Dying to Tell You,* which DeWitt was going to order for you on Amazon only it all went horribly wrong, whose Product Description on Amazon (written by the dude himself) says: What was Orpheus dying to tell his wife, Eurydice? What was Judy dying to tell her beloved, Scottie, in Hitchcocks *Vertigo*? What were the previous one-night wives of King Shahrayr dying to tell Shahrazd? What was the Christian God dying to tell us? What were the faces of the candidates in the 2000 parliamentary election in Lebanon dying to tell voters and non-voters alike? While writing *(Vampires): An Uneasy Essay on the Undead in Film* and *Undying Love, or Love Dies,* I, a mortal to death, was dying to tell these books' readers and myself about diegetic silence-over, which produces a dead stop and reveals the occasional natural immobilization of the living as merely a variety of movement; and an unreality that sometimes behaves in a filmic manner (for example, lapses in hypnosis, schizophrenia, and undeath permit editing in reality), inducing the undead to wonder: Am I in a film?; as well as a significant number of other anomalies. This new book contains two or three additional things I am dying to tell its readers as well as the poet Lyn Hejinian and myself. Jalal Toufic.

Amazon says: Better Together! Buy this book together with *(Vampires) An Uneasy Essay on the Undead in Film* by Jalal Toufic today! BUY TOGETHER FOR $46.00. Buy Both Now. Since you ask, the price of *Two or Three Things I'm Dying to Tell You* is $20, and the price of *(Vampires) An Uneasy Essay on the Undead in Film* is $26, so buying both now does not actually save you any money, though the $20 book does then qualify for Super Saver Free Shipping (offered on purchases over $25). What are you waiting for, you morons? Buy! Buy! Buy!

Diegetic silence-over. Diegetic silence-over. *Diegetic silence-over,* you fucking morons, the book is worth the $26 for this alone, Jalal Toufic is a fucking GENIUS! Buy! Buy! Buy!

On page 58 you come across *for vampires animal flesh is chewing gum* which you had presciently underlined before you met DeWitt, and there is the mother of all footnotes, footnote 211

> With the concomitant implied blankness, suggested absence of any elements in the section that will function as a matte: there are no Palestinians ("In Israel today it is the custom officially to refer to the Palestinians as "so-called Palestinians," which is a somewhat gentler phrase than Golda Meir's flat assertion in 1969 that the Palestinians did not exist" (Edward Said, *The Question of Palestine,* 2nd ed. (New York:Vintage Books, 1992), pp. 4-5); "The Zionists made it their claim that Britain was blocking their greater penetration of Palestine. Between 1922 and 1947 the great issue witnessed by the world in Palestine was not, as a Palestinian would like to imagine, the struggle between natives and colonists, but a struggle presented as being between Britain and the Zionists. The full irony of this remarkable epistemological achievement— . . . the sheer blotting out from knowledge of almost a million natives—is enhanced when we remember that in 1948, at the moment that Israel declared itself a state, it legally owned a little more than 6 percent of the land of Palestine and its population of Jews consisted of a fraction of the total Palestinian population" (ibid., 23)) Jean Genet relates in his *Prisoner of Love* (page 24) a game of cards he witnessed in which the participants, Palestinian fighters, played, gambled without having any cards in their hands.

You're gambling with no cards in your hands.

No cigar

1

It's the first week of December. Fresh snow has fallen each night for two weeks.

Everything happened a long time ago. In the Inbox now are 13 e-mails from close personal friends and 35 things of wonder from the Wizard of Oz, one of which I read:

rachel, i am around the corner if you at sorrotti, lets meet up for perhaps a walk or talk or lemonade. alcohol free has shifted to coffee free too...also i want to go to poland tomorrow… interested? thinking 'frankfurt oder' then a walk across the border...several reason for this departure but could be a nice day 'out' ....

misha

The phone rings.

It's the Wizard. He's around the corner in Mehringdamm.

—Hey Zozanian, do you want to go for a walk? Is this a bad time?

—No. No.

Snow is falling, it has been falling steadily for days, the Ice Queen is in her domain.

—Want me to come to your place? Kannst du mir ein Moment geben?

—Yes. Yes. Good. Yes.

Diegetic silence-over, yes, yes, and he walks up and down the cold handsome room.

—Hey cool, Mozart chocolates, cool, OK if I have one?

—No, um, sorry, it's my lucky box of chocolates. Do you like Ritter Sport? Quadratisch, praktisch, gut. I have Pfefferminz, Amaretto, Bailey's

—Yeah, OK, OK, so, Frau Zozanian, was denkst du, wir spazieren ein Gang?

You talk too much.

—Yeah, OK, yeah, sure.

I like the silence of the snow. We walk up Grossbeerenstrasse to Victoriapark, which is built on a steep slope. It is empty in the falling snow. We slip and slide on the icy paths. He is wearing brown shoes with a split up the back and a bright red coat.

Do you need money for shoes, I say, he says Nee, Nee, alles klar. Es ist die Mode.

He says he's applying for a job on a paper in Cambodia. He's applying for a PR job with an NGO in Ethiopia and something else in Sudan. I talk about my first suicide attempt, a misjudged overdose like Plath's. He's very sweet.

We go to Sarotti for coffee. He starts talking about Australia, government scandal, ripple of muted public concern, UN oil for wheat, kickbacks to Saddam, no one gives a fuck.

I say: What?

He says: The only time there will be a revolution in Australia is if the breweries are closed.

I say: ¿Qué?

He says: It's just the same old crap. After the Gulf War the UN introduced economic sanctions on Iraq, so members of the UN couldn't buy Iraqi oil or sell food, pharmaceuticals, blah blah blah, to Iraq so millions of Iraqis died, so this would have been a highly effective measure if Saddam had happened to give a fuck about the death of a million Iraqi kids. Right? Many bleeding-heart Western liberals were somewhat concerned about the dead babies, after an unseemly scuffle for control of the remote Clinton got change of channel, the UN adopted an oil-for-food stance in 1995 under which Iraq could sell oil in exchange for humanitarian necessities such as food, medicine and such requirements for the preservation of infant and other life. So, the AWB, that's the Australian Wheat Board, started selling wheat to Iraq, except the only way to do business in Iraq was to pay kickbacks to Saddam.

He's standing the paperwrapped Sarotti chocolate on the short edge, flicking it over with a finger, standing it up, flicking it down. His nails are bitten back into the flesh, thin slivers of horn in the freckled skin. Stands the chocolate on edge, flicks it down. Stands it up, flicks it down.

He says: They were told they had to use a Jordanian trucking company, Alia, to transport the wheat, the cost jumps from $12 a tonne to $50 but AWB just claims the extra expense back from the UN so *no worries, mate.* It turns out Alia doesn't actually own any trucks, it's a joint venture between an Iraqi businessman, Hussein al-Khawam, and the Iraqi government, that exists to take payments from foreign contractors and pass them on to the Iraqi government after taking a commission. So the wheat is transported by Iraqi government trucks and the money goes straight to Saddam, 300 million Australian dollars, that's about a hundred million pounds, for about 3 billion Australian dollars in wheat exports.

Turns the chocolate end over end over end, long edge short edge long edge short edge.

So now there's this so-called scandal because it appears 21 cables were sent from the UN starting back in 2000, pointing out that Australia could be in violation of international law, and John Howard—the PM—says he doesn't remember seeing them, Mark Vaile—the Trade Minister—doesn't remember, Alexander Downer—the Foreign Minister—doesn't remember. So you've got the Prime Minister, the Trade Minister, the Foreign Minister, all in this mysterious informational black hole such that apparently nobody thinks they need to know? So if it's not dishonesty it's incompetence on a scale inconceivable outside Australia, but hey, they're good Aussie blokes and the breweries haven't been bombed so alles gut, alles klar, who gives a fuck!

It feels good to hear this (and there is more, and yet more, and yet more, the UN commission released its findings in October and the AWB was at the top of the list of payers of kickbacks to Saddam and he is OUTRAGED at the iniquities of the Australian Wheat Board). I think this is what it's like to have a country. I have three passports in my own name, but it was writing *Lotteryland,* writing a book in a state of OUTRAGE at post-Thatcher post-Major Big Brother Blairite Britain that made me feel the way I thought you were supposed to feel.

He drinks his double espresso like a shooter and orders another.

He says: So Australia's motivation for supporting the invasion of Iraq becomes klar, nothing to do with weapons of mass destruction, they just wanted to ingratiate themselves with Bush to guarantee their monopoly on the Iraqi wheat market.

He says: But what the *fuck*.

His double espresso comes. He drinks it like a shooter, unwraps the accompanying chocolate and wolfs it down, unwraps the chocolate of the previous espresso and wolfs it down, pulls a book from a pocket.

He says: Have you read this?

He's reading Bernhard's *Correction.*

I take the book and leaf through. Thick pencilled underlines mark passages expressive of Bernhard's loathing of Austria:

> such a country needs people who are not angered to the point of rebellion against the insolence of such a country, against the irresponsibility of such a country and such a state, such a totally decrepit, public menace of a state, as Roithamer said again and again, a state in which only chaotic conditions, if not the most chaotic conditions, prevailed; this state has countless men like Roithamer on its conscience, it has a most sordid and shabby history on its conscience, it

> is no better than a *permanent condition of perversity and prostitution, in the form of a state*

> he has to decide whether to stay and go under, to grow old in misery and without ever achieving anything in his own country and his own state, watching his own mind and body die a horrible slow death, whether to accept this lifelong process of decline while remaining in his country, under this government, or else whether to get up and out as soon as possible, and by so doing save himself, save his mind, save his personality, his nature

I say: When Bernhard died his will specified that none of his work should be published in Austria.

He says: Let them order Kuchen off Amazon.de.

I have a sense of foreboding. I'm charmed and disarmed, yes, by my star's previously unguessed-at revulsion for the Australian Wheat Board. But. But but but but but. It's not that Simon would not read Bernhard; he might well. But the reason Simon has the luxury of reading Bernhard in his very own personal $2 million loft in Greenwich Village or his very own personal $1 million beach house in the Hamptons is that he would *never* in a million *years* present this sort of thing to the American public. Never in a million years failing alien abduction from a crop circle and brainwashing. If such aliens exist I have yet to be reassured by an encounter of the third, or, indeed, any other kind. I have a sense of foreboding.

Snow is still falling from the grey Prussian sky. On the LCD in Sarotti the faux flames die down, it's time for a video, the Pet Shop Boys lip sync to "Suburbia."

2

It's the second week in December. Snow falls each night and is cleared each morning from the streets. The Germans are unashamed of efficiency in the clearance of snow, though the Deutsche Post disowns the Führer and all his works by sending every third letter astray. The broad avenues are divided by plantations of trees; the uninitiated pedestrian, crossing a road when the green man says Go, finds itself halfway across the central divide when the red man says Stop. The initiated knows it has a choice between sprinting and crossing the road in two changes of light. A traffic system inclining to the Deusche-Post end of the efficiency spectrum. But after two weeks of snow all is forgiven, the central plantations are not cleared, there are enclaves of snowy trees and soft snowfilled paths between snowclad bushes and benches and swingsets, and at night one can walk in the silent tracts of snow and hear no footsteps. There is no word from Simon.

I get an e-mail from Gina explaining that all five children have solved the new puzzle!!! Might they be geniuses? Could I send a cheque for $250?

Patrick has also solved the first puzzle but did not understood the clue!!!!!!! Should he go to a magnet school?

80 people are dying a week in Iraq.

I walk up and down the handsome apartment. I am wearing two pairs of tights, thermal underwear, cargo pants, three sweaters and a scarf.

I should call Simon.

I pick up the phone, press three numbers, put down the phone.

If I talk to Simon, beloved friend of my childhood, I don't know what words will leave the mouth.

I write to Simon. I delete the first ten drafts. The 11th states politely that I am not an agent but two months have gone by.

An e-mail appears in the Inbox: Rachel darling, mea culpa, mea maxima culpa, i KNOW i KNOW i KNOW, the language sizzles on the page, he has an extraordinary talent but the text was somewhat fragmented and i was nervous and procrastinated, we should TALK

I forward this e-mail to the Talent. The Talent has revised. The Talent sends a new draft to Simon, a Battle of Champions, Henry Miller kicks Gustave Flaubert in the balls with Nietszche as ref and Warhol as commentator. The head is not clever, it is not at all clever, I write Simon an e-mail and mention Flaubert and an e-mail comes back explaining that he will forward the ms to a sympathetic editor. I knew Flaubert would be the kiss of death.

It's a comfort that my only gun is buried 3000 miles away.

3

There's a gallery at Tate Britain, the Clore, that houses the Turner collection. Its curator, Ian Worrell, has access to the whole of the Turner estate, drawings and paintings in the possession of the painter at his death, and though he can only display a selection at any one time he himself, of course, can see everything that's there. He does not have to coax and cajole Turner to let him see the odd drawing.

I had 40 or 50 e-mails by now, and I sucked new ones from his fingers by writing daily, sometimes twice a day, until I forced him to reply, but there were, there must be thousands more. I would have paid him $10,000 for the password to his Hotmail account, but he didn't keep the e-mails he sent, they were scattered in Hotmail accounts and hard drives of the hundreds of people who had drifted into the Thornhill orbit, and if they were not retrieved they would be lost. Sooner or later he drove everyone crazy; sooner or later they walked away.

Simon would not have had to do much coaxing or cajoling, an offer of publication has its own magic. What to do, what to do, what to do.

From: “Rachel Zozanian” <zozanian@onetel.com>
To: “Misha Kropotkin” <returntosender@hotmail.com>
Subject: bizkitz
Date: Thurs 15 Dec 2005 01:05:23 -0500

misha

simon sez he has passed your MS on to a sympathetic editor. god knows what that means. look, here’s an idea. let’s do a book together. your e-mails plus my oxford hustlers, was denkst du? just give me anything you’ve got, e-mails about wheeling and dealing as tabloidista, chasing angelina, travelling in middle east, anything. i think this is really part of something larger, the sale of souls.

rachel

From: “Misha Kropotkin” <returntosender@hotmail.com>
To: “Rachel Zozanian” <zozanian@onetel.com>
Subject: RE: bizkits
Date: Fri 16 Dec 2005 11:29:04 +0000

sure, let’s make a million fucks!

misha

4

X-Originating-IP: [84.188.239.166]
From: "Misha Kropotkin" <returntosender@hotmail.com>
To: "Rachel Zozanian" <zozanian@onetel.com>
Subject: everyone is crazy or just us?
Date: Sat 17 Dec 2005 14:23:58 +0000

oh dear! it could be said from the list bottom, everyone is a pyscho or i am close...

In research on psychopathy, it is often necessary to identify groups of inmates with high, medium, and low levels of psychopathy using specific cut off scores (Wong, 1988). Analysis of variance indicated that the overall difference between low, medium, and high psychopathy groups was highly significant, $F(2, 298) = 208.9$, $p < .001$; post hoc comparisons (Scheffe) revealed that each group differed significantly from the other (Schroeder, Schroeder, & Hare 1983).

The items can also be summed to yield scores on two distinct, yet moderately correlated (.5) factors (Harpur, Hakstian, & Hare, 1988). The two factors have proven to be reliable and are replicable across institutions and countries (Hart, & Hare 1989). Factor 1 of the PCL^R reflects the affective and interpersonal features of psychopathy. Factor 1 has been labeled the Selfish, Callous, and Remorseless Use of Others.

The items in this factor are concerned with impressions and inferences about interpersonal processes and are typically scored using both file information and impressions formed during the interview. In particular, this factor reflects the psychopath,s verbal and interpersonal style.

Factor 2 reflects social deviant behaviors and has been labelled Chronically Unstable and Antisocial Lifestyle (Zagon, & Jackson, 1994). The items that define the factor predominately depend on identifying the occurrence of specific behaviors, most often using the inmate,s file.

Items in the Hare Psychopathy Checklist - Revised

Item Factor Loading:
Glibness/superficial charm
Grandiose sense of self-worth
Need for stimulation/proneness to boredom
Pathological lying
Conning/manipulative
Lack of remorse or guilt
Shallow affect
Callous/lack of empathy
Parasitic lifestyle
Poor behavioral control
Promiscuous sexual behavior -
Early behavior problems
Lack of realistic, long-term goals
Impulsivity
Irresponsibility
Failure to accept responsibility for own actions
Many short-term marital relationships -
Juvenile delinquency
Revocation of conditional release
Criminal versatility

Let's have our own circus!

1

[though rachel pitched the idea as something commercial, misha's reading of bernhard, beckett, makes her want to do something different, she wants to write something like the books he reads in his empty room, the books he carries in his pocket, books with dog-eared pages and sentences underlined in thick soft pencil.]

1.1.1.1.2.1.1 = ١.١.١.١.٢.١.١

There is a language on the verge of extinction, once spoken in northwest Australia, called Mati Ke or possibly Marti-Ke or Marri Ke or Magadige or Magadi ge. It is described by Mark Abley in *Spoken Here: Travels Among Threatened Languages,* who states that in the culture of its speakers a brother and sister may not converse after puberty. This is really very clever and civilised.

It does nothing to address the problem of growing up under surveillance. Thoughts pace the skull. It would be better if each child was taught a language and script unknown to its parents and siblings. This would enable each child to keep a record of its thoughts without fear of discovery. One might have a conventional order: for example, the eldest child of non-Russian-speaking non-Chinese-speaking parents would be taught Russian, the second Chinese. The eldest child of Russian-speaking non-Chinese-speaking non-Arabic-speaking parents would be taught Chinese, the second Arabic. One might leave the matter to random selection to achieve greater variety. I suppose that if Uyghur were one's private language one would have some sort of bond both with one's fellow private speakers and with native speakers of the language (who, in turn, would include a brotherhood of speakers of Chinese, of Russian, of Tamil).

Without these mechanisms, the members of kinship systems turn to subterfuge and camouflage. Still, there is always the need to confide. And confide. And confide. There is no need to send cheques or fill forms. No forms were filled. No cheques came.

As Adam Smith says, though, the butcher and baker do not provide for my needs out of benevolence but in pursuit of their own interests. The invisible hand is our friend. The invisible hand that sells alcohol and tutti frutti pharmaceuticals to adventurous punters is a girl's very best friend in the world. Duty Free wrote a 10,000-word severely cash-hungry classic of the nouveau new journalism on the Oxford sex trade for Eduardo (the best-selling issue ever of a magazine which is not getting free publicity in this book).

Strange things began to happen. I went sometimes to watch the Stepford freshers at their rowing. An olive green felt hat with a small bronze feather appeared in peripheral vision; its owner said: I'm looking for kiltsters.

I said: Sorry?

He said: I wrote to kiltsters@hotmail.com and got no reply. One gathered this was the stomping ground.

A denim jacket stood beside me and uttered a sentence that appeared to include the term "kiltfucking." A black wool coat stood beside me and said something about the kilt that I did not catch. A waxed jacket stood beside me and said something about a magazine I had not heard of.

2

[it's somewhat depressing to work on, especially as she knows other people are having a good time]

From: "Misha Kropotkin" <returntosender@hotmail.com>
To: "Stephanie Lambert" <slam222@yahoo.com>

Dear Stephanie
I am dancing like the Indian God Shiva or perhaps a
more appropriate scene
would be Frederich Nietzsche dancing naked believing
he was Indian God Shiva
all as his Turin land-lady watched through the key
hole worried these/those
last days before infirment, will see lacking
renumeration.
Take a pick as to which of these three characters you see as most appropriate, for me they all seem to form the current triangle of my existence.
Good for you with your outlined notions of success.
Glad to hear the guns are firing. Take Dalston.

Trying to get to Paris..

misha

3

[but there is work to be done. she wants to write something clinical and cold, like manet's olympia. she wants to place manet's olympia next to aristide bruant dans son cabaret]

1.1.1.1.2.1.2 = ١.١.١.١.٢.١.٢

It was early November. I had transferred liquidity to the Bursary. I had put the box of Mozart chocolates in a drawer for a rainy day. The kinship system remained illiquid, wretched. I went down to the river. I don't like buying clothes; I wore the Black Watch kilt I always wore.

I don't remember anyone watching me or following me.

It was not clear how long the liquidity from Duty Free would need to last. If there is a disappearance or breakdown it's important to have a line of credit; it was not clear that books should be bought on the small number of credit cards acquired since the last purge.

I went to Blackwell's to look at books.

[but there is a problem. inflation makes the money problems of the past look surprisingly manageable. Mr Darcy's £10,000 a year would be £750,000 a year in 2005. look at it this way]

Here's an extract from the Oxford University Gazette for 13 October 1937, p 67:

New College

1. Ella Stephens Greek Scholarship

The College has received a legacy of £15,000 to be devoted to the furtherance of Greek Studies. The donors, husband and wife, did not wish their names or addresses to be known. The bequest, which is due to the wife's indebtedness during a long illness to the medicinal and spiritual value of Greek Literature and particularly of Plato, will be known as Ella Stephens Greek Scholarship Fund, and will enable the College to offer Scholarships of the annual value of £125, tenable for three or four years, to boys who are natural-born British subjects, and show proficiency in the language and literature of ancient Greece. Any surplus which from time to time may be available will be applied for the provision of post-graduate travelling scholarships of not less than £150. In awarding the Scholarships the Warden will, other things being equal, have regard to the need of the candidate for pecuniary assistance.

If the Ella Stephens Greek Scholarship Fund is still helping out deserving young natural-born-British-subject male Hellenists in 2005, just shy of seventy years after its establishment, the lucky boy can sprint down Holywell Street to Blackwell's and run WIIIIIIIIIIIILD!

He can buy a Greek-English Lexicon for £140! YES! YESSSSS!!!!!!! YESSSSSSSSSS!!!!!!!!!!!!!!!!!!!!!

Or he can, more sensibly, remain in his room, go online, and purchase this indispensable work of reference for a paltry £81.99 LOW PRICE off Amazon, secondhand doesn't qualify for Supersaver Shipping so the boy is left with, say, a cool £65.

He can THEN buy Vol. 1 of the Oxford Classical Text of Plato (Euthyphro, Apologia, Crito, Phaedo, Cratylus, Theaetetus, Sophista, Politicus, 1995), discounted from £21.50 to £14.19, Vol. II (Par., Phil, Symp., Phrd. Alc. I, II, Hipp., Am., 1963) for £22.50, Vol. III (Thg., Chrm, Laches, Lysis-Euthyd, Prot, Gorgias, Meno, Hp. Maj. et Min., Lo, Mnx, 1963) £21.50 or Used and New from £14.50 (i.e. not qualifying for Supersaver Shipping).

At this point he has used up his Scholarship for the year. He can either turn to St Barclay or, perhaps, postpone Vol .III to the following year and instead buy

Vol. IV (Clitopho, Respublica, Timaeus, Critias 1905) for £21.50. If the boy is in his first year he will not be reading the Republic for at least another year, but surely any serious Platonist must own the Republic. It probably depends which texts are being set for the first part of the course: if the Protagoras or Meno, he must buy Vol. III, if Symposium, Vol. II, if Phaedo, Vol. I. Vol. V, by the way (Minos, Leges, Ep., Epp., Deff, Spuria, 1963) costs £37.50.

In 1937, since you ask, the Greek-English Lexicon sold for 42 shillings (2 pounds 2 shillings).[7] OCT Plato: Vols. I–III, 7s6d apiece; Vol. IV, 8s6d, Vol. V, 9s6d. In other words, the entire works of Plato could be had for 33 shillings 6 pence, or £1 13s6d. The Ella Stephens Greek Fund, remember, offered £125 a year for four years. A boy who bought a Greek-English Lexicon and the complete works of Plato for £3 13s6d would have £121 6s6d left over at a time when you could buy a Greek-English Lexicon and the complete works of Plato for £3 13s6d. To put it another way, if the lexicon and works of Plato were roughly 1/36 of the value of the prize, and the lexicon and works of Plato cost the same, adjusting for inflation, in 2005, the prize would need to offer £4,464 a year in 2005. But to put it yet another way, the lexicon plus Plato at full price in 2005 would be £264.50. A scholarship representing 36 times the value of these books would come to a princely £9,522.

Let's stay with that clinking clanking sound. Martin Amis's first novel, *The Rachel Papers*, was set around 1970, just after Britain had decimalised its currency. In 1977 the lexicon cost £25 and the complete works of Plato cost £22.50—over a third of an Ella Stephens scholarship, as opposed to 1/36 of the scholarship 40 years earlier. You could still have bought something useful with the money, but it was no longer a princely sum. Princeliness would have required a scholarship of £1710, over ten times the amount of the original scholarship. 30 years later, as we've seen, the scholarship would have needed to be 75 times the original amount. A House of Commons Research Paper[8] shows that the value of the purchasing power of the pound in 1998

7. £1 = 20 shillings; 1 shilling = 12 pence.
8. "Inflation: the Value of the Pound 1750–1998" http://www.parliament.uk/commons/lib/research/rp99/rp99-020.pdf

was about 1/36 of what it was in 1938—but that is not, clearly, purchasing power for academic books.

In 1937 the value of a Greek scholarship rested not only on the strength of the pound but on the large pool of schoolboys who studied the language. The Oxford Classical Texts were designed specifically to provide cheap editions of texts, based on sound scholarship, so that an interested schoolboy could build up a small library that went beyond the excerpts studied at school. It was possible to have cheap editions because there was a large pool of potential buyers, and because a text, once established, could be reprinted more or less indefinitely without alterations. Because of the very large pool of buyers, there was also a large pool of even cheaper secondhand editions of the most popular books, so even those who did *not* get an Ella Stephens could pick up books on the cheap. This cheapness, in other words, relied on a hidden investment: the school fees and scholarships that enabled boys to go to public schools and grammar schools, where classical languages were widely taught.

You may think this is not worrying. Perhaps you think there is no point in studying dead languages, why not study a living language? Or perhaps you think what's needed is a cure for cancer. But the princely sum of nine grand is not on offer for anyone, and the corpus of cheap texts made possible by a market of teenagers is impossible in fields where rapid advances are made and texts have a short life.[9] Time that might be spent grappling with difficult subjects not taught at school must be spent as a barista (bad news) or bartender (good news) or McJobber (bad news) or four-star waiter (good news) to make up the shortfall. But there is not much advancement for an academic in helping a barista or McJobber get up to speed, there is hot competition for posts with minimal contact with these lowlifes, maximum time on research and publication. So the best chance of contact with the hot shots

9. While a newly-edited Vol. I of the OCT Plato was issued in 1994, Vol. IV was first printed in 1905 and is still on sale; Crick, Watson, Wilkins and Franklin discovered DNA in 1953 and no biologist, however impoverished, can scrape by using a text from 1905.

is to read the publications, which requires if not book acquisition then time, time in libraries, time online, time even a bartender or four-star waiter cannot always find. On the other hand, to take an example, in 2005 the wholesale price of a kilo of cocaine in the UK was $50,036, and the street price of a gram was $79. So Ella Stephens Greek Scholarship equivalents can be found, if you know where to look.

The liquidity from Duty Free was about half an Ella Stephens Greek Scholarship 2000 equivalent.

When you are very very young you think you study a subject to find out about the subject. After a while you find the people you know are shadows of their possible selves, because other shadows of possible selves, those parents, those politicians, never thought about Darcy's £10,000 a year, never thought about the Ella Stephens Greek Scholarship Fund.

You live among shadows in shadowland. You don't want to be a shadow. What happens if you fight against being a shadow? That's what you find out.

[rachel is failing to achieve even the cold clinical cashlessness of manet. she tries to get back to the story.]

A man was now standing beside me. He wore a pale green tweed jacket with chestnut flecks and dark green corduroy trousers with a very deep wale. He wore a brown knitted tie. His shoes would outlive the present occupant by a century; this was the bumptious confidence of the aggressive shiny orange-brown uppers and tough stitching.

—Strapped for cash?

—Sadly.

—Tell you what. If you'll come back to my hotel and suck my cock I'll buy 'em for you.

I was not dressed for streetwalking. So this did not sound like a genuine proposition, but the verbal equivalent to sticking one's hand down one's trousers and jiggling below the waterline.

—£43. Golly. That's a handsome offer.

—Is that all? Why the fuck don't you just—

—Look, I'll take care of it. And they say chivalry is dead.

—That's OK.

—No, I mean it.

—That's OK.

He said: I didn't know they were only £43. That's silly. Is there something that wouldn't be silly?

His face was like a potato, bulging slightly at the forehead and jaw, with a squashed nose in the middle and a very small mouth with a curling upper lip. His hair was a sort of boyish brown thatch. He had one of the Sloane Ranger accents, one that garotted the words as they came off the tongue. He used the words cock, suck and fuck in that public schoolboy playing-at-grownups way. He had none of the louche charm of Duty Free.

I had read that Soho tarts charged £300. So £300 would not be silly. I stated this fact.

He said: I'm staying at the Randolph. D'you want to go now?

I said: £300 would not be silly but I don't want to do it.

He said: Is there something that would make you want to do it?

I said: No.

It is in *Extension de la domaine de la lutte* that Houellebecq's narrator contemplates our unhappy fallen world, a world where the physically repulsive, once assured access to sexual pleasure, are condemned to celibacy. Bonjour tristesse, Mistah Houellebecq.

1.1.1.1.2.1.2.1 = ١.١.١.١.٢.١.٢.١

Yes. Exactly. I walked out of Blackwell's, and the pleasure of having no further conversation with Mr Tweed was there for the taking, so I took it.

A girl with a pimp doesn't indulge herself in this way. A girl with a pimp develops, probably, resistance to repulsiveness. I did not realise that I was picking up bad habits. No no, I walked out into the Broad thinking Ho Ho Ho Ho.

I went back to my college thinking Ho Ho Ho Ho in the soft afternoon air.

I walked up and down my room, thinking nothing very much.

I stopped in the middle of the floor.

I said: Kilt.

I turned on my computer, went to Hotmail.com. My fingers typed kiltsters@hotmail.com as the address and whitewash as the password.

A mailbox sprang open. It had 100 messages, only 20 for penis enhancement.

4

[but it would be so easy just to have a good time]

[plucking news from the air]

news update, i have information rich air now, the techno sphere enters my world with a wireles contection floating from neighbours or simply the currents of hte wind...strange shift in geo politcs now- dont really need to leave the house now but this cruelly relies on the invisible source so once again i am impositioned by subservence to stronger invisible forces but i enjoy my new 'office'

[killing pain with a pill]

rachel, the nurofen worked a treat, by the time i was near currywurst 36, the dehydrated absorption and dull raw pulsation of neural path ends wrecked started to dissolve...ok more to come...hang on
misha

[streetwalking, selftalking]

my genre of late has been a bill of health. hoisting the windows shutter a flutter open and singingthe sun's praises...a friend rented out la dolce vita for me and i went to her house to watch it but it was a german edition so i couldnt watch it...i then walked to wedding from elberswelder strasse (where we met once and alighted for our recent abra-kebab-ra at babel...) and on this walk was thinking about this stroke of genius or this and i must get my dictaphone out more....message to sell (original word sell is incorrectly spelt or missed typed -slippage?) shoudl read message to Self, though i had to write it on a scrap of paper.

[nursing a sickly pc]

yes, funny sin-chroni-city this little guy sometimes needs a green aligator clip on the side of the screen to keep it fully a glow. i like the idea of your mac, and am warming to jump ship to attack, but there is a story in the end of the first book of don quixote where two ships come up against each, moors versus christians and when the christians ramm the boat the narrator jumps to attack the other ship but somehow his boat then veers off course and no one else joins him and he becomes a hostage/prisioner of the moors making him row their boats...this is a convulated metaphor for my frustrations/fears/ anxieties of shifting from pc to mac for all those reasons unsighted above.

[but there is work to be done]

1.1.1.1.2.1.3 = ١.١.١.١.٢.١.٣

An online search turned up the piece Duty Free had written while doing background investigation on the Oxford-Cambridge Boat Race. Sexual practices of the Greeks, Romans, Egyptians and Phoenicians performed by kilt-clad nymphomaniacs, chemical potency enhancers mixed by bug-eyed buggered molecule-mixers at Keble, this was the gist. E-mail address of source allegedly under surveillance by CIA & MI5 following alleged multiple partner incident involving a mullah, a rabbi, a monsignore, three senior civil servants and the Provost of Oriel.

Three days went by. The Hotmail account had 400 messages, only 50 for penis enhancement and cheap pharmaceuticals. Out of the hundreds a handful were offering extremely interesting prices.

It had been so strange and pleasant in the weeks after Duty Free, reading Plato's Symposium, working through a reading list on the Symposium, writing an essay on the Symposium. How extremely nice it would be to live that way always, how extremely nice not to turn to the kinship system for liquidity... But for this one would need to know sexual practices of the Greeks, Romans, Egyptians and Phoenicians.

Or rather . . . That is, if you tell a client that a sexual practice has been handed down through the millennia from the ancient Phoenicians he is probably not going to say: Just what is your evidence for that? But . . .

And anyway, some of these messages seemed to be written by raving lunatics. *Give it back you bitch if you know what's good for you,* what's that about? You'd have to be crazy to have anything to do with these people. But . . .

But it would be so frabjous to walk the silent spaces of thought, to go to lectures, read books and write essays during term, and spend my vacations with my dear, brave friend, poor wheelchair-bound suffering Lily Marlowe.

I bought a scratchcard which revealed the sums

£100,000	£100,000	£10
£1	£2	£10,000
£50	£20	£50

Better luck next time.

The phone rang whenever it was not in a lecture or library; concern was expressed in varieties of pricelessness.

I wrote to 20 applicants explaining that the service was heavily oversubscribed, only a very small number could be seen, and therefore the price was £1000 for straight sex and £10,000 for sexual practices of the Greeks, Romans, Egyptians and Phoenicians. 19 thought this was ludicrously overpriced. One was willing to pay £10,000 for sexual practices of the GREP. I wrote to another 20 applicants; 19 thought it was ludicrously overpriced, one was willing to pay the grand for the Prada of prostitution. I arranged to meet him at the Randolph.

His head is covered with tight yellow curls. His eyes are bright blue. His cheeks are a startling bright pink. His mouth, too, is very pink.

The chest is covered with curly fluff, through which freckled skin can be seen. The thighs are covered with denser curly fluff. Perhaps his cock is not really the pink of a cocktail cherry, perhaps it is memory that brightens it to maraschino. Perhaps it is.

I think that it would not be pleasant to be a girlfriend with the obligation of physical contact with all this fluff, one would always be hoping that one's boyfriend would keep his clothes on and the fluff out of sight. One would always be having headaches or one's period. Exams would be coming up. There would be family crises. One would have essays to write.

Perhaps this is the moral. The number of unattractive men is so very large, this underexploited resource can be used to fund the higher education system.

He says: I think I'd like you to unbutton your blouse but not all the way, and could you roll the sleeves up, yeah, I like that, that slutty schoolgirl look, it would've been better if you'd worn a tie, but that's nice, yeah, nice, and could you take off your knickers and sort of flip the skirt back and forth, but leave the shoes on, the black Converse high-tops are a nice touch, I like that, that sort of give-us-a-spliff-and-I'll-give-you-a-blow-job behind-the-bikesheds bad girl mentality, yeah, yeah, that's nice (all this time I am unbuttoning sloughing flipping turning flipping while he tweaks and twiddles and talks but then the talk stops and I turn still flipping the kilt but he has stopped tweaking and twiddling and he says)

Look, is there some kind of problem?

I stop flipping the kilt.

You can get a girl to do the business for 30 quid and they just lie there and it's like eating a kebab from a van at 2:00 a.m., you don't want to know what's in it, you wouldn't normally give it to your dog but you're drunk and it's the middle of the night, but at the other end of the scale if you don't mind paying over the odds you can get something absolutely mindblowing [talk talk talk talk] thought that piece by [Duty Free] was a fucking fantastic piece of gonzoism always been a big fan so there's a buzz obviously in tracking you down but I thought you'd be more

He would have done better to track down Duty Free's mixture of pharmaceuticals. He seems to have underestimated the role of monosodium glutamate as a flavour enhancer.

I say: OK. Look. I am leaving the envelope with you. I'll be back in 15 minutes. You don't have to wait.

I buttoned the shirt. I left the underwear on the floor. I thought he'd like that.

There is a Victoria Wine in George Street. I bought a bottle of Bushmills. I bought a packet of Solpadeine Max (paracetamol laced with codeine), a packet of Nurofen Plus (ibuprofen laced with codeine), and a plastic change purse with a picture of Homer Simpson at Boots. I bought an institutional tie at Castell's in the Broad. I bought two whisky glasses in Boswell's. I put on the tie and pulled it loose; I popped two Solpadeine Max and two Nurofen Plus out of their plastic casings and put them in the change purse.

That was 20 minutes. The client is still in the room, glum under the bedspread.

This was the best I could do at short notice, I say. I open the bottle and poured triples. I shake the pills onto the bedside table.

What's that? he asks.

Something to blow your mind.

Are you a bad girl?

He pops a pill between bright moist lips, raises the glass, sips, china blue eyes on Lolita of the Bikesheds.

Finish your medicine.

He sits under the bedspread sipping Bushmills.

You have expensive tastes.

Which must be paid for.

I pull back the cover and sit astride him. I unbutton the blouse.

He looks happier. Pale freckled fingers squeeze my left breast.

Yeah, nice, I think I'd like to fuck you up the arse, I liked the rear view.

That was not what we agreed.

Yeah but fuck's sake it's a fucking grand

Do you want me to go?

No no no no I'm not complaining, and he tweaks at the nipple, but the whisky bubblewraps the sensation.

I take a condom from my front pocket and he naturally asks if we have to use it, it's a fucking grand, he's not complaining.

I think this is what he wants, the mind sinking into a swoon, luxuriating in a pre-Raphaelite languour in which all colours are bright all details finicked, while someone sluttishly goes to work below. I tweak and twiddle where he had tweaked and twiddled before; Cherry Ripe stands alertly to attention, a child submitting to scarf and mittens for a romp in the snow.

His eyelids droop; Death's cousin holds him in a slack embrace.

What the fuck did you give me?

I want you inside me, I say, fuck me fuck me fuck me you son of a bitch, and I sink tensely onto the waiting cock.

Unh, he says, unh, oh yeah, nice, you don't often get a tight pussy in a tart, nice, nice, unh, this is an unusual situation, unh, having my dick boldly going where the dick of King Gonzo has gone before, unh, what was that actually like, unh, oh yeah, yeah, did he do a lot of damage?

He was an animal, I say. I thought he was going to kill me. But he was *extremely* generous.

I think we had better finish this off before he passes out. I roll sideways pulling him on top of me. Fuck me, I say. Enter me enter me *fuck* me yes yes now

His eyelids creep down, blink, open wide in alarm, but his cock says he loves this.

What the fuck did you give me, you bitch?

I say *Fuck* me *fuck* me *fuck* me and he starts saying Did he do this? Did he do this? Did he do it like this? Unh unh unh unh oh yeah, but he keeps forcing his eyes open, a bunny on the wrong battery, so I start screaming You fucking animal and thrusting my pelvis up in some sort of simulated uncontrollable frenzy and he shrieks AAAAaaaaaaaaah and 80 kilos of fluff-clad flesh collapse on top of me. I shift him to one side, courteously removing the condom and dropping it in the bin.

[£952.17 after expenses. Never seen again]

and there's always the novel, ha ha ha ha ha, there's always the novel ha ha

N E L A R D T L Y O T

38. THE END OF THE BEGINNING

1.

We're not saying this is for everyone, said Jake.

We just think whatever you do, you should go into it with your eyes open, said Mona. Remember, your luck is what you make it.

The motivational open-access luck-improvement segment of the evening was over. Jake and Mona went off to one end of the room with a group of conventionally goodlooking freshers who wanted to make something of their luck.

I sat gloomily on my chair.

Fatima said: Blimey!

She said: You know, I had a hard enough time just persuading my dad to let me go to a university that had mixed seating in the lectures.

I said: You think you've got problems. I've got two sisters. My grandmother doesn't even want them to watch *Top of the Pops*.

Something told me my grandmother would not take well to the idea that my sisters' strictly sheltered girlhood had served only to safeguard a valuable asset which could be used to fund a university career.

Something told me the rest of the family would not be more openminded.

I said: They're going to expect me to provide for them. And I'm not even conventionally goodlooking, how am I going to provide for my sisters to the tune of £3500 a year each when I'll be lucky to get a lower second?

Fatima said: No offence, but I promised not to talk to any boys unless there was at least one other girl in the group.

Fatima walked off to join a group of girls who had no future with escort agencies. An extremely reasonable facsimile of Johnny Depp caught my eye, hesitated, crossed the room to sit beside me.

He said: Look, it's not as bad as it looks. What's your name?

Ephraim.

Ephraim. I'm Nick. Look, I'll be straight with you, if you're not conventionally goodlooking it can be an uphill battle.

He said: But to tell you the truth, it's a two-edged sword. People aren't really prepared for it when they come up, the schools could be doing a lot more to educate people. As it is people can't necessarily deal with it. Maybe they've had a meaningful sexual relationship in the past, for example, well we've all got to grow up sometime but it's never an easy process. Or people might not have had the chance to mature sexually at school. Commercially that may be an advantage, granted, but it can be quite difficult moving straight into sexual relationships with people who in all probability are older and less attractive.

He said: Also, you've got to remember there are a lot more incidental costs. You've got to keep in good shape, that takes time you can't charge for, you've got to have clothes, and also frankly the money does go to people's heads. They may think, why should I bother with a degree when I can make this kind of money? The thing people forget is there is always going to be someone younger.

He said: I'm not denying if you stack boxes in Tesco you'll find it a hard slog, but it's not easy for the rest of us either, however it may seem.

I said Sure, I know.

I said It's just funny, because when I got my dodekadiamond I thought all my problems were over.

He said You got a

He said You mean you're the one who got the

He said I heard about that. You mean you actually got a dodekadiamond?

I said Yeah

He said Look, there's got to be something we can do about this.

He said Look, I know a guy who runs a restaurant. He keeps telling me he's tired of hiring drop-dead gorgeous waiters because they just leave. I'll put in a word for you. You never know your luck.

2.

Leave everything to me, said Nick, striding ahead of me through the streets of Cambridge. Don't worry, Eph, I'll take care of it.

OK, I said panting.

Now the thing is, Nick said seriously, shortening his stride, I want you to go into this with your eyes open.

Yeah OK, I said.

It's a commitment. They're not going to tailor the shifts to suit your convenience. You've got to be prepared to do your part, yeah? What I mean is, you're not necessarily going to to be able to go to the lectures you might want to go to, other things being equal, because obviously they're going to have an observation period, they're not going to put you on the evening shifts straight away, I'll be honest with you it's going to be a lot of lunch shifts to start off with until you've won their confidence.

Yeah OK I said. But um

But after all it's no better at Tesco's or McDonalds, believe me they're not going to sit down with you and your lecture list and ask what times would suit.

OK, I said.

But it's not as bad as it looks. You got a dodekadiamond, for fuck's sake. They haven't extracted the brain from the cranium, for fuck's sake, as long as you don't fuck it up with Tescoidal activity you'll be all right lectures or no lectures. I mean Christ you could even buy some books.

OK OK I said.

And remember, said Nick, and he gestured eloquently with one hand, this is a four-star restaurant. The skills you pick up will be with you all your life.

He hesitated.

Look, don't take this the wrong way, he said. Would you mind taking off your anorak? Thanks. We'll just leave it behind this bush.

3.

Nick then introduced me to Michel, proprietor of the eponymous Chez Michel. Michel took one look at me and gave Nick a look that seemed to say You can't be serious.

Nick said: Look, Michel, I know what you're thinking but I can explain.

Michel said: Does he speak French?

I said: Pas beaucoup.

Nick said: Look, Michel, there's absolutely no need to discuss this in French. He knows he's not conventionally goodlooking. You need to show some imagination. I mean look, I know the clothes are pretty ghastly but take away the clothes and what do you have?

Michel: An ugly nude?

Nick: Someone who'd look absolutely fine in Toby's kit, and who, unlike Toby, can be relied on for a three-year course. You said you were tired of training people.

Michel said gloomily Jesus, Nick, I don't know. You and your crazy ideas.

4.

You're not thinking, said Nick.

Think Kafka!

Think Liszt!

I dunno, said Michel.

Rimbaud by Picasso! urged Nick.

Michel sighed deeply. OK, he said. There's a uniform in the office. Put it on and we'll see how it looks.

I emerged presently.

Egon Schiele! said Nick.

5.

Merde, said Michel.

The Larrikin

1

From: “Rachel Zozanian” <zozanian@onetel.com>
To: “Misha Kropotkin” <returntosender@hotmail.com>
Subject: klicken Sie hier
Date: Sat 17 Dec 2005 03:52:01 +0000

misha

here are the first 30 pages or so. hope you think this is a project you want to be associated with. if so, it would help if you could send me some e-mails from yr time as tabloidista. there is no point in sending a ms to publishers now b/c no one will look at anything before the new year but if we can get it finished by the end of jan we can send it to agents and it can be taken to the London bookfair in early march, which is a big deal

rachel

From: “Misha Kropotkin” <returntosender@hotmail.com>
To: “Rachel Zozanian” <zozanian@onetel.com>
Subject: RE: klicken Sie hier
Date: Thurs 22 Dec 2005 14:09:09 +0000

Rachel
\sure, sounds and reads great, no problem with sending down the line some mails from when in the mud, fighting for tabloid glam glam. anything in particular you desire? Any idea of how you see this developing?

from the first sound of things i was a wash with hesitations, but this is cool, good, great, when you said it would be about oxford i thought it would be Stephen Fried-like, something twee about punting, soggy biscuits and buggery with those rugger buggers or chaplins et al. this is fine, much going on, will send e-mails when time to revisit the past permits.

From: “Rachel Zozanian” <zozanian@onetel.com>
To: “Misha Kropotkin” <returntosender@hotmail.com>
Subject: Xmas cheer
Date: Sat 24 Dec 2005 08:41:19 +0000

hey misha
it wd be great if you cd send the emails as i think it is better to alternate between your voice and mine, Merry Christmas in case I don’t see you

From: “Misha Kropotkin” <returntosender@hotmail.com>
To: “Rachel Zozanian” <zozanian@onetel.com>
Subject: meme and me me und u u
Date: Wed, 04 Jan 2006 13:19:35 +0000

ms zozanian

well i have a found a new cafe to email from and this one has the lime green and straight furniture feel making sitting uncomfortable but somewhat fashionable as seems the path these days. thought the juxtaposition between red tulips placed on tables and the right corner housing an indian women dressed in sari, reading and chatting occassionally with the hyper obiese owner adds a lynchian surreality i hope iced by similar email correspondence/dance

for the past two nights i have been awake until 5am dotting around the internet, writing bits and pieces, listening to jonathans music selection i should have culturally known, chewing my nails...too much coffee and perculated thoughts...now back on my trusty steed the z-y problem inverses itself and i am flickering incorrectly .... got in touch with mary, who is in the front line trench of ICM, i know her from london and last time i saw her she was hassling me to send her something, she actually makes two parallel annoymous appearances in *drinking bleach* - that i hope is appreciated...she takes me to see martin amis but this is simply a sentence or two...she liked some stories i have previously sent - two stories from pakistan, so i am now in ‘dialogue’ with her...havent sent anything just said hello and explained my situation...

ok well i have included another chapter to come, ‘and there she was’ obviously needs a spell check. i have already sent this to my friends computer so i can send through but obstenibly *it is* the stephanie, London snowballing out of control Stephanie. More money more access to problems mau mau... perhaps this idea not fleshed out enough??? Well, story stories all wrapped into one ...also with the bountiful collection of emails gillian sent me, i have, cut and paste, started eradicating the ‘oh’s’ and ‘ahs’ and am forming a stream of coconut-sense around all the needed little tid bits of court action and comments seared into the shimmering incandescent worn-worm memory,, more vodka, please.

will send requested e-mails, much going on

ok well a lot to re-read so apologies but it seems awfully close....

misha

2

I had sent presents and apologies to the kinship system—my poor brave friend Lily Marlowe was now bedridden and alone over the holidays, and I felt my place was at her side.

Three weeks went by with little of wonder upon the screen of the iBook. I picked up the phone, punched 11 numbers fast, uttered sounds into the mouthpiece

—I think maybe we should meet, go to an internet cafe, send messages back and forth through the ether, adjacent laptops communicating via Hong Kong Singapore Sao Paulo

—yeah cool

—a real working meeting

—cool yeah fine ok

3

X-Originating-IP: [84.190.1.242]
From: "Misha Kropotkin" <returntosender@hotmail.com>
To: "Rachel Zozanian" <zozanian@onetel.com>
Subject: desperately seeking p-seeko
Date: Fri, 23 Jan 2006 11:18:20 +0000

ok let's talk when we arrive together, this would be a great time to do msn messenger, simply download at msn.com or skype, that is another futuristic internet device bringing our nodal souls together while not saying much or having the great desire to communicate...

i do like the idea of clothes sscattered all around london and desperate pleas, i sent kats email with this in mind...here are some more, will like to look at them and then perhaps edit appropriate, rewriting history is a fun project, albeit doomed to inevitable rewriting itself!

well, i think they suggested the time i spend in sorgen pause café using their internet doesn't equal, or equate to, the money i spent - so i am thoroughly disastisfied and will assert my consumner sovereignity elsewhere... what happened to berlin?

ok ok one minute then we decide a spot to meet

misha

X-Originating-IP: [84.190.1.242]
From: "Misha Kropotkin" <returntosender@hotmail.com>
To: "Rachel Zozanian" <zozanian@onetel.com>
Subject: alcoholism in the Jung
Date: Fri, 23 Jan 2006 11:43:26 +0000

ok, i am going to get out of the cafe and pick up a book and perhaps we meet at 2pm at rosa luxemburg platz? there is a monolithic cafe distributing internet waves and cafe culture where everyone is chatting/typing /reading ther compiuters - they look healthy smart and silver. ok well lets do it - any glitches in the system then call the psyops

misha

4

We sit in a café called Sankt Oberholz. This is trendy Prenzlauerberg, so a thousand keystrokes thicken the air, a softly whirring cloud of cicadas born aloft above the pale pine, shiny white iBooks and dull silver PowerBooks are their hatching grounds, there is not a PC to be seen. He's chippy about his plebeian Fujitsu, wants to ban Macs from the face of the planet.

He brings a cappuccino and a latte. I am morose, demoralised. I think now we're going to work, he will summon the tabloid world from its Hotmail cave, he will forward e-mails through the ether and we shall have at last the Felliniesque thing of sordid glamour—but neither of us can get connected. We have a slip of paper with strings of numbers; the remorseless ambient clicking tells us it is not cool to be clueless. WEP, WPA—*NFI*?

I approach the silver ranks of PowerBooks along the far wall. Dog-owners bond with owners of a similar breed of dog; could the PowerBook be a virtual pet?

"Ähm, ich weiß nicht warum, aber ich kann keine Internetverbindung."[10]

Several rapid sentences assail the ear to the effect that one gets the relevant data on a slip of paper at the till. I make helpless noises. He takes the PowerBook from my hands, a competent obedience trainer accustomed to dim owners. He clicks, types, clicks, Danke, I say fervently, Danke, but Misha has no one to turn to. We smile at each other helplessly. Someone passes the window. Misha waves. We are joined by a pale man with a mouth like a rosebud.

Misha says: Hey! Ziggy!

and Rosebud says Hey! Misha!

Misha says So did you talk to the dude?

and Rosebud says Yeah, yeah, same old same old, he'll get back to me, yadda

and Misha says yeah yeah hey do you know how to get this online

---

10. Um, I don't know why, but I can't (get) an internet connection.

and Rosebud says he thinks so, & while he clicks & types he says I want to move into journalism, I was talking to a guy from Albania who does the false papers for the girls they bring over from Ukraine, he's based in Brussels, I think there's a story in it what do you think?

click click click click

yeah, I know I know says Misha everybody thinks that but if there's no British angle there's no story. Tabloids love this sort of organized crime story but unless the prostitutes are headed for Britain they don't give a fuck. I met these Ukrainian girls in Trabzon, it's like a rite of passage in Turkey, before they do their National Service the 18-year-olds go with their mates to the Black Sea, to these brothels full of "Natasha," you ask them about it and they say these Russian girls, they just like sex, so I wanted to do a story but the editor's like sorry mate that's not news we've heard all that before, sex sells but gets stale too

click click I think that should work

hey cool, thanks, give me your e-mail address

& Rosebud says it's Z-y-g-m-u-n-t@deadnet.de

& he says but I'm going fucking manic, I was at the gym with the guy who is personal trainer to Vessarova on the set of *Stake VI,* she put on a lot of weight when she was in detox so then she started working out and taking steroids but she overdid it or maybe they reacted differently because her body had been through so many chemicals? so she turns up on set and, I don't know, there's hair where you wouldn't normally expect to find it on a chick or something and she's, like, better built than the male lead

& Misha says you wouldn't happen to know the name of the trainer? this is the life I lead, snatching crumbs from the air

& there's a glimmer in his eye

the scent is smelt

but he's still nonchalantly clicking and typing

& Rosebud says Not sure, I don't want to get him in trouble

or the gym, maybe, they like details, there could be some money in it

& Rosebud says How much

& Misha says Dunno, couple of hundred bucks, maybe? if you think of anyfink send us an e-mail, I'll send you an e-mail so you have my e-mail address

& Rosebud says you going to Sasha's installation tonight? I think there's some videos in English, maybe

& Misha says yeah maybe maybe see you there

& somehow this arrival is standing and smiling without having a coffee

Misha is online. He tells me to set up MSN Messenger so we can chat. The Mac hates this, it says five times that a new version is available, do I want to install, first I say No and it refuses to sign me in and then I say yes and it gives the message that a new version is available do I want to install, then something briefly changes & a figure like a glowing green pawn or Michelinised Parcheesi piece appears in a pale blue panel. I add Misha as a contact. He adds me as a contact. At the bottom of the panel appears the announcement Misha is typing, and in the panel appears

Now we can chat

I type

Yes. The thrill of it.

He types

The medium is the message/massage

I say: Are you going to this thing, then?

He says: Not sure, thing about Ziggy, he starts talking, it's like incredibly über take no prisoners juggernaut onslaught and when he's on cocaine, which seems every time i see him, it's worse, if everyone is taking cocaine, jabbering on and on, it's ok, it doesn't really get to me but otherwise it's just too fucking much, look, let's go, are you ready to go?

& we're walking the streets of trendy Prenzlauerberg, Schönhauser Allee or something. He gets out his mobile & he says:

Hey, Jonathan, hey, hey, it's Misha, look, I was just talking to someone about the new Stake *film, yeah, it seems the female star has been bodybuilding & taking steroids & she turned up with a moustache or some such thing & basically they're really worried cause it makes the star of this action film look like a pussy, give me a call*

& we walk on & maybe this is what the book needs, maybe so, I'm laughing, but if the book were finished & we had a deal he could stop hustling this shit so why is he such a lazy prick?

His phone rings & he answers & he says yeah, yeah, it was a friend of mine who knows the personal trainer, they work out at the gym, yeah yeah, she put on a lot of weight in detox and this was to take it off only there was some kind of drug interaction or something, yeah yeah, yeah, & she came back really built & with the moustache & so forth so they're talking about recasting or something, don't know the name of the trainer, no, but obviously the movie is in this big crisis, yeah, yeah, ok, so yeah, I'll see what I can find out, cool.

We go to a monstrous store on Alexanderplatz, & we pick out a printer after much deliberation over laser versus bubble jet, & we go with bubbles, & in the street he asks if he can scam a loan, & I say sure but it's tiring, this feeling of someone all this time wondering when to ask & not giving me the e-mails and being a lazy prick but hey

So I'm tired from all this purposeless talk, we walk back toward his place across railroad tracks and the desolate expanses of Alexanderplatz & his phone keeps ringing, it's Adam, it's Nick, it's Sandy, it's Mark, and the answers to the eager questions are MOUSTACHE! & NIPPLE HAIR!! & TOTAL

FUCKING CRISIS!!! he says yeah yeah yeah he says playing for time & his silicon-enhanced tabloid Muse whispers FIVE-O-CLOCK SHADOW!!! & WHOLEBODY BRAZILIAN!!!!!!! in his ear, he's making it up, dancing with triviality, more alert and alive than he's been all day, yeah yeah yeah, he says, SHOCK HORROR! he says, HORRIBLY WRONG, yeah, talk soon, we pass Hugo Boss with its blood red window dressing, he's talking about Kate, he doesn't want to talk to her again till he's a success

I say Have a good time in Köln

There seem to be no good times in store

I walk up the stairs to Eberwalderstrasse & I write on the back of my ticket Zygmunt@deadnet.de

I switch to the U6 at Stadmitte. Einstein says insanity is doing the same thing again & again and expecting a different result.

I get off at Mehringdamm. I go to Yorkschlosschen & go online. I write an e-mail which says: Dear Zygmunt, we met today at Sankt Oberholz. I was very interested by this man who sells false papers. Do you think he would talk to me? I'm doing research for a book. Rachel.

5

I sit in the handsome apartment reading Julia Kristeva, *Le soleil noir*. At midnight I go to Yorkschlosschen to check e-mails. They sell Walker's crisps: Ready Salted, Smoky Bacon, Salt and Vinegar, Cheese and Onion, Prawn Cocktail, Roast Chicken, BBQ Rib. I order a Jever and Smoky Bacon crisps.

From: "Misha Kropotkin" <returntosender@hotmail.com>
To: "Rachel Zozanian" <zozanian@onetel.com>
Subject: I hope you larfed
Date: Sat, 24 Jan 2006 11:20:38 +0000

oh dear

www.http://sentinel.co.uk/article/0,,2003400213,00.html

STAKE NIPPLE HAIR CRISIS has a two-page spread, an inset on the drink, the drugs, the self-harm and a by-line for James Crossman. I run a search for Vessarova on Google News. The STAKE NIPPLE HAIR CRISIS gets 7,300 hits. China Daily, New India Post, Globe and Mail Canada, Sydney Morning Herald, Malaysia Star, editors across the world thought their public needed to know. To be fair, Darfur gets 12,000 hits, Gaza gets 29,000, Afghanistan gets 78,000 and Iraq gets 220,000, so the world has not gone stark raving bonkers, it has merely had PMS on top of a bad hair day.

Interesting. Interesting. So, he could have done it. If I'd sent him an e-mail from Niagara, given him an exclusive, he could realio trulio have outsmarted sharpshooters and all my faux friends. Interesting.

From: "Rachel Zozanian" <zozanian@onetel.com>
To: "Misha Kropotkin" <returntosender@hotmail.com>
Subject: hardy har har
Date: Sat, 21 Jan 2006 01:10:16 + 0000

misha

and they say fiction doesn't sell. hope this helps yr cash flow situation. sorry there's still no deal for the book.

just out of interest, why didn't they mention the connection with jake noszaly? is that because he's not newsworthy? he's been talking to me about doing a film of lotteryland, and every time he gets on the phone or sends an e-mail he tells me what a hot shot he is, but if he's such a hot shot seems to me the betazoid would be acting as if she was my agent even if she wasn't instead of acting as if she wasn't even if she is. surely if vessarova had gone the whole eating disorder self-harm multiple suicide attempt trajectory as a result of early close encounters with polanski it wd have been brought in? so presumably no one is actually interested in the sordid Lolita-llving past of the self-genannte hot shot apart, of course, from the man himself?
rachel

From: "Misha Kropotkin" <returntosender@hotmail.com>
To: "Rachel Zozanian" <zozanian@onetel.com>
Subject: RE: hardy har har
Date: Sun, 22 Jan 2006 09 :20:38 +0000

Rachel

Yes! Indeed never let the facts get in the way of a good story. and with the world crumbling apart i feel it my ever-present duty to add my bit to this post-apocalyptic fan fare/fair.

nipple hair, breast hair, chest hair this is my life! My *life*, my *wife*

noszaly is definitely top fodder… where have you/i been? fucking brilliant rachel, why didn't you say this before?/ i loved Count but everything from there was down hill/ ok great didnt know this before, reckon i can get some miles out of this/him.

sorry to bring you down to my impecunious ways but would you be interested in burning some embers, thowing some coal into the tabloid flames of hyperbole? better our pockets touched then theirs, i guess.

so whatchya got? anything for this mangy dog? have you slept with him? please say a thousand times *yes*!

misha

p.s, this would definitely be great for any potential suicide story!

From: "Rachel Zozanian" <zozanian@onetel.com>
To: "Misha Kropotkin" <returntosender@hotmail.com>
Subject: RE: RE: hardy har har
Date: Sun, 22 Jan 2006 11:10:16 + 0000

misha

well as you know hearsay is not evidence. Simon saw vessarova in count and wanted her for Bat-Mitzvah Boy, but he said Noszaly's producer had tied her up for something like the next 6 films and wanted an insane amount of money to release her. she was 14 when count was made but very thin so able to play a child because starving when discovered in dnipopetrovsk, hence wistful look of early hepburn (a). went to hollywood, couldn't stop eating, would eat 10 Big Macs in an hour and throw up afterwards. she gave an interview on Oprah when she was 19 (maybe you cd find it on YouTube), in which she apparently said Noszaly said he would use her in another film if she lost weight. he stopped returning her phone calls. she said she knew she shouldn't call but she couldn't help herself, if she called and he didn't call back she would make a cut on her arm with a razor to teach herself a lesson. there is a notorious scene in Stake III where you see an arm with 100 scars. Simon says they had an affair during count. I don't know if there's any evidence for this. anne (my friend who had the first option on Lotteryland) says noszaly gave an interview on the letterman show 10 years ago, was asked about the relationship, said he would have loved to work with her again but the drugs made it impossible, she would call him up and it was the drugs talking not the human being.

Sorry I don't have any inside info, it's not the kind of thing he'd discuss with me. Not sure I want him to make a film of lotteryland even if he is the next Polanski and even if he is a hot shot, though that clinking clanking sound is always a source of good cheer.

Rachel

From: "Misha Kropotkin" <returntosender@hotmail.com>
To: "Rachel Zozanian" <zozanian@onetel.com>
Subject: rint gones
Date: Sun, 22 Jan 2006 13:20:38 +0000

hey rachel
listen, i mentioned this to the wise men of the newsdesk and they were keen for me to get moving on this. Do you have a contact number? Preferably the mobile number, just for a quick quote on what you suggested. I promise no heavy breathing and, as always, it didnt come from you...

misha

From: “Rachel Zozanian” <zozanian@onetel.com>
To: “Misha Kropotkin” <returntosender@hotmail.com>
Subject: RE: rint gones
Date: Sun, 22 Jan 2006 19:23:36 + 0000

Misha
Sorry, I don’t have a number, he calls me I don’t call him. I will make a point of getting it off him, though, if the Black Dog howls. I wouldn’t want to leave you high and dry with nothing better than a Z-list suicide to flog
rachel

13
Under My Thumb

You're on page 475 and you still have no idea what's going on. Zozanian has embarked on a book with your character, so now we have a book-within-a-book-within-a-book-within-a and you seem to be the minimost perestroikist in a nest of Gorbidolls. A cast of extraneous characters seems to be multiplying like rabbits. Rabbits in a Viagra trial. Rabbits in a Viagra trial designed to tackle the freak four-hour erection problem. Who are these people? What are they doing here? It's like the finale of *Blazing* fucking *Saddles*.

Something is bothering you.

You go online and Wikipedia makes alles klar.

Dr Wiki propounds:

> A **Chekhov's Gun** is a literary technique in which a fictional element (object, character, place, etc.) is introduced early and in which the author expects the reader to invest. That investment must 'pay off' later in the story even if the element disappears offstage for a long interval.

Exakt. DeWitt has lost the plot.

Scroll down scroll down scroll down and here is the Master's voice:

- "One must not put a loaded rifle on the stage if no one is thinking of firing it." Anton Chekhov, letter to Aleksandr Semenovich Lazarev (pseudonym of A. S. Gruzinsky), 1 November 1889. [*verification needed*]

- "If in the first act you have hung a pistol on the wall, then in the following one it should be fired. Otherwise don't put it there." From Gurlyand's *Reminiscences of A. P. Chekhov*, in *Teatr i iskusstvo* 1904, No 28, 11 July, p. 521.'
- "If you say in the first chapter that there is a rifle hanging on the wall, in the second or third chapter it absolutely must go off. If it's not going to be fired, it shouldn't be hanging there." From S. Shchukin, *Memoirs* (1911)

In other words, the book is fucked.

But wait. It may not be too late.

From: "Ilya Gridneff" <anarchicus@hotmail.com>
To: "Helen DeWitt" <Helen.DeWitt@gmx.net>
Subject: cheekyhov gun: BANG BANG
Date: Fri 15 Sep 2006 11:01:03 +0000

Dewitt,

Wow, this is great! So strange to see oneself and to be konstrukted as 'oneself' through a *text.* Well, will make some comments and justly mark down the notes in red pen, is red still industry standard? But, by the way, I was wondering... my promised 'libidinal excesses' or 'prowess' or 'prowesses" (prowess excesses?) are raised but never displayed. And while my thoughts lie with the HitchCOCKeyan anxiety about the "unseen" OBJECT/ other, etc etc, I think this is like going to Paris and not seeing the Awful Tower, or, the '*throbbing uncircumcised member*' perhaps some omitted exploits for the reader could be submitted, could be helpful in *firming up,* shall we say, the narrative structure?

A way to better enhance character development? bathos, pathos and chaos and all that Greek stuff. As Chekhov says, if a rifle is placed on stage it must be fired in the next act – The Chekhovian Gun – or Gridneff Phallus, is perhaps what the reader would appreciate. Is our 'Springtime for Hilter'. The gun cocked and loaded, fired once, blank as those bullets may be, could be the way to loop things back in on itself?

Ilya

Windows Live™ Messenger has arrived. Click here to download it for free!
http://imagine-msn.com/messenger/launch80/?locale=en-gb

From: "Helen DeWitt" <Helen.DeWitt@gmx.net>
To: "Ilya Gridneff" <anarchicus@hotmail.com>
Subject: RE: cheekyhov gun: BANG BANG
Date: Fri 15 Sep 2006 17:47:02 -0100

Ilya

was thinking more along the lines of a MacGuffin (term & device popularized by Hitchcock) Here's Wikipedia:

> A **MacGuffin** (sometimes **McGuffin** or **Maguffin**) is a plot device that motivates the characters and advances the story, but has little other relevance to the story....
> The element that distinguishes a MacGuffin from other types of plot devices is that it is not important what object the MacGuffin specifically is. Anything that serves as a motivation will do.[citation needed] A true MacGuffin is essentially interchangeable. Its importance will generally be accepted completely

by the story's characters, with minimal explanation. From the audience's perspective, the MacGuffin is not the point of the story."[citation needed]

The technique is common in films, especially thrillers. Commonly, though not always, the MacGuffin is the central focus of the film in the first act, and then declines in significance as the struggles and motivations of the characters take center stage. Sometimes the MacGuffin is all but forgotten by the end of the film.[citation needed]

helen

From: "Ilya Gridneff" <anarchicus@hotmail.com>
To: "Helen.DeWitt" <Helen.DeWitt@gmx.net>
Subject: MacGuffinitis
Date: Sat 16 Sep 2006 10:32:45 +0000

Dewitt

To be fair, this book is just one macguffin after another. I am wondering which is the real mccoy and whether macguffin after macguffin just becomes another macguffin. Do we need to clarify more? Or be clearer? Is it my journalistic background searching for *clarity* or is the opaque device with minimal explanation the motivating force behind all great work/s? No, I am not aggrieved nor outraged simply wanting to see the light at the end of the tunnel is not a locomotive train.

Sure, our previous discussion alluded to fears one (me) may be perceived as a sex-fiend, or sex addict, sex pest pepped up on modern life/strife, a violent Jekyll and Hyde, or a 'kold killer' who hadn't had enough Quinine or a Byron-esq Don Jaun desperately seeking salvation in female flesh, how this could lead to tawdry thoughts and undermine their judgement to the prescribed texts offering hope and sexual liberation for all! But, perhaps the reader would actually revel in such DeSadian logic? Sensitivity, a lust for life.

So as your ever loyal and hard working co-conscriptor, I have included a story I wrote the other day. Of course, it is fiction, all this is another clever device of simply showing a whole new unseen other/Object. Don't want to shoot myself in the foot or worse. Incriminate, ahem, cough cough. moving right along. thank you very much.

ilya-esquire

From: "Helen DeWitt" <Helen.DeWitt@gmx.net>
To: "Ilya Gridneff" <anarchicus@hotmail.com>
Subject: RE: MacGuffinitis
Date: Sat 16 Sep 2006 20:08:55 +0000

.

ilya

thanks for raising these concerns. ok, look, i think this has really clarified some issues. have been looking at a couple of other entries on plot devices in Wikipedia. They have an entry on plot vouchers, a concept used by Nick Lowe to describe the narratology of science fiction (characters collect plot coupons and trade them in at the end for a denouement, i.e. an object is collected early on and cashed in at the end, often to ludicrous effect).

At the arthouse end, on the other hand, we have: **Unexposed contents** is a film device originally used primarily in Avant-garde film but that has penetrated into the mainstream during the 1980s and 1990s. A container is shown by the author/director, but the contents are intentionally never revealed. Alternatively, an important door may be shown but never opened. The technique is used to stir curiosity in the audience and to create ambiguity. Unlike a red herring or a MacGuffin, the contents may be important to the characters, the plot and possibly the audience, despite the fact that the viewer never finds out. Directors who commonly use unexposed contents include David Lynch and Luis Buñuel.

Well, why settle for just one device? why not have a chekhov's gun AND a MacGuffin AND Undisclosed contents AND a plot voucher? amid the rampant artifice we have something like life as we know it (the great Plotmaker in the Sky has not gone through the world putting Post-Its on significant objects (Plot Voucher - Lose it and you'll be sorry! &c.)). we already have a MacGuffin and Undisclosed contents and a plot voucher, so it's great that you are firing chekhov's gun. thanks for the story, i think there is definitely a place for it.[11] everything is going to be all right.

helen

So this is great. This is great. This is great. You're working with a writer who turns to Wikipedia for inspiration.

The book is fucked.

Your character needs a new alias.

11. p. 493.

The Klinger klings—
—Hallo?
—Herr Gridneff? ein Pakett—
—Wow! Toll!
It's the new Toufic!!!!!!!!!!!!!!!!!!!!!!

From: "Ilya Gridneff" <anarchicus@hotmail.com>
To: Helen.DeWitt@gmx.net
Subject: the wrong double O man
Date: 21.09.06

dewitt

There is full faith here on this side of the united nations. not impatient, just know or think i know what needs to be done in these moments that goes and goes on and on.
toufic is terrific or tourific, and the hitchcock talk in there made me think about also suggesting names: roger thornhill or george kaplan, north by north west...
perhaps the superfluous man finds himself a hitchcockian "wrong man", (or a third man, Larry Lime?) Roger thornhill mistaken for non-existent spy George kaplan? Cary grant allegedly told hitchcock 'this is a terrible film, we're a third of a way through the picture and i can't make head or tail of it...'
roger
over and out

24 Frames a Second

1

He does not know what to do. He earns money describing medical symptoms in English from a preprepared card for German doctors keen to improve their English. He earns money hitting the Play button on a DVD player at a Hollywood film studio's stand at the *Berlinale*. The films are shite films, he didn't know there were so many shite films in the world, he makes a comment and someone says it is good for its genre, *exactly*, there are so many shite films in the world. The people he's working with want to be cool about clothes, he turns up wearing his clothes and the people aren't cool, he has to go home and change to look good to hit Play. Everyone wants to be a player. Someone asks him a question and he says 'I don't know, I'm just the monkey, here to press Play,' outrage outrage even if you're not a player you're supposed to aspire to be a player. Later that day he shakes the German Chancellor's hand.

Frau Merkel Was gehts, Digga?

2

X-Originating-IP: [84.191.209.249]
From: "Kaplan Thornhill" <nxnw@hotmail.com>
To: "Rachel Zozanian" <zozanian@onetel.com>
Subject: RE: the field 'to' can't be expanded
Date: Mon, 13 Feb 2006 18:01:32 +0000

Berlinale, its ridiculous and absurd. And have been taking notes. feeling misanthropic, was going to knock on yer door today so glad i got this at this. nick has been difficult and this wholemonth has been poor compared to jan. hope all is well in oxford. drop me a line when back...

i am surrounded by those people,,,, occassionally having fun.
ilya

3

But perhaps and perchance he can write a piece on organised crime! If there's a British angle.

X-Originating-IP: [84.191.209.249]
From: "Kaplan Thornhill" <nxnw@hotmail.com>
To: "Ryszard Wysokowski" <Ryszard@ReWind.com>
Subject: film bizzle shizzle drizzle
Date: Wed, 15 Feb 2006 20:08:45 +0000

Ryszard,
how you doing? still got leprosey? all well here, a few aches and brusies as ever but have just done a week working with you film business people at the Berlinale. Actually, was facilitating their egos while lubricating the wheels of kapitalismus by pressing the play button on a remote controller for DVD trailers of their latest offering. Oh, and smiling a great deal…
anyway, heard something, somewhere, from someone, you may be able to give me a small indication as to whether is good or bad idea, someone suggested that there is a lot of dodgy money going into film projeckts that dont get up or past the initital pre-production stage. if that at all, like buying options on dodgy films, while of course your strict sense of justice would prevent you from this behaviour, have you heard anything about this or on the lines?

I am interested to pursue this, heard there is a eastern european connection... **Money laundering via Hollywood**.. Can you help me with this, no names of course.

hope you are wearing sunglasses inside, at night with knights. as the future is bright. Always…
kaplan

From: “Ryszard Wysokowski” <Ryszard@ReWind.com>
To: “Kaplan Thornhill” <nxnw@hotmail.com>
Subject: RE: film bizzle shizzle drizzle
Date: Fri 17 Feb 2006 16:24:02 +0000

Kaplan
you cold pilmeny, you think all us eastern europeans are kriminals? hoolygany>? well yes i pay less with cash, now it’s ‘eta *Prada,* net eta praVda.’ Eastern europe or ‘former Soviet States’ or the C.I.S or the ‘new europe’ as former soviet bloc is popular gaining with movie business. Cheap and hard working cultural peasants! We make Praha look like anywhere in the free world. But of course there are many hungry (Hungarian) sharks and Hungarian shark with hunger is not good thing when you like to swim in such waters.

I have heard there are dodgy people, fake options, fake accounts, fake companies and fake boobs! But i don’t know these people and prefer to stay with no bullet hole meeting me early one morning. stick to pressing areshole remote control for arseholes, you arsehole!

So, when we clinking glasses again?

ryszard

Download the new Windows Live Toolbar, including Desktop search! http://toolbar.live.com/?mkt=en-gb

4

Or perhaps make contact with a friend in Oz who done good

From: "Kaplan Thornhill" <nxnw@hotmail.com>
To: "Andrew Farrell" <afarrell@semaphore.com>
Subject: deutschland salutes you
Sent: Sat 18 Feb 2006 02:02:54 +0000

Andrew,

ahoy from the sweltering decay of the fourth Reich. Yes, the americanised berlin resisting the new world's attempts to USArabia. i met merkel actually and she is impressive with that mummsy going to make every phink better kinda way.. vive *Hartz IV*!

You have done well for yourself, even jockeying to be considered Aussie's christopher hitchens, i see. Oh, the contarian's life amongst the barbarians. well done and get the bad guys no matter how ambigious it is these days. they have moustaches, i think, no beards. *SAVE OUR SOULS/SHAVE THE BEARDS*

i see the ever loyal/ ambivalent australian flower shining with the 'she'll be right mate no worries' sinecure for a culture continuing on as ever incredulous as before, race riots on Sydney's Cronulla beach, terror in every kebab/ chinese meal/ poor unwashed living the aussie dream in the sydney outskirts, stealing cars and burning 'abos', all wonderful days. Johnny and the boys, perhaps if nothing AWB did was illegal, some of those new happy IR laws could be inacted for such gross inadequecies?

If only the 1950s were so joyous as it seems today. I want to go even farther away. sad i guess cause i miss bits and pieces of it, sometimes. It's all those fucking muslim jews ruining this cunt-try, i hear them yell, and what, they lost the cricket! Send in the troops, invade bangladesh, that leg spinner has WMDs (the moustache is clearly a provocation, the beard evidence)... well, so my purierent evidence proposes....

Well, I have become a tabloid hack, chasing Britney Spears around Europe but now the story is Angelina Jolie. I find myself making up stories that hurt no one and pepetuate the complexities of our post-modern melange. I was briefly in Iraq and Iran and Pakistan and and various other dens of evil post card post cold war scare mongering. I see it as the stabilising forces of a acephalus-hypercapitalist market working endlessly to terrirotorialise all the last frontiers before MCarabia (coded collapse with Marxist tendancies) ... if only there was an alterantive, black blood oil and coke (cola). time travel perhaps? was working for a few newsagencies over in London, shifts at the *Sunday Mirror* and now freelancing for national enquirer but moved to ber-lion

I've been meaning to write since i first saw your clean-shaven blog pic on the Sydney Morning Herald page. I have to say i didnt read too far down as it concerned matters not for me, but now i am procrastinating with onanistic celebrations of self, do you remember me? i was a fiesty copy boy at the Sun Herald, didnt get a cadetship cause 'yar karn speel' amongst other mediocre self-failings, i guess. oh well. It was a magnificent call to arms and had an amazing six years since such provocations ... life dazzles, endlessly and all seems good as i settle for a life removed from such petit bourgeois desires such as a free and fair press....

Ok, well knock 'em dead, and if you have time correpoDANCE is desired, the metony of this email exactly. No, i am not mad this is how i write these days.

kaplan

5

The phone rings. The phone rings. The phone rings.

She lies on the bed. She turns her face to the wall.

Noises Off

On 22 Feburary 2006 the Golden Mosque of Samarra, a site of exceptional holiness to Shiites, was bombed. Sunnite mosques were bombed in reprisal. Sectarian violence broke out. The Prime Minister assured the press that this was not civil war, it was just your basic sectarian violence, a point affirmed by Bush, Blair, Chirac, Merkel and many others in a position to want not to know.

If every man, woman and child in America had woken up a fluent Arabist it would have made no difference to the tit-for-tat mosque bombings, the kidnappings, the murders, the torture, the rogue militias and vigilantes. In the short term it might have made a difference to a few soldiers. In the long term, as Keynes said, we're all dead.

I had an idea. Noszaly was a certified Hot Shot. *Damascene* was being billed as a cross between *Lawrence of Arabia* and *The Quiet American*. An unlikely hybrid, you say? But the Hungarians have strange powers. You are perhaps casting your mind over the actors of our day; who could be Michael Redgrave? OK, Ralph Fiennes, and sure enough he had Ralph Fiennes. And the Peter O' Toole and Omar Sharif of our time would be who, exactly? Not to be unkind, let's just say he worked with the material available.

The point is, though, Sharif always said he picked up bridge in sheer self-defence; it gave him something to do in the endless longueurs between takes. If Noszaly's A-list stars were to start working through a Hollywood guide to Arabic in the longueurs, better yet if their progeny were to do the same, might the puzzles not rival sudoku in popularity? Thereby sidestepping the many obstacles in the way of putting such things in a book? The betazoid had not flatly refused to negotiate on behalf of such a book, no, she had simply said No Publisher Will Allow and sensed lack of confidence, so I had done the deal myself and got Simon's signature on the sort of thing No Publisher Will Allow and it had not ended well. Mr Clever had told me he would be thrilled to represent me. It had not ended well. But on the one hand if Hollywood stars were whiling their longueurs away over Arabic there would be no need for a book, and on the other hand if they were whiling their longueurs etc etc I would find a new amenability in the book biz, I would have people telling me 9/11 changed *everything,* it's not about *money* it's about reaching *out,* there's a longing for *authenticity*

So why not offer Noszaly a deal? Instead of going around in circles over percentages and strike prices tell him he could have any terms he wanted as long as he passed on the abovementioned guide? Which presumably he would think worthwhile *anyway,* given the preoccupations of *Damascene*?

I put the book with Mr Fabulous on hold, I cobbled together a sketch of the Hollywood Guide, I wrote a friendly after-all-we're-all-on-the-same-side-aren't-we there-are-more-important-issues-than-box-office-bonuses 9/11-has-changed-everything e-mail to Noszaly. To which answer comes there none.

From: zygmunt@deadnet.de
To: "Rachel Zozanian" <zozanian@onetel.com>
Subject: RE: false papers
Date: Sun 26 Feb 2006 17:40:19 +0000

sorry not to get back go you. kaplan really fucked me over, so i don't want to give out any of my contacts. if you go to the Albanian quarter of Brussels you might turn something up.

zygmunt bialystok

From: "Rachel Zozanoan" <zozanian@onetel.com>
To: "Kaplan Thornhill" <nxnw@hotmail.com>
Subject: research
Date: Mon 27 Feb 2006 23:02:54 +0000

hey kaplan

i have to go to London for a few days. my friend lily marlowe is on her own b/c the nurse got a cheap flight to ibiza. she has ms so it's hard for her to cope. hope all is well

rachel

[Meanwhile Rachel discovers a flaw in the proposal. Her half of the book was supposed to display a whole Threepenny Opera of Oxford hustlers, the strippers, shoplifters, phone sexers, forexers, the writers of porn hard and soft, the drug dealers, meths-makers, poker players, yes, and there's always the tabloids, yes yes, and there's always the novel, ha ha. But most of what she knows comes from readers, the hundreds of readers of *Lotteryland* who wrote saying Yes, that's what it was like, and Nobody ever talks about it and I felt so alone. Some of them were people she knew. But she has a phobia of the spoken word so she never talked to people, and anyway it was not a world where people talked about what they did. It could not aspire to the Habermasian ideal speech situation, because McJobbers spend so much time making Chicken McNuggets they are ill-prepared to discuss Habermasian ideal speech situations and the many hustlers, though well prepared to discuss Habermasian ideal speech situations, have too many other things they can't talk about. They're always better off telling a few jokes. How is she to show a world where no one knows what anyone else is doing? Aren't omniscient narrators passé?]

14
The Robot's Guide to Self-Defense

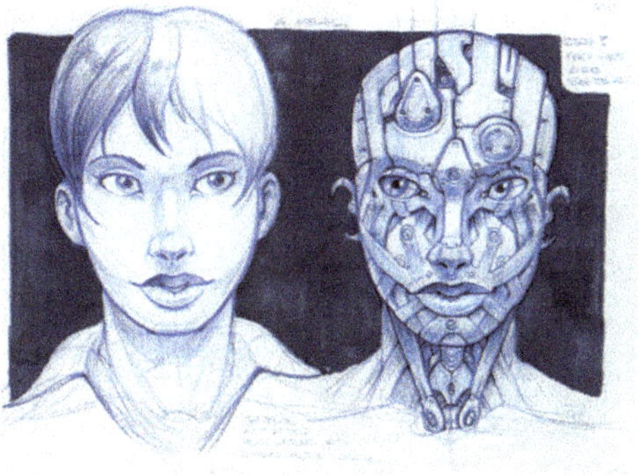

[http://spinefinger.netfirms.com/Characters/Android_Head.JPG]

You're reading *Your Name Here,* the new novel by Helen DeWitt. You're not a typical reader. Sometimes you wonder if you're a robot. Not only do you wonder if you're a robot, you *hope* you're a robot (and what force do "wonder" and "hope" have if you are?), because if you're the kind of robot that's capable of wondering whether it's a robot and *hoping that it is a robot* you're an exceptionally sophisticated robot, the triumph of an unknown Frankenstein, a creation that raises profound philosophical questions about the nature of consciousness, the self, persons, rights, language, if you watch pornography, play with kittens, explore philosophical questions this shows that you are a miracle of cybernetic art. If you're not a robot, wondering if you're a robot shows you're the kind of person who sits around wondering if he's a robot. If you're a robot, it's even more impressive that someone came up with a robot that could worry about whether it was the kind of self-obsessed geek who sits around wondering whether he's a robot, your creator is a genius, you'd like to meet him, even though he's probably the kind of person who sits around wondering if he's a robot. Is the fact that you'd love to meet him proof that he exists? You remember that Turing was persecuted for his homosexuality and committed suicide. Maybe you're gay. A gay robot. Are there other robots like you?

Maybe this is not the best book to be reading. A self-referential book that raises metaphysical questions as a pretext for talking about itself, doesn't the book simply replicate the very neurosis that makes it so hard for you to be spontaneous except in the calculating, premeditated way that made you wonder whether you were a robot in the first place? You should read something simple and funny, something with characters, something that will teach you some jokes. You've heard that *Lotteryland,* by the reclusive misanthropic Zozanian, is funny. You think you should be reading *Lotteryland* instead.

LTTEOYARDLN

39. THE BEGINNING OF THE END

1.

I was marooned for the first four weeks of term in the morgue shift at Chez Michel. 10:30–17:30 Monday–Thursday. A shift which coincided with an unsurprising number of lectures. Michel had not had the vision to see that a waiter whose appearance called to mind Kafka, Liszt, Rimbaud and Egon Schiele could be an asset to the evening shift.

I was not really making the tips I needed, and meanwhile more and more of the conventionally goodlooking mathematicians were buying new clothes and fast cars. There are substances to ease the pain of being an escort agency hack; there are substances to ease the pain of being ineligible for escort agency shame; there are substances to facilitate 24/7 revision by the underclass of physically repulsive Tesco wage slaves. More and more conventionally unattractive chemists were driving fast cars.

My comrade in misfortune, a reasonable facsimile of Joe Pesci, had also failed to break the monopoly of the conventionally goodlooking waiters on the evening and weekend shifts. He turned up an hour late for the fourth day in a row, but as luck would have it Michel's was empty. We stood at the back brooding darkly.

Steve was working on an M.A. because he had got a lower second and he thought it was bad luck.

It's worth bearing in mind, said Steve, I mean, just because you're not conventionally goodlooking doesn't mean it's the end of the world. It may hold you back, but even if you get a lower second you can always do an M.A. They don't tell you that kind of thing when you start out, so it's easy to get discouraged.

He said: In my opinion far too many people rush into the escort agency route without thinking things through.

He said: Of course, you and I are the beneficiaries. This time of year you get all these girls signing up with the agencies, the reality comes as a bit of a shock, you get all these girls overreacting. They don't want to shag guys who are conventionally goodlooking because they assume they're all doing it commercially, on the other hand they have this feeling that it doesn't mean that much anyway, they go through this stage where they'll shag anyone who asks.

I said: Are you serious?

He said: It comes in waves. After the first exams you get a lot of people with disappointing results going to the agencies and then you get another wave of it.

I said: How long have you been working on this M.A., anyway?

He said: About five years, why?

I said: Oh, nothing.

He added: Of course in my opinion what we're seeing is a very shortsighted policy. It can't last. Sooner or later we're going to run out of unattractive people who are able to pay.

2.

I did not really believe Steve but events began to bear him out. One day after work I ran into Ellen, one of the girls with good tits. She explained that she had just been to a lecture on topology, Fucking brilliant, mate, she enlarged, and asked if I would like to go for a coffee.

I said: Sure.

She said: Or we could go back to your room for a quick shag if you like.

I said: What?

She said: It's entirely up to you.

I said: So you decided to go with one of the agencies?

She said: What's that got to do with it?

I said: Oh, I don't know. Um. Maybe a coffee?

She said: Fine.

I did not want to spend three hours' waiting revenue on customized caffeinated lactinated beverages and I did not think Ellen was in the market for a conventionally unattractive toy boy. Which left religiously sanctioned beverages in the home.

3.

So what can I offer you? I asked. Instant coffee? Our special blend of rat droppings and finely ground cockroach? Certified kosher in the last millennium?

That's OK, said Ellen, scoping 10 or 20 mugs of mould cultures from instants past.

I put on the kettle; no means no, but you can never rule out a last-minute change of heart.

So how's it working out? I asked.

Ellen paced up and down the narrow path of carpet between pages of problems awaiting the dodekadiamondic brilliance of a tragically underappreciated Egon Schiele lookalike.

Oh it was absolutely the right thing to do, she said.

A startlingly reasonable facsimile of Kim Basinger as a reasonable facsimile of Veronica Lake in *LA Confidential,* she had the ineffable air of a mathematician who has been spending anachronistic amounts of time on mathematics. She said: The thing is, when I started out, you start out with some things you don't want to get involved in, and they don't put any pressure on you. But after a while you realise you're not getting the work, and it just doesn't make sense.

She traversed the four feet of carpet for the fourth time, kicking aside the odd book.

Actually I think I'll have some of that rat shit.

I held out a steaming mug of the house brew.

4.

We sat on the bed sipping mugs of hot rat shit.

You know it's actually not bad, said Ellen. If you're not expecting it to taste like coffee.

The ground cockroach gives it that certain je ne sais quoi, I said. You were saying?

Yeah, well, the thing is, Eph, she said, say you've got an asset people will pay good money for. I mean, I can see their point. I mean, your body is obviously just luck of the draw. Well, say you get one people are willing to pay for, that's already one piece of luck, why should other people pay so I can keep my body to myself? What I mean is, from their point of view, if I don't want to make use of an asset that's obviously my decision, but why should they subsidise it?

She lit a cigarette and inhaled deeply.

Fancy a quick shag? she asked.

I said apologetically that I did not have much experience.

Ellen shrugged.

I said actually I'd never actually

Ellen said What, you mean you're still a virgin?

I said And the hell of it is it has no commercial value whatsoever.

Ellen said Oh, Eph, that's just so *sweet.*

5.

I had been trying not to take advantage of the situation but Ellen said Come on, Eph. I'd really like to.

I said Well, if you're sure.

Of course I'm sure, said Ellen.

I put my hands on her shoulders.

Would you mind not kissing me? said Ellen.

Oh, I said. Sorry.

I don't like them to kiss me, she said.

Sorry, I said.

It's all right, said Ellen. You weren't to know. Just take off your clothes.

She was unzipping her dress down the back. She pulled it off over her head. I stared. Mona had said she had good tits; this was obviously an example of English understatement at its finest.

Aren't you going to get undressed? said Ellen, unhooking her bra.

I took off some clothes, resisting the temptation to turn my back.

Come on, said Ellen. Don't be shy.

I wasn't sure this was really such a good idea but it was too late to stop. I took off the rest of my clothes and sat on the bed. Ellen came and sat beside me.

Don't worry, Eph, she said. Everything is going to be all right. Leave everything to me.

I was staring at her breasts. I bent my head.

Would you mind not doing that? said Ellen.

Sorry, I said, straightening up.

It's just that I really hate being slobbered on, they always do it and I really hate it.

Sorry, I said.

And would you mind not touching me there? said Ellen.

Sorry, I said, hastily retracting my hand. Um

What? said Ellen.

Well, um

What?

I thought the, um, woman needed to be, um, lubricated?

I have a commercial product, said Ellen. I don't like to use physiological methods.

She opened her bag and took out a little tube and a packet of condoms.

6.

Ellen applied some of her commercial product to herself and soon had a condom in place.

Oh Eph don't tell me you're going to be one of those, she said. You get these blokes they go into a big song and dance about wearing a condom well excuse *me*

I said hastily that it was not going to be a problem.

There is a famous scene in *Star Wars* where Obi-Wan Kanobi teaches Luke Skywalker to fight with his eyes closed, directing the Force with his will. This was sort of like that and it was also sort of like trying to inflate a balloon by power of will alone.

After a while she said *That's* more like it.

7.

At least I didn't have to worry about my biggest worry. The concept of 'premature' did not really seem to apply to ejaculation in the circumstances.

Ellen said: How was that?

I said: It was *fantastic. Brilliant.* I didn't realise it could be like that.

15

Return of the Hot Shot

Most people want to think life has got some structure, form and that you can distinguish the past from the future, and the present. I don't think it's true, I think Fellini admits to that and allows all of these things to enter into the process. Faces always coming at you—he's got the money, he's got everything, but he doesn't know what he's doing and everyone's coming at him. They're all wanting answers. They're all wanting something from him. I think one of the first times I was really aware of the camera as a partner in dance, because I think the film is like a dance. He shoots like a dancer would shoot. It's all moving, it's shifting. Things are coming in and out of frame. It's never still. It's what life always seems like to me. It always feels like the passage through life.

Terry Gilliam

1

You went back to Paris in March to write some new scenes. The cards from the preview of *Damascene* had come back with "hard to follow," a recurrent motif. THE top guy at the studio said he was behind you one thousand percent but this was too important for anyone to get left behind, he knew you would find a way to achieve that without compromising your vision because this is what really great artists do, Jake, they're *communicators.*

You flew Virgin Premium Economy to Paris and you locked yourself into a sixth-floor apartment on the Rue Mouffetard. You slept the soft heavy sleep of jetlag, the only drug that never pales. You woke up at some improbable time, 6:00 a.m., but this is Paris, the boulangerie was already open. You asked for deux baguettes, s'il vous plaît, dix croissants, dix pains au chocolat, dix brioches, and then you just started pointing at one government-authenticated bread after another because when you're working you don't stop. The girl is looking at you like who is this lunatic because why would you want to stock up on bread in Paris when you can buy freshly baked bread tous les matins du monde but when you're working you don't fucking stop.

The fromagerie was open. You bought an unpasteurized Camembert, the kind of thing that not only can't legally be sold in LA but can't be bought from even the most resourceful of dealers, and then you started pointing at one obscure regional cheese after another until you had about thirty of the fuckers and the guy's looking at you like who is this crazy-ass spendthrift American when realistically this was maybe the equivalent of two lines of cocaine.

The charcuterie was open, well-stocked with the succulent corpses of happy airbred cornfed farm animals and unhappy forcefed geese. You bought five organically reared cornfed roast chickens. You bought three motherfucking hams (a jambon de Bayonne, a jambon d'Auvergne, and a jambon d'Aveyron). You pointed at a two-foot slab of paté de campagne and the girl said Combien and you said Tout and she looked at you like who is this lunatic so you pointed at the four patés on display and said Je veux tous les quatre, I want all four, and then you made a gesture with your hands, two feet apart, this is what really great artists do, they're *communicators,* and that was maybe the equivalent of three lines of cocaine.

The Parisians go shopping with wheeled plasticized shopping bags but you just brought your suitcase. The coffee guy was open. You bought five kilos of their darkest roast, ground for espresso, and that went in the suitcase with the bread, the cheeses, the hams, the chickens. The patés, *obviously,* were not in the fucking suitcase, they gave you a box tied with string for the fuckers, only a *moron* would put paté in a *suitcase,* you're rewriting your screenplay for the kind of 20-watt intelligence that needs to have it *explained* that the fucking patés went in a box with a string. And that the fucking chickens came in foil-lined thermal *bags, no,* you did not put three greasy roast chickens in the fucking suitcase. The wine guy was open. This is not about alcohol, it's about self-affirmation, your Muse is not a fucking Valley Girl.

Your cellphone has a wine advisory service but why bother. You stood looking at the shelves of obscure regional wines, wines not available in LA even from the most resourceful of dealers. There were three dusty bottles of Bordeaux: Saint-Émilion, Château Cheval Blanc 1er Grand Cru Classé A 1990. 650 euros. 800 bucks. You're not a barbarian, this is not a wine to put in the suitcase on top of the motherfucking hams. It's not a wine for this occasion. You left, wheeling your suitcase.

The supermarket was open. You bought five jars of moutarde de Beaune à l'ancienne, because a ham without wholegrain mustard is like a day without sunshine.

You climbed the six flights of stairs with your roadrunning delicatessen. When you opened the door the phone was ringing.

You picked up.

Only four people knew you could be reached at this number. This wasn't one of them.

You put the phone down.

2

There's a looooooooooooooooong e-mail from Noszaly saying he has to have an answer, he needs to know what his next film will be, he has three ex-wives and four children to support, there are helpful e-mails from friends and friends of friends and friends of friends of

It's still snowing in Berlin. It's still bombing in Baghdad. Is there a Snow Queen? Is there a Bomb Queen? I think we should meet.

It's a mistake to write about things you don't want to think about.

The Vessarova story keeps surfacing. Noszaly's former pet psychologist gave an interview explaining that Vessarova used to intercept her and talk to the dogs. A former au pair had a story about Jake screaming abuse down the phone: Look, Nadezhda, I've bought a gun, if I have to I'll use it. The Wizard said he had found a few other bits and pieces to feed them. It was like watching a Boy Scout build a bonfire by rubbing two sticks together.

I ask the Wizard for e-mails from his days as a tabloidista, it's crucial to the book, I say, this is the life of our generation, commodification, alienation, it's all in *Adorno*

3

X-Originating-IP: [217.83.26.160]
From: "Kaplan Thornhill" <nxnw@hotmail.com>
To: "Rachel Zozanian" <zozanian@onetel.com>
Subject: a knife kept/keeps following me, life begins at Oxford circus
Date: Sun 5 March 2006 13:35:59 +0000

hey rachel,
was thinking may be not today. just not in the best mood for several reasons (nothing life threatening). maybe all simply lack of sugar...just dont want to be socialable- have some work responsibility too.

i will get on with the task (collating emails etc) and call you incase you dont read this, ring ring..

the Simon stuff is frustrating and oh, well, i appreciate your efforts, we can drink champagne from a shoe, one day...

more to say but not right now. think i'll try to get Munich to visit my friend for some time out of Berlin.

kaplan

From: "Kaplan Thornhill" <nxnw@hotmail.com>
To: "Lothar Strunk" <lstrunk@gmx.net>
Subject: dodgy deals done dirty cheapy
Date: Mon 6 March 2006 11:07:49 -0300

Lothar,
just a short one to ask if, in your celluloid travels, you have come across dodgy dealers buying scripts or options in books but the plan is not to go ahead with the production for it was a scam to begin with? Basically, films as

a money laundering process . . . I am looking into this story and thought you may have heard something that may help?
all the bestest,
kaplan

Windows Live™ Messenger has arrived. Click here to download it for free! http://imagine-msn.com/messenger/launch80/?locale=en-gb

From: "Lothar Strunk" <lstrunk@gmx.net>
To: "Kaplan Thornhill" <nxnw@hotmail.com>
Subject: RE: dodgy deals done dirty cheapy
Date: Thurs 9 March 2006 12:16:32 +0000

Kaplan
thanks for getting in touch, it has been such time. Well, interesting angle you present me. Unfortunately, I am very much involved in low budget productions that need every dollar possible to make them happen! So, there is no dodgy deals I am aware of. If anything, I'd love someone to launder money through one of our films as it would help us reach our artistic goals/dreams. Well, good luck with the story.
Lothar.

From: "Kaplan Thornhill" <nxnw@hotmail.com>
To: "Sally Marchbanks"<sally@marchhatter.com>
Subject: laundrymat of love-lies
Date: Mon 13 March 2006 12:19:04 -0400

hey Sally

hope all good with you right now. Just a short one here to get straight to the point. I have been doing some research into the film bizz and heard that there are not just wonderfully talented people who passionately love cinema, some are just in it for the money!

that is, there are organised criminals /gangs using film to launder money. have you heard anything like this? in particular through eastern european channels. was hoping considering your London background you may know something or someone who may someone of something...kind of looking for a UK story, though things like this can lead all the way around the world, so maybe the american's would be interested too... well anyway, let me know, and when i am back in london i'll buy you a main meal (no entree / desert though)
kaplan

Be the first to hear what's new at MSN - sign up to our free newsletters! http://www.msn.co.uk/newsletters

From: "Sally Marchbanks"<sally@marchhatter.com>
To: "Kaplan Thornhill" <nxnw@hotmail.com>
Subject: RE: laundrymat of love-lies
Date: Fri 17 March 2006 10:54:02 +0000

Kaplan
Sorry, can't help you with this. I don't know anybody who could. off to South Africa for documentry. When in london call me,

Sally

4

From: "Kaplan Thornhill" <nxnw@hotmail.com>
To: "Rachel Zozanian" <zozanian@onetel.com>
Subject: Karnival
Date: Thurs 23 March 2006 23:14:22 -0200

Hello unternet user,
short one. today van loads of those stoic green uniformed police were stopping bike riders (illegally) riding along the 20 metre strip of road outside my house to then interogate them and check their bike serial numbers. Oh, nothing wrong with this very (very) short arm of the law but there were sooooo many police simply to control those pesky bike criminals (terrorists?) It seemed a tad over the top and falling into old german stereotypes DAS IST NICHT RICHTIG...and it did make leaving my house seem a litte, paranoid creating.

ok *Adaption* sounds good. and let's have it!

printed out *Drinking Bleach* (one black printer catridge gone! RIP) and it is placed sectioned around my living room. Actually must congratulate Zozanian on how good an idea printing out said book, mental note.

wrapped up the affair with Beatrice, who is in Morocco now. all very adult and it is amazing how much of the real stuff lurks underneath the veneer of social. breaking up reveals the underneath carriage and somewhat far more interesting flesh of life. a fiercer pleasurable intensity lacked in holding hands and brunch. And well, as they say, the best part of breaking up, is making up.

Ryszard Wysokowski has opened up a contact Eva Tapanninen interested in the sound of *drinking bleach./* so we see. slowly. slowly. am going to ceremonously buy a red pen.,,,

Layla M respodned to my email with many 'do not understands' 'what does bemused, void and haunting echoes mean???' ...along with a totally new face/approach of i am a humble farm girl different tone to previous rightousness. I agree with your comments and sent a soothing response.

i am always a very gentle gentile gentlemen, i thought. feeling good, hair looking better everyday, reading *three penny opera* and have more Zola on the way..

more gold fish aquatics, 'little fish, big fish, swimming in the water…'

mouth gestures a 'yes.'

From: "Rachel Zozanian" <zozanian@onetel.com>
To: "Kaplan Thornhill" <nxnw@hotmail.com>
Subject: emergency
Date: Wed 29 March 2006 24:04:19 +0000

Kaplan, sorry, have to go to London. My friend Lily is very ill, sorry book taking so long, many things to deal with. Good that you printed out DB. Yes. Great that Ryszard has put you in touch with someone, if she likes his work that may be a better jumping-off point than people who cashed in on ll. How do you feel about book readings? Joyce is giving one at the babylon, maybe go when I get back? or we cd go out and have fun.

Rachel

From: "Kaplan Thornhill" <nxnw@hotmail.com>
To: "Rachel Zozanian" <zozanian@onetel.com>
Subject: RE: emergency
Date: Thurs 30 March 2006 11:17:03 +0000

k, doesn't sounds so good. I do hope the script gets together for you when you see fit. and from our last meeting i understand how difficult things can be, so not sure what to say…

re: reading. yes, perhaps a waste of 6 euro and our cat calls, boos hooting noises like pachyderms on heat could be unsettling for all involved. i would like to meet another 'real' writer and i did a little looky looky on the interwebby about Joyce so am interested to meet her or hear a little more about the book that i saw. It sounds a dichtomy from diffidence to dazzling (self) distinction...

two things i do want to do but haven't achievied are a) ten pin bowling and b) the melancholie exhibition at the Neue Kunst gallerie. maybe we can combine everything or everyone into this.

perhaps this a far better pursuit than readings. i mean the bowling could be fun in that oh the simple pleasures of simple life with some others or simple Zozanian v Gridneff or Gridneff and Zozanian vs XXX in a battle of banality and fine motor skills vis a vis ten pins.

ex Berliner magazine told me how to write and made some suggestions that seemed a little hypocritical, contradictary and above their station. as well they were going to print a story about my time as a waffle seller (waffleverkaufer) but decided it was "an advertial" but I said they missed the point that we didn't have any customers. It's just that sort of small mindeness I have to deal with on a day to day basis, and I told them they're just king of the english speaking berlin fiefdom...contraversal or cool or crazy cause they have a tatoo, beard, piercing and live in Derrr-rlin.

I am well, i didn't mention this but i took a large quantity of magic mushrooms at Wansee, with a canadian friend and her american journalist friend and her visiting lesbian sister. Potsdam is a wonderful park built by Kaiser Wilhelm and in the belief of my own aristocracy, I had a wonderful day laughing and appreciating the breeze, leaves, trees and sun setting on endless expanding spaces, lakes. Some highlights were discussing joyous circles, smoking platipus, and creating an "indigital" music group incorporating digerido with electronic beats and various other peaks light lightness....my conclusion, i need to tread more lightly, stop parrying the blow... be like a leaf,

and the winter hidden, your Yorkstr thoughts, is an interesting thought cause it did all seems so ephemeral the other day that such thoughts become clearer stronger///

o

k

well to add insult to berlin injury a friend broke his foot playing badminton, i have to get out of here. and one place thinking is Israel, not cause of our sniper friend but an old friend from London suggested she could sort me out something or other...but it changes like the breeze/season.

\

got a compliment from the Mail on Sunday that there were v. impressed at how well the Fred Perry football hooligan article was written but still it is not clear the pay, prominence or byline. So strange, while i no doubt always feel a disappointment with the product the process is always worth more than the rewards.

oh and i think i do need to scam some money of you. I haven't paid the rent and the cheque is still in the international financial limbo world or virtual bank space. So now Beatrice has some access to laud over me financial impecunity meaning the very ungermanic way of right and wrong with responsibilities. she rang and asked if i was upset at her and in my round about way i said yes but after all the mushrooms i should just not even indulge her in my thinking. So was light and said there is no time waste on these things, explained her missing the point - she remained firm in her position said something like ;'you don't do this' or ' you dont say nice things to me' . incredulous, i rolled my eyes and said ok ok bye bye and then she asked for my friends' phone number and i explained what i explained to you about his poor form in context to being flummexed by Berlin attitude and she made a funny noise with her mouth like i don't care. Pffff. Well, I don't know. Care. Blah blah blah blah more more more to come

kaplan

From: “Kaplan Thornhill” <nxnw@hotmail.com>
To: “Sandra DiAngelo” <sandra@dealwiththedevil.com>
Subject: 24 frames a second
Date: Wed 5 Apr 2006 13:04:19 +0000

sandra
Sandra- SANDRA!
I worked for one of the world’s leading film production and distribution companies at the Berlinale and met a guy who told me about gangs using film as a way to launder money- that is using the paper work for costs of pre-producing a film that is never made? are you aware of this? so far i’ve got people telling me yes, this is the case but no one wants to go on the record or can steer me in the right direction. something british would be great/.

kaplan

From: “Sandra DiAngelo” <sandra@dealwiththedevil.com>
To: “Kaplan Thornhill <anarachicus@hotmail.com>
Subject: RE: 24 frames a second
Date: Sat 8 Apr 2006 16:47:38 +0000

kaplan
yes i know a bit. phone is better. call me.
sandy

Find Singles In Your Area Now With Match.com! msnuk.match.com

5

You were back in Paris mixing the sound for your new scenes. Vessarova was still in free-fall; the press wouldn't leave it alone. The three au pairs had resigned without notice the day *People* rerererereran the story. Nothing to do with the facts and everything to do with the fact that you're now hot shit, but try telling that to an AAA-battery-brained au pair.

You filled your suitcase in the Rue Mouffetard, carried the fucker up six flights. You heard the phone ringing while you fumbled for keys. It was 9:00 a.m., 12 midnight LA. Some crisis you could do SFA about from Paris, France, which was one good reason to be mixing sound in Paris. You opened the door, let the phone go on ringing.

At 10:00 a.m. the phone rang again. You looked at it. You let it ring five times. You picked up.

It was Mary Poppins. It was the Wicked Witch of the West. Depending on your point of view. It was Caroline DeVere, THE numero uno at Paramount. It was 10:00 a.m. in Paris which meant it was ONE AM in LA. THE numero uno at Paramount got your number which was theoretically known to only five people on the planet, she knows you know she knows you know this does not present a problem for THE numero uno at Paramount, and she called you at ONE O'CLOCK AM LA time because she knows you know she knows you know she would only do this as an indication of her conviction that you're Hot Shit. So THE numero uno explained that when she heard the pitch for *Damascene* she thought you were *bonkers* but this is a work of *genius*, Jake, we need to *talk*, she said, that's all I ask, let's just sit down eyeball to eyeball, Jake, I want to hear your ideas, you've got balls, Jake, you're not afraid to take risks, I'd like to see what you do when you have total artistic control, Jake, we can offer $4 million for your next screenplay sight unseen but gosh, I know you're not interested in money, this is not about money, it's about freedom, we'd like to Concorde you back so we can discuss this on a person-to-person basis.

You explained your situation and she said Let me say just one thing. Your life is too complicated. We can simplify it for you.

You said What do you mean? and Mary Poppins said what she meant, she could snap her fingers at complications that looked like purely personal problems and they would disappear. Just think about it, said Mary Poppins, and she said Let me give you my direct line.

Poppins did not specifically mention Nadezhda Vessarova. She knows you know she knows you know it was one of the things she meant.

Your friend Dillon had been telling you it's time to move on. It's time to aim higher. Do the impossible. Film an unfilmable book. Forget *Lotteryland,* he said, have you seen *Your Name Here,* the new novel by Helen DeWitt? I was talking to Johnny Depp and he *loves* it, he'd love to work with you, what are you waiting for?

As a matter of purely academic interest Mary Poppins loves Johnny Depp.

Still. You've been obsessing about *Lotteryland* for years, it's a very personal project, you definitely want to make this movie, the material is definitely great.

Sometimes you do things people totally don't get. You left the apartment, slid down the wrought-iron bannister for six flights, went to the wine guy and bought three bottles of Saint-Emilion Château Cheval Blanc 1er Grand Cru Classé A, 1990, for 2400 bucks.

16
The
Impure
Propagandist

What become of her new straw hat that should have come to me? Somebody pinched it; and what I say is, them as pinched it done her in.

George Bernard Shaw, Pygmalion

Wäre also nicht die Menschen im grunde gleichgultig gegen das was mit allen anderen geschieht außer dem Paar mit dem sie eng verbunden sind, so wäre Auschwitz nicht möglich gewesen.

If people were not fundamentally indifferent to what happens to others apart from the couple with whom they are closely bound, Auschwitz would not have been possible.

Theodor Adorno

1

From: "Kaplan Thornhill" <nxnw@hotmail.com>
To: "Rachel Zozanian" <zozanian@onetel.com>
Subject: sugar cubes dropped from great heights
Date: Tues 25 Apr 2006 13:34:53 +0000

So you back? hope London was productive and exciting being back. I didn;t make it to Hamsterdam for several funny reasons will relay in full ancedote mode - got a story so kinda of worth it.

felt pretty strange all weekend actually.

well if you are back i am going to be in Kruezberg to participate in the simulation of a violent angry protest against everything oppressive except of course violent angry oppressive protests simulations/ MAY DAY MAY DAY MAY DAY . . . not sure exactly when the revolution pertains to begin/have begun, revolutions, but its a yearly affair on this May first and apparently is fun to watch the argy bargy - um, well ok it goes and it goes. Throwing stones. In glasses houses.

the treadmil at varying speeds continues its varying speeds. ok hope you well
kaplan

From: “Rachel Zozanian” <zozanian@onetel.com>
To: “Kaplan Thornhill” <nxnw@hotmail.com>
Subject: RE: sugar cubes dropped from great heights
Date: Tues 2 May 2006 01:11:01 +0000

kaplan
London ok, didn’t go out much because i was staying with Lily. feels good to be back. hope you had a good revolution. have the cheques cleared yet?
rachel

From: “Kaplan Thornhill” <nxnw@hotmail.com>
To: “Rachel Zozanian” <zozanian@onetel.com>
Subject: kreuzberg howl
Date: Tues 2 May 2006 14:37:20 +0000

Yes! It was quite a nice day wondering around - like a mini version of London’s Carnival just without any black people. i do find Berlin a city without smiles. I tested it out today and gave ten generous smiles in a row to varying ages sexes gender and received nothing other than a stare or darted look away. this didn’t help my dwindling resources towards berlin - the PR campaign lost but i do say when it comes to throwing bottles, rocks and inanimate objects they do a good job at it and I was pleased and happy at a far more vigourous carnival of theatrics...at the end of the day i was in the thick of it all - whizzing bottles, bircks and cheers and thumps – all a little unusual without a camera or concealed weapon. the odd feeling that the people outnumber the police but that focualtian notion that the self police kept the majority at bay . . .

have now hit a rocky patch somewhat and while some people call it ‘becoming german’ i wonder what there is in life without alcohol or drugs. oh my pasta and pesto is ready, how exciting -- ok well lets meet sometime this week. Everything is pegged to the blood sugar levels these days and also the fact those US cheques haven’t cleared. ok well hope London was great . . .

and yes, my pasta is ready but yes, we have no banannas
kaplan

2

[rachel gets nowhere with her manetian mametian fairy tale. in march the british government had announced that universities would be allowed to charge £3000 top-up fees beginning september, in line with the recommendations of the russell group. it had explained that this would in no way diminish access and everything was under control.]

Not to be unkind, the Charge of the Light Brigade, the Battle of the Somme and Gallipoli are not rare, uncharacteristic examples of snafus on the part of British higher-ups which send gullible lower-downs obediently off to die. An 18-year-old raised from infancy in the Amazonian rainforest might be reassured by a Government pronouncement on educational funding. As it happens, the number of Tarzans in the pool of university applicants is small; the average British 18-year-old has grown up in, um, Britain. Blair would like to see some smiling faces for a change. Tarzan, where art thou?

The Russell Group, anyway, is rivalled only by the Australian Wheat Board and Thermazopam as a cure for insomnia, which is, of course, one reason a formerly cash-strapped young author decided to go the gloriously Mel Brooksian naming-no-names-let-alone-quangoes route with *Lotteryland*. Since 50 percent of the authorship of *Hustlers* remains cash-strapped to this very hour it's a bit self-indulgent of the cash-cushioned 50 percent of the authorship to resort to gratuitous discourses on the Russell Group instead of, as it might be, gratuitous sex, drugs and violence. Ha ha. Ha ha. Ha ha.

The show trials of the Stalinist Soviet Union are notorious: eminent undesirables confessed publicly to ludicrous crimes after behind-the-scenes persuasion. Eminent British academics are not taken from their homes at night, subjected to cattle prods, water cannon, sleep deprivation, beatings that leave no mark and hauled out to face the press. They are not subjected to sexual humiliation: Blair does not "invite" the Regius Professor of Virtual Reality to 11 Downing Street and tell him to suck dick. So if you talk to someone from the Czech Republic, if you talk to someone from the former Soviet Union about pressure they will laugh in your face.

British academics are subjected, instead, to intellectual humiliation. If the underfunding of certain university departments is to look fair, overstretched staff at even the best universities must divert time from research and teaching to paperwork—paperwork proving their excellence in teaching and research to the kind of moron who draws up forms with separate headings for aims and objectives.

A professor at Yale does not have to waste time proving that Yale is better than Flagler. The kind of hotshot who is in the running for a Nobel prize does not have a lot of time for timewasters; the hotshot looks at the facilities and salary and absence of administrative crap on offer across the water, spares a brief glance for an inbox where the British bull has shat, and vacates the premises. Or looks for ways to get more money into the system.

The Russell Group, anyway, is a group of British universities who think they should be allowed to cover some of the cost of teaching students by charging fees, capitalising on their market value as is done by, say, Yale, Harvard, Princeton, Stanford, or the University of Chicago.[12] £3000 (about US$6000) looks paltry when a year at Yale might cost $30K. Yale and its cohorts, however, have an uninterrupted history of endowment going back to their foundation. British universities, on the other hand, have endowments like the Ella Stephens Greek Scholarship Fund, scholarships that looked superfluous to requirements for a period of twenty years when all British university students received a maintenance grant. Some American students can't afford to go to Yale or Harvard; some go as second-class citizens, scrambling to pay their way; for about twenty years anyone who was accepted to Oxford or Cambridge or Imperial College London could afford

12. Readers new to the machinations of the Group will be relieved to know that it takes its name from the Russell Hotel, where it hatched its schemes; it does not profess adherence to the principles of Bertrand Russell.

to go, where "go" is defined as spending vacations reading, as it might be, the whole of Homer and Virgil or tackling a mathematical Everest of similar height, vacation jobs being strenglich verboten. With the result that the first two years of undergraduate study were the equivalent of the first two years of graduate study at American institutions with a more flexible approach to funding.

Only about 10 percent of students went to university; the aim was to raise this to 50 percent. Government funding could no longer provide a grant for all, and the much larger number and size of universities could no longer be funded on the same scale. So, on the one hand, universities were forced to compete with each other for funding by performing various assessment exercises and, on the other hand, a a system of student loans was introduced to be supplemented by the previously forbidden vacation jobs. So access was widened to something, but not to university as an Everest expedition, which was no longer available to anyone.

Makes the Australian Wheat Board look exciting, no?

Look at it this way. A young chemist who can manufacture MDMA in the lab should have have no pressing financial worries.

Look at it this way. My body is an asset. If I choose not to exploit that asset, that's my decision. Why should I expect other people to subsidise that decision?

1.1.1.1.2.1.4 = ١.١.١.١.٢.١.٤

£50	£1000	£100
£1	£100	£1000
£1	£20	£50

Better luck next time.

The client is wearing a charcoal grey Hugo Boss coat, a charcoal grey Hugo Boss suit, a black shirt and black silk tie. The high, narrow lapels of the suit permit only a glimpse of shirt and tie.

He takes a slim gleaming black leather wallet from an inside pocket of the suit. He removes six 50-pound notes. I count them and put them in my bag.

Presently the suit and its owner are briefly parted. The jacket is hung upon a thick wooden hanger, one of five suspended by locked rings from a rail in the wardrobe. The trousers are hung by their cuffs, is there not a piece by Ana Maria Pacheco of a naked man strung up by the ankles? Called?

A narrow black belt coils on a chair.

Some sort of effort appears to be being made at spontaneity; the tie is loosened, tossed carelessly over the TV, as is its companion, the shirt. Labels now visible declare provenance: the tie owes allegiance to Calvin Klein, the shirt to Paul Smith. A white Calvin Klein T-shirt and boxer shirts leave the unbranded body to the air.

There is a thick pelt of silky hair on the chest and back, a tight trail of hair to the navel, a black fur rug below. Lolling in the black fur is a naked cock. There are light throws of loose black hair on the forearms, hair creeping up over the hands to the first knuckles. There is an abundance of black hair on the plump thighs and narrow shins.

This is the sense: of a scene in *The Fly*. Is there not a recurring American Werewolf theme in Jack the Modernist? I think there is. There is a sense that it would be more interesting if this were a werewolf.

He says: I'd like you to suck me first. Take off your clothes.

I say: OK.

I put the kilt and the sweater on a chair. I put my bra and pants on top.

He says: You need to lose weight.

I say: Why?

He says: You need to lose at least a stone.

I say: Why?

He says: There's nothing worse than a fat tart.

I say: I don't think I'll ever be worth more than 300 pounds in this line of work.

He says: You're not worth it now.

I say: OK. Do you want your money back?

He says: You're a piece of shit.

I say: You'd better have your money back.

He says: You piece of shit.

His arm goes back very rapidly. The hand slams across the side of my head. I fall to the floor and begin to get up and he hits me again.

He says: Do you like that? Do you like that? Is that what turns you on?

I say: Yes. That's what I like. I like violent sex. I want you to fuck me.

The thought is something like: He does in fact have quite a long penis. If he goes to public toilets he must see that it is longer than most of the competition. There does seem to be quite a lot of hair, more hair than a man with a liking for Hugo Boss would perhaps have chosen if the body, too, could be bought off the rail. But could he not take solace?

The thought is something like: It could be better to play the game.

He says: I will most definitely fuck you.

He hits the side of my head again.

I think this is very bad for the head. I do not want to damage such mental faculties as remain. I allow the momentum of the blow to carry me plausibly a long way across the floor. He takes two or three quick steps after me, his cock bouncing against the fur, draws one foot back and brings it swiftly forward. Of course as soon as I see the foot going back I know I must catch it on the kick. I seize it as it comes. He staggers, hopping on the grounded foot, trying to wrench the captured foot back (and this too has tufts of hair on the toes), then falls sideways. I leap to my feet, to the door, snatching at the chairful of garments and coming away with my bag. I scrabble at the door and then I am in the corridor walking fast.

The side of my head feels as though a piece of ice had been held against it.

The head is not very clever. It seems as though this is likely to cause problems, making it difficult to use the hotel.

Although it was rational to take the bag rather than clothes (the latter cd be replaced for under fifty pounds), it is not common to buy clothes wearing none.

Could my boyfriend be a Hooray Henry? Could he be a fucking arsehole?

I have no clothes to undermine my claim to have such a boyfriend.

A magenta jacket and black trousers with a satin stripe up the side approach.

I say: My boyfriend is being a fucking arsehole.

He says: I'm sorry to hear that, madam. We can't have you wandering about like this though now then can we? It will disturb the other guests.

I say: I *know*, I *know*, 'snot a fucking nudist colony, mustn't wander round starkers, be an *angel*, let me into one of the rooms and I'll lie doggo while you rouse my clothes. They're in room 114.

He says: Oooh, I don't know about that madam, I can't go barging into the rooms without so much as a by your leave and remove *clothes*, which *may* or *may not* belong to you—

I say: Well, you'd better park me in one of the rooms while you make up your mind.

He opens the door to a broom cupboard and says: Wait here.

I say: Isn't there a spare uniform I could borrow?

He says: The uniforms are hotel property, madam. They are not permitted to leave the premises.

I say: Oh. Right.

I say: Well, look, if I give you £100 could you nip round the corner and buy me a fig leaf?

He says: I don't know about that, madam—

I say: You can keep the change. I just want to get away from this fucking arsehole.

Open sesame.

He came back in half an hour with a black pullover and a black and white houndstooth skirt from which the labels had been cut out.

I said: Cheers.

I walked out into St Giles.

[£300. Never seen again]

1.1.1.2.1.4.1. = ١.١.١.١.٢.١.٤.١.

£100	£50	£1
£20	£100	£50
£1	£20	£10,000

Better luck next time.

The client says: I don't normally do this kind of thing.

He's walking up and down the mean little room which he gets at the Randolph for £90. There's a double bed and a bit of carpet beyond the foot of the bed to pace.

He says: We've had another baby. There's that book by what's his name, isn't there, there was a big stink when it came out, but i read it and I thought it said things that simply weren't being said. We're sexual beings—we've known that since Freud. it's one thing to give the mother of children economic security—I see the value of that. But why should I be condemned to

He says: I'd give up everything I have if I could walk out the door. But look. I'm paying you for sex. You have something I want. I'm paying for it. I understand that we may or may not think it's a good thing but it's comprehensible. What I fail to grasp is, why should I have to pay *not* to sleep with my wife?

I say: If you put it in those terms it sounds irrational and unjust. It is the choice of terms that is under debate.

He says: No, actually, that's exactly what it's about. The streets are full of unattractive women; no one expects me to pay for the privilege of not having sex with them. Why should any sort of legal ceremony convert not having sex with someone into something one has to buy? 200 pounds is quite a hefty sum to pay for sex with you, but it's nothing to what I'd have to pay simply to place my wife on the same footing as all the other unattractive women in the street.

Talk talk, talk talk. Not included.
I say: Are you here to talk or to fuck?

[*£300. Never seen again.*]

1.1.1.1.2.1.5 = ١.١.١.١.٢.١.٥ *[£550. Never seen again].*

Even heavily discounted, the Prada of prostitution is perceived as ludicrously overpriced. The clients like taking their engorged members where the Gonzo has gone, but it's never enough; despite accepting the offered discount for silence they are unable to restrain themselves, asking eager questions about their anti-hero, digging for details, wanting to know the totally disgusting too-sordid-even-for-the-[Name Withheld] Magazine perversions and debaucheries. The possibility that fact might be less interesting than the fiction of a pharmaceutically-enhanced pathological liar does not occur.

1.1.1.1.2.1.6 = ١.١.١.١.٢.١.٦ [£575. Never seen again.]
1.1.1.1.2.1.7 = ١.١.١.١.٢.١.٧ [£420. Never seen again.]
1.1.1.1.2.1.8 = ١.١.١.١.٢.١.٨ [£525. Never seen again.]
1.1.1.1.2.1.9 = ١.١.١.١.٢.١.٩ [£360. Never seen again.]
1.1.1.1.2.1.10 = ١.١.١.١.٢.١.١٠ [£495. Never seen again.]
1.1.1.1.2.1.11 = ١.١.١.١.٢.١.١١ [£320. Never seen again.]
1.1.1.1.2.1.12 = ١.١.١.١.٢.١.١٢ [£345. Never seen again.]
1.1.1.1.2.1.13 = ١.١.١.١.٢.١.١٣ [£415. Never seen again.]
1.1.1.1.2.1.14 = ١.١.١.١.٢.١.١٤ [£240. Never seen again.]
1.1.1.1.2.1.15 = ١.١.١.١.٢.١.١٥ [£330. Never seen again.]
1.1.1.1.2.1.16 = ١.١.١.١.٢.١.١٦ [£210. Never seen again.]

and there's always the novel, ha ha, ha ha, and there's always the novel, ha ha

3

[but 50 percent grew up in oz, where graduates do not rack up debt, they simply pay a higher tax if they earn more than $15,000 a year (which perhaps accounts for the happy-go-lucky nietszchian jouissance of the black-market boy), and his response to the machinations of the russell group is roughly that of the average reader to the wheelings and dealings of the australian wheat board]

From: "Kaplan Thornhill" <nxnw@hotmail.com>
To: "Rachel Zozanian" <zozanian@onetel.com>
Subject: figures in flux
Date: Wed 3 May 2006 14:45:42 +0000

i uynderstnad this and perhaps one needs to show the elastic values of cash money value. i learnt about this with the national enquirer, where 3500 euros was spent on a 25 minute private jet hire from athens to santorini when chasing the bum lead of angelina jolie bread shit being in santorini. three of us stayed in 50 euro a night hotels ate drank and i spent the 2000 us spending moeny on various made up things..with flight from london to athens it worked out to be around 10 000 on nothing but i got a four night holiday.

i think then you need to illustrate the varying comforts or ease or liquidity of this figure wherever it lies. 1000 for me opens up endless months of exotic travel, ok maybe a month or two but for some guy it is one night for another it is several nights fucking a prostitute. a week of crack cocaine use or a few nights drinking fine wine...then there is the politics of do you get your money's worth, i do think some guys are going to expect more - like some specifiic desirs the others won't do...

what are we/you trying to say in this exchange? sex for money - the figure is in flux but demonstrating what?

not sure about the relentless sexualisation of the narrative - perhaps a tad too long?

kaplan

4

This was not very heartwarming, but everyone knows some things are best passed in diegetic silence-over. It's easier to make a friend of a stranger than a stranger of a friend. DSO, baby, DSO.

17

?
Afternote to LECTURE ON NOTHING

In keeping with the thought expressed above that a discussion is nothing more than an entertainment, I prepared six answers for the first six questions asked, regardless of what they were. In 1949 or '50, when the lecture was first delivered (at the Artists' Club as described in the Foreword), there were six questions. In 1960, however, when the speech was delivered for the second time, the audience got the point after two questions and, not wishing to be entertained, refrained from asking anything more.
The answers are:

1. *That is a very good question. I should not want to spoil it with an answer.*
2. *My head wants to ache.*
3. *Had you heard Marya Freund last April in Palermo singing Arnold Schoenberg's* Pierrot Lunaire, *I doubt whether you would ask that question.*
4. *According to the Farmers' Almanac this is False Spring.*
5. *Please repeat the question . . .*
   And again . . .
   And again . . .
6. *I have no more answers.*

[John Cage, Silence, *p 126]*

1

[there's no reply. this is somewhat worrying given the cashflow situation. but perhaps and perchance]

X-Originating-IP: [84.188.232.142]
From: "Kaplan Thornhill" <nxnw@hotmail.com>
To: "Rachel Zozanian" <zozanian@onetel.com>
Subject: please mention the war we are German
Date: Mon 19 June 2006 14:38:36 +0000

below is a call to arms for the Mail on Sunday and Sunday Mirror . . . forgot to mention former stasi bureau krauts working as train bus ticket inspectors.

yes, i was thinking of including the farsi of 'do you have pain killers' and more unusual arabic in the text . . . perhaps talk of making a guide book for travelling with no guidebook!

but i will think of a few arabic words worthy of noting. . . .

reading Sadie Plant's 'writing on drugs,' which is fucking phantastic, so much ! And one story well known but interesting is the word *assassian,* coming from Arabic meaning hashish smoker *hashishiyya*..cause they took a lot before going out and killing to enter into the paradise they saw when on hash (supplied by a cunning overload yadda yadda)

ok more to come- as ever-oh, also that cheque hasnt cleared and despite a US -UK pact in their coalition of Willing against the axis of evil - yadda yadda, i think they still are suspicious of each other's currency - perhaps simply the very precepts of global capitalism itself.

but this leaves me somewhat in between impecunious and archiac/anarchicistic technologies...for i am now sweeping up dust from my house with a broom and dust pan and broom as the vacuum vampire has a fulll bag and also i need to buy more blank CDs as i am sending over to Australia all my pictures of travels here and ther for her assessment as to whether there is a good back drop for say 50 000 words of travel yarns like in pakistan and iran ad turkey - the third of the two year trilogy, kill em all and let god decide- (mis) adventures through the orient...three cds full and only one is, also milk for coffee otherwise it is a bitter sweeet brew tough on the old tum tum...so, i was wondering can you spot me hard currency? Until alles klar, until alles gut, sent between our banks. perhaps this can underline our next encounter work related or social, whichever comes first.

danke, & Tanks

kaplan

2

[still no reply]

Nadia was sitting in Schonwitte Bar with her friend Christian. This outdoor bar annexed a corner in Mauer Park, east Berlin, where seasonally laid sand gave it a feeling of being in a golf course bunker not desert island. I sat along the wooden seating thinking she and the two tattooed Norwegians were part of our group massing around the table behind. Drunk and excited, sand and candle light, I exchanged my German hellos then explained to the inquiry I was another cliché in Berlin. *ICH VICE*, I Know, *ICH VICE*, I Know, JA JA, JA, Writing that GREAT/EST UNPUBLISHED NOVEL. Trying to avoid the cliché of Hack Journalism in London. The Hack in Hackney living off (Night)Mare St and Murder Mile. Now on Sonntag Strasse . . . every day is Sunday street

They laughed. Her friend said his friend was also writing a book but started three years ago. Genau, (exactly) Genau, and now he figures serving behind the bar, Wilkomme zu Berlin. Exactly. The Norwegians begin singing almost: RABBIT PROOF FENCE , a film telling one story of Australian Aboriginal girls fleeing the state sanctioned ethnic cleansing child care seen in the 1930s. The stolen generation, we call it. Nadia explained she was a 21-year-old Venetian writer/painter who works in a Schöneberg ice cream shop. The best apparently.

It's 50-cent deposit on each bottle. I find three (empty) to exchange for one (full). . . . Christian has gone and Nadia is buying a beer next to me. We sit together and I wobble on about this and that about my new arrival in Berlin.

The bar empty, the beers finish, no more errant bottles to exchange for new fresh ones. Even with exact change the bar is not interested in trading.

FIRE ABEND

WAS IS DAS? ICH MOCKTE FILA BEIREN.

NEIN. FIRE ABEND

WARUM? ICK VICE NICHT RICHTIG.

The bar guy wearing a They Might Be Giants T-shirt ignores my shit and suggests better places to be. Nadia says FIRE ABEND means the bar is shut, the end of the night. So I casually ask her if she would like to come with me for another roll of the dice. She smiles and ums and Rs. I smile and she smiles and whines her body in a coquettish fashion. I say 'well let's leave it and work it out on the way. Where do you live?'

We leave through the sand, a dry desert once filled by drinking shadows, I stumble into the darkness without any excited hop step or skip. I have to find the bike I have locked somewhere, six beers ago.

She disappears for her bike into the darkened edges of a fence covered by foliage. I wheel my (t)rusty steed along the white sandy gravel and think she's absconded.

I turn round the corner and see her shadowy form wheeling a bike towards me. The bike's headlamp shines a limp orange dot ever so slightly expanding in the darkness, this increasing glow like a burning hole in paper is beside the full moon's spotlight around her. It seems a dream. Closer and closer she comes to me in a direct line. We walk straight into each. We merge face to face, we meet in the fluid embrace of a kiss. Gently, kissing, her bike drops with a dramatic crash of metals, I tentatively suck her coy tongue and then I let go (of my bike) following is another crash as if there is no return.

Her mouth tender and gentle with my play. Little kisses building the blood's need for oxygen, more and more, slowly, spiralling to wider mouths and thirsty tongues dotted for and by taste. These desperate confident hungry meshings of lips evaporate every thought I've ever had, tongues, saliva and hips grind as if breathing is the distraction. Teeth biting each other. Panting breaths, soft moans. We stand kissing passionately in the path's centre, the bar's employees leave with CHEW-SY,

AUF WEIDERSENS

and BIS MORGANT,

I lick her lips and edges of her teeth. She is stroking my face as I squeeze her soft arse and stroke her hard flat stomach. I lick her neck and she moans ever so slightly then I slightly bite her neck and she whimpers. I lick the mark as if a wound my saliva can heal, then move back to her mouth with tiny little kisses. The kiss move up the gears to become a vicious gnashing of mouths 'kissing.' Our breathing reaches a peak of necessary departure. We break.

giggle and let out those deep searching exalted exhalations of what was that . . . Maybe we should sit down I suggest, we move into the near by field, a few steps off the gravel path, she throws herself on the ground, her opening her legs invite me to move between.

I am watching her outstretched arm, hand gripping the weeds and grass, she pulls with oscillating intensities and I watch it correlate to my gyrating and thrusting hips. The earth holds it grip against such destructive forces, I am pulled into her and she pulls at the earth's hair. She grips the closest bunch of weeds then lets it go with concurrent thrusts of my push further into her. Her fashionably green pleated skirt has been lifted up coagulating around her waist, she had whipped her black pants off in one movement and now I see her Argentinean Jesus sandals, straps tied around and up her ankle and shin, sway and bob in my peripheral vision. She has her legs so desperately wide open and up in the air, so open, so wanting of me to push deeper into her. Her wetness soaks the tightness, contracting muscles contract as I pull her shoulders down and thrust deeper into her. She is screaming in my ear.

OH MEIN GOT, OH MEIN GOT, YA, YA,

She is so lost in screaming, makes me want her to say FRICK ME DU AUSLANDER SCHWINE, but I realise she has probably forgotten my foreignness, now I'm inside her.

My jeans undone at the top but fully on, restriction and restraint as I hunger for more. I pull my balls out from their unbranded underpant cover and with my cock in as far as possible I push harder against her. I pull down on her shoulder and her back arches towards me, she catches her breath then I slide back as if out then quickly forward to begin a furious chord of fucking. She arches almost the opposite to how she was, screams into the lidless night. I keep laying into her feeling each thrust bringing me closer to orgasm. She is pulling grass out of the ground writhing around as if the last moments of the deer's life during a lion's consumption. Would you like to fuck a lion? Be devoured by one? The eater and the eaten.

We fuck on. Then again and again with similar passion. I hold underneath her arse and roll my hips into her while pulling it up with each thwack of my coccyx against her vagina. She kisses me frantically making louder noises that fill the field's empty space. Such a wide-open field with the late late night or early early morning light. The ugly coarse Mauer Park, now there is a hint of felicity in the air, the space allowed with another early summer morning, I applaud Soviet Architecture as my groin slams repeatedly into her and she keeps speaking, sort of mumbling, in German.

I shoot again, NORMAN MAILER stabbed his wife, BURROUGHS shot his, Bukowski, the list goes on . . . I just hold her jaw with one hand while realising/releasing her hair from the other. She nuzzles in close to my neck. Don't I am not that good. The German word for misogyny is der Weiberfeind. Passion is leidenschaft. Ich bin fremd hier. Why am I thinking this now?

She calms her volume to sighs and deep breaths drawing me down with her chest, then up I go with its expansion. I roll off to the side sweating and dizzy, she doesn't move just lies there, limp, hypnotised dead, gently stroking my brow with her hand. We lie/lye there for a while not talking. The sun brings the new day's light. We laugh, she rolls her body over and kisses me. Looks me in the eyes in that you've seen it all and it's just begun. I playfully push down her skirt and realise I hadn't touched her breasts. I play with the left nipple through the fabric of her white top and breath out little sighs of satisfaction. I tell her I have never fucked in a field, never like this before. All while Mitte and P'berg sleep in their renovated apartments. I've had sex in public, in alleyways, car parks and in darkened East London streets in full view of Nouveau Riche apartments but never felt so open with someone I've just met. Her too she says with a laugh and squeeze of my chest. She says she liked it when I put both my hands into hers and held them down above her head. We laugh and kiss like old lovers. Depart like new friends. As if nothing happened retrieve our scattered bikes still lying in the middle of the path. With no hands I ride my bike down the hill and towards home in the early morning light steering me safely.

3

[still no reply]

18

Guildenstern

No, I am not Prince Hamlet, nor was meant to be

You came to Berlin on a recommendation from a friend who died a long time ago.

It was September 1992; you were a shy 15-year-old in 10th grade at the Colegio Jorge Washington. Your father was a simple businessman working in Cartagena, Colombia—the kind of simple businessman who scoffs when asked if he works for the CIA. You spent a lot of time hanging around the pool at the conspicuously consumptive residence of Hro Zozanian—the kind of simple businessman who does not get asked if he works with the Cartagena Cartel. The ostensible reason was Rachel, your first and last girlfriend.

The Zozanians had glamorous visitors, Simon Crawford who made movies and ran art zines, his significant other Krzysztof who traded Forex and owned a gallery in Hoxton, Jake Noszaly who had directed the to-die-for *Count,* the fabulous Vessarova, your age and already a star.

Krzysztof was dying amid recriminations. He sat in a cushioned wicker chair reading *Du coté de chez Swann* while Simon cried passionately: You are *destroying* everything we *had.* You are *obliterating* the *past.* But if it never *happened . . .*

Krzysztof said: You know, I kept *saying* I'd get round to reading this and putting it *off,* but it's actually *Not.* at *All.* *Bad.*

Simon said: J'abandonne.

Krzysztof sat quietly in the wicker chair for three hours.

He said: It was stupid to wait this long. I should have

He said: I've always loved KaDeWe.

He said: Fortnum's—well, it's *all* very well in its *way,* but the *attitude* is, what you do in the privacy of your own *home* is *your* business. Just because we *sell* the stuff doesn't mean we can have you *eating* it on the *premises.* They have a poxy little tearoom at the back where you eat the sort of thing the British *do* eat, bless them, in public spaces. You can get a cream tea. You can get fish and bloody chips. Whereas if you go to the sixth floor of KaDeWe, well, there's the same jolly feeling of stumbling on the *Galapagos* of

He coughed. He said: Fuck. He coughed. He said: Fuck. Fuck. Fuck. He turned his head away and transferred a bloodstreaked clot of green sputum to a man-sized Kleenex, which he dropped into a wicker basket by the chair.

this mini-Galapagos of *conserves,* and of course the *Wurst* are

Cough. Fuck. Cough. Fuck. Spit.

what they've got is each little *département* or whatever you want to call it has its own little *counter,* with high *stools,* so you can *sample,* as it were

Cough. Cough.

one could spend the night making the rounds of a series of rather seedy gay bars off Nollendorfplatz and then make one's way over to Wittenbergplatz for *elevenses,* as it might be, one had the sense of rejoining *civilisation.* One shaved, one turned up with one's toes turned out, as who should say 'I washed my hands and face before I came.' *Luvverly.* And it's on the sixth floor, you see, and there's a, what's the word, a well, maybe? this fucking big block of empty space going up to the roof, so you can look down to the ground from any floor, or, of course, up to the roof from the ground. One could have done the deed in a couple of seconds. Should have.

Well, that was sad. And it was sad that he spoke Polish till the age of six and then forgot it because his mother took him to Britain and it was sad that he grew up in Walthamstow answering to the name of Chris and it was sad that he never knew his father until it was too late. And it was *tragic* that he never explained Forex to Simon, it wasn't the *money,* it was the betrayal of *trust.* But you loved the sheer unabashed sense of occasion, the poolside deathbed drama, all so gloriously different from the tightlipped upbuttoned self-effacement of your father the suit. You made a mental note to make the pilgrimage.

—

KaDeWe, the Kaufhaus des Westens, that monument of materialism, has seven floors, as it turns out, the seventh offering an overpriced cafeteria and the Palmenbar, a bar with towering plastic palms, from which one could also presumably do the deed in a couple of seconds. There were tall stools with green plastic seats overlooking the drop, though the void was walled off by glass panes beneath a brass rail; you liked to sit there once in a while with a Long Island Iced Tea; you'd been meaning to read *Mephisto* for years and kept putting it off, but it's actually not at all bad.

You'd seen people writing snatches of Arabic on napkins, Filofaxes, agendas,

بانانا

appears on the yellow legal pad next to you while the speaker fires the first Powerpoint bullet, followed by

- تيتيكاكا
- بيكيت
- كافكا

and then the scribbler rather sweetly runs out of words and it's back to

- بانانا

You'd seen people reading *Your Name Here,* the new novel by Helen DeWitt. You think it misses the point.

You taught yourself Arabic years ago. You love Abu Nuwas, Baudelaire of the Abbasids. It's not just the poetry, it's not even just the wine, the boys, addicted though you've always been to this winsome threesome. The thing you love is that fucking Abu Nuwas wrote fucking *poetry* about getting drunk, chasing boys, within an Islamic society where wine and homosexuality were strenglich fucking verboten, this was back in the 10th *century*, for fuck's sake, but Abu Nuwas was both a lunatic and a genius and he just *did* it. Without benefit of swoosh. So whenever you hear some sensitive soul telling his coming-out story you either keep stumm or make yourself unpopular by talking about Abu Nuwas, Baudelaire of the Abbasids, and of course then there's the whole *Galataseray*, because homohomophobia is such a *cliché*, you've had this discussion a gazillion times each more stultifying than the last, if you want to know just how much Xanax the human body can absorb before tipping over into a catatonic trance this is a way to find out with embossed goldleafed copperplated gothicscripted vellumfetishisted fuckfisted testimonials, motto, keep on poppin', but long story short this is your *hero*, this is a writer everyone should *know* about because we *need* to *know* that it is *always ALWAYS ALWAYS* possible not just to stand *up* to oppression but to *celebrate*—to *CELEBRATE*—to

CELEBRATE

—this is your spiel after the cocktail course, the white wine course, the red wine course, the dessert wine course and the cognac-plus-El Presidente course (Abu Nuwas would have understood).

You were initially captivated by Berlin. You were in a city with three operas. Barenboim was at the Staatsoper, Rattle at the Berlin Phil. You'd read Fried on Menzel, you went to the Alte Nationalgalerie and saw room after room of the work of this underknown genius, this dwarf who used the constraints of his stature to transform realism. You saw Nefertiti! You got a loft in P'berg for the price of a shared closet in Queens. You made the rounds of seedy and not so seedy gay bars.

Then things went sour. There was a boy you liked, you went to a lot of trouble, he treated you like a piece of shit. If you could stop the fucking war in Iraq by living on, being treated like a piece of shit, you might do it, fact is the Army's "don't ask don't tell" policy expelled you into civilian life when addressing the shortage of Arabists was of the quote unquote utmost importance to national security.

You'd never been the suicidal type, but now you were ready to take the drop. You planned the multiple meals you would enjoy before the leap. And the goddess of wisdom whispered in your ear: Ahem. Joe. Do you KNOW this will work?

We-e-e-e-e-l-l . . . Krzysztof knew a lot about carpets; he knew a lot about wine; he knew his divas; was this in fact someone you would trust to sit down and calculate the rate of velocity upon impact of a body falling from the seventh floor of KaDeWe?

We-e-e-e-e-e-e-e-e-e-e-e-e-e-l-l-l-l-l-l-l-l-l-l-l-l-l-l-l-l-l-l-l-l-l-l-l-l . . .

You'd read *Ethan Frome* at an impressionable age. You did not repeat not repeat *not* want to attempt suicide only to find yourself a living on as a cripple, only too possibly a cripple living on in the bosom of its loving family.

You dug up the formula. You plugged in a highly speculative figure for the length of the drop and arrived at a velocity that appeared to be that of a car travelling in a built-up area. Your grasp of differentiation is not something on which you would want to base this kind of death-threatening decision, given the extracurricular activities which took up your time the year you got a D- in calculus at precocious 16 (Abu Nuwas would have understood). You did some more research online and found a site which claimed that there was only a 90 percent mortality rate for bodies falling from the sixth floor. With your luck, you just would be the 1 in 10 to survive. Fuck that.

It seemed a pity to miss out on the meals you'd planned out with such care. You went to KaDeWe, no longer your suicide spot of choice. Funnily enough, on one of the stools at the Palmenbar, you saw another alum of Colegio Jorge Washington. Zozanian sat with her hands palm up on the lap of a short black skirt. Had she, too, come to Casablanca for the waters?

You bought an El Presidente to smoke in memory of your faux friend. You might give Cuba a try.

COOGAN GIVES UP

The book is fucked.

19

Hot Shot Take 8 1/2

I don't know. I think Fellini just told me things about my future.
He told me things about the process of life.
He told me things about memory that all seems true and honest and believable, even though he lies the whole time.
That's what I love about Fellini, he's a liar.
He's a constant liar. He twists and distorts the truth.

Terry Gilliam

1

You felt very very good about the way you'd developed your second-person narrator. You were definitely the Mastroianni in the book. Mastroianni was not afraid to take risks. He was not afraid to make a fool of himself. There's a vulnerability to Mastroianni, there's a versatility, there's an unerring sense of style, this was what you had managed to capture in a relatively small number of pages. (Some of your best scenes were cut, but an editor may well want to cut back some of the other characters to have you on-page longer.)

They hadn't raised the subject of Arabic for a few hundred pages, though you would definitely have been open to doing more with it. You mentioned this casually in passing. They said, "The situation has progressed."

You said, "In what way?"

They said, "What do you know about John Negroponte, Jake?"

You said, "Went to Iraq as Ambassador after the handover. Currently Director of the Office of National Security. Why?"

They said, "Let's just put it this way. On September 11, 2001 the man in charge of counterterrorism at the FBI did not know the difference between Shiites and Sunnites. *He still doesn't know*. Out of 12,000 FBI agents, 33 have some knowledge of Arabic; six are fluent. A fluent agent has recently been *taken off counterterrorism*."

You said, "But surely you don't think Negroponte was behind it!"

They said: "Don't call me Shirley."

This was the level of sophistication.

They then said: "Joking aside, Jake. Negroponte has not contacted us directly. *But then he wouldn't, would he?* Suffice it to say, we've been given to understand that the ambitious program backed by our initial sources would be unwelcome in other quarters. Let's just leave it at that."

From: "Jake Noszaly" <noszaly@gmail.com>
To: "Rachel Zozanian" <zozanian@onetel.com>
Subject: Call me
Date: Sun 25 June 2006 09:09:57 +0000

Rachel, We need to talk. Call me on my cellphone. The number is 342 759 2292. (Please don't give this number to anyone.) Jake

2

From: "Rachel Zozanian" <zozanian@onetel.com>
To: "Kaplan Thornhill" <nxnw@hotmail.com>
Subject: Zitty ist schuld
Date: Mon 26 June 2006 09:01:37 -0400

Kaplan
Sorry about delays, cheques. a few problems. let's meet, don't want to leave you high and drigh.
i may have to go to Dresden, any interest?
rachel

From: "Kaplan Thornhill" <nxnw@hotmail.com>
To: "Rachel Zozanian" <zozanian@onetel.com>
Subject: RE: Zitty ist schuld
Date: Mon 26 June 2006 11:38:01 -0200

OK WELL DRESDEN SOUNDS GREAT. STILL OFF THE GROG. LETS DO TOMORROW NIGHT- THERE IS MUCH TO TALK ABOUT. ALSO A FILM NIGHT ON AT THAT BOOK SHOP IN PBERG BUT I WAIT TO SEE WHAT IS ON. MUCH TO TELL. I DO HOPE THE GUARDIAN BUDGE A LITTLE -

I HAVE BEEN GETTING A LOT OF FEEDBACK ABOUT THE ZIZECKY LECTURES IN LONDON A LOT OF EXCITEMENT THERE. FEEL THERE IS SOME INTELLECTUAL VALOUR DESPITE THE STRATEGY OF BRUNCH.

BOOK STUFF SOUNDS GOOD - MAYBE BONO COULD GET INVOLVED IN SOME FAUX WAY. MONEY FROM PRODUCTS SPENT GOES TO ARMING THE INSURGENCY.

OK WELL I THINK I AM ALIVE AGAIN. LET'S MEET

TOMORROW. DAY OR NIGHT I AM A BREATH AWAY (WATCHING WITH THE CAPS LOCK ON) _IT FEELS LIKE I AM TALKING TO YOU OVER A FENCE BY STANDING ON MY TIPS OF MY TOES WITH THIS CAPS LOCK

KAPLAN

3

We meet at the Rat Pack, a bar in Yorckstrasse with murals of Sinatra and Dean and Sammy Davis Jr which reminds him of what passes for a bar in Dortmund. I give him 400 euros in an envelope, say I hope it will see him through till the cheques clear. Should it be less? More? I give him a copy of John Fante's *Ask the Dust*.

He says: I want to get out of Berlin, it's very nice but the people here, it's like this is the achievement, getting to Berlin. And getting *out*.

He says: I was trying to work on this story, this girl the Berlinale told me there's some scam, you know in *The Producers* the idea is, who's going to look at the accounts of a play that flops, well, nobody's going to look at the accounts of a movie that never gets made. It seems there is some such practice afoot, production companies set up around options on scripts and so forth as a way to process drug money and such, a lot of it going on in Berlin cause there's 20 percent unemployment. It would have been a great story if I could have found a British angle but I couldn't make that connection.

He says: Hey, all those books you said you wrote that got optioned, did you ever think maybe alles was not klar? This producer who's living in Dubuque, wher'e Dubuque?

I say: It's in Idaho.

He says: Genau, the sticks, did you ever think vielleicht sumfink rotten in the state of Idaho?

I say:

He says: And Tulsa, where's Tulsa?

I say: It's in Oklahoma.

He says: Genau, the sticks, the Dortmund of the West, didn't you tell me the producer of *The Tetragrammaton* was in Tulsa?

I say: The producer of *The Tetragrammaton* is in Pierre, South Dakota. The producer of *Hypno* is in Tulsa. The producer of *The Severed Hand* is in Roanoke, Virginia. There's a friendly deal with someone currently based in Buenos Aires, there's someone in Bangalore, there's someone in Urumqi, you can do an option on the basis of a few chapters people move with jobs they don't want to places they don't like you don't need a conspiracy theory to account for inefficiency and incompetence. It's important not to be paranoid.

He says: But you met these people in Shanghai

I say: Hong Kong

He says: And Colombia, didn't you say you lived in Colombia, didn't it ever seem strange to you that all these people would be buying up books, chapters, whatever, from someone who'd never been published?

I catch the eye of the girl at the bar. Ein Jameson's mit Eis, bitte, ein doppel, do you want something?

Just Apfelschorle, ein Apfelschorle bitte

He says: And this first look agreement, didn't you tell me they all wanted a first look agreement, isn't that somewhat suspicious if someone who can't get even one film off the ground wants to buy up everything else you're working on?

The drinks come. Oh, danke, danke.

He says: There's no story in it, if there's no British angle nobody in Britain gives a fuck unless there's a celebrity angle, but if there was a celebrity angle they wouldn't be films that couldn't get made, makes no difference to me one way or the other, I'm just speculating

I say: Could we stop talking about this?

The former smartass is thinking A*ha*! I always *thought* there was something fishy about the novelization rights. And maybe there was something fishy, yes, perhaps, about so *many* close personal friends having the same brilliant idea. And not to be unkind, there were many many many former 29-year-olds, and it would not have been unlike my father to offer a convenient arrangement with Peter Chan or Nicky D as part of a friendly severance deal. And then, of course, my father grew up on the shores of Lake Van, where the girls weave carpets that tell stories to take with them to their new homes upon marriage, and when a previously nomadic tribe is forbidden to roam, when it is forced into mountain settlements where the flocks die and there is no other source of income (straight out of Virgil!), it's quite common to sell the girls' carpets if a buyer can be found (and my father can always be found). So it would not have been unlike my father to be unsentimental about the disposition of the progeny of a youthful smartass.

But look. What does Jameson (Fredric, not John) have to say? Neurosis is simply this boring imprisonment of the self in itself, crippled by its terror of the new and unexpected, carrying its sameness with it wherever it goes, so that it has the protection of feeling, whatever it might stretch out its hand to touch, that it never meets anything but what it knows already. In other words, forget it. In other words, step into the floating world.

I say: Why don't we go somewhere, do something?

He says: I'm supposed to be meeting my friend Wlad at Gorlitzer Tor at 11, maybe some other day?

4

If close personal friends had been using options as a cover for money laundering it would, perhaps, be good to know, but I could not see a way to find out. Perhaps it would be good not to know.

But perhaps

It would be good not to know, probably, because it would not be nice to think of the years of hustling and scrounging and scrambling from credit card to credit card in the context of close personal friends living comfortably off the convenient source of income. But it would be dangerous not to know, possibly, because the point of ducking new contracts and dodging phone calls was the thought that sooner or later even the friendliest of options expires. Books like *The Tetragrammaton* and *Hypno* and *The Severed Hand,* books written back when a precocious smartass was a real storyteller, would revert to the person legally identical to that smartass, thereby freeing up a source of income for a person who might never tell such stories again.

If all this ducking and dodging was likely to cause problems, though, not just for close personal friends but for Peter Chan and Nicky D, they could save themselves a lot of trouble by arranging a power of attorney and commitment to a mental health facility. By the time the former smartass knew how much trouble they could save themselves it would be too late. Commitment to a mental health facility would be one route, an unfortunate accident and a forged will would be another. Life offers fewer last-minute escapes than fiction.

I stood in the handsome apartment by the phone. I picked up the receiver. I punched 13 numbers fast.

There were four rings, then a message. Hi! You've reached Gina, Dongsuk, Patrick, Megan, Jennifer, Brendan and Jacob! We can't come to the phone right now, but if you'd like to leave your name, number and message we'll get back to you as soon as we can!!!!!

—Hi. This is Rachel. My number is

—Rachel?

—Gina?

—I hate picking up during the day, you get these telemarketers and you *know* it's some kid making minimum wage so you don't want to be mean but then you talktalktalktalk

—I wanted to ask you something. I'm a bit worried.

—Oh, Rache, of course anything we can do to help, but you do tend to

—Someone told me Lyndall's option on *Hypno* was being used for money laundering, wondered if you'd heard anything.

She starts talking very fast.

I say so anyway I was a bit concerned by some of the investors who were mentioned in connection with

and she talks even faster, these people are businessmen, she explains, if they see a genuine business opportunity, a movie with real potential that will actually get *made*, they're happy to put some money into it, but obviously there are some projects that are never going to go anywhere, for them that's just another business opportunity and *Lyndall*, well *really*, talktalktalktalk

I don't call anyone else because it would be bad to be known to have asked questions.

It seems it would be a good career move to do a deal with the self-appointed heir to Polanski. At 6:00 p.m. it's only 9:00 a.m. in LA. At 8:00 I punch 13 numbers on the phone very fast.

5

The phone rings. The phone rings. The phone rings. A voice says: You've reached 342 759 2292. Please leave a message after the tone.

MEEEEEEEEEEEEEEEEP

Hi.

This is Rachel.

The number iiiiiiiiiiiiiiiiiiiiiiiiiiiiiiiiiiiiiiiiiiiiiiiis 0049, 30, 212, 36, 305.

6

X-Originating-IP: [84.188.245.237]
From: "Kaplan Thornhill" <nxnw@hotmail.com>
To: zozanian@onetel.com
Subject: a life full of Swis-spellings
Date: Wed 28 June 2006 20:25:18 +0000

Frau zozanian, good to exchange thoughts/foughts on Fante. I like it when you swear. Fuck, you fucking kan't fucking swear e-fucking-nuff these fucking fucked days.

Yes, I also liked the letter writing between writer and publisher, the desperation for cash felt something like our relationship and both (for me) the arrogance of Bandini with such little achievements amid such obvious failures and here was a guy and here i am parading around Berlin distancing myself from other 'writers in Berlin' yet still waiting for that telegram to come to announce some achievement . . . and would Bandini get mad cause the Mail on Sunday rejected his 'topless swiss male models milking cows set to lure english birds lonely during World Cup' - it has been rejected and surely the headline: 'Dear John, good luck in Germany - i'm going to SWiss you' - is genius and another tabloid triumph, no? but I am ILYA GRIDNEFF, a throbbing purple member and Ralph Steadman will illustrate my works and and and and . . .

for the record I have no problems with organised social gatherings around flames - nor domesticated and named animals chasing and retreiving balls, plastic items or sticks of various sizes for the lack of emotional / human contact -It is more the human's actions around said objects i find the most irratating. a woman talked to her dog like it understood or even her (innocent) belief said K9 has the capacity for language 'annoys' while (long unwashed hair foreigners too!). Three men arguing in Spanish about flame height and slab of meat time over said flame are not the most inspiring backdrops of humanity whilst immersed in literature reaching you regarding the difficulties faced by both author and reader with humanity not getting it, death of the author, death of the novel, the death of Walter Benjamin amid the dearth of Benjamins, baby . . . but i managed to sunburn myself which makes me proud in the vain fact I may turn a more desirable brownish colour but i did catch my internalised parental police system, but it was mere silent voice of felt shame for red headed mother and pale slavic father always warned one about the perils of the SUN RA!

i bought some bottle green cordorouy traditional german 'shorts' today - the ones extended past the knee and tightened with little draw strings at the side and already it, i and they have caused a stir. Since you funded these excursions you are implicated as facilitating homeless albeit loved pets- that i like and for sure more to come. perhaps with my correspondences with Morocco, Palestine, Jerusalem, offers for baby showers in Stockholm if I were to be kidnapped the released images of me looking like Isherwood/ Hemingway/ Hitler Youth would hardly garner the sympathy 'true blue aussies trapped down a mine/mind for 14 days does or would -

'After be-heading that prick they should hang, the queer bastard,' they shout at the tele...

'oh, pet, that's a bit tough, surely just a simple execution style bullet in the back of the head would suffice?' says wifey dishing out clumps of mash potato

i feel with summer everything seems farther away while on the surface closer. a sweaty alienation rather than cold annoynomous(e). Though i do recognise this comes from a man wearing traditional German trousers with a funny 1930s hair cut. *Don't mention the war.* A high bench mark for any frau to hurdle. but the test ist there.

this below made me laugh and i think it may amuse you for specific reasons, it is in response to my inquires about this man's desire to re-create Arnold Schwarzenegger's Commando film to celebrate the film's 21st birthday on June 21. it was advertised in a little advert planned for Hyde Park. He is seeking out people to play the characters, he will play arnold's character, i told him i am otherwise engaged but interested none-the-less . . .

oh to milk some topless cow, i mean . . .

From: david lennon <davidplennon@yahoo.ie>
To: Kaplan Thornhill <nxnw@hotmail.com>
Subject: Re: arnie
Date: Tues 20 June 2006 17:15:20 +0100 (BST)

hey man, this is gonna happen and Its gonna be great. unfortunately, i dont believe that your a journalist, first of all you spelt it is "journlaist" and a real journalist would never make such a mistake. you also wrote "ting" instead of "thing". im afraid i just cant believe you.

im sorry.

david lennon

ps i would love if you could get one of your newpapers to cover the event!!!!

best wishes!!!!

7

The phone rings. What time is it? 17:00:00.

The phone rings.

The phone rings.

The phone rings.

The phone rings.

Once more into the breach, dear friends.

She lifts the receiver and manipulates air with larynx, tongue and lips.

—Hello.

—Hi. Is that Rachel?

—This is Rachel.

—Hi.

—Hi.

—Hi. This is Jake.

—Hi.

—Hi. Look, Rachel, I've called the house 17 times and I keep getting some woman trying to pitch some kind of pornography, if that's what you want to do that's your decision but this is not what I do. This is not what George Clooney does. This is not what Nicole Kidman does. This is not what Ben Affleck does.

—

—My agent called your agent 15 times and he can't get a straight answer.

—Did she say she was my agent?

—Didn't you tell me she was your agent?

—I think I thought there was a reasonable chance she would turn out to be my agent if your agent called. An option, though, a 10 percent commission on $20,000 is only two grand, she may have sensed hesitancy, confusion

—I keep getting calls from Anne and I don't want to talk to Anne. There are people I might show my screenplay to, but that's different from having a lot of language in the contract, that's completely insane.

—¿?

—I don't want to encumber myself with a producer, if people have ideas I'm happy to hear them, but that's different from being a producer.

—¿?

—I get $3 million for a screenplay, if Anne wants to come to me and pay me $3 million for a screenplay, fine, I'll be happy to talk to her. Look, it's fine for Anne to help you with your contract as a friend, but that's not being a producer.

—¿?

—It's fine that she got your book published, that's not being a producer.

—¿?

—That's not casting. That's not doing contracts. That's not setting up locations. If someone wants to be part of a film they have to earn it. If she can come to me with an idea, fine, I'm happy to hear ideas, if it's a good idea I'll be happy to use her. I'm always open to anyone who has a good idea.

DJD XXX lies open on the bed. The opportunity cost! The opportunity cost!

—Look, I don't care about money. I'm not interested in money. I can get $3 million for a screenplay. I'm buying the rights with my own money, I don't want to get locked into agreements about producers, any producer, let alone someone who knows nothing *whatsoever* about the movie business, they had the rights for about five *years*, if they knew how to get a movie made they would have gotten it made, but this is just a Mom in Dubuque and a guy who was the business manager of a fucking computer games manufacturer, these are not producers. If you want to come to me with an offer from Scott Rudin, fine, I'll be happy to talk with him. This is a producer.

"I sense rage" speeds through the brain. It's stopped at the lips.

—

It's not that she is unsympathetic.

—I can't go to people and say my producer is a Mom in Dubuque.

There is more. Then there is even more. And yet more. The $3 million screenplay is mentioned 17 times.

She has no words to send forth to assuage affront.

Her head hurts.

She does not like the sound of "Mom in Dubuque."

She likes the sound of "$3 million for a screenplay." It is mentioned a few more times. How good that sounds.

But Fitzgerald, didn't Fitzgerald like the sound? And Faulkner? Was that not the big draw? The thing that wrote *The Sound and the Fury* died young, and a drunk named Faulkner turned up to claim the prize that it had won.

She's talking to a moral Munchkin. A Munchkin with a hard-on. Which would be how big?

The homunculus struts and frets his nanosecond.

—Look, we're talking about ten minutes' clerical work. Call my agent. My agent would love to talk to you.

—Yikes! Something burning on the stove! Got to go!

8

From: "Kaplan Thornhill" <nxnw@hotmail.com>
To: "Rachel Zozanian" <zozanian@onetel.com>
Subject: [Snoop Daddy]
Date: Thurs 29 June 2006 14:10:04 +0000

Frau zozanian,
was thinking of some additional stuff for the email pursuit of money- maybe add to the banker with fake tits email - 'i am in beirut, can you send me a lazy 1000 i want to go to iraq; see it as a high risk investment. (bank details below or perhaps western union? there is a similar email where she replies- *get fucked*)

also what is the legal on the intellectual property situation considering real and assumed and made up emails from real and assumed and made up people - eg can someone be pissed that the ending of a sentence with 'you wanker' is their personal property sent to me, does an email, letter become mine where i can do what i like?

i thought last night perhaps some people may be pissed off farther- or seen as betrayed- of being shopped out; while i see this as their great moment in literary history, for them the colour maybe difference; i also see how it could fartther rectify me to the outskirts of their rectum - ratifying me along with the hordes of history's scoundrels as not a koala bear good guy but rather a finely manipulated or orchestrated media personna; which is a zero sum game, i guess- though does one become the same shopping friends out to the press as secret celebrity mole/publicity agents etc etc...

http://hitlercats.motime.com

kaplan

From: “Rachel Zozanian” <zozanian@onetel.com>
To: “Kaplan Thornhill” <nxnw@hotmail.com>
Subject: RE: [Snoop Daddy]
Date: Thurs 29 June 2006 15:53:19 +0000

Herr thornhill

you hold the copyright to anything you write. If you send a letter, the recipient owns the physical object but the content remains your intellectual property. they can’t publish it without your consent. we can’t just help ourselves to e-mails people have sent you, probably better to rewrite them. you automatically have the right to veto use of e-mails from you (you don’t need a contract guaranteeing that right).

good thing you brought this up though. i shd give you something in writing giving you the right to use my half of the book in case i crack up, jump off a cliff, fall under a bus, same old same old. right to finish it, access to papers & so on.
rachel

From: “Kaplan Thornhill” <nxnw@hotmail.com>
To: “Rachel Zozanian” <zozanian@onetel.com>
Subject: RE: RE: [Snoop Daddy]
Date: Thurs 29 June 2006 21:09:11 +0000

rachel

look, stop being so melodramatic. i’d be pissed if you died, but all this talk about suicide is just bullshit. thanks for making alles klar on the legal

kaplan

9

You flew Virgin Premium Economy, LA–London. You were late checking in, they'd overbooked, so it was upgrade city for Courakis.

You're still reading *Your Name Here,* the new novel by Helen DeWitt. You're on page 577 and what you want to know is, what happened to the banker with the fake tits e-mail? Was it removed to make space for three pages on the Russell Group??????!!!!!! Or do you find yourself unexpectedly back in a travesty of Calvino's incomparable *If on a winter's night a traveller,* with key sections of the book inexplicably removed?

You glance across the aisle. Wow! It's Jake Noszaly, director of the incomparable *Count*! He seems to be reading *Lotteryland,* by the reclusive Rachel Zozanian. You play it cool, act unimpressed.

10

But *you* flew Virgin Premium Economy to get some work done. Just before you left for the airport you got a text message, HARI KAPUR DEAD. You called the texter, who said Kapur, the Sharpshooters accountant, had been gunned down at his home in West Egg but it was nothing to worry about, it was under control. Now someone across the aisle is rubbernecking. Great. Fucking great.

Nobody ever talks about what you went through to get Vessarova out of Dnipopetrovsk. Nobody talks about where you found her. Nobody knows the kind of people you had to deal with. You don't want to go through that again.

At the airport you got a call on your cell from Mary Poppins. Poppins said Dan Brown said he was *thrilled* with the movie of *The Da Vinci Code* but he would have loved to have seen what you would have done with the material, he'd love to see what you'd do with *Angels and Demons*, we'd give you $6 mil for the screenplay, Jake, said Poppins, it's not about the money, I know you're not interested in money, it's about respect, it's about our commitment to your talent, let us simplify your life for you.

You picked up a copy of *Angels and Demons* at the airport bookstore but you left it in your bag after takeoff. You turned instead to the end of *Lotteryland*, by the reclusive Rachel Zozanian

92. PERSEVERANCE

I still had the business card I had been given all those years ago. I called the number on it and I was told that the Generous One was no longer there. I asked where he had gone and the girl said she was not at liberty to disclose that information so I had to persevere.

I called the new number and a secretary asked May I say who is calling?

I gave her my name and I said I was the one he had given a £15,000 violin.

The Generous One came on the line and said What can I do for you in a tone of voice that said Piss off.

I said I wanted to talk to him and he said I was talking to him. I reckoned with all his advantages he was still probably my match for perseverance if he really wanted to make an issue of it, he would not have got where he was without it, but when I said I wondered if I could come and talk to him he suddenly relented. He consulted his diary and gave me an appointment. I thought O please o please o please because I knew I could never make it as a writer and I would never be a mathematician and the violin was absolutely out of the question.

93. PERSEVERANCE

I went to see the Generous One at the appointed time and he seemed to be in a softer mood. He said Well, what have you been doing with yourself?

I had been thinking about Gaby's comments and this time I was determined to be sympathetic. I said: I've been thinking a lot about your offer. I'm sorry I reacted the way I did, it's not that I don't appreciate it.

He said But?

I said It's just

He said What?

I made a real effort this time to make him understand about the violin and what it would be like to play it with an orchestra. I said: The thing is that as third violin, say, you have no significant say in the choice of conductor, who may be a complete tosser. Even as first violin you wouldn't have a say in the conductor or choice of programme. The conductor is selected by the management who in all probability are a bunch of complete

I was about to say wankers when it occurred to me that this might not make quite the right impression. Tossers also, on reflection, did not sound mature.

That is, I amended, they have in all probability risen to their present positions through commercial acumen rather than musical sensibility, and their, um, areas of expertise are likely to be reflected in their choice of conductor, the conductor, also, may not have complete freedom in his choice of programme, pressure is likely to be brought to bear by the management who in all probability will not be influenced by purely musical considerations.

In other words you haven't changed your mind, he said.

I want to be a banker, I said. Isn't there some way I could be a banker?

He sighed and settled back in his chair. All right, he said. I think I understand why you don't want to be a professional musician. But I think you're under a slight misapprehension about banking.

I said Oh really? Why is that?

He said: You're not the first by a long shot. We see this sort of thing all the time in young people, they think banking is about making a lot of money.

I said Oh really?

He said The thing is, Ephraim, we're really not looking for people who just want to earn a lot of money. We're looking for people with a genuine interest in banking.

94. I thought: I give up.

95. PERSEVERANCE

I got home and I thought: Wait just a minute.

96. PERSEVERANCE

It was obvious that I had improved my chances with the Generous One by being more sympathetic, the problem was just that he had gradually seen that my interest in banking was purely mercenary. This was exactly the problem I had had all along with my book. But help was to hand. I didn't know how I could have missed it—it was in the most obvious place of all.

I had worked out weeks ago that you could use the lottomonitor to run microchecks on whether someone was snogging you because she wanted to or because she could not think of a polite way to tell you that she only really liked snogging people who were conventionally good-looking.

My father had worked out years ago that you could use the lottomonitor to tell whether your son was likely to get into an argument with the rabbi or just scowl Byronically from a corner.

It should be possible to do exactly the same thing with a book!

Suppose I just wrote it down sentence by sentence, running luck checks as I went along to see whether each new sentence had maximised my chances of appealing to the maximum possible audience! If a sentence was off-target I could go through it word by word! The result would be a book that was as nearly sure to win a Golden Ticket as any book could be that was not by someone conventionally good-looking!

You're probably thinking: Wait a minute, if it's that easy why don't the professionals do that with every book?

Excuse me, but that's completely obvious. The fundamental Rule is that you never talk about the lottery.

97. PERSEVERANCE

I sat down by the screen with a pad on my lap and I started all over again.

I would write a sentence and hit DRAW and if the news was good I went on to the next sentence. If the news was bad I changed the sentence and hit DRAW again.

98. PERSEVERANCE

I gave Gaby a sample chapter to send in.

A week later she said He really likes it Eph.

She said He'd really like to see some more.

99. PERSEVERANCE

I went on sentence by sentence. I took out perseverance. I took out the lottery because it turned out to be bad luck to talk about the lottery. I took out the Impossible Dream. The point was not that nobody would like it but that the odds were that 45,999,920 would not. I took out all the advice about maths and English because it was too much like talking about the lottery. I took out talking about the book with Gaby because that was too much like talking about the lottery. Since that was the main thing we had talked about by the time I had taken it out we were not doing much talking.

After a while I looked back at what I had so far and even I was amazed. I couldn't believe how sympathetic I sounded.

100.

31:05:01 1005

APPEARANCE OF SINCERITY

Congratulations!!!!!!!!!!!!!!!!!!!!!!!!!!!

There were just a few loose ends to tie up. I was going through the last few pages with the lottomonitor one last time when the phone rang.

Gaby said: Eph, can you come downstairs?

I said: Where are you?

Gaby said: I'm downstairs. There's something I want you to see.

I went downstairs. Gaby was standing on the pavement. A big, long red car stood in the street beside her.

Ta *da*! said Gab.

What's that? I asked.

I *told* you all you had to do was make the effort, said Gab. It's a brand new *Lamborghini,* Eph, and it's *yours. Now* what do you say?

I said: You mean this is one of the prizes you claimed?

Gaby said: That's *exactly* what I mean, oh ye of little faith. Isn't it *lovely*?

If the lottomonitor was anything to go by, once my book hit the bookstores I'd be able to buy a hundred Lamborghinis.

I said: It's fantastic, Gab. But I think you should have it. You're the one who did all the work. If it wasn't for you it wouldn't be here.

Gab said: Yeah but *Eph,* it's *yours.* I did it for *you.*

She looked at it longingly.

I'd love to drive it just once, she said. Maybe you'll let me drive it one day.

I said: Look, Gab, the least I can do is let you drive it. Tell you what, why don't you take her out on the road for her maiden run? See how she handles. I've just got one last page that I've got to get back to.

Gab said: You mean you don't want to come?

I said: I just want to get this in the post first.

Gab said: You'd let me take it out on my own?

Sure, I said.

Gab said: Oh, Eph, that's so *sweet.*

She ran a finger along the gleaming metal.

Well, if you *insist,* she said at last.

I insist, I said.

She got into the car, buckled her belt and turned the key in the ignition. The engine made a noise like suave thunder. I kept looking at it incredulously. I'd never known anyone to get the actual prize they'd won in a commercial prize draw.

The car pulled out from the curb and disappeared round the corner.

1717 PERSEVERANCE

I looked up from the screen. It was late, and Gaby still wasn't back. Perhaps she'd gone out one of the motorways and got caught up in roadworks. Perhaps she'd just decided to keep the car.

The main thing was, I'd finished. My luck had finally changed.

I wrote:

THE END

There was a knock at the door.

Hello!

20

The normal euphoria of a healthy person

One of our rules during production was that when it was fun versus realism, fun won. There were several well-established gaming conventions that we embraced, like the fact that despite the caliber and country of origin, weapon types (pistols, rifles, submachine guns) all shared the same ammunition; you could carry over 100 pounds of gear and never get tired; and, most importantly, you could come back to life as many times as you wanted after you'd been hit in the head with a German Panzershrek bazooka.

Hirschmann (from Game Creation & Careers, *Marc Saltzman)*

1

So ja. Ouais. Si Si Si Si Si (Castilian Catalan Portuguese Italian Romanian). Da. Да. Or in the words of the universal language (understood in each of the 25 countries where *Lotteryland* was sold), yeah yeah yeah. Yeah. Whatever.

In Italy students have a saint, San Precario, for the feckless luckless jobless young of today, and they take to the streets to march for the saint once a year. In France last year students rioted in protest against Villepin's solution to unemployment, namely the employer's right to fire within the first two years without explanation. In Germany the entry to almost any career lies through a Praktikum, an unpaid internship; once upon a time a Praktikum might lead to a paid job but companies spotted a cost-cutting opportunity, why not simply syphon off a range of tasks to this abundant renewable supply of unpaid labour? It's not uncommon for jobseekers to do one Praktikum after another until well into their thirties, living on support from their parents, a route into the job market that puts good jobs well out of reach of anyone who cannot afford to work indefinitely without pay (i.e. all working-class candidates).

The system of unpaid internships is equally popular in the US and UK; naming no names, why not have a look at *Harper's,* that bastion of liberal self-righteousness, and see the generous package offered to would-be interns? A package ideally suited to give a break to the sort of person who can live rent-free in New York City, one of the most expensive cities in the world. Chin chin, Lewis Lapham. (It would be easy to go on at *some* length but not for another 265 pages, why not read Anya Kamenetz' *Generation Debt,* Riverhead Books (some sort of subsubsubsidiary of Penguin), 2006? Buy! Buy! Buy!)

Though *Lotteryland* was set in Big Brother Blair's Britain, it had a universal theme—AND some excellent Lubavitch jokes. AND a 24-year-old former smartass of an author, dark of hair, flashing of eye (I believe the French term is jolie laide, which translates roughly as "not dissimilar to the ugly weird mutant in an adventurous boyband but on you it looks good, fancy a quick shag?").

So the good news was that its author was suddenly entitled to a lot of money. The bad news was that Anne had made a flying trip to Oxford because she was *worried,* spotted the defenceless manuscript on the unguarded desk, took it to her hotel, read it at a single sitting, and was back the next day with the sort of contract that is full of standard language that basically just expresses faith in talent and commitment to the project. I explained that this time I was going to a *publisher,* and she explained that of *course* it should be published, but Sharpshooters *had* an imprint, they were *looking* for fresh young talent and so on und so weiter, yes yes.

That was bad news, yes, and look, we're on page 588 and far too much space, I would guess, has already been spent on bad news of that kind. Bad news I could have dodged if I'd been sharper, smarter. The real bad news, though, was that though I now had an entitlement to half a million pounds or so, I could not buy a ticket back to 1999, or 1998, or 1997, or even 1992, because that's the one ticket nobody ever does win.

2

From: "Jake Noszaly" <noszaly@gmail.com>
To: "Rachel Zozanian" <zozanian@onetel.com>
Subject: Time out
Date: Mon 3 July 2006 09:08:57 +0000

Rachel

I definitely want to make a movie of your book, but I get the feeling this is not a good time for you. The last thing I want to do is jeopardize your life or your mind. The most important thing is your health. No movie is worth placing that at risk. Let's take some time out, talk again when it feels right.
Take best care
Jake

3

My character did come to Casablanca for the waters.

Krzysztof had made KaDeWe sound very good.

In the inbox of the verdammte iBook are 200 e-mails from close personal friends. Also an old old old e-mail from a stranger in a bar.

Orson I turned 24 the other day. Not that much changed but the stagnant point of calendar time and place-space rah rah rah met the dot conception occurred time before I am in the present.

I used to read it when things went wrong. Then there more, and yet more, and more and more. The fabulous anarchic voice appeared on the screen of the iBook day after day, and I thought that I too could live in the floating world. But if you have lived too long at absolute zero, if the blood has frozen in your veins, perhaps you cannot come back to life.

Krzysztof had failed to perform the calculations for the velocity upon impact of a body falling from the seventh floor; KaDeWe had lost its charm.

What does Britain have to offer? Barry Island, a stone's throw from Cardiff, has fast tidal currents; it's a popular spot. The Clifton Suspension Bridge in Bristol has a drop of 75 metres, representing a velocity upon impact of 122 kph or 86 mph. The cliffs at Beachy Head, on the south coast, have a drop of 180 metres, representing a velocity upon impact of 211 kpm or 132 mph. Excellent news. It's 4:00 a.m. I book a one-way ticket to London Luton on Easyjet.

It is the day of the semi-final of the World Cup. France is playing Brazil. For a month the dour Berliners had been happy, sitting in the biergartens, cheering, groaning, while tiny figures cavorted on small screens.

Easyjet has its own check-in hall on the ground floor of Schoenefeld, where every check-in counter serves all flights. All lines are twenty passengers long. I have no bags to check. I have the laptop.

Easyjet is promoting itself on, through, prepositions begin to be cumbersome, the generosity of the size and weight of its hand luggage allowance. The bag can be any weight WITHIN REASON. Orange stands, racks, tubular frames permit one to determine whether the bag is small enough. The stupid mind blunders over a page. This is a bad system, but once on the plane one is better off. The seats are large & pleasant & one is on a whole planeful of strangers. Does the T-shirt stink? Probably.

I'd like to live in the floating world.

There are trains from Luton that go to King's Cross. Others go all the way to Brighton. There's a bus from Brighton, the 12, that goes through various Sussex towns, and another bus, the 12A, that goes through Sussex towns taking in Beachy Head.

The body gets on the plane; it gets on the train; it gets on a bus. At Eastbourne it gets off the bus. I would have liked a clean anonymous hotel with plump white pillows, but here the invisible hand provides B&Bs.

I take a taxi to a B&B. They have no single, only a double for £40. I say I will stay two nights. I can't imagine anyone choosing to visit the town for any reason other than suicide, so that I am sure the proprietors must know where I was headed, but they are jolly and proud of their decor.

Upon the hall table is a thick stack of leaflets about local attractions. It is hard to believe this is not camouflage for the principal draw, but perhaps a visit to the place is not the suspicious circumstance I suppose.

In the morning it is not necessary to ask for Beachy Head; it is the first thing recommended. The woman speaks of the beauty of the cliffs; the bad pub; the good pub in East Dean with its excellent wine list. One could walk up or take the bus from the pier.

I take the 12A, which goes through an ugly shopping centre reminiscent of Dalson, quaint pubs, fields of mown hay in bales, it climbs, it climbs, the sea opens out to the left, and here's the bad pub! I walk up toward the brow of the hill. To the right one can see glimpses of the white cliff below the grass. Walkers, jolly walking parties amble across the turf. There is a low fence with a warning of cliff erosion, and then a little patch of grass past which one looks straight down. There is a white stone beach far below. A wooden cross in the grass bears the name Maggie. I lie on the grass on my stomach. It's a 6.060606-second drop. Good news.

I lie in the grass because there's no particular hurry. I think of a story, one of the useless stories I read for my useless impractical degree. Here's the story.

In Book XIII of the *Odyssey* Odysseus wakes up alone in a cave on a shore. The Phaeacians had said they would take him to Ithaca, along with the loot he picked up from the King of the Phaeacians. Now he wonders whether they tricked him. He is very very very very tired. First he fought in Troy for ten years; then he angered Poseidon and was forced to wander the seas for another ten. Now he's tired.

Athena, who loves him, was afraid it would go to his head if he knew he was home. She has transformed the place so that it is unrecognizable. Instead of comforting her favourite she appears to him in disguise, in the form of a young shepherd. She asks him who he is, where he's from, and he spins her a story. He talks and talks and talks and talks and talks, he's a Cretan, he fought in Troy, he got in trouble, he was trying to get to Elis, where is he? Speaking as a shepherd Athena says he must be very ignorant if he does not know he's in Ithaca—but then she can bear it no longer. She throws off her disguise, appearing as the goddess she is. Skhetlie, she says, you scoundrel, you're always the same, always spinning the same lies, no one, not even a god, could surpass you for deceitfulness, it's his cleverness and canniness and wheelerdealerness that she loves, this is why he is her favourite, and because he can wheel and deal from the depths of despair the grey-eyed goddess of wisdom will never desert him.

I think: Is there really no way to cash in on this?

Suddenly I have a brilliant idea.

There are people who don't see the need for a false passport until it's too late. There are people who don't see the need for credit cards under a variety of aliases until, again, it's too late. These are friendless orphans, alone in the world. These are the very people who also see no need for a shell company in the Channel Islands until, once again, it is too late. They may, perhaps, see *The Importance of Being Earnest* and giggle at the jokes—perhaps they even see it at an early age—but the wisdom of the work is lost on them. They see no immediate need for a Bunbury and this too they fail to set up early on. They neglect to send themselves letters from Bunbury care of persons whose suspicions may later need to be lulled. They don't call home using an assumed accent, ask for themselves, and leave the message that Bunbury called. They don't set up an address to which they themselves can be sent post care of Bunbury. They don't set up a range of *dummy* Bunburies to avoid exposing the real one to unwanted attention when the time comes.) These are people who in all likelihood have read the entire oeuvre of John le Carré without taking necessary precautions. They read Greene and go comfortably on with their lives.

Sometimes their luck holds out. Sometimes, like Plath, they run out of luck.

Time for a well-earned Mozart chocolate. I take the box of lucky chocolates from my bag. My nails are chewed to the quick; I tear the cellophane with my teeth, claw at the bright red and gold box, remove a chocolate in its red and gold foil with the portrait of Mozart on the wrapper, prise open the foil. I sink my teeth into the dark chocolate. They close on something powdery, crunchy. What's this? Instead of the promised marzipan the chocolate is filled with dense white powder. Excellent news, Duty Free, excellent news.

I shake out the powder onto the lucky box. I draw lines with a credit card in the name of C. K. Dexter Haven. I roll a fresh twenty-pound note into a tube and inhale.

I'm going to learn how to fly, high, fameeeeeee!, I wanna live forever—and so and so.

Your luck is what you make it.

There's no place like home, Toto. There's no place like home.

By Kaplan Thornhill

Hollywood director Jake Noszaly has been linked to the suicide of writer Rachel Zozanian who never recovered from an alleged underage affair.

Today the *Sunday Sentinel* can exclusively reveal the shocking events of wunderkind writer Zozanian who went missing last week.

The writer's suicide note was found on her laptop where she outlines how the 'brief' affair 15 years ago tormented her to the point of break down.

If the allegations are true Noszaly may face a criminal investigation.

The letter addressed to 'Jakes' suggests their affair happened when she was 15.

In the letter she states: 'It's not your fault. I know you never meant to hurt me. But I can't go on like this. I've tried to put you out of my head and I can't.

'Fifteen years is a long time, too long, but our brief time together still haunts me. I've never met another man like you and I never shall.

'I hoped your interest in *Lotteryland* meant something more; now I see this for the madness it always was. I know I'll hurt the many people who love me, but I can't go on.

'When I am laid in earth
may my wrongs create
no trouble in thy breast.
Remember me, remember me,
but, ah, forget my fate
with all my love, as always,
Rachel'

Zozanian's clothes and passport had been found on the shore at Barry Island, a well-known suicide spot. Her body has never been recovered.

Her laptop then arrived at the *Sentinel* by Federal Express where the note was found.

Notorious ladies man Noszaly refused to comment specifically on details in the letter. But denied any relationship with the writer other than professional.

His agent in a written statement said: 'This year Zozanian and Noszaly had spent months negotiating the rights to her cult classic book: *Lotteryland*. But I was unaware they had ever met before.'

The *Sentinel* has passed the letter onto UK police. And the investigation continues.

Sunday Sentinel, 16 July 2006

By Zygmunt Bialystok

A bidding war broke out last week over the rights to *Hustlers,* by Kaplan Thornhill and Rachel Zozanian. Zozanian's apparent suicide has given rise to a frenzy of speculation concerning her relationship with Jake Noszaly, which the book is rumoured to describe in detail. Simon Crawford of MKM, who won the auction for a reputed high six-figure sum, said the book offered "startling insights."

"Sometimes a book is absolutely *of* its time, yet *ahead* of its time, a book that will be cherished for years to come. We felt at once that *Hustlers* was one of that rare breed, a book that would live in the hearts of generations, a *Catcher in the Rye* of the 21st century.

"The portrayal of Rachel's life as an Oxford prostitute—told with the cold, clinical savagery of a *Flaubert* of the MTV generation—takes us behind the scenes to the *forging* of the black humour of *Lotteryland*. There's an almost unbearable *poignancy* to the narrative, read as it now inevitably is in the shadow of the tragic *denouement*—one whose seeds lay in a doomed relationship years before. And yet it's not a book without hope. It has given us an extraordinary *new* talent in Kaplan Thornhill, a chance-met Australian who *sweeps* the reader along in a breakneck literary *joyride,* a take-no-prisoners frontal *assault* on the feverish *hedonism* of the London art world, the *machinations* of celebrity tabloidism, the hellbent *gravitation* of the journalist to enter-at-your-peril *war* zones—a drunken *orgy* of a voice that's *utterly* unlike the well-behaved products of the MFA factories.

"And then there's the *engagement* of the characters with *Arabic,* something that would have been *unthinkable* fifty, even ten years ago. But what we see these days is that readers have a desperate *longing* for *authenticity,* something the beancounters simply hadn't the imagination to *recognize.* One can't say it too often because it's the simple *truth*—September 11 changed *everything.*

"It's Manet meets Mamet meets Miller meets Mailer meets Plath meets Hunter Thompson meets *Tarantino*—a book that transcends all the hype."

The deal is said to include options on two of Zozanian's unpublished books, of which at least 10 are said to exist in substantially finished form. The Zozanian estate has been bequeathed in its entirety to Lily Marlowe, a close friend of the notoriously reclusive writer. Lily Marlowe was unavailable for comment.

Publishers Weekly, 31 July 2006

21

Curtains

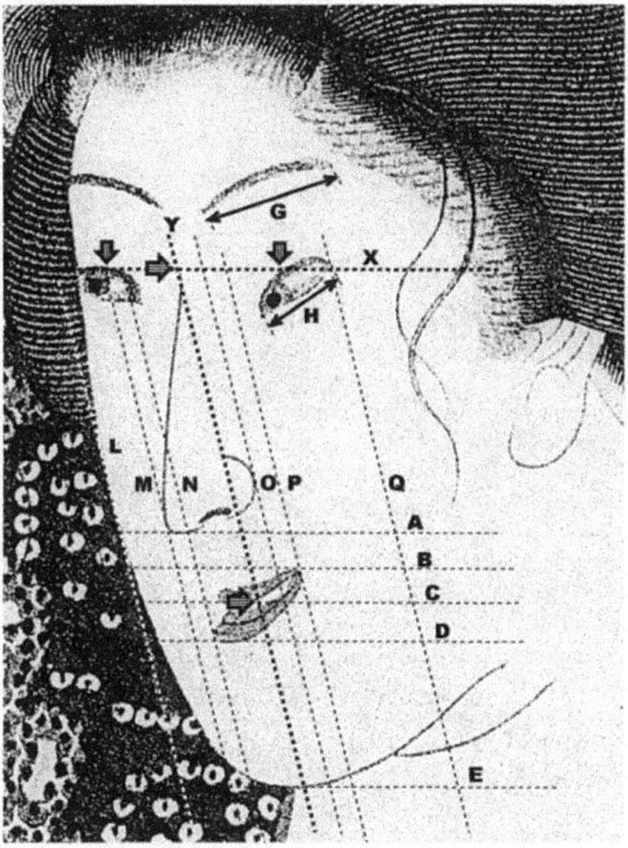

From: “ilya gridneff” <anarchicus@hotmail.com>
To: “helen dewitt” <Helen.DeWitt@gmx.net>
Subject: pappa razzle dazzle
Date: Fri 22 Sept 2006 21:02:59 +0000

Dewitt,

Yes, all good here despite the on going ridiculous. read the end and like it, and i dont need to have the final (s)word. though with all these other characters does it take away some of my limelight, i mean it was or *is* about me, at the end of the day, and depsite a 50 50 kontrakt i was under the impression i was the *STAR*? So - what exaclty brings, all these other people into the ending? This is the serious question, the limelight star stuff was my impersonation of Steve Coogan.

Please can you send me the WHOLE book, or have it printed for me this weekend? this is no ego but serious narrative-critique.

From: “Helen DeWitt” <Helen.DeWitt@gmx.net>
To: “Ilya Gridneff”<anarchicus@hotmail.com>
Re: YNH
Date: 15 October 2006

Ilya

Last-minute extras are vorbei. Not sure it helps. Going beserk.

Months of e-mails from Indiana at QBQ saying how great it wd be to do for Arabic what Tolkien did for the languages of the elves, loved The Last Samurai, loved YNH, this, that, EXPLAINED to her THREE MONTHS ago that you were going to Ramallah and access to money wd in all likelihood improve yr chances of not getting blown up, cd we do a deal. Finally thought I cd not take any more of the biz, booked Easyjet to London Luton which has a direct train to Brighton which has a bus to Beachy Head. Thinking how lovely to leave it all behind.

Got e-mail from Indiana saying YNH was experimental (yes, let’s run an experiment to see whether anyone has read those 18th-century prepostmodernist time travellers Sterne and Diderot), STILL not answering the question. Wrote pointing out that if I had simply played online poker and won a satelite tournament on PokerStars & gone to the WSOP to do battle for $1 million, this apparently insanely long shot wd at least have been a fast track to an actual book deal and been an an easier way to resolve financial issues than trying to get a simple answer to a simple question from her. Knew how to play poker. Terminally incapable of extracting an answer to a perfectly straightforward question. Response: resounding silence. So I think we are now not on speaking terms.

Has to be saner to walk away than leap on next bus to Beachy Head.

I’m sorry things didn’t work out with Your Name Here. I think the Arabic will simply have to go on a website; all the things we discussed never made it into the book because there were too many disruptions dealing with the biz. It's my fault that YNH didn't turn out to be a million-dollar baby; you gave me some amazing material to work with and I failed to do it justice. You were definitely the best thing in the book.

Hope all is well
Helen

From: “Ilya Gridneff” <anarchicus@hotmail.com>
To: raphaelmarx@hotmail.com
Subject: the immense dimensions of a rodent’s inner experience
Date: Mon 30 Oct 2006 09:56:01 +0000

Privyet Raphael,
There was a reason why I couldn’t get to sleep. Lucid dreams of Lucian Freud, painting and trying to organise my fiscal situation despite an undercurrent thought that everything was... sorted. Waking today, in Bishkek, I walked through wet drizzle, I slotted my Nat West bank card into the Bank of Kyrgyzstan machine and on the screen a dollar bill character with an unhappy face waved his hand backwards and forwards expresses his No, No, NO... and no doubt the bank’s deep regret ‘I had insufficient funds for the withdrawal’. I reduced the amount by half - was farther disappointed - then laughed at by the queuing locals as schlept away.

Once again, I have run out money well before I thought I would. I am down to my last 300. So the 300 squids you have held in your keep so adequately, I need it transferred into my account, details below. Fuck Western Union they’ve excised too much. For some reason 50 cent’s ‘21 questions’ keeps looping my head; ‘Would you love me if I was down and out?’

I guess I wanted this. I mistakenly asked the ‘Gods of Experience’ for destitute Russia and now as the arse falls out of my former Soviet pants in Bishkaka. I want my MTV. Though this feeling (*this feeling*) has been the re(o)ccurring nightmare, intermittent since January 16 in Amman, Jordan when I inadvertently cancelled my bank cards after believing three Algerian Celine Dion fans stole my wallet, nope just cash, mobile phone and camera.

‘Guys you said we were brothers!’ as I ran down to the hotel lobb. Unimpressed, the Palestinian refugee clerk said: “Hey Mister, put pants on.”

All my own doing. ‘if I was flipping burgers at burger king would you still love me...’

if only, for the past two weeks the Bishkek guys I’ve been living with have cooked the 40kg of potatoes - that they bought for US$1- in two alternative yet tender ways. I've been buying the odd treat (sugar, sausage and cheese) but they seem content with potato kicked in alternative ways. I now have a greater understanding of this little chap's important role in history, as your Ire-rish lot know all to well. Hunger and repetition, Knut Hamsun- chic-anary.

I met some Americans. I even ducked into these new friends house for 'lunch' where they discussed lazy prostitutes, then listened to how if he was in London he would still go out with these two local girls he goes out with, who apparently look like models and want to marry him, all to borrow 50 fucking som (a bit over 10US dollars) all this to the back drop of fashion TV and the impasse of comments like: 'nice tits, corr look at dat arse...' roaarr, phoaarr, noarrrr, boar..etc etc... Though as the former US marine explosives expert told me, teaching English is an excellent cover for a spy. It is not worth it I tell you. English teachers here are exiles, Vikings, fat failures seeking the currency of exchange, virus... then I had to look for the pen I dropped on the road as such a loss would ruin my financisl situation... I have learnt a lot. The most symbolic gesture of late has been using newspaper as toilet paper in the cold Soviet apartment. Apparently, I learned mid-shit, Becks had an affair, shocked they seemed so happy.

Soooo Raphael, the coolest of ninja turtles, I have 13 Som in my pocket, roughly enough to get to and back from tomorrow's Russian lesson with Svetlana, (no chance at all she's gonna sleep with me) and the change buys three single Russian brand cigarettes, if I was smoking that is, (extra tar for the Slavic masculine mentality). As the dysentery affected cabin boy said to gangrene lad: "All part of the adventure". Holly Valance seems more fake on Bishkek television. Real.

I am borrowing money for this email, nothing has changed, even in developing worlds I can justify mooching. But all this money talk is not the real issue. The issue is what to do with this last 300! (300 of the banks 650 overdraft) My thoughts are finish this month in Bish-kaka and then head to Moscow for work and more Russia, though this is a real throw of the dice. I may score free accommodation with Lena's (the Russian Doctor you met one 3am at Kingsland Rd Russian Pub) her parent's live in Moscow, she has mentioned it and from what I gather her father always wanted a son, especially a boxing son, though I feel too much of a cliché turning up from the provinces with no money, wanting to live in Moscow like Chekhov's 'Three Sisters' - I am a writer, what's in the fridge? Moskva, Moskva, Mosvka. Vodka Vodka Vodka!

But again not sure of the politics, logistics, can't get in contact, her email is full of junk or the pictures I sent of me having a good time. Could try and out do Orwell - live on Moscow streets with out his Parisian finance source when life got too rough... I could return to London where shoes and haircuts oscillate wealth on the cultural scale like Witches brew and tiger penis aphrodisiacs, where capital is the obscure and esoteric... re-engage with the fray get more work as a stylist for photo shoots in the elevatorrrrs of exclusive hair salons: "*The light in here is amazing,*" work somewhere/somehow, avoid the lure of the 'centre of paralysis,' the excessive culture of diversion, sleep on couches and then scoot back to Moscow? Slightly interested in this though feel it would stifle the Russian and getting money in London is not as easy as it sounds- everyone has gone a bought a fucking house with sofas designed to purge friend's like me. I could call those fucks at Flatline news agency. Re-enter the tabloid news agency hack zone; 'he puts the hack in hackney', *Ferrari Press* may be the alternative, the Sentinel, Sunday Mirror, back outside celebrity houses waiting for a quote, going through garbage to make more garbage, asking how people feel after the death of a loved one?

Oh, what a tattered flag I wave as the Chilli Peppers sing 'Californicaton', the last time I was Californicating in LA, my then valley girl's father (ex-CIA) at the dinner table said:"That fuck Che, yeah, when I was down in Panama I was listening in on his Commie conversations" then at dessert "those Afghans are animals, we should nuke em all" - funny he is now doing security at the Bikonaur Cosmodrome in neighbouring Kazakhstan, thought I may pop in, though when I suggested this at the time he asked if I had a 'security clearance.' I said no and thought about the night I spent in a Newcastle police cell for spraying ketchup in the kitchen of pub after I had been asked to leave, for intoxication. And, this woman, told me recently in my email inquiries as how she was getting on with my previous departing gift: "It's hard to read Crime and Punishment in Los Angeles," but I digress...

Oo minya net kapoosta
I have no cabbage (slang for money)

That's right. Money - the flow was there. Walking down Tschyu Prospect, down town Bishkek. I realise money is the extension of your body. When you have it you don't need to walk, eat, drink, sleep or fart, it takes care of that. Everything comes to you. And how. I had to walk to the city like so many times I had to in the stinky knife fight of London. What upsets is I was relishing the thrill of the chase, I was, I was, but perhaps on super indulgent terms. I pushed the dream too far and now like revolutionary Russia the wheels fell off. The question keeping the right dinner table talking all night, where did it all go wrong? - I blame January 16 others will say it began at my birthday... I blame Celine Dion and the Algerians who robbed me in Amman. They say Western Imperialism. France the Colonial overlord. Despite a man in space and atomic energy, four months abroad scooting about countries the government suggests you do not attend: 'cause they're dirty A-RABS', worse too – Muss-limbs,' the constant being different realities, now the real pregnant poignant dormant lacunae, as I also answer my Russian wife's email, springs itself back to the fore front. Money. I have to return to London. This didn't happen to Hummingway, no doubt he had a plethora of one-armed gun runners ready to sponsor more adventures. Though I heard he, Hemmingway, once trapped pigones in Jardin Luxembourg for food...

I feel the amniotic juice sucked out of me. There I was ducking, diving, skiving, pretending to be a journalist/spy/man of leisure. Now the story has run out of gas, my last 300. My last 300. Enough to get into Heathrow and the Piccadilly back to Hackney.

Yes, indeed you are correct, all these emotions are the result of me fleeing the coup, the problematic of why most enjoy being inside 9-5 or sitting on the roof when an insouciant red head leaves the door open. Oh, wise man of the north, what to do? Life was going up, I was even making new jokes in Russian:

"Oo minya deva novosta padruga - moy oochebnek e moy tetrad!"
"I have two new girlfriends, my textbooks and notebook,"

Much to the delight of Svetlana and the girl's in the office (they like their men crisp, clean and sharp, scruffy doesn't cut it here) ... my boxing was getting better, chin up - eyes straight, I was starting to build a vocabulary for fuck sake. I can explain in Russian why a man with a Russian name can't speak Russian. Ya espweeteevyuashi (I'm disgusted).

But it's strange here. Vlad the boxing coach say: *ilyousha,* the soft Russian deminative for Ilya, the same soft way my father called me when I was a little cosmo-naughty in Sydney and then receiving boris' left right punch into my face; a slight transference of the realites faced in the real world and the parent's protected world they try to offer...

300 squid will not perpetuate the dream it will prolong it! It will make it more desperate – Ya espweeteevyuashi - a granny on life support Ya espweeteevyuashi ... pull the plug or push through? Ya espweeteevyuashi...

I do not ask for money though cheques are tax deductible. I need support/advice. Will I be Napo-I-leon/Hit-I-ler determinedly/madly pushing onto Mos-I-cow? Heroic Will? Invincible Megalomania, or simply the arduous point of the trip? Will I make it? I know the answers just voicing frustrations...

...Crimean Tom, that stuffed cat we saw at London's Imperial Museum shirking the day's responsibilities and visting the relics of war, he turns in his grave or the soul of Tom retches as his stuffed body lets out a collective "Arghhhhhh" making the whole War Museum and South Kensington shudder with a: 'Geeee-zuz, someone got it bad...'

Strange also as this momentum builds. I wonder do I really want this Russian language? It's not going to come over night, it's going to be, like Stalin, a five-year plan over 40 endless years, not really this long but simply a trope for historical inter-textuality. It is like carrying a heavy ball backwards? I was studying, writing out words like a schoolboy wanting the gold star. The Red Crest. Excitement in shedding light in this the darkness, but I choose to be in the darkness, a choice for what reasons? And when there was a power failure in our building I studied under candlelit, second to writing under candlelit when my hotel in Gilgit Pakistan controlled Kashmir had a power failure - I wondered why they gave me so much hash, for free? The paranoia kicked in…

My situation reminds me of the Indian guy I met on the train from Mumbai (Bombay) to his home in Jaipur. He wanted to become a model, and/or Bollywood actor and being a smart kid his back-up plan was… to learn guitar so if he never made it as a model he could always make it as a musician… I encouraged him and wrote down my email address, if he was ever in London/Moscow.. If this journalism/writing gig doesn't kick off perhaps I could become a professional athlete.

I realise you're not a great emailer. More of a Norman *Mailer* but can you please (please please) transfer funds into my account either electronically or physically. Oh, my boiled potatoes are ready. So, Reverend Brother Raphael, High Priest of the East London Temperance Movement what do you say to this, again, one of my darker moments of confession? My Russian soul – russkaya dusha - my Russkaya douche – my Russian shower, as I've been mispronoucing, will prevail. I will handsomely push onto Moscow, he says with a bottle vodka under him. In him. Halp..

Give and afford what you can
Natwest Finsbury Park Branch
Acc number 9555 1923
Sort code 600 822

Ends

You are a thetan. You are not your mind or your body or your name. You are You.

"L. Ron Hubbard"

Helen DeWitt is the author of *The Last Samurai,* which has been named one of the best books of the twenty-first century by multiple publications. She is also the author of *Lightning Rods,* as well as a collection of short stories, *Some Trick,* and a novella, *The English Understand Wool.* She lives in Berlin.

Ilya Gridneff was born and raised in Sydney, Australia. As a journalist, his work has appeared in the *Financial Times, Politico,* and *The Baffler.* Since 2015, he has helped craft foreign policy for numerous governments. This is his first work of fiction.

www.ingramcontent.com/pod-product-compliance
Lightning Source LLC
LaVergne TN
LVHW021946060526
838200LV00043B/1938